© 2025 Anne L. Dean

Far Side of Revenge: Prince Brian Boru, Future King of Ireland

All rights reserved.

No part of this publication may be reproduced in any form, by photocopying or by electronic or mechanical means, including information storage or retrieval systems, without permission in writing from both the copyright owner and the publisher of this book.

Published by: GladEye Press
Interior Design: J.V. Bolkan
Map Illustrations: Sydney Therrell
Cover Design: Sharleen Nelson
ISBN-13: 978-1-951289-22-5
Library of Congress Control Number: 2025935768

This is a work of fiction. All names, characters, places, and events are either a product of the author's imagination or are used fictitiously. Any resemblance to real persons, businesses, organizations, or events are totally unintentional and entirely coincidental.

Printed in the United States of America.
10 9 8 7 6 5 4 3 2 1

The body text is presented in Garamond 11 point for easy readability. The header font is Jana Thork. Chapter titles and dropcaps are Dublin.

Far Side of Revenge

Prince Brian Boru, Future King of Ireland

A HISTORICAL NOVEL

Anne L. Dean

Springfield, Oregon

Glossary of Names, Places, & Things

Name/Place/Thing *Pronunciation.* Definition

Áed *EE (Irish), Hugh (English).* Son of Mahon & Úna.
Ailill *(AYE-leel).* Son of King Eóghan.
Ailill Olum *AYE-leel OH-lum.* Ancestor of Clan Dal Cais.
Armagh (Ard Mhacha) *AR-magh.* See of Saint Patrick.
Bebinn (Bébhinn) *BAY-vin.* Brian's mother.
Belach Lechta *BAH-la LEKta.* Battle site.
Beltane (Bealtane) *BYOWL-tinna.* May festival.
Bobbio *BAH-bee-oh.* Irish abbey in Rome.
Bórama *BOR-ah-mah.* Fortress at juncture of River Shannon and Lough Derg.
Bóraime *BOR-ah-mah.* Irish spelling of Boru.
Brat *BRAHT.* Woolen, fringed cloak.
Brehon *BREY-un.* Judge.
Brigit *BREEDge.* Úna's infant daughter.
Brithem *BRI-them.* Judge of highest rank.
Blat *BLAHT.* Monk at Holy Island.
Brunhild (German name) *BroonHILD.* King Donobhan's wife, Ivar's daughter.
Buí *BWEE.* Druid wife of the god, Lugh.
Cashel (Caisel) *CAH-shel.* Traditional fortress home of Munster overkings, on Cashel Rock.
Cathal *CAH-hal.* A Connacht king, Úna's brother.
Callaghan (Ceallachan) *CEH-la-ha*n. Munster overking, rival to Brian's father.
Cennétig (Kennedy) *KIN-ah-juh.* Brian's father, clan king.

Cian *KEE-an.* Son of Dal Cais rival, Molloy.
Clonmacnoise (Cluain Mhic Nóis) *CLON-mac-nosh.* Famed monastery on border between Meath and Connacht.
Colum *KUHL-um.* Abbot from Cork.
Conaing *CON-ig.* Brian's nephew.
Connor (Conchobhar) *COH-nar.* Connacht king, Úna's brother.
Conn *KAHN.* Priest at Holy Island.
Corccarán *KOR-car-on.* Brian's messenger to Molloy.
Cormac *KUR-a-mac.* Son of Deisi King Fáelán.
Corcu Bascind *KOR-ku BAHSH-cind.* "Seed" of Bascind, King Donal's people and territory.
Cúchulainn *KOO-hull-in.* Demigod son of Lugh (mythological).
Currach *CUHR-ah.* hide-bound, canoe-like boat.
Dal Cais (Dal gCais) *Dal Gosh.* Brian's clan.
Deichtre *Deck-truh* Mother of Cúchulainn.
Dún *Doon* A fortress.
Donobhan (Donnubán) *DON-uh-van.* King of Uí Fidgiente.
Eíden mac Clérig *A-den mac CLErig.* Mór's father, King of Uí Fiachrach.
Eíden mac Donncuan *A-den mac DonKOOan.* Coning's twin brother, Brian's and Mahon's nephew.
Edgar *ED-gar.* King of Wessex.
Emly *EM-uh-lee.* Large monastery in Munster.
Eóghan *OH-wen.* King of Eóganacht Caisel.
Eóganacht(a) *OH-wen-ack-ta.* Clan(s) in Munster; dominant before Dal Cais.
Eric *EH-ric.* Son of Ivarr of Waterford; grandson of Donobhan, Uí Fidgiente; great-grandson of Ivar of Limerick.
Fáelán *FAY-lan.* King of the Deisi.

Fáelán mac Cáellaide *FAY-lan mac Kelly*. Abbot of Emly.
Félim *FAY-lem*. Rory's charge; Mahon's and Brian's spy, scout.
Félim mac Ruadh *FAY-lem mac ROO-ah*. Elder; Long-Beard.
Fergal (Fearghal) *FAR-gal*. King of Uí Briúin Bréifne, in northeast Connacht.
Find (Fionn) *FINN*. Brian's recruit for caves.
Finnian *FINN-i-an*. Irish saint.
Flaith *FLA*. High ranking members of society (king, poet, scholars, lawyers, etc.).
Gilla Padraig *GEE-ah PAH-drig*. Son of Osraighe king.
Holy Island (Inis Celtra) *Inish CEL-tra*. Monastery in Lough Derg.
Haroldssons *HAROLDSONS*. Ivar's Norse enemies.
Henri *AWn-ree*. Donal's manservant.
Ivar *Ivar*. Norse king of Limerick.
Ivarr *Ivarr*. Norse king of Waterford.
Kincora *Kin-COR-a*. Brian's fortress on River Shannon.
Lachtna *LOCK-na*. Brian's older brother.
Lugh *LOO*. Old god; Cúchulainn's father
Lughnasa *Loo-NA-sa*. August festival, start of harvest season.
Mac Liag *Mac LIG*. Poet to Mahon and Brian.
Mag Dún (Dúin) *Mag DOON*. Site of battle between Kennedy and Callaghan.
Magh Adhair *MAHG-air*. Dal Cais inauguration site.
Mahon (Mathgamain) *MAY-on*. Brian's brother.
Marc (Marcan) *MARK*. Brian's monk brother.
Molloy (Maolmhuadh) *Mah-LOY*. Eóganacht king at Rath Rathlainn; Mahon and Brian's chief enemy.
Mór *MORE*. Brian's first wife, mother of son Murrough, daughter Sadb.
Murrough *MURR-ah*. Son of Brian and Mór.

Óenach *EE-nuk.* Assembly.
Órlaith *OR-la.* Mahon and Brian's older sister, Cennétig's and Bebinn's only daughter.
Osraige *AHS-rah.* Kingdom contested by Munster and Leinster.
Pádraig *PA-drig.* Foster father to Sadb, Brian's daughter.
Rónan *RO-nan.* Brian's novice monk friend.
Rory (Ruairi) *ROR-ee.* Mahon's manservant.
Sadb (Sadhbh) *SAHV.* Brian's daughter.
Scattery Island (Inis Cathaig) *IN-ish CA-taw.* Site of Saint Sénan's monastery.
Seanchaie *SHAN-a-kee.* Tale tellers.
Slipe (*Slipe*) Flat, metal sledge for moving heavy objects, pulled by horses and oxen.
Stefan *STEF-an.* Eric's brother.
Stirabout *STIR-about.* Cooked cereal.
Sulchóit (Solchóid) *SUHL-kit.* Battle Site.
Tadgh *TIED.* Úna's father; king of Uí Maine; **Tadgh** *TIED.* Dal Cais chieftain, loyal to Mahon.
Tuamgraney *TOO-am-grainee.* Cluster of farmers' ringforts; home to Rónan's brothers and Sadb's foster family.
Úna *OO-na.* Mahon's wife, daughter of Connacht King Tadgh.

—MAC LIAG—

I am Mac Liag, poet and scribe for King Mahon mac Cennétig of clan Dal Cais, Munster Kingdom, Ireland. In my one score years of service, I have penned one hundred praise poems for my king. In only one did I pen a verse praising his younger brother, Prince Brian mac Cennétig. Some months ago, Prince Brian asked if I would write the tale of his lifelong trials and triumphs with King Mahon. Had I known what he would say, I might have begged off from his plea. Yet the deed is almost done and it is my turn to plead with you. If King Mahon still rules here at Cashel, pray put these calfskins back into the round tower where you have found them and tell no one. The king will not take kindly to his brother's words or my treachery in writing them. If it comes to pass we are all dead—the king, the prince, and myself—pray carry the calfskins to honest monks who can copy my words and spread them throughout our island. Irish forever after will deem you a hero.

Muircheartach mac Con Ceartaich mac Liag
Cashel, Munster Kingdom, Ireland
The last day of March, the year of our Lord, 976

PART ONE

—Chapter One—

I was in my mother's womb when my sister's husband, the high-king of Ireland, chopped her head off. I heard whisperings about Órlaith when I was a child, and I knew she had been my only sister who died young, but I was ten before I prodded the bare facts from Mahon, my brother six years my elder. Our father, Cennétig, king of our clan, hated that Mahon had witnessed much of what happened, and he threatened my brother with banishment if he breathed a word to me. Had both of us known, or both of us not known, my father might have treated us both the same. But as it was, our father slighted Mahon and favored me. That made all the difference in our lives.

My first memory haunts me still, like a dream that comes back time and again. I am three years old, walking across courtyard stones at dusk, holding my father's hand. The top of my head scarce reaches the bottom tip of his jewel-studded knife sheath, and I can see his fair-haired legs stretching down from under his tunic to his leather shoes—red, blue, and green, the kind only kings wear. We are at Kincora, his fortress on the River Shannon, and smells of roasting pork and baking bread tell me we are heading toward our hall for evening meal.

Laughter drifts from behind us—nine-year-old Mahon and his friends in the king's house hearth room. A man lights the night torches and the courtyard bursts into a warm circle of fire.

Most nights this is a magical time for me, when nursemaids' tales of druids changing children into swans and women into fawns tumble through my mind. But this night, a gust of wind blows my mother's sick house torches out, and I hear a wail—loud, soft, loud, soft—eerie, like an animal cry.

My father stops and whispers, "*Aevil!* Pray not now, fairy woman!"

I do not know what he means, but I tug on his hand, wanting to run back to our house and hide. He tightens his huge fingers around mine and bids me stay. I cry out, yet he grips my fingers tighter. Sharp pain runs up to my elbow.

On the far side of our courtyard, three men step out from my mother's sick house—our priest, my older brother Marc, already a monk, and Lachtna, my oldest brother, who lives in his own dún upriver. From their sad faces, I guess my mother has gone to Heaven. I do not know what Heaven is or where, but Mahon has sworn no one ever comes back from there.

"Mahon," my father booms. "Come."

The laughter from behind us stops and I hear Mahon's shoes clapping up across the stones. My brother reaches for my hand, but I snatch it away and beg my father not to leave me.

He kneels down and pulls me close. "I will never leave you, Brian. Go with Mahon now. I must tend to your mother."

My father lifts me into my brother's arms and strides away. I wiggle free, but Mahon catches me and whisks me back to our house, the king's house, then empty of his friends. I throw myself on the floor, slide under my wooden bed frame.

"Aevil," I sob.

Mahon crouches down and looks under, his blue eyes peering at me. He sticks his arm out to grab my foot. "Do not say that name." I jerk my leg away.

"Come out. If you even think of our fairy woman, the priests will punish you." Those words scare me and I cry more.

Mahon snares my foot, drags me out, and carries me over to a shelf. For the first time in my life, he says I can touch his ash wood hurling stick, banded in bronze for a prince. I put my finger to the cold metal, scarce believing my good fortune. When I look back at his face, it is streaked with tears.

"Why are you crying?" I say.

He puts me down and wipes his eyes. "I am not."

The next day, I am up on my nursemaid's shoulders in a sea of people outside my mother's sick house door. Out she comes atop her funeral bier, her shroud stark white against the gray sky, the only color the yellow gorse flowers heaped on top. Mahon holds up one back corner of the bier, but he trips on the threshold and the bier tilts down. My mother slips to the ground, the yellow flowers fallen with her into the dirt. My nursemaid sets me down and covers my eyes with her hands. I cannot see, but I can hear my father's angry voice cursing and chiding Mahon. I am crying, my face wet and slimy from snot.

When next I can see, my mother is back up on the bier, off down the path. My nursemaid and I chase after her, past animal pens, gardens, houses, the pigsty, but she disappears through the gate before we can catch her. Pitying faces stare at me as we go, even the dogs and cats. I try to think what will happen if all the people and animals in the fortress are sad at the same time. My nursemaid carries me to the top of the wall, but I see only the yellow flowers moving down the hill, higher than heads in the crowd. I want to follow, but my nursemaid will not let go.

That night, Mahon says he and my father tied a stone to my mother and threw her body into the river. He swears she sank straight down to the bottom. I believe him, until a day soon after when my father takes me to the river to fish. I think of my mother and fear I will catch her on my hook.

"Mahon says you threw my mother into the river."

My father looks down at me. "Mahon tricks you, Brian. Your mother is here." He guides me over to the graveyard by our river chapel, traces his finger over new stone-carved letters. "See? Her name. Queen Bebinn."

"Aevil took her?"

My father squats down, covers my mouth. "Do not say that name so close to the chapel. Our Lord God might hear you."

"But you said it."

"You must not."

"Will she take you?"

He swipes my nose with his big rough hand. "She does not take people. She warns when death is near."

I burst out crying. Death is all around us in the graveyard.

My father pulls me close. "Only simple people believe in fairies, Brian, not kings or princes. My nursemaid told me she saw our fairy woman dance at Grey Rock on Samhain Eve, the night fairies show themselves to humans—old goddesses, she said, who fled to the mounds when humans came to our island. Truth, she did scare me, and even now I think I hear a wailing. But Samhain Eve is not for fairies. It is the night when the air turns cold and the harvests are in, when we remember the dead. I believe in only one god now, our Lord God, not goddesses who turn into fairies. You should, too."

"I heard Aevil wail."

"That was the wind." He stands up, towers over me. "Enough now. The fish are waiting."

Back in our house, I find Mahon playing chess with the blacksmith's son. "My mother is not in the river," I say. "You lied."

Mahon pushes me away. "Who would believe that anyway? Only a fool."

I want to kick Mahon, but he is much bigger. Instead, I kick his board and knock the pieces everywhere. He chases after me, but I run faster.

That night, my father drags my bed from Mahon's side of the king's house, all the way across the rush-covered hearth room floor to his sleeping nook behind his cowhide curtain. He puts our beds so close they touch. That way, he says, if I imagine I hear wails from outside, I will not need to wake him.

Mahon teases me and calls me a baby, but I do not care. Kincora is my whole world. My father is like a god watching over it, and I am his most favored son.

—Chapter Two—

I once heard my father say I followed him around like a duckling when I was small, but truth, for those three years after my mother died, I remember only my certain belief my father loved me, deemed me special, and would always keep me safe.

I was six the day my father left me in the care of my nursemaid, promising he would be back by nightfall. She left me alone in our house, free to do what I wanted.

I stood before my father's giant chest at the foot of his bed, tempted to open it, even as he had forbade me not. My mother's two blue-dyed jugs were in it, her most precious things and his too, now that she was gone. Many times my father promised he would show me the jugs when I was older, but I was older, and I made up my mind that day to take one quick look. No one, not my nursemaid or my father, would ever know.

The heavy lid took all my strength to push up and back. I dug through the fringed woolen brats my father wore in cold weather, but felt nothing like a jug. Leaning further in, so far my feet left the floor, I touched two hard cloth-wrapped bundles at chest bottom. My nursemaid nowhere in sight, I tossed brats from the chest onto the floor, climbed in, and took hold of one bundle. I dove out and carried the bundle to the hearth room for better light.

I had peeled off the cloth and was admiring the jug's sky blue color, running my hand along its curved neck and silky smooth skin, when Mahon burst through the door. Startled, I dropped the jug onto the hearth stones. A loud crack, and the jug shattered into many pieces. I went stiff, struck dumb by the horror of what I had done, in Mahon's plain sight. He stopped and stared. "Our mother's jug?"

My eyes squeezed tight, I readied for a blow, but heard only a swish from Mahon's cowhide curtain and a rustling noise in his sleeping nook. My eyes open a slit, I saw him step out with a leather pouch in his hand. He held it out to me.

"Put the pieces in here. I will bury them for you in the forest. It will be a long time before he looks for his jug. Perhaps never."

I gripped the pouch tight, not moving. I had never defied my father, nor could I think what would happen if he knew I had gone into his chest, taken the jug, broken it, and hidden the pieces from him. Mahon set about pulling on boots, strapping on his knife sheath, grabbing up his spear, readying for a deer hunt with his friends. The empty pouch dangled from my hand, shards of sky blue jug at my feet.

"You will not tell him?"

"Why?" he said. "He would only blame me."

"He will know."

"He will know if you leave those pieces lying there. If I were you, I would bury them in a deep hole before he comes back." Mahon started toward the door.

I moved to block him. "Pray take me hunting with you."

"You?" he laughed. "The little prince? Our father's pet?"

Pet? Heat crept into my face. "I am no pet. I can hunt better than you." Mahon had hurt my pride, calling me a pet.

"Oh?" He stepped back behind his curtain and handed me an old wooden stick the length of my arm, sharpened at one end—his childhood spear. "You can come this once if you pick up those pieces."

I swept the broken shards into the pouch, catching my finger on a sharp edge and drawing a drop of blood. I sucked it, stabbed my wooden spear into my rope belt, and ran after Mahon to the fenced-in horse pen, the pouch tight in my grip. He pulled me up behind him and we galloped out the fortress gate to his waiting friends. Around the back of the fortress, past the forest tree line, I dropped the pouch into a pile of leaves the same brown color as the leather, praying no one would find it.

We took a trail through the woods to an old oak grove where deer foraged for acorn mast in autumn. Skilled at tree climbing, I perched on a strong leafy limb to hide from our prey. In little time, a family of deer trotted into the grove and stopped below me—a buck, a doe, and a fawn. I hurled my wooden spear down at the buck, but missed. The deer bounded out of sight.

Mahon and his friends slid down from their trees, stood beneath my limb and hooted with laughter. Mahon swore I had ruined the hunt. I should have known my little spear could not kill deer, or indeed anything. It was a toy. His friends smirked, and I felt shame greater than any pain I had ever known. Down from the tree, I could not hide my pouty face.

Mahon's voice softened. "You tried, Brian. You will do better next time."

Those words cheered me some, but could not heal the hurt from Mahon calling me my father's pet, giving me a toy spear, laughing at me, even as he had said there would be a next time.

Riding back into the fortress at dusk, we could see my father pacing the wall. He climbed down and met us at the gate, his face knotted up under his bushy eyebrows.

"Where have you been?" he demanded of Mahon, his voice strained and high-pitched.

"Hunting deer," Mahon said, fearless.

"Hunting deer? How dare you take Brian into the forest without my leave? Where anything could happen."

Surely Mahon would tell him I had thrown my toy spear at the buck. But no, he only shrugged. My father held up a sky blue shard. "Next time you thieve around in my chest, Mahon, put my brats back in and close the lid."

The skin on Mahon's neck turned red as his hair. There would be no next time if I did not confess. I jumped off the horse and held up my cut finger. "I broke it. I am sorry." I waited in terror, staring at my father's boot.

His voice rose in surprise. "You, Brian? You went into my chest? You broke your mother's jug?" Those words stabbed into my heart like knives. My father put his hand under my chin and lifted it up, a wry smile on his face. "You are a good friend to your brother, Brian. Swear you will spare the mate?"

I swore and a great weight lifted off of me. Mahon would thank me and my father had already forgiven me. "Brian will make a good hunter some day," Mahon said, "but he needs a real spear and a horse of his own."

I had never ridden a horse alone or held a real spear. "A metal spear," I said so Mahon's words would not fade, "and a fast horse."

"A lad must know how to hunt," my father said. "Shall we visit our metalworker for your spear, Brian? And Bórama, for your horse?" Yes! I wanted to shout with joy, but I held it back. Mahon had been ten when my father gave him a horse of his own. I was only six.

I believed my father had forgiven us both, but I was wrong. The next morning, in the hall for stirabout, he spewed out a list of chores and duties for Mahon.

"I have given our shepherd boy leave to go home, Mahon. You will pen the sheep every evening, and when you are done, you will take evening meal here with me and Brian."

A dark scowl covered Mahon's face. With chores and duties, he could no longer do as he pleased with his friends, hunting or anything else.

"I will call in learned men to tutor you," my father went on to Mahon. "You will pay them close heed when they are here, and when they are gone, you will practice reciting what you have learned."

Mahon gave me a hate filled look, pushed back his chair, and strode away. I guessed he imagined the tutors were punishment for insulting the ancient seanchaie who came in for storytelling at evening fires. I hung on every word those old men said, most of all about Cúchulainn, demigod son of the old god, Lugh, and Princess Deichtre, sister to King Connor of Ulster. But usually Mahon snuck away or fell asleep.

"Mahon swore I could hunt with him and his friends," I said to my father after Mahon had gone, hoping he would command Mahon to keep his promise.

"You can learn to hunt without Mahon, Brian. You will have your horse and spear, but your brother must tend to his chores and his tutors."

My father did not understand. I wanted Mahon to know I was not a pet, that I could wield a real spear and ride my own horse. I could scarce tell my father that.

That first week of Mahon's chores, he came in late for evening meal, mouthing one excuse after the other—a lost lamb, a rainstorm, a loud noise that scared the sheep. One night, my father tired of waiting, sent me out to fetch my brother.

I spied Mahon shouting and waving his stick, scattering sheep everywhere save the pen's open gate. I envied the rippling muscles in his bare arms and legs as he ran back and forth, but I could scarce believe he did not know sheep move only in a clump. I ran to get our sheep dog and the smith's son who tended him. Together, we four penned the sheep in little time. If Mahon thanked me, his voice was so soft, I did not hear him.

Back in the hall, I held my tongue. But the smith's son followed us in, and the whole story poured out. My father's blue eyes twinkled and he slapped the table. "Twice Brian's age, but only half his brains, eh Mahon?"

Mahon went still and lowered his mutton leg onto the table. From his trembling chin, I could tell he was trying not to cry. I was pleased my father thought me wise, but more, I wanted Mahon to take me with him and his friends, hunting and whatever else they did.

Alone in our house with me, Mahon spat. "Our father favors you now. But one day he will leave you to the wolves."

Wolves? I squeezed up my nose, pretending not to care. "I will be king before you," Mahon said. "Your turn will never come."

I believed I would be king like my father, but had never thought Mahon and I would take turns. Hearing the hurt in his voice, I did not answer.

He lay down on his bed, put his face in a pillow and pulled another over his head. I stood next to him and spoke loud for him to hear. "If you take me hunting, I will sit with the tutors in your place. I will beg our father, and he will agree."

Muffled words came from the pillow. "Go away."

"When the seanchaie come," I said louder, "I will not tell when you sneak away." A plan made in haste, but I thought it perfect.

A long silence from Mahon, and then a grunt. "Go away."

Tutors did start coming into Kincora, experts in everything known to man. At first, Mahon sat with them. But as time went on, he learned to read the signs they were coming and made haste to the forest before they rode through the gate. My father was bound by our laws of hospitality to give the learned men food, beds, new boots, brats, hats, leather pouches, and even horses for their journeys home, no matter if Mahon showed his face. When he was nowhere to be found, my father's face turned red like a ripe holly berry, ready to burst.

One day, when I was eight, I called up my courage and begged my father to let me sit with the tutors in Mahon's place. To my great delight, he agreed. I learned numbers, letters, measures, months, seasons, Greek and Roman fables, names of celestial bodies, foreign lands, animals, plants, music, poems, and laws. The tutors and my father were proud of the vast knowledge I mastered. His face calmed and he no longer looked like a ripe berry. Mahon kept on with his old ways, and from time to time, invited me hunting with his friends, with my own dappled horse and my own metal spear.

Once again, I thought all was well, but once again, I was wrong. Our father and the abbot at Clonmacnoise, a wealthy monastery far upriver, had agreed a pact—tutoring for Mahon in return for cattle from my father's plentiful herd. Joy poured from Mahon's face when he heard he would at last be free of our father, and he rushed to tell his friends. But I fell into an angry fit.

The day of Mahon's leaving, strong envy came up in me watching him on his frisking black stallion in the courtyard, readying to ride out with my father's manservant and bodyguards. I would not meet his gaze, even as I knew he was looking to tell me goodbye. He touched his yew rod to his horse's cheek and nudged the animal out the gate. Tears burned behind my eyes at the sound of horses galloping down the hill.

My father sat next to me on my bench, put his arm around my shoulder and pulled me close. "When can I go?" I sulked.

"When you can recite from memory every Brehon law in our books, every number fact in our mathematical tables, every verse in our priests' gospel books."

"I can already."

"You must know the names of every plant in the forest, every animal that lives on land or in water, every bird that flies in the sky, every great man who has ever existed since time began. Then I will send you to the monks."

"My tutors cannot recite all of that. No man can. Mahon cannot recite anything."

He shrugged. "You must know every note of every song our minstrels sing, every move our chess masters make, every line in every poem our bards compose ... and you must know the mating habits of bees."

I stood and kicked my foot against the courtyard stones. "I want to be a king like you, not a keeper of bees."

My father stood next to me and pressed his big hand down on my shoulder. "Ah, Brian, to be king like me, you must teach your beekeepers the mating habits of bees."

For the first time, the thought came my father did not speak truth to me. I did not believe all kings knew the mating habits of bees, or even that he knew. But still I searched out our beekeeper and begged him tell me. When my turn came to be king, I would be ready.

With Mahon at Kincora, I enjoyed my father's favor. But with Mahon away, I chafed at my father's constant biddings—most of all his commands to sit with him and the chieftains at council meetings. The stench from their body sweat and the animal fat candles sickened me. I could scarce breathe in my chair by the smoky hearth, while my father and his chieftains sat along the sides of a long table, taking in good air from the open door and wicker window.

"Pray may I leave?" I said to my father. "I do not care about the weather and the harvests."

"You will when you are older."

"Mahon does not know."

"No matter. You are Brian, and Mahon is Mahon."

When the chieftains came in with talk of thieves stealing from our monasteries, my spirits lifted. The chieftains begged my father to take hostages from among the monks, to threaten if their abbots did not try harder to chase the thieves away.

But no, he said, "You fight the thieves. The abbots will reward you well."

"Do not all great kings take hostages?" I blurted out. "Do you not fear thieves will hurt Mahon at Clonmacnoise?"

As soon as I said those words, I prayed my father had not heard me. Yet the ruts in his forehead grew deep as ditches in our vegetable gardens. "Mahon is warrior age. He can fight the thieves himself."

Did Mahon have a sword? I had never seen it. Yet I doubted my own doubts and vowed never to speak them out loud again.

I was close to ten before I truly challenged my father. We were watching cowherds from Munster's overking, King Callaghan, drive our best cows and bulls across the river to Callaghan's fortress on a big rock called Cashel. With Mahon at Kincora, I had paid close heed to the cow drive so I could tell him what he had missed. But with Mahon away, new thoughts came to my mind.

"Why does Callaghan take our cows and bulls and never give any back?"

My father tossed words at me like so much gristle from his plate. "More cows would only mean more grain to grow."

A falsehood I could not let pass. "The ancients say great kings cannot have too many cows."

"The ancients know nothing of cows."

"They speak of cows in every tale they tell."

My father fell silent, and I did not say more. Instead, I imagined myself Cúchulainn, turning my wasp-spasm kick against Callaghan's cowherds and holding them off with my magic barbed sword, until our chieftains swept down through the forest and stole our cows and bulls back. It did matter to me that Callaghan took our cattle and never gave any back.

That same day, the chieftains came into Kincora with urgent news. I followed them to our council house, but my father's manservant swore I was not wanted. I yelled, but my father stepped out, commanded me away, and banged the door shut.

My eyes blurred with tears, I made haste to the king's house, to my sleeping nook. To my surprise, Mahon was back from the monks in talk with a friend.

He spied my wet face. "You have heard about our brothers?" Mahon's deep voice surprised me, as did the rust-colored hairs sticking out from his chin.

"Marc and Lachnta?" The only two brothers I knew, save Mahon.

"No, Echtigern and Donncuan." I sighed relief. I had heard those brothers' names, but they had been long away by the time of my birth.

"They were killed in a skirmish against King Ivar's warriors in the west of our kingdom." King Ivar? I was shamed not to know of him. Mahon shot me a surprised look. "Do you not know of the Norse King Ivar of Limerick?" I did not answer. "You know of Órlaith? Our sister?"

"She died young," I said to Mahon. That was all I knew.

Mahon's surprise turned to pity. "You know how she died?"

"No."

Mahon sighed. "No matter. There is no need for you to know. Not yet." I vowed the next time my father lied or hid a truth from me, I would challenge him more.

The day I turned ten, my father and I set out for a walk in the hills behind Kincora, our wont on fine summer days. That morning, he had given me his father's knife and jewel-studded sheath. It was right and good I should have them, but I knew better than to stir Mahon's envy. So I hid the knife and sheath in my father's chest.

On our walk, my father started in telling about beasts who roamed the hills and ate men. I had never seen such beasts, and I said so. He smiled and said they only came out at night.

We stood on a jutting rock and looked out over hills and valleys. Always in that same place he told the same tale. "Long ago, I sang songs to your mother across this valley, a princess in Connacht Kingdom. When she sang back to me, I knew we would wed."

I had once loved that tale, but I could no longer bear his lies. "Mahon says a man cannot throw his voice from Kincora to Connacht. It is too far."

I stayed silent, thinking he would try to sway me. He tilted his head. "I cannot fool you anymore, eh?"

"Cúchulainn did not lie," I said. "Why do you?"

"Cúchulainn? A mere tale. I am a real king who keeps the peace." He stepped off the rock, back onto the forest trail.

I stayed close behind him. "You do not keep the peace. Echtigern and Donncuan died fighting your battles, and I know who killed them ... and I know about Órlaith."

"Oh?" He turned and glared at me.

"Mahon told me. Those same Norse murderers will host here next."

His voice menacing, he said, "No king dares attack Kincora, Norse or Irish. I am strong and feared. That is how I keep the peace."

I hurled a rock against a tree trunk. "How does any king know you are strong?"

He shrugged. "You will know when you are older."

"I am older. I am ten."

"You do not know all the stories." I didn't want to hear his lies. But he sat me down on a log and put his foot up.

"Before you were born, I fought Callaghan at Mag Dún for the Munster overkingship." He waved his arm out wide. "The field turned red with the blood of Callaghan's warriors, but I spared him. I granted Callaghan the overkingship for a vow to always leave me and my sons in peace. Peace through strength, Brian, that is my way."

"Callaghan takes our best cows and bulls twice every year. He does not leave us in peace."

His eyes narrowed. "You doubt me. Kneel down, Brian."

He pulled out his short sword, touched me on the head with his blade. I slipped off the log onto my knees. "Listen to these words Callaghan said to me at Mag Dún," he said. "'Praise God and you, King Cennétig, merciful king of Dal Cais. I swear to always leave you in peace.' Say those words back to me, Brian."

"Praise God and you, King Cennétig, merciful king of Dal Cais," I said. "I swear to always leave you in peace."

My father raised his short sword in the air, shook it over my head. "If you break your oath, Callaghan, I will kill you." He turned and walked off down the path.

I sat back up on my log, struggling to fathom what had happened. Perhaps my father was strong. Perhaps other kings did fear him. I chased after him and begged him tell his story at evening fires. Surely the seanchaie did not know of his glorious victory against Callaghan at Mag Dún.

"No. Evening fires belong to the ancients."

Back in our house, I dragged my bed's wooden frame and straw mattress from my father's side back to Mahon's nook—not so easy across the rush floor. When my father asked me why, I said I was ten, not a baby anymore.

That night after evening meal, my father disappeared into his council house, alone. Save for his manservant who brought him food and emptied his stinking pot into the cesspit, he let no one in, not even me. He stayed there alone, all that night and for five days and four nights after.

—Chapter Three—

The fifth night, something woke me. I opened my eyes to blackness. For a blessed moment, I could see nothing, hear nothing, remember nothing. A long, mournful wolf's howl, a whistling snore from Mahon next to me on his bed, and all came rushing back. Another snore, a whiff of ale from Mahon's breath, and I sat up, hoping to hear any sound from my father's side—a scrape of his boot, a creak from his bed frame, a clearing of his throat. But no, only that same dreaded silence. I lay back down, fighting tears. All my life, we had not been apart so long.

A screech pierced the night. Not a wolf, but what? I flipped onto my stomach, pulled my pillow over my head. If that was Aevil, I did not want to hear her. I had not forgotten her wails the night my mother died. They meant death.

"Brian. You again?" Mahon! Ach! He had threatened to throw me out if I woke him.

I stayed quiet on my bed, praying for dawn. When birds chirped and light grayed outside my window, I crept silent as a cat around the end of my bed and slipped out into the courtyard. On the stones, in my breeches, I clutched my arms around my knees and rocked. Only a small spotted dog was about, with his tail between his legs. He sniffed over and licked me. I did not have the will to stop him.

"Why does my father hide?" I whispered to him. He wiggled his back end. I held his face, stared into his eyes. "Who are you, dog? Hound of Chulainn? Cú-chulainn?"

Sometimes when I pictured my demigod hero in his chariot, his tunic white and gold, his magic barbed sword sheathed at his waist, his long black hair blowing straight out behind him, I could think thoughts wiser than any mere boy. A wise thought came to me.

Your father hides from you, Brian.

My nose in the dog's neck, I breathed a silent scream. It was so. I had angered my father, calling him a liar, challenging him and moving my bed. The dog nuzzled his cold nose into my lap, his tail gone still.

Go down to the river and catch a fish. When you come back, Cennétig will be waiting for you at the hall door, like every other summer morning.

I tiptoed back into our house, pulled on my tunic and shoes, picked up my spear and crept back out. No dog in sight, I climbed to the top of the mud wall and spied a black cloud rising between hills in the distance. The smell of rain in my nose, I raced down through the ditch, over the berm, and down the hill to the river. A salmon shimmered under the deadfall, but it swam away before I could take aim. I crouched, ready to strike again, but minnows taunted me, swirling in waves in the shallow water, flashing silver.

I paced, whispering, "Praise you, worthy king of Dal Cais."

A big trout swam by and I snagged it as thunder sounded and the heavens opened up with a mighty downpour. My hair and tunic clinging to me, water filling my shoes, I started back up, the fish limp on the end of my spear. Only a very strong clan king could command a vow of peace from an overking. My father trusted only me with his tale, not my brothers, not the ancients. I spoke his brave words out loud. "If you break your oath, Callaghan, I will kill you."

Almost back to the fortress, a plan came to mind so wise I knew it had to have come from Cúchulainn. I would take my fish to my father's manservant waiting outside the council house door and bid him bring it in to the king. I would have him say, "Brian praises God and you, merciful king of Dal Cais. He prays that with this fish you will forgive him all his doubts and foolish questions."

Good cheer came into my heart, even as lightning flashed and the rain poured so hard I could scarce see.

When I spied Mahon waiting for me in the rain outside our hall, his jaw set tight, no smile on his face, my good cheer left me and I dropped my spear and fish onto the ground. Mahon pushed me across the threshold to my brothers, Marc and Lachtna, sitting at a table with my father. I scarce knew my father in his leather vest, short sword sheathed at his waist, his spear, long sword, leather helmet, and round wooden shield on the table. He motioned me to a chair beside him.

"King Callaghan's army is near. He comes with Norse King Ivar from Limerick. I have summoned the chieftains and we will fight, but my victory is not certain. You will go with your brothers to the monks at Holy Island and stay there until it is safe."

I clutched my father's arm, but he pried my hands off, waved my brothers away.

"I prayed this day would not come until you were older, Brian. Hear this from me, not from those who would gossip in half-truths and falsehoods."

I willed myself to listen between my thunderous heartbeats.

"Your sister, Órlaith, betrayed me, else this battle would not be happening." His voice dropped lower. "Heed your women well when you become king. Do not make my same mistakes."

"I will never be king. Mahon swore it."

My father swiped his brow. "You will be a great king."

Lachtna shouted in through the hall door. "Warriors, longboats, horses. Close."

My father pushed back his chair and stood. I lunged and tried to stop him, but he held me away. "Pray forgive me when I am gone."

His helmet pulled down, the leather reaching down to the tip of his nose, big holes for his eyes, he strode to the door, spear in one hand, shield in the other. He stopped and looked back at me.

"Pigsty, Brian. Remember it."

Without another word, he vanished. I sprinted after him, but Mahon waited outside and blocked me. "No. Come with me."

I dodged around him but had scarce gone five steps when he knocked me from behind onto the ground. "Fool. You want to die? You heard what he said. Holy Island. Stay with me."

My arm in Mahon's grasp, he dragged me across the rain-soaked ground into our house, stuffed clothes and shoes into a sack, and took down his hurling stick from the shelf.

"Take a last look, Brian. You will not see this house again."

Screams came from outside. "Norse warships in the rapids."

Mahon slung the sack over his shoulder, shoved me out the door in front of him. People streamed past, yelling. Pigs, chickens, and goats ran wild, let loose from their pens, squealing, squawking. Mud splattered everywhere.

"Pigsty," I shouted. "He is there."

"No," Mahon yelled. "This way."

"But he said pigsty."

Mahon tried for my wrist, but I dashed back into our house, and snagged my knife and sheath from the chest. I fumbled about for a leather string, threaded it through my sheath, tied it around my waist, and slipped my knife in.

Mahon threw open the door, stared at my knife. "What are you doing? Where did that come from?"

I squeezed the hilt. "My father."

"You stole it?"

"He gave it to me."

Mahon started toward me, but I backed away, pulled out my knife and waved it at him. I would fight my way to the pigsty, if need be. "Put that away, Brian," he growled, "or I will take it."

Mahon dropped his sack and took another step toward me. I sheathed my knife and put my arms out to stop him. He grabbed me and pulled me out the door toward the fortress back wall, my knife flopping against my thigh.

Marc and Lachtna paced behind a house, waiting for us. "Mahon!" Lachtna said. "Where have you been?" Mahon tilted his head toward me, rolled his eyes.

Lachtna's gaze found my knife. "Ready to fight, eh Brian?"

"Are you not? Our father said 'pigsty.' He waits there."

"Forget the pigsty. The fort is burning," Lachtna said.

A few steps toward the back wall and we heard a whoosh— the thatched roof of the house gone up in flames. A shower of sparks rained down on our heads as we raced away, Mahon pushing me always ahead of him. Scrambling over the wall, we ran across a field and through trees, circling down to the river path. The way was clogged with people, most fleeing the fortress. Chieftains I had seen at council meetings pounded by on horses toward Kincora, hastening, I prayed, to my father's side.

A short way down the path, we climbed a hillock. A huge rainbow filled the morning sky, and beneath it, a red glow from Kincora burned like a sunrise. The smell of smoke filled my nose, and tears rolled out my eyes. I heard a wailing.

Aevil! Not now, fairy woman!

An urge welled up inside of me to tear somebody, anybody, into small pieces. But I could only weep.

—Chapter Four—

The path to Holy Island ran next to the river from Kincora to Bórama, our father's fortress where he kept his boats, cows, and bulls. There, the path took a sharp turn inland, twisting through forest, sheep fields, tilled farmland, more sheep fields, farmland, and more forest. My brothers swore we should stay out of sight in the day and walk at night, so we stopped at a forest stream, gulped down water, ate berries, and waited for dark.

Night come, we hastened down the trail by moonlight, passing by sheep who stood sleeping as if that night was no different from any other. I held tight to Mahon's rope belt.

"Beasts roam in these woods," I said.

"What beasts?"

"Beasts that eat men, at night. Our father told me."

"No beasts," Mahon said, "just sheep."

I quieted, until the beasts came back to mind. "Say it again, Mahon. No beasts?"

Many times I begged, and many times Mahon answered me. "No beasts, just sheep."

The last time I asked, he pointed to the sky. "Look. The stars. Can you say their names?"

I said as many names as I could, panting along behind him. "I know the mating habits of bees. Do you?"

"No, but look." Up ahead, Lachtna had turned off the main path and was running up the ridge.

"I tried to stop him," Marc said when we caught up, "but he will not go without his chessboard."

"What chessboard?" Mahon said.

"Our grandfather Lachtna's. Go after him, Mahon."

Mahon shook his head, whispered to Marc. I caught the words Grey Rock, Aevil.

I dropped to my knees. Marc took hold of my armpits and pulled. "Get up, Brian. I will carry you if I must."

I stayed down, covered my head, limp with fear.

Marc raised his hand. "Need I beat you?"

"No." Mahon pushed Marc's hand away. "I can name more animals than Brian." He pulled on my hair. "Beaver ... badger ... deer."

I stumbled after him down the path, scarce able to see through the wet in my eyes.

"Fox," Marc said from behind us.

"Bird." I breathed out.

"A bird is not an animal," Mahon said over his shoulder.

"It is," I said.

"A bird is an animal," Marc said. "What else would it be?"

"No matter," Mahon said. "I named more animals."

"You did not," I said. "Cow, hedgehog, wolf, pig, dog, badger, cat, chicken, horse ..."

"I give up," Mahon said. "Now plants ..."

Further down, the path forked at a grove of trees with roots like bent legs, growing above the ground. One way led toward the lake and a fisherman's path, the other to Tuamgraney, a cluster of farmers' ringforts. Marc bade us wait at the fork for Lachtna, saying we would take the fisherman's path by the lake, around Tuamgraney—longer, but safer.

"Why?" I asked.

"You do not know?" Marc said.

I shook my head. Something else my father had not told me. "The Tuamgraney have not been our friends since our father and his brothers took the Dal Cais kingship from them. They would like nothing better than a chance to kill all four of Cennétig's living sons at once."

Leaning against a tree, my eyes closed. When next I looked up, Lachtna stood over me, his chessboard and pieces in a sack over his shoulder.

We picked our way along the fisherman's path. Had it not been for bullfrogs' croaks, wind-whipped waves lapping the shore, the light of the moon breaking from behind clouds and streaking across water, I might not have known we were but an arm's length from falling into Lough Derg, a giant lake made by the River Shannon.

"What else can you name?" Mahon said from behind me.

"Laws?" I said.

"You lie," he said.

"I do not."

"Then do it."

I could recite laws learned from my tutors. My honor price as a prince was higher than most Dal Cais, and I could rid myself of a wife if she let my household fall to ruin or did not bear me children. But truth, why did I care? My fortress was burned and my father likely dead. No law could change that.

By the time I named all the laws I knew, we were back on the main path toward Holy Island, on the far side of Tuamgraney.

"You know the mating habits of bees?" Mahon said.

"Our beekeeper told me."

"Well?"

"Thousands of male bees chase one queen bee in the air, and the ones who catch her stick their flutes into her stomach and die."

Mahon laughed. "Poor fools. But we are here."

Marc and Lachtna had turned down a well-trodden, tree-rooted trail toward the lake, where a clutch of monks in brown tunics stood waiting by currachs, leather-wrapped wooden boats tied to tree stumps. Moonlight and stars filled the sky, and far away, I could see a tiny speck of land I knew must be Holy Island.

"Did I not tell you?" Mahon said. "No beasts. No fairies." He put his arm around me and pulled me close. My brother had tricked me to name everything I knew, to forget the beasts and fairies. Kincora had burned and I suspected my father was dead. Yet with Mahon beside me, I would be brave, even as tears always seemed to threaten behind my eyes.

—Chapter Five—

The going was hard against the wind, and the waves turned our currachs sideways. Marc and a giant-sized monk struggled to keep our small boat pointed toward Holy Island. I pulled my woolen brat tight around my shoulders and fixed my gaze on Mahon and Lachtna in the boat ahead of us. A wave wet my breeches and shoes.

Our currach scraping bottom, I jumped into shallow water and splashed onto the rock-pocked sand. Monks in brown wool tunics lined the shore, all silent and staring. The abbot whispered to the giant-sized monk from our boat, who took me by the arm and led me up a forested path to a field filled with anthill-like huts, woven tree branches covered in mud. He opened the wicker door to one and nudged me into a space so small I could not stand.

"You will sleep here," he said.

I was shaking in the dark when Mahon's sack came flying through the door, Mahon crouching down behind it. He tossed me a mat and a blanket, commanded me to lie down and sleep. But I could not stop my trembling.

Moonlight filtered in through cracks in the walls, enough for me to see Mahon's long, thin body stretched out next to me, his tangled hair covering his face. His quiet breath and hands behind his head told me he stayed awake. I touched his arm.

"Our father is dead?" I said.

"Yes."

"Who were they?"

"Callaghan. And the Norse."

"How do you know?"

"The abbot."

"The abbot was not there," I said. "How does he know?"

"He has spies."

I touched Mahon's arm again. "Our father said to remember the pigsty. Perhaps he hides there."

Mahon turned over on his side, faced me. "You cannot wish him back alive, Brian. A Norse warrior speared him through the neck and they threw his body into the fire. No pigsty. No fortress. Only ashes, burned flesh and bones."

A sob escaped my throat. "It is not true. You left him to die. You and Lachtna and Marc."

"We could not have saved him. He bade us save you."

"Coward," I said, tears flooding my face. "You did not try."

Mahon reached over and put his hand over my mouth. "Quiet. Do you think those raiders will not come for us? This is no time for tears."

I squeezed my eyes shut, pulled my blanket tight around my neck. After a long while, I opened my eyes again, saw Mahon still awake. "Tell me about Órlaith."

"Órlaith?" He sounded vexed. "Now?"

"Our father said the raid would not have happened, save for her."

Mahon stayed silent a long time. When he spoke, his voice strained. "Did he tell you he forced Órlaith to wed a brute? The high king of Ireland? Against her will?"

"No." My father would have boasted his daughter had been wife to a high-king, powerful across vast territories north of us. More powerful than Callaghan.

"I was only six," Mahon said, "but I remember Órlaith hiding when the high king came in. Her wedding tunic was covered in filth when our father found her in a slave's hovel. She wept at our chapel door, taking her vows. So did our mother, who was so heavy with you, she could scarce stand."

"Órlaith betrayed our father. He told me."

"He would say that, but truth, it was revenge Órlaith wanted. And she got it, lying with her husband's son that first week. No doubt she imagined the high-king would send her back to her father, like any other wayward wife. But no—he commanded her head chopped off."

I gasped loud. Mahon slapped his hand over my mouth. "Hush. Monks are all around." He lowered his voice. "The high king's manservant dumped Órlaith's head at our gate." Mahon took a big breath. "It was gray and it stank. It was horrible. I remember our father yelling and cursing, and our mother ..." Mahon's voice caught.

"What?"

"She cradled Órlaith's head in her arms and sang to it." A sob escaped Mahon's throat. "Rocked it ..."

I scarce breathed. "She birthed you right after in the sick house. She screamed so loud I covered my ears. The midwife caught you ... Truth, Brian, you should have waited."

Waited? "The midwife tried to give you to her, but she wanted only Órlaith. For weeks she raved like a madwoman. Even after she calmed, she stayed in the sick house, withering away until she died." Mahon went quiet.

"Did I visit her?"

"How would I know? Our father forbade me from visiting her. He said he would whip me if I told you why she was sick.

I had imagined my mother's soft voice in my mind, whispering my name, her warm hand touching me, her wet eyes smiling up at me—all made-up memories. I had not known I was born into grief, a torment to Mahon.

Mahon went on. "The high king never sent the warriors he promised our father, but Cennétig hosted against Callaghan anyway, at Mag Dún, with his pitiful army. He never stood a chance."

I forced words from my throat. "He said he won at Mag Dún."

Mahon let out a sigh. "Well, now you know. He lied to you every day of your life. He escaped Mag Dún, but our brothers, Finn and Dúb, were not so fortunate. Callaghan never forgave the insult."

A monk stuck his head through our doorway and wagged his finger for us to quiet. "You knew?" I said when the monk was gone.

"Knew what?"

"That Callaghan and the Norse would come against our father."

"Not until he called me home from Clonmacnoise." Mahon stayed quiet for a moment. "I was surprised he had not warned you. You were the one he made up stories for. You were the one he lived for." Mahon rolled over, turned his back to me. and began to snore.

I wanted to kick him and wake him, but I could only pick up my shoe and throw it against the hut door. Mahon sat up with a jerk, and two monks stuck their heads in. I feigned sleep, as warm breaths hovered over my face.

"Sleeping?" one monk said.

"Yes," Mahon whispered. "A noise woke me."

"A mystery," another monk said.
"A bat," the first one said.
"Yes, a bat," they all agreed.

The monks padded away. Mahon lay down and went back to snoring. I slid closer to his body to feel his warmth. The rhythm of his breath soothed me, and I fell asleep.

—Chapter Six—

It was still dark when a bell woke us. Marc stuck his head in and bade us up for morning prayers. We followed him across a field filled with monks' huts, and in the distance, we could see candlelight glowing from the windows of a stone church. Climbing over fence stiles, we came up to monks kneeling outside a church overflowing with other monks. I could scarce see the lake, the air was so heavy with fog and mist, but thunder told me rain was coming. Mahon fell on his knees next to Lachtna, mumbling.

"Kneel. Pray," Marc said, his hand on my head. How could I? I did not know the words. I slipped behind him.

He pulled me out. "This is Holy Island, Brian. You cannot hide from our Lord God."

A blast of wind ruffled the lake water. The monks rose in haste and hastened toward the refectory—a long, low building with a smoke-bellowing chimney rising from the middle. Marc pulled me along beside him, and I could smell food. I was hungry. Monks at long tables stared as we came in. I felt naked, even as I wore my dirt-smeared tunic.

"Why do they stare?" I whispered to Marc.

"They pity you."

"Bid them stop."

"They will pity you if they want. Come."

He nodded toward a raised platform at one end, where Mahon and Lachtna sat at the abbot's table. We took the empty chairs, and straightaway, I readied to pour my milky stirabout down my throat.

The abbot put up his hand. "No, Brian. Wait for my blessing."

Blood rushed into my face and I set the bowl down.

The abbot said words, my brothers and all the monks in the refectory said words back, and everyone set to slurping and scraping. My gut soured and my hunger fled.

"I thank the good Lord you are safe," the abbot said. "Your father did well to bid you here. A pity he could not come himself."

"Leave Kincora without a king?" Lachtna said, ripping a piece of hot baked bread from its loaf.

"He stood no chance," the abbot said. "Why wait to be killed?"

"A king does not run from his enemies," Lachtna said.

I caught his eye. "You left him to die."

The abbot and my brothers set down their spoons. "Hold your tongue, Brian," the abbot said, "else Brother Blat will cut it out." Brother Blat? The giant-sized monk at the table below us turned his head, aimed his gaze at me.

"Pray, may I go?" I pleaded.

The abbot waved me away. "Go if you must."

I raced back to my hut in the pouring rain, shook myself like a dog, and wrapped myself in my blanket. I had known nothing about Órlaith, or the high king, or Callaghan, or the Limerick Norse, or Mag Dún, or the Tuamgraney, or why my father hid in his council house, or the words to pray, or that Brother Blat would cut out my tongue. Only two days before, I had believed I knew everything and was special, like my father. But truth, he had been a liar and a fool and I wanted to be nothing like him.

A wise thought came. Cennétig was not my father. I was son of a god, a demigod, like Cúchulainn. I did not need Cennétig anymore.

The storm had passed when the bell rang again, many times. I covered my ears, but to no use. Mahon shouted in through the hut door. "Norse. Get up."

I stumbled out to monks streaming in from fields and four longboats heading for the island—sails down, oars beating water. I grabbed for Mahon, but he was steps ahead of me.

"The church," he shouted back to me.

"Kneel over there," the abbot said as I came through the door. He tossed me a robe and pointed to novice monks in a corner.

I slipped the robe over my still damp tunic and knelt next to one. When I looked back for my brothers, he nudged me in the side. "Do not move. You will get us all killed."

A voice speaking Norse came through the door. The abbot said something back in Norse, and then Marc spoke. "I am Marc, son of Cennétig. You seek me?"

Nei. Brødene. "Not you, Marc," the abbot said. "Your brothers."

"No brothers of mine hide here," Marc said. "The first place these murderers would look?" Scuffling noises, more words back and forth in Norse.

"Stand. All of you." The abbot's voice.

The novice monk put his hand on my shoulder. "Swoon. Cover your hair."

My hair was longer than the novices'. I clutched my hood tight around my throat and fell to the floor. Feet shuffled up and kicked me in my side. I held my breath, brave and stoic like a demigod. More grunts, Norse talk, shuffling feet.

"They are gone. Thanks be to God," the abbot said.

I sat up and looked around. Mahon? Lachtna? As if they had heard my thoughts, my brothers strode through the chapel door. "That well water almost froze me to death," Mahon said, dripping wet. He stepped over and ruffled my hair, a smile on his face.

"Better freezing water than those mice in the granary," Lachtna said, swiping straw from his tunic. I burst into tears. A coward. Again.

⊕

The Limerick Norse stole every bit of gold and silver at Holy Island, save for the little hidden in the round tower.

"The Norse grow fat and lazy," the abbot said as we gulped broth at his table. "They do not trouble themselves climbing our round tower. It is human booty they are wanting for the slave markets." He chomped on bread. "Our tower holds little treasure anyway. Cennétig kept his secreted away at Kincora."

"Where at Kincora?" Lachtna asked. "If we could find treasure, we could trade it for cattle."

"We have cattle," I said, proud to know that. "At Bórama."

Marc cleared his throat, stared at me. "Do you think Callaghan and the Norse would burn the fortress and kill our father but leave our cows?" I aimed my gaze at a bump on the dirt floor.

"We leave on the morrow, Mahon," Lachtna said. "Else Norse thieves will strip Kincora bare, whatever is left of it."

I looked up. "What of me?"

"Be glad you have food and a hut here," Lachtna said. "We cannot be burdened with you at Kincora."

I glanced at Mahon, certain he would shake his head and swear I would be no burden. He set his bowl down, met my gaze. "We will visit, you will be safe here. No beasts, no fairies."

No!

"You will learn to pray," Marc said. "I will teach you the words."

The abbot studied me, one eye half closed. "Do I see a novice monk in the making?" No monk. I would be a great king. I held my tears until I was inside my hut, sobbed myself to sleep.

At sunup, Mahon stuffed his sack with clothes, strapped his knife and short sword around his waist. I watched from my mat. "Such a long face, prince?" he said. "Heed Marc. He will teach you to pray."

He stepped out the door, walked fast across the field toward the church. I ran after him to Lachtna, Marc, and the abbot, standing together. Mahon and Lachtna lifted their sacks over their shoulders, started off toward the strand, tall and slim like trees.

I followed and watched them climb into a currach with a boatman. He pushed off, but the currach stuck in the sand. As he reached out his oar to push off again, I splashed into the water and threw myself in, almost turning the currach over. I prayed Mahon would grab onto me, fathom my grit.

"Good God, Brian," Mahon said. "Throw him out," he said to the boatman.

Strong arms lifted me and dropped me into the cold lake. I stood in water up to my knees, helpless to stop the currach gliding out of reach. My legs numb, I walked wretched back to my empty hut.

Weeks went by with no news of Lachtna and Mahon. Every day, I questioned Marc and the abbot, but they swore they knew nothing.

One day, I made a plan to steal a currach and row myself to the mainland, in the dead of night when the guard was sleeping. Before morning prayers the next morning, I stole under a full moon down to the water, only to find the guard awake.

"You, Brian?" he said. "Trouble sleeping?"

I lifted up the spear I held in my hand. "I come to fish, before they wake."

"You would spear a sleeping fish?"

"I would wait for them to wake."

"And the fish?"

"I will take it to the abbot."

He laughed loud. "That would be a sight." He peered at me from under his eyelids. "Running away, eh? Shall I tell the abbot? Brother Marc? Brother Blat?"

I dropped my spear, fell on my knees, put my hands up in prayer. "Pray no. I beg you."

"The abbot will have my head if you sneak past me. Swear you will not." I swore, my mind searching for any other way to escape the island.

"If it is Kincora you are looking for, it is not safe there."

"Why?"

"Ruled by rats, I hear." His grin showed missing teeth, top and bottom.

I grabbed my spear, raced back up to the church as the bell sounded for morning prayers. I put myself next to Marc.

"Do rats rule Kincora?"

I did not wait for his answer, but knelt next to Rónan, the novice monk who had saved me from the Norse raiders. He put his hand on my arm, solacing me once again.

—Chapter Seven—

I had no choice those months but to follow Brother Blat's commands to pray eight times a day, tend the animals, sweep the church, study my lessons. At mealtime I sat with the novice monks, forbidden to speak save for prayers. In the morning, we downed stirabout, and in the evening, barley bread, root vegetables, bird, the occasional fish. On special feast days, the mutton, beef, and hog we hacked and ripped to pieces with our knives and fingers only teased our guts.

After evening meal, at the abbot's signal, we rose from our refectory tables and followed each other out the door across a grassy space into the candlelit church. A voice carrying words of absolution sounded from behind a half wall of mud and stones. I could not see the speaker's face, but Rónan told me he was Father Conn, the priest. For a long time, I had nothing to confess, but Father Conn blessed me anyway and muttered my sins would come to mind when I was ready. Every night, I fell onto my mat in the hut I shared with novices, thankful I had escaped our Lord God and the priest one more night.

Yet I could not escape Brother Blat and his rule of silence. One night, back from Father Conn, I asked my hut-mates' names. They whispered them. I asked where they lived, the ranks of their fathers, the ages of their brothers. They started whispering all at once, and worse, they laughed. I threw my pillow sack over one boy's face to quiet him, but too late. Brother Blat swung open the hut door, commanded us out into the night, lined us up, thrashed our bent-over naked bottoms with his strap. A week went by before I could sit without pain.

I vowed Brother Blat would never get another chance to beat me. If he tried, I would set my demigod self against him.

✠

One summer afternoon before vespers, the abbot called the novices to the refectory for Bible stories. He waved me away, swearing Bible stories were only for monks. Truth, I was glad for the time alone, and crept down to the lake to watch birds, insects, and fish I could see through the clear water. I knew a trout from a salmon, but not a starling from a blackbird or a swallow from a sparrow. Mahon might have known, but he was not there to tell me. I contented myself watching big fish chase little ones, fish of all sizes chasing insects on the water surface, birds swooping down and snagging fish, ducks turning themselves upside down in the water and coming up with little fish, swallowing them whole.

Those sights soothed me, the way of the world, an order to things, until ripples in the water changed the face of a little fish into my father's face. I blinked, but his face stayed. I stood, ran back and forth, keeping sight of the father fish darting below the water's surface. I started back up the path, my mind conjuring a bigger fish with my face on it swimming up behind the father fish and eating it.

In my hut, alone, I lay on my mat and gazed at the ceiling. A trail of ants came from a crack between the floor and wall, went up across the ceiling and down a wall into a corner. My mind turned them into monks, Brother Blat in the lead, and then into monster Norse ships rowing across our lake to Holy Island. I bolted up, ran outside and wrenched a leafy branch from a tree. I raced back in and smashed ants, swept them across the floor, beat them down, stomped on them, joy flooding my chest as I crushed them beneath my feet. I was a demigod like Cúchulainn in his battle rage, killing everything in sight with my wasp-spasm kick and stomp, reciting words he spoke for every head he chopped off in battle—*Like the sands on the strand* (swipe), *the stars in the sky* (swipe), *the dew in May* (swipe), *snowflakes and hailstones* (swipe), *leaves of the tree* (swipe), *buttercups in the meadow* (swipe).

I sat up on my mat, my chest heaving, my heart pounding, daring the ants to show themselves, swatting and stomping any that poked through the crack.

That night, my turn come for Father Conn, my sins poured forth. I knelt beside the half wall of mud and stone, readying for a long stay. "Father, all these nights I have kept silent. Now I yearn for penance. I can no longer bear the pain of my sins."

"How have you sinned, my son?"

I let my words out in a burst. "I wish to kill my father's murderers and I wish to harm my brothers who left my father to die."

"For those wishes you have just cause. I can give you no penance."

Sweat broke out on my forehead. "But Father, at Kincora, I believed myself good and worthy. Here, I have killed and maimed. This very day I smashed ants that crawled up the walls and across the ceiling of my hut—hundreds of them, so many I feared they would crawl into my nose in my sleep. I took joy in smashing them." My hands turned cold waiting for Father Conn to speak.

"Have you nothing more to confess, Brian? Your only sin is killing ants?"

I squeezed my fingers tight, took a deep breath. "I sometimes imagine I am like Cúchulainn, beating back ants with my wasp-spasm kick."

Father Conn hesitated. "Wasp-spasm kick?"

"His battle rage, Father."

"Ah. What boy does not imagine such things? Is that all, Brian? Killing ants? Wasp-spasm kicks? You waste my time."

Fright swept over me. Father Conn would not give me penance. "Father, I pray you. I have harmed other creatures here. A lamb bleated alone in the heather. A lost lamb. I left it to die. I fear a wolf tore it into pieces—wool, skin, insides."

"No doubt it did, but your sin?"

"It thrilled me."

Father Conn stayed silent. I went on, set on prodding penance from his mouth, even if it meant lying. "You know that lame dog who follows me everywhere, who sleeps outside my hut, tries to sit beside me at evening meal? I cannot bear to tell you what I have done to him, many times."

"God shall forgive if you repent."

"I kicked him, many times. Each time I kicked him, I thought of my father, or my brothers, or Brother Blat. I took pleasure kicking him, until my shame made me stop. Punish me, Father. I beg you."

Father Conn paused. "You have just cause to kill ants in your hut if they ruin your rest. But for the joy of killing and kicking a dog, you will fast for two days and recite the Pater two score times every hour, on your knees in this church. One may have just cause to kill or kick, but never to enjoy it. Remember that. Now go."

"Thank you, Father. But pray, may I finish?"

"The night grows short."

"My worst sin?"

"Yes?"

"At the lake, I saw Cennétig's face on a little fish, and I pictured myself a big fish swimming up behind the little fish and eating him. Father, have mercy on me, that I wished to swallow Cennétig whole."

For the longest time, I heard Father Conn turning the pages of his penitential, back and forth, back and forth. "I find no such sin in my book. If you strive to be a great king for the good of your people, our Lord God will look kindly upon you. Take yourself away now."

"But Father, pray, one more sin? I swear it will be the last."

"The monks are waiting."

I took a deep breath and spat out the words. "I told a half-truth, Father. It is not so I imagine myself like a demigod. I am a demigod, like Cúchulainn, son of the god, Lugh, and my mother, Queen Bebinn. Cennétig swore he was my father, but he lied."

I imagined Father Conn would take many breaths and triple my Patters. But he softened his voice.

"It is right and good you solace yourself in your time of grief, Brian, and for that I can give you no more Paters. Surely you know we are all children of our Lord God, no matter what else we believe."

"The priest at Kincora said so, but he died in the rout."

Father Conn paused. "His truth did not die in the rout. We are all children of our Lord God, no matter if any priest lives or dies. He will forgive your wrong thinking until you become wise enough to know better. Then you must beware of such notions. Remember that when the time comes. Now go. I will hear no more of your idle talk."

Monks shifted their feet outside the church door, no doubt tired of waiting their turns for Father Conn. He had heeded my words and forgiven my sins, and I was glad. But most of all, I was glad I could be a demigod, without sin, until I knew better.

I was kneeling on the hard church floor reciting my Paters, blood oozing from my knees, my head spinning with hunger, when the abbot's feet came into sight, shuffling up next to me. He set a cup of milk and some bread on the floor, put his hand on my head. "Come," he said. "Our Lord God will forgive your sins." I looked up into his face and sobs came into my chest and my throat, one after the other. I could not stop them. He reached down and wiped my face with his robe.

"We have no rules here for a prince, only monks. I was wrong to bid you away from my Bible stories, Brian. They are the word of our one and only true God. Our ancestors believed in many gods, the old gods, but we believe in only one, the new God. Is that not so?"

Had Father Conn shared my confessions with the abbot? The thought frightened me so, I could not raise my head. "It is so," I muttered.

"Come, Brian," he said again, pulling me up by the hair.

I stumbled to my feet and followed him to the refectory, where I sat with the novice monks. The abbot spun tales of Adam and Eve, their bites from the apple showing them naked; of old Abraham, who so trusted in God he would have killed his son Isaac had God commanded it; and of Cain, who swore to God he was not his brother's keeper, as his brother Abel's blood pooled around his feet. I had not heard those stories, not from anyone. When he finished, I stayed back to question him.

"The priest at Kincora did not tell Bible stories like those. Only tales of Jesus and Patrick. Why?"

He smiled. "Your priest, bless his soul, did not know the stories himself. Our Bible is a rare treasure on this island. A scribe carried this book to me on pilgrimage from France, all the way across the sea."

He opened the cover of his Bible. "Look. The pages are warped with sea water. Some of the ink has run."

I stared at the page, imagining the book floating in the sea, rescued by the scribe.

"Do you read Latin?" the abbot asked.

I lied, pointing to the only three words I knew. "Et … Deus … Magnificat."

He smiled. "Three Latin words shall not a Great Abbot make."

I had not known a Great Abbot or even what one was, but I was grateful the Holy Island abbot thought me worthy of one. Indeed, I was not surprised when he bade me learn harp playing from my novice monk friend, Rónan. Every night before vespers, we plucked metal strings on our handheld harps, side by side, making music pure as nightingales' songs in spring. Close, I could see Rónan's dark brown hair thick as a cow's coat in winter, his skin white as a sheep's face and spotted with brown freckles. He knew harp playing and the rhythms and chants from the old monk who had played before him, and I copied his fingers and voice as best I could. I could feel Rónan's yearning to talk as strong as mine, but Brother Blat had forbidden it, and I would not give him more reason to beat me.

One day in autumn, the leaves red, orange, and yellow all in one tree, I spied Rónan sitting on a milking stool in a cow pen. Brother Blat nowhere in sight, I crept in and squatted beside him. He smiled wide, and we set to pulling teats together, our whispered words tumbling out on top of each other. He was son of a farmer at Tuamgraney and had many brothers. I was a prince who had escaped a rout that killed my father at Kincora, saved by my brother, Mahon.

"Will you become a monk?" he asked.

"No."

"Why not?"

I hesitated. "Truth? I am a demigod. Son of Lugh ... like Cúchulainn."

Rónan's teat pulling stopped. His eyes widened. "Truth?"

I nodded. "You know of Cúchulainn?"

"All his tales."

"They are true, no matter what anybody says."

Rónan leaned in closer. "Do you know how Cúchulainn was made?"

"Lugh followed King Connor's sister, Princess Deichtre, to a poor man's hut in a storm and put his seed into her. She gave birth to Cúchulainn the next day."

Rónan shook his head. "No. Lugh came to Deichtre as a mayfly in her cup of wine, at her wedding feast. She drank it down before she knew it was there."

"A mayfly cannot make a baby." I was certain of that.

"No, but a mayfly can turn a princess into a bird that can fly to a poor man's hut and turn back into a princess."

"Then we can both be right?"

Rónan nodded. "Yes." It was then I knew Rónan would be my friend. We went back to pulling teats.

"When did you know you were a demigod?" Rónan said.

"How did you know?"

I squeezed one eye shut, tilted my head. "Sometimes I have demigod thoughts wiser than any mortal."

"Like what thoughts?"

I could not think of any thoughts right then, not with the sight of two big feet planted in the slop on the other side of the cow, just past the teats.

"Sacrilege," Brother Blat boomed over the cow's back.

"Run!" I grabbed Rónan's wrist and we leapt over the pen's back fence, dove behind haystacks and listened as he shuffled about, looking for us. When at last he strode away, we set off running across fields, fences, and stone walls to the abbot's house, hoping to reach him before Brother Blat had a chance to tell of our sacrilege. The abbot was my friend and I prayed he would save us.

The abbot's door stood ajar, his house empty, but his underwear, robe, and shoes lay on the bed. Water splashed behind the house, and I guessed the abbot was bathing.

Feet rushed up and the splashing stopped. "I caught them whispering about demigods." Brother Blat's voice.

"Who?" the abbot said.

"Brian and Rónan."

"Ah, if you find them, bring them to me before you beat them."

I whispered to Rónan. "The abbot is coming. Look away." I pulled Rónan into a corner, facing the hut wall.

The door pushed open. "Brian?" The abbot's voice.

I looked around, my face burning hot, my gaze fixed on his bony body. I had thought him fat under his robes.

"There you are. Your brothers are coming."

"My brothers? When?"

"Today."

"May I watch for them? At the strand?"

He reached for his undershirt. "What do you think, Rónan? Can we spare Brian?"

Rónan shrugged, trembling and staring into the corner.

"Brother Blat will not hurt you, Rónan," the abbot said. "If he tries, I will help you whip him. Now go, Brian. Bring me your brothers."

I leapt to my feet, raced out the door.

—Chapter Eight—

Day fading, Rónan, the abbot, Marc, and many monks gathered on the strand. A currach came through the water, bearing Lachtna, Mahon, and an oarsman. Mahon first, the three men stepped out onto the strand. It had been many months since I had seen them, and I was a head taller than before. Both of my brothers seemed thin and worn, their matted hair pushed back behind their ears.

We clasped hands. "A man now, eh Brian?" Mahon said.

The pride in Mahon's eyes cheered me, and I yearned to say I was a man and a demigod, but the words stuck in my throat. I scarce knew what to do, so I nodded and shrugged.

We walked to the church, where Lachtna spoke to all the monks in a deep, steady voice. "Dal Cais chieftains have chosen me king of our clan. Prince Mahon will be my warrior prince and chief counselor at Kincora."

He turned to me. "I pray for your blessing, Brian, a most worthy novice monk." *I am no monk*, I whispered to myself. *I am a man and a demigod.*

"Praise God." Words from the abbot, behind me. The monks nodded and murmured. We strode to the refectory, and the abbot beckoned me to his table with my brothers. I waited to pick up my bowl.

"Thank you, God, for thy bounty," Marc said, "and the strength you have granted Lachtna and Mahon to raise Kincora from ashes. Protect them from thieves and murderers. And pray look with kindness on our brother, Brian, who will make his home here at Holy Island. Help him forsake all worldly desires and offer his life to study and prayer."

Never. I had thought the abbot was my friend.

Lachtna's face turned dark. "King Callaghan ravages all of Munster." Marc put down his knife. Lachtna chewed and talked at the same time.

"He will come against Kincora again," he said, "with his Norse allies. I will not fight them. I will submit."

Submit without a fight? I was shocked. What king would do that?

"You have built Kincora back?" the abbot asked.

"God willing, it will be done," Lachtna said, "if Callaghan spares us."

"He will not spare you without hostages," Marc said. "He will want Brian, a worthy Dal Cais prince."

Hostage? Me? Lachtna would not dare give me hostage to Callaghan!

"What he wants," Lachtna said, "I will give, else risk another rout."

I stole a quick look at Mahon. He met my gaze and looked away. Mahon too? I would bash my brothers' heads with my magic sword, with joy, no matter how many more Paters I would need say.

⛨

Time come for Father Conn, I confessed my murderous wishes, but not my joy.

"A wish is not a deed," Father Conn said, "but take care, Brian. Jesus preached we should be our brothers' keepers."

"Forgive me, Father, but Cain said he was not his brother's keeper."

Father Conn drew in a deep breath. "Jesus wanted all men to be their brothers' keepers, whether he said it or not."

"But the abbot said ..."

"You doubt me, Brian? It is a sin to doubt a priest. Now go. Think on what I have said."

I did not know what Father Conn meant. Where should I keep my brothers? A sword's length away?

Stepping out from the church, I spied Marc pacing in the courtyard, and I pressed my body against the wall, praying he would not see me. Monk after monk passed by, flushed from their confessions, but still Marc stayed. Caught in the light of night torches, I had no choice but to show myself.

"You hide from me?" Marc said.

"From you who would make me hostage."

He reached for my arm. "I would rather you take your vows. It is time."

"Monk, hostage—the same." I snatched my arm away.

"Lachtna must give you to Callaghan if he demands it."

"What do you know? A monk who prays all the time? I will be king of Dal Cais."

Marc huffed. "Lachtna will rule Dal Cais, and his son after him. If something happens to Lachtna, Mahon will rule and his son after him. You will never be king."

"Cennétig swore I would be king. A great king."

"Our father swore many things he wished could be true."

"I will never be a monk."

"Then you will be the ninth of our father's sons to die fighting useless wars—Anlon, Flann, Cormac, Corcc, Donncuan, Eichtergen, Finn, and Dub—you will follow them all to the grave, and for what?

"He did not tell me of eight slain brothers." I knew of only four, and a sister.

"Our father begged us not to tell you. Do not waste your good life, Brian. Take your vows and Lachtna will name you an abbot somewhere. Perhaps even abbot of Emly, strong as any king, if one day Lachtna takes the overkingship of Munster from the Eóganachta."

"I will not."

"Think, Brian. With your wit and courage, you could become the most powerful cleric in Munster ... stronger even than the Great Abbot at the See of Saint Patrick at Armagh. You could become known as the first Great Abbot in history from Munster."

"I will not be a Great Abbot. I will be Munster overking, king of all Munster kings, and then high king, over more territories on this island than you know exist."

Marc put his face up close to mine. "You will say penance forever, for all the killing that will take."

"I will not be your keeper."

Marc slapped me across my face. I turned and sped away to my hut, to my mat, my only safe place. From their silent breaths, I could hear the boys in my hut stayed awake. They envied me, a prince who could sit with the abbot at his table. And well they should. I was a demigod.

A wise thought came to me just then—Lie. I turned onto my side, closed my eyes in blessed silence and sleep.

The next day, I put myself next to Marc at dawn prayers. "Forgive me, brother," I said. "I will beg penance for my angry words."

"Ah," Marc whispered back. "As will I, for striking you."

"You will be proud of me when I become an abbot."

Marc let out a great breath. "You have chosen the church?"

"Yes." A lie spoken steady and firm.

Marc put his arm around my shoulder, hugged me close. "Our abbot will be pleased." That same day, Mahon and Lachtna left the island. I did not follow them to the strand, nor did I bid them goodbye.

✟

At Christmas, the monks prayed not eight, but ten times a day. Rónan and I plucked our fingers raw praising the baby Jesus. I had been at Holy Island for two years, and even as the abbot prayed I would devote myself to study and prayer, he had not demanded I take my vows. Perhaps I could stay until I became old enough to know what I was and do what I wanted.

Leaves sprouted on trees, the air warmed, and birds sang. Days began to pass with sun and no rain. Mahon and Lachtna visited with smiles on their faces.

"King Callaghan is dead," Lachtna said loud at the abbot's table. "From a lightning strike last month, trying to shelter from a storm under an ash tree." Gasps went up from monks in the refectory.

"Callaghan's mother forgot to tell him lightning bolts do not favor kings over slaves. A bolt hit the tree and Callaghan died a cooked king."

"A cooked king," a monk squeaked. A titter of laughter started at the novices' table. Soon the whole refectory set to laughing, so hard they could scarce eat their stale bread and sinewy hare.

"You will not give me hostage to Callaghan?" I said when we could speak again.

"Not to a cooked king," he said. Another bout of laughter started up, but I only smiled, relieved I would not be made hostage to Callaghan.

"Callaghan may be dead," the abbot said, chewing his carrot, "but his sons live, and many others from Eóganacht clans who claim Cashel as their right—King Molloy, for one. I will hold my laughter until he and all Eóganachta are struck by lightning."

Lachtna frowned. "You are not pleased Cennétig's most hated rival is dead?" The abbot rolled his eyes and downed his cupful of ale.

—Chapter Nine—

Lachtna and Mahon visited often, sometimes every week. They ate with great speed, as if they were starving. The work at Kincora was hard, they said, and time too short for hunting or fishing. But when weeks went by and my brothers did not appear, I sensed trouble. So did Marc and the abbot, who spoke in hushed tones.

"They will come soon," Marc said.

"The rains slow them," the abbot said.

"Ah yes, the rains," Marc said.

But what rains? We had had little rain those last weeks.

Another week on, I had closed my eyes for sleep when the boatman's horn rang out. I threw on my shoes and brat and hurried to the strand with torch-bearing monks. Oars slapped the water nearby, but the fog was so thick we could not see the boat. I called my brothers' names, but no one answered. At last, the boat up on the strand, a tall, thin man with a rough brown beard stepped out.

"Who are you?" our boatman said. "What is your business?"

"I bring news for the prince, from Kincora." He lifted his tunic, showed his naked skin—no sword, knife, or spear.

"Your name?"

"Rory."

"Who sent you?"

"The king."

"Speak your news." The abbot's voice sounded from behind me, Marc by his side.

"My news is for Prince Brian," Rory said.

"I am Prince Brian." I stepped farther forward.

Rory fixed his gaze on me. "Your brother Lachtna died yesterday."

"Died?" The abbot gasped.

"Set upon while out fishing. By rival clansmen and Norse." I stepped back and clutched Marc's arm. "I spied your brother's dog and went looking," Rory went on. "He was close to dead when I carried him back to Kincora." Rory bore his gaze into me. "Pus oozed from his wounds, and he shivered and shook for three days. We wrapped him in cooling clothes, bathed his lips in herbal potions, and poured water down his throat. At the end, he shouted and raved, and called for his mother. We buried him next to Queen Bebinn. Prince Mahon is king now. He bids you to Kincora."

"Mahon cannot swear himself king," Marc cried. "He must be chosen." Rory glanced at Marc and me, sorrow in his face.

"Mahon cannot command Brian," Marc shouted. "Only God commands Brian. Why did you not come sooner? You waited for Lachtna to die? You speak to Brian and not to me?"

"I do what King Mahon bids me."

"Come, Brother Marc." The abbot put his hand on Marc's shoulder. "Lachtna's death is the will of our Lord God."

The abbot reached for my arm, but I stepped around him and raced up the path, past my hut, through stiles, over rock walls, through the sheep and cow pens, past monks' huts and gardens and into the copse on the far side of the island. I fell to the ground behind bushes, gasping for air. I had not meant to bash Lachtna's head, or for him to die. I had no magic sword like Cúchulainn, and truth, I was no demigod, only son of my flawed mortal father, Cennétig. Why did Mahon call for me? I could not fight for him. I was only twelve.

I burrowed into leaves and curled my body into a ball. Soon my mind was elsewhere, in a forest filled with man-eating beasts, a rock wall stretching high and wide, blocking my way to Kincora. I spied an opening to a cave I could crawl in to die. But when I walked closer, the cave turned into two with tiny points of light at both of their ends, one cave wet, the other dry. Hope came up I might find my way home. A few lengths into the wet cave, my feet sank into a thick runny muck—blood. I raced back out, ripped off my shoes and tunic, and stepped naked into the dry cave. I had moved closer to the point of light, when laughter started up. Monks. I kept on, my hands over my ears, but could not hide from their faces, pitying me, hands grappling my skin. I ran back into the wet cave, to streams of blood flowing into a mighty river. Mahon stood naked on the far bank, ready to dive in.

He spied me. "Come, brother. We will swim together through this river of blood, to the light."

A foot nudged my side. "Brian!" I looked up into Marc's face, not remembering where I was.

"We searched this whole island for you."

I flung my arm out, grasped my father's knife. Mahon's words still in my head, I stood and walked with Marc toward the church. Buildings, graveyards, huts, fields, rock walls, animals, trees, water, the well, all looked the same, but not.

In the refectory, I stared back at the monks and marched up to the abbot's table.

"Brian, my son," he said. "I thank our Lord God you are found. Brother Marc tells me you have chosen the church."

"You would have me shun Mahon? You would have him be the tenth of my brothers to die?" Marc and the abbot traded looks, brows knitted. "Mahon calls for me and I will go."

"You are but a lad, Brian," Marc said. "Who will protect you? Counsel you?"

"Mahon. And my hero, Cúchulainn."

Marc cast a worried glance at the abbot. "Forgive him. He forgets where he is."

The abbot shook his head. "Brian is not one of us, Brother Marc—no matter how much we might wish him so. Mahon is alone and Brian must go."

Marc drew in breath. "He is not yet fighting age."

Anger flooded over me. "I will swim with Mahon through a river of blood, Marc, while you stay here like a coward and do nothing but pray one hundred times a day."

He started toward me, hand raised, but the abbot took his arm. "You will go with Brian to Kincora, Brother Marc. He will be safe in your holy presence."

I did not want Marc's holy presence. Yet the abbot cared for me, and I would not refuse him. Marc frowned, but no matter; Mahon had called for me and I would go.

PART TWO

—Chapter Ten—

The monks pushed our currach into choppy waters. I kept Rónan in sight until he shrank to a speck and disappeared, the only friend I had ever known. On land, I ran ahead, stopping only at forks to wait for my companions. Marc carried the chessboard Lachtna had rescued from his dún, and Rory carried a harp gifted to me by the abbot. I carried the clothes on my body, and my father's knife. He had known his knife would better serve me than a corpse.

Almost to Bórama, Rory caught up to me. "I leave you here, Prince Brian. We are near to my house and my wife will beat me if I do not hasten home."

"House?" There were no houses anywhere around.

"A small house, hidden in the trees." He lied with a voice so sure, I did not question him. I took the harp, nodded my thanks, and waved him off.

✣

At the hillock close to Kincora, I raced to the top. An evening mist skimmed through the tops of trees, cloaking my sight of the river. Kincora leapt in and out above the mist like a teasing ghost. I smelled burn, but thought it a memory.

Marc puffed up beside me. "Turn back, Brian. There is still time."

"You turn back, Marc. I will not deny Mahon." I hastened down the hillock, Marc following after me, silenced.

Close to Kincora, I stopped to listen, expecting sounds of people waiting to greet me on the wall. But not even a leaf quivered in the forest. The sun low in the sky, I ran out onto the hill into a clump of sheep eating weeds by the riverbank. They scattered, opening a space between me and our river chapel. One wall stood amidst heaps of broken wattle and thatch.

Marc put his hand on my shoulder. "Callaghan broke God's house, he and his Norse friends."

"Where are the people?"

"Slain," Marc said. "Or fled."

"Mahon?" I howled.

Halfway up the hill, I stepped in fresh horse dung, a trail of piles leading to a gaping hole in the wall where the gate had been.

"No guard," I said.

"No gate," Marc muttered.

Inside the fortress, mounds of burned wood and wet-sodden straw stinking with animal waste blocked our sight. Only the four walls of our stone church stood upright, open to the sky. A rat ran in front of us, stopped, looked, and kept going, its nose guiding it across the filth.

"Ruled by rats," I murmured. "Mahon called me to this?"

"Voices," Marc said. "Listen."

Two dirt-smeared boys ran into sight, spied us and raced away. We followed them around piles of waste to two women sitting side by side on a yard bench. The two boys crouched in behind them.

"King Mahon?" I said. "He is here?"

"Pray no," one said, her arm up before her face.

"I am Prince Brian, son of King Cennétig." I set my harp down, pointed to my jeweled knife sheath. "Look. My father's knife."

"Do not take our sons," the other woman whispered. "They are all we have."

I raised my voice louder. "I am Prince Brian, no thief. And this is my brother, Marc. A monk. We are looking for King Mahon."

"There is no king here," one said. "But Prince Mahon's house is there." She pointed behind her.

"Where?" I saw only ruins.

"Back there." She pointed again.

"Come," Marc said, "we will find him."

We stepped around a mountain of rubble to see a newly crafted thatched roof. I sprinted toward it and peered into a cold, dark room, stinking with ale.

"Mahon?" Truth, I hoped not to find him there. But something moved in a pile of pillows by the unlit hearth—Mahon, jug in hand, ale dribbling down his beard.

"Mahon!"

"Ho. Is that you, Brian?" I stood over him, looked down.

"It is you, Brian," he slurred. "You came."

"I did."

"Here." He handed me his empty jug. "Today we drink. Tomorrow, we die."

"Die?"

Mahon thrust his arm out to grab me, but I stepped away. He slumped backwards, hit his elbow on a hearth stone, groaned and cursed.

I set the jug down and backed out to Marc, sitting cross-legged on the ground, his back against a bench, my harp and chessboard in his lap. His tired face told me not to speak. I slipped down next to him, wrapped my brat tight around me, and lay my head on his leg.

☩

Morning come, I woke to the sound of loud voices. Marc's brat bunched up under my head, I raised up and looked about, but did not see him. Two bone-skinny men stood outside Mahon's house, one holding a large metal spike, the other, a hammer. A pole lay beside them. I had known those men before the rout as cowherd bondsmen from Bórama.

"Good day," I said, walking over, faint from hunger.

They looked at me, wary. "Remember me? Prince Brian?" They shrugged. "Have you food? A cook?"

"Cook?" one grinned. He reached out to touch my jewel-studded knife sheath, but I stepped back.

"Snare us a hare and we will be your cooks," the other said. Both howled with laughter. Mahon appeared from his doorway, shaded his eyes. The cowherds picked up the pole and started pounding.

"Ah, see?" Mahon said. "My slaves. They fear me."

Mahon reached out to hug me, but I pushed him away. "You forget your drunken words so soon?"

"What?" Mahon said. "A newborn colt? No father to protect him?"

"Liar. I need no one to protect me."

Mahon shifted his gaze to Marc striding up behind me with the chessboard sack and harp. "This fortress is a mere carcass," Marc said, "picked to the bone."

Mahon sneered. "So the little prince brings his bodyguard and his weapons." The cowherds coughed, covering laughs.

"We must talk, Mahon," Marc said. "In a safe place, away from prying eyes and ears."

"There is no safe place," Mahon said, his sneer faded. "Thieves were here yesterday and they will be back today." He turned back toward his house. "Wait here."

He stepped back into his house and came out with two half-eaten mutton legs, tossed one to me and one to Marc. I bit into mine, noticing worry lines in Mahon's young forehead, tangles and filth all through his hair and beard.

We followed him down the hill and leaned against the standing river chapel wall, a pile of charred wood blocking our sight of the river. I calmed at the sound of the rapids, the feel of my brothers close, the warm sunshine.

"No one came to help," Mahon said, "no chieftains, no farmers, only those two slaves. They do my bidding and I give them leave to stay here at Kincora."

"You swore this fortress was built back," Marc chided. "You lied to the abbot."

"That was Lachtna's idea, to spread the rumor. But chieftains and thieves believe their own eyes more than rumors."

"I see no thieves," I said. "Where are they?"

"Everywhere," Mahon whispered back.

"Do not tease him," Marc said.

"But it is so."

My calm ruined, I stood and walked toward the river. Marc reached out to stop me, but I escaped his grasp. "He is young yet," I heard Marc say to my back.

I sat in the sun next to a currach tied up on shore. A thumping noise came into my ears I thought was my heart, but it fast turned to shouts and hoofbeats on the river path, coming from Norse Limerick way. I slid over the side of the currach and curled up in the bottom. Horses pounded past me up the hill, bringing screams from inside the fortress.

Pray God, Lugh, Father Conn. Let me live. I will do penance forever. I will keep my brothers forever.

The hoofbeats pounded back downhill and stopped near my boat. I shook, picturing men readying ropes to bind me. A woman wailed, a man cursed, the wailing stopped, and the horses galloped away. I peered over the boat's side, but saw no brothers to keep.

"Brian? Where are you?" Mahon's voice.

"Brian?" Marc.

"Come out," Mahon shouted. "They are gone."

I jumped out of the boat and ran leaping into Mahon's arms, unable to stop tears flowing down my face. The force of my weight knocked us both to the ground.

Back in the fortress, the cowherd slaves crept out from their hiding places. "They stole the harp and chessboard," one said.

"My things?"

"Forget them," Mahon said. "Be glad they did not steal you."

"You heard the screaming?" a cowherd said. "They took another woman."

The abbot had spoken truth. The Norse thieves were after human booty, women and children, for the slave markets..

Mahon pushed me through his door. "They will take you if you let them. You would bring a good price."

"Who are they?" Marc said, collapsing into a chair.

Mahon sank into his pillows. "Who knows? They circle around for fresh meat every day."

"Our father would have stopped them," I said.

Mahon shot me a look of pure scorn. "Like he stopped Callaghan and the Norse?" He hurled his cup across the room. "Are you blind, Brian. I am poor. No one will fight for me."

I backed out the door, sick of Mahon. No swimming through a river of blood for him. The cowherds grabbed up the pole and started pounding. I kicked a rock hard across the ground. They stared.

"Do not stare at me. I am a prince."

I stepped back into Mahon's house. "Those cowherds will never pound that pole into the ground. Send them away."

"The only men who help me?"

"We will die," I said.

"No doubt," Mahon whispered.

I sat down hard on the hearth stones. Could I still be a monk? Holy Island had no women, no children, little treasure, only monks' huts, sheep, cows, chickens ... "There is treasure here," I said. "Our father hid his booty at Kincora. Do you remember? The abbot said so. Did you look for it, Mahon?"

Mahon wiped his brow. "There is no treasure here."

Marc pulled on his beard. "Cennétig fought many battles, Mahon. No doubt he took booty."

"There is no booty here."

"No king hides booty in plain sight," I said. "We must look for it."

"Our mother's brooch," Marc said. "Remember it, Mahon? Gold, with jewels—rubies, emeralds and diamonds? You would be rich if we could find that."

I shook my head. "He would have shown it to me." Or would he have?

"Or hidden it," Mahon said, in a tone of grave doubt. "Like our mother's jugs. But where? His chest burned in the rout."

"The pigsty!" I shouted.

"Do not yell," Mahon said.

I lowered my voice. "He said to remember the pigsty. His last words to me."

Mahon leaned back on his elbows. "There is only slop in the pigsty."

"But why would he say pigsty, Mahon?" Marc said. "We must at least look."

Mahon leaned back further. "If thieves know we dig for treasure in the pigsty or anywhere, they will be back tenfold."

Naysayer. Small wonder he sat in sloth. "I will dig the pigsty," I said. "Alone, if I must." I stood straight and tall before my pitiful brothers.

Marc rubbed his chin. "I will help you, Brian. If we find treasure, all could be set right. If not, nothing will be lost."

Mahon stayed back in his pillows. "You are both mad."

"Treasure could buy us cattle to sway clansmen to help rebuild this fort," Marc said.

"Cattle from where?"

"The abbot's flock, all along Lough Derg. One gold band could raise a man's rank, gain him a better wife, buy him a slave. Chieftains everywhere will want treasure."

Mahon swiped his hair back, sat up straight. "We will not find treasure, but I suppose we can look." He stood, flicked weeds and straw from his tunic, set his shoulders square.

My heart lifted. But what shame to dig the pigsty and find nothing—another of my father's lies?

The two cowherds spread word of our plan around the fortress, and a small clutch of old men, women, and children gathered outside Mahon's door. He stood on a bench and spoke of treasure in the pigsty—King Cennétig's booty—silver, gold, gems, who knew what else. People gripped arms and held each other close.

"If we find treasure," Mahon said, "we will trade it for cows to sway men to help us rebuild." Mahon waved his arm at the two cowherds. "If we find treasure, I will grant these men freedom, with land and cows of their own."

The cowherds smiled so wide I imagined the skin on their faces would crack.

"If we find treasure," Mahon went on, "I will be clan king. Prince Brian here will be my warrior prince. Brother Marc will tend to our souls. We will all be the better for finding treasure. Raise your arm if you will help dig." All arms raised, as did my hope and pride, brother to Mahon and Marc.

We marched to the sty with our shovels. With no pigs in the sty for two years, the slop had turned hard and stone-like, a thick, smooth crust on top, covered with small rocks and pebbles. We tried to dig, but our shovels made dents, not holes. Glances of sorrow shot forth from the few people watching us. Some turned and walked away, shaking their heads.

"We look like fools," Mahon said, tossing his shovel onto the path. "Did I not tell you? We should stop this now."

"Only fools give up so soon," I said.

Gloom settled over us and we sat on the path without speaking, watching the sun turn red and sink, its rays shooting out from behind a cloud.

Mahon spoke the words we all dreaded. "No treasure here. Stay if you want, but I am leaving." Yet he did not move from his spot.

"We will dig the horse pen on the morrow," Marc said. "The sheep pen the next and the gardens the next. No doubt our father misspoke."

"No." I picked up my shovel and stepped back out onto the hard crust. I bent down and ran my finger along a thin line, poked my shovel tip into it, wiggled it around, scraped out dirt, opening up a crack.

A cowherd spoke from behind me. "You could break that open with a hammer."

I looked around. "This ground is too hard for hammers."

"Wait—I will show you."

He hastened off, and came back with a hammer and a chisel. "Watch me." He stuck the chisel tip into the crack, lifted the hammer and struck the chisel's blunt end. The crack deepened and widened a bit.

"Do it again," I said.

He struck it again. The chisel went through the crust. He pulled it out. "Again?"

Over and over the cowherd pounded, breaking off a chunk, another and another, until a big hole opened up. I reached in and touched wet.

"Slop!"

I bade the cowherds go in search of all hammers and chisels in the fortress. We had scarce any time before dark.

Mahon and Marc watching, the cowherds and I broke off crust, shoveled it into heaps and poked our shovels into slop. We found no treasure, and with daylight gone, we could scarce see, even with torches. I was fighting gloom when I heard a sound. A rock?

"Stop!" I emptied our shovels onto the path, and saw only mud.

"No, look there," Mahon said, "I see something." He stepped to the far back corner of the sty, stuck his arm deep into the slop. His arm covered in mud, he pulled and out came a skinny jug, covered in slop like his arm. The shape was the same as the one I had broken.

"Bring it here," Marc said.

Mahon cradled the jug to his chest.

"Shake it," Marc said. "Turn it upside down."

Mahon did Marc's bidding, and we all heard it—thumps.

"Something in it!" I shouted.

"Open it," Marc said.

Mahon climbed out and set the jug on the path, pulled on the stopper. It shredded in his fingers.

"Push it in," Marc said.

"It is stuck," Mahon said.

"Smash it," I said.

"You." He handed me the jug.

"Pray bring the torch." I said to a cowherd. Warm light shining over me, I lifted a stone high and brought it down hard on the jug, cracked it open. We leaned over and stared.

Gold bands glittered amongst tarnished silver bands, ring pins, clasps, and our mother's brooch—bright gold, studded with diamonds, rubies and emeralds. Our father's treasures, sparkling in the torchlight. The cowherds cheered, hugged each other, danced arm in arm.

The pigsty was truth. My father's truth. Such sorrow and love came into my heart for him, I let tears course down my cheeks, no matter who was looking.

Scooping up the treasure, we hastened into Mahon's house. Piece by piece, Mahon stuffed the treasure, brooch and all, into a leather pouch. He took his good time, paying close heed to each piece, wiping it clean with a wet rag.

"Now what?" Mahon said when he was finished.

"Now I will carry this pouch to the abbot," Marc said. "No thief will think to rob a lone monk on his way to Holy Island. The abbot will choose pieces for himself and send his monks to trade the rest for cattle. Once the cattle are gathered, you will herd them to Bórama."

Mahon and I looked at each other, both waiting for the other to speak. Our monk brother alone with the treasure?

"What do you think, warrior prince?" Mahon said. "Do we agree?"

Mahon asked my counsel? Hope and pride swelled in my chest, even as the picture of my brother drunk in his pillows stayed bright in my mind. Surely it would fade.

I nodded. "Yes, I think we do."

—Chapter Eleven—

Mahon and I waited a fortnight, time enough, Marc had said, for the abbot to trade treasure for cows. Indeed, Rónan, Marc, the abbot, and a half-score monks stood waiting in the cow pasture on the mainland across from Holy Island, with three score cows and bulls, and two horses. A shiny gold pin clasped the abbot's brat at his neck as he counseled us to go the Tuamgraney way. The fisherman's path was too narrow, he said, and cattle might lose their footing and fall into the lake. Even as the Tuamgraney had been our father's rivals, if we put them in mind of my friendship with Rónan, they might well agree to help us.

I fixed my gaze on Rónan, somber and thoughtful in the abbot's presence, but I could see the spark in his eye, his wish to come with Mahon and me. One day when I was able, I would call for him to join me at Kincora.

✛

Mahon and I had gone some distance toward Tuamgraney when we stopped to rest, the cows content to graze in a field. I rode up beside my brother. "At Tuamgraney," I said, "we will promise half a cow to every man who agrees to help us at Kincora."

"No."

"What? Why not?"

"We are princes. Chieftains give cows to their farmers."

"Most of our father's chieftains are dead from the rout," I said. "Any chieftain who still lives has no cows."

Mahon gave me a long look. "Do as I say, brother. I will soon be your king."

"You will not be anything if we have no men to help us."

Mahon nudged his horse away from me. I shouted after him. "Who will tend these cows at Bórama? You?" He paid me no heed as we rounded up cattle and kept on.

☩

A farmer's ringfort in sight, I dreaded what Mahon would say to the three farmers standing in the widened path.

"Good day," Mahon said, his voice lifted in good cheer. "I am Prince Mahon. This is my brother, Prince Brian. We are sons of Cennétig, slain king of Dal Cais."

Our cows and bulls had smelled fresh grass and trampled on past the ringfort without us, knocking over buckets, frightening chickens and children. "Forgive our cattle," Mahon said to the men. "They know no better."

Meantime, more men gathered in the road. "For every man who helps rebuild our father's fortress," Mahon spoke in ponderous tones, "we will give one-half a cow." Not one glance or wink came from him as he spoke my words as if they were his own.

The men stood in a circle and put their heads together. From the bits I could hear, they marveled at Mahon's offer. Only chieftains gave cows to farmers in exchange for crops, labor, and willingness to fight, yet their chieftain had been killed and any cattle he had owned had been stolen by his neighbors. Perhaps they should agree to Mahon's offer? But no, another man spoke of the brithem, the master of laws, who would judge them lawbreakers, another of the priest who would deem them sinners.

I nudged my horse over. "Are any of you kin to Rónan, novice monk at Holy Island?" No one spoke or nodded, but their likenesses to him told me yes.

"Rónan is my friend," I said. "He begs you to help us."

The men looked one to the other, each waiting for another to answer. "No one will fault you for taking our cows," I said. "My brother will soon be Dal Cais king, and if you help us rebuild Kincora, we will forget all differences between us."

The men went back to their huddle. More worries flew out about the brithem, the laws, the priest. I dreaded the moment we would ride away with no men to help us. By then, our cattle were grazing in a field further on.

I had turned my horse's head away, when a hollow-chested boy raced out from a nearby hut, his mother after him. More hollow-chested boys and girls followed, and more mothers, who whispered to each other in high-pitched bursts, scowled at their husbands. The men went back to their huddle and came out nodding yes.

That day we left five cows at Tuamgraney ringforts—one-half cow for each of ten strong men we took with us to Kincora, on horseback. But the next time Mahon spoke my words as if they were his, I would demand he admit they were mine.

☩

Word spread and Dal Cais men of all ranks, from chieftain to base freeman to slaves, hastened to help. Among the chieftains were our fiery-haired twin nephews, Eiden and Conaing, sons of Donncuan, our much older brother I had never known. They grumbled we had broken laws, promising cattle to their farmers, but their frowns turned to smiles when we pledged more breeding cows, milk cows, and bulls to them than any of their client farmers.

For months, we chopped down trees, dried branches and grass, pounded poles, planted gardens, fattened pigs, bred chickens and goats. I rose each morning with hope for the day Kincora would be a fortress again and Mahon truly chosen Dal Cais king. When that happened, my smile would shine brighter than the moon, stars, and sun put together.

Late afternoons on those days, Mahon and I strolled to the river to talk. Truth, the more our fortress rose from rubble, the more I worried about another rout. The Limerick Norse were close by in their island fortress downriver, and surely Ivar, their king, had spies to tell him Kincora would soon be a threat. Yet I bided my time with Mahon, wanting us to be brothers with the same wit and purpose. But when weeks passed and Mahon said nothing about Ivar or his Irish allies, I made up my mind to question him.

One summer night, we sat cross-legged on the grass, wrapped in our brats, chilled by the river mist. "What will you do first when you are chosen king?" I said, fiddling with a twig.

Mahon did not hesitate. "Seek a wife."

Surprised, I hesitated. He smiled and winked at me. "A wife before Ivar?" I said, my voice betraying shock.

"Ivar can wait. A king must have a wife." A smirk covered his face. I snapped my twig. Was I not to be his warrior prince?

"Ivar will not wait," I said. Mahon's stubbornness stirred certainty in me. "The Limerick Norse will raid here any time now."

"Oh? Where are they?" He put his hand over his brow, scanning the river rapids.

Heat crept up my neck into my face. "They stalk this river, Mahon. You know that."

Mahon threw a stone hard into the rapids. "When I am king, I will seek your counsel if I want it. Take care not to give it unless I ask for it."

I threw my twig pieces at him. "Fool. You have dung in your ears." He spat, rose to his feet, and walked off up the hill. Mahon might not seek my counsel, but I would give it anyway.

—Chapter Twelve—

The day after we hammered the last nail into wood, Mahon bade me join him and his chieftains in our council house, bigger than in my father's day. We sat around a long wooden table on chairs cobbled together with wooden boxes and straight plank backs, Mahon facing the door, the rest of us along the sides. An animal fat candle stood in the corner, tall as a man on its wide brass base.

"I welcome you," Mahon said, lifting his cup. "I have raised Kincora from ruin and made us whole. Nine of my brothers and my father have died fighting for Dal Cais, and as Cennétig's oldest living son, save for my monk brother, Marc, it is only right I be chosen Dal Cais king."

I had expected smiles and wishes of good fortune from the chieftains, but no. "Why you, Mahon?" Conaing said. "Why not me? Or Eiden? We have the same rights to the clan kingship as you."

Mahon scratched his head, seeming to ponder Conaing's words. Would he give way to our nephews? Not after all we had done. "My brother promises three milk cows," I said in haste, "to every man here who raises his hand for him."

"Milk cows?" Conaing sneered. "I would rather a bondswoman who can cook, weave, grind, and tend to my flute. Milk cows give only milk."

I cast a worried look at Mahon. We had cowherds at Bórama, but our father's bondswomen had only just begun to drift back from their hiding places in the forest.

"You will have bondswomen, milk cows, and much else from our battle spoils," Mahon said, "when I am king."

Ah, but what battles?

"What can you promise me, nephew," Mahon said, "if I raise my hand for you?"

Conaing put his finger to his cheek. "An ox. No, half an ox, the other half to Brian here." Mahon and the chieftains laughed and shame came over me. They had been jesting, and everyone knew it, save for me.

"All for King Mahon, raise your cups," Conaing said. We lifted our empty cups, my face burning hot, my smile feigned.

Mahon stood and spoke the words he and I had crafted for the occasion. "I, Mahon mac Cennétig, king of clan Dal Cais, swear to honor our laws, punish wrongdoers, and protect our clan from all enemies."

"Norse enemies," I whispered loud, "and Irish who lend them aid."

"Of course," Mahon said. "All enemies. And I forget to mention Brian. He will be my warrior prince, and already I am the better for it." Mahon and I touched cups and walked side by side to his enkinging feast in the hall. On the way, he gave me a pleasant thump on my back.

Soon after, Mahon and I set out for Magh Adhair, to our sacred oak tree on our clan's inaugural mound. We rode in the company of one score bodyguards, farmers who had never wielded a sword or spear against a man. Mahon was in high spirits, and he laughed and joked with his bodyguards, leaving me to worry about ambushers and thieves. Every sound in the forest set my heart racing, but we crossed through the mountains without harm. Down into flat fields and pastures, we came to Magh Adhair, where a throng of Dal

Cais chieftains sat waiting on a half-circle berm, lower ranked clansmen crowding in the field behind them. Marc, come from Holy Island, broke a branch from the sacred tree, handed it to Mahon, and turned him around three times, bidding him to bless our land and our people.

I studied the faces of chieftains on the berm, musing about who among them had ridden with Callaghan and the Norse to kill our father and burn our fortress, or ambushed Lachtna? I was young, but I knew smiling faces could hide schemers, more dangerous than thieves who raided in plain sight.

I had hoped Mahon would praise me for all I had done to help him. Yet he so reveled in the smiles and cheers of his clansmen, he did not glance in my direction. No matter—we both knew he could scarce piss without me.

PART THREE

—Chapter Thirteen—

Mahon stayed true to his word; he would only seek or heed my counsel when he wanted. His first full day as king, so many commands spewed forth from his mouth, I could not keep them all in my head.

"Ready Prince Brian a house," he ordered our carpenters. "A king does not share sleeping space with his brother."

Ah, relief. No more of Mahon's snores to trouble my sleep.

To his servants, he said, "Heat my bath water with hot coals—not so many as to scald, but not so few as to leave a chill. Bring oils, for a king must have sweet smelling feet. Comb my hair sleek and shiny like the locks of a newborn infant. Be quick with my clothes in the morning, but take care not to wake me until I call."

To me, he said, "At mealtimes, you will give up your chair for my queen." I bit my tongue so hard I could taste blood. Already I had moved my chair two arms' lengths from his, as was our custom, but my chair for his queen? What queen?

One day, he and I met by chance at the cesspit. "I will ride north to the kingdom of Connacht," he said, "to the overking's dún. His name is Tadg mac Cathal, and he has a young daughter, Úna. I mean to wed her." I took my turn at the hole, troubled that he once again spoke of a wife before Ivar.

"Can you not be content with our milkmaids?" I said.

A smile crept over his lips. "Ah, Brian. You are young yet. Milkmaids can succor my flute, but they cannot give me ties to powerful kings."

"I desire no woman tied to me by law," I said. "Nor should you—not before we cleanse our river of Norse." Mahon took no more heed of my words than fire takes of mist. We strode away to better air at the vegetable garden.

"I will take a poet from Connacht as well," Mahon said. "He is distant kin to Úna, and his name is Mac Liag. He is your age or about, but already he is famed for his clever verse."

I wrinkled up my nose. "My words stink?" Mahon said.

"Our father took no poet."

"True, and our father will be but a name and a death date in the monks' annals—if that." Dust motes sparkled around Mahon in the setting sun.

"A king must have a manservant," Mahon went on. "You remember Rory? The messenger who came for you at Holy Island? Long ago, you kicked his chessboard over in a snit. Rory cares for a young Irish boy he found tending pigs in Norse territory near Limerick. They live together in the forest."

I remembered Rory well, but Mahon thought so well of himself, I could not bring myself to answer.

"I have not forgotten you, Brian," he said. "You are a prince, it is so, but with your home here at Kincora, my fortress now, you possess no land, no cattle, no client farmers, no slaves. You may sit with me and my chieftains at council meetings—if you take care never to speak against me."

I kept my face straight. "That should be easy enough, Mahon, since you and I so often speak the same words."

Mahon smiled. "We are brothers, are we not?"

Mahon called a council of the same chieftains who had chosen him king. He started, like Cennétig before him, with talk of the dry summer just passed, the scorched barley and wheat in the field, the too skinny people, and the cattle weak from winter sickness. The chieftains nodded, grave looks on their faces. But when Mahon took a breath, they swooped in, wanting to know which enemies Mahon most feared, his own rival clansmen, or Eóganachta, traditional enemies of Dal Cais, whose kings had ruled Munster from Cashel fortress for centuries, Callaghan the last of them.

"Eóganachta are so busy fighting each other," a deep-throated chieftain croaked, "they will scarce notice you."

"Yes, and rivals who fight each other make good prey," Eiden said, shooting Mahon a smug, all-knowing look, "if a new king is hungry enough."

"Indeed—courageous, wise, and ambitious enough," Conaing said.

Mahon fingered his beard, a faraway look in his eyes. "My enemies can wait," he said. "I can scarce call myself king unless I take a wife, a poet, and a manservant." The chieftains' rickety wooden chairs squeaked as they turned their bodies and faces toward Mahon, like dogs finding the scent. Mahon repeated all he had said to me at the cesspit and vegetable garden about Úna, Mac Liag, and Rory. I cringed.

"How will you sway Úna's father?" Eiden said. "Your name is little known, even in Munster."

"I will raid Clonmacnoise, the famed monastery where I studied as a youth. The abbot there is kin to Tadg, the Connacht overking who protects that same monastery. When I show myself a strong warrior, the abbot will speak well of me to King Tadg."

"You misspeak, Mahon," Conaing said. "You will not win the overking's favor raiding a monastery he protects." Conaing's same words on my lips, I gave silent thanks he had spoken them first. Raiding Clonmacnoise was the last thing that would endear Mahon to King Tadg.

Mahon shook his head. "Did I say raid? I meant trample on his holy ground. I will neither harm nor steal."

The chieftains glanced one to the other. "Wise," the deep-throated chieftain said. "I will ride with you, Mahon. Your enemies can wait, as you so wisely say."

Every one of the flattering, fawning chieftains smiled and nodded. I shouted. "We must save ourselves for the Limerick Norse. Ivar is on our doorstep, spying and readying another rout." My voice cracked and my face flushed.

"Ah, Brian," Eiden said, "did your tutors not teach you the wisdom of the druids? If an animal sleeps, let him sleep?"

"Sleep? Ivar has killed more of my kin than I can count."

"Norse are content in their towns, Brian," Conaing said, his nose in the air. "No need to stir them from their nests."

I stood so fast, my chair fell over backwards onto the floor. "I will not ride with you, Mahon. A wife and a poet? You are fools not to heed Ivar."

"Do as you will," Mahon said, fingering the silver pin on his brat. "There are many young princesses in Connacht ..."

"They would be as poison to me."

"You swore not to speak against me, brother."

"I swore not to speak your same nonsense." I kicked my fallen chair out of the way. Almost out the door, I tripped on the threshold, but caught myself in time, praying no one had seen me.

—Chapter Fourteen—

Under a full moon, Mahon and his chieftains rode out of Kincora for Bórama. From there, they planned to take our few boats up through Lough Derg and the River Shannon to Clonmacnoise. Peering down my long body to my feet hanging over bed's end, I could see I was a man, no longer a child, yet I felt like one, weak and powerless.

Mahon gone, the fortress quiet, I battled with myself *Go, Brian. Spy on the Limerick Norse. See if Ivar threatens Kincora. Perhaps he truly does sleep?* No. The Norse have guards, spies, and dogs. I pulled my blanket tighter around my neck.

Coward, are you? No coward. Only wise and careful.

Cúchulainn would not stay back. Why do you? Cúchulainn had special powers and a magic sword. I have neither.

Did he not put wise thoughts in your mind? I know better now. Those wise thoughts were my own.

All the more reason to spy. Your wise thoughts will sway Mahon.

I threw my blanket onto the floor, strapped on my knife and short sword, and pulled on boots and my wool brat. The fortress asleep, I made my way to the kitchen, stuffed pouches with water, dried pork, berries, and nuts. A dog barked, but I was up and over the back wall before anyone came looking.

Far down, the river path ended in scrub. I turned uphill and forged a path through an oak forest. I crouched, crawled, and slithered through grass, vines, and weeds, listening all the while for Norse. At a stream, I lay on the ground and slept to the sound of running water.

Dawn come, I stripped naked and lowered myself into the cold stream water, soothing my cuts, scratches, and scalp, my long hair floating around my head. I was gazing up at oak tree branches arching over the stream when something moved in my side-sight. Sinking down under the water, I caught a glimpse of a doe and a fawn drinking from the stream. Coming up for breath, I scared them. They crashed back into the forest. *Fool, Brian. If those deer had been Norse, you would be dead.*

I pressed on, the river on one side and the mountain ridge on the other. Shafts of sunlight pierced the dark forest up ahead, heralding an open space, a field. Turning down through trees to river's edge, I peered around the trunk of a massive oak. Downriver, Ivar's fortress rose up high on an island, its giant earthen walls standing stark against a sunset streaked sky. Boats and warships of all sizes and kinds floated from ropes tied to posts on the island and far shore.

Night coming on, I crept up the hill to rock outcroppings, stashed my sack in a small cave, and climbed a tall tree. Torchlight flickered across the metal on guards' helmets and shields as they stood watch on the walls, and a glow rose from night fires inside the fortress. I climbed down, squeezed into the cave, downed food and water from my pouches, and wrapped myself in my brat for sleep.

At first light, I crept down through trees and out into a shallow bog close to the river bank. Praying I would look like a log, I lay still on my back, gazing at sleek longboats bobbing in the river water, pocked with oar holes, serpents and beasts threatening from their prows, twice the size of the warships my father had kept at Bórama before the rout. Seeing the Norse boats struck terror into me.

I was still lying in the bog when the wooden gates of Limerick creaked open. Three Norse warriors stepped out with bows and quivers of arrows slung over their shoulders, stood on the edge of a field next to the fortress, and shot arrows into the air, aiming away from the sheep and the cows. The ancients had told of Irish using bows and arrows long ago, but I had never seen them or fathomed their deadly power.

Turning blue with cold, I dashed back into the forest. But I had gone no more than a few steps when loud noises came from across the river. I crouched and watched leather-armored Irish on horses push through trees onto the river path. Limerick's gate flew open and a short, big-bellied, bearded man stepped out, his long brown hair tied back with a leather strap, his face as wide as it was long, a circlet on his head. If he was Ivar, he was not the fearsome man I had imagined. He sauntered around to the far side of the fortress, and came back in a few moments with six Irish, one a king or chieftain from his bright-colored tunic. They walked into the fortress, banging the gates shut behind them.

I had seen enough. Ivar schemed with Irish, and with his longboats and archers, he could waste Kincora in no time. I had climbed the hill to my cave when four more Irish burst out from the woods, another king and three others. Caught in the open, I flattened myself on the ground, wetting my breeches from fright. Ivar came out and all happened as before. My chance at last come, I raced back to Kincora at top speed, reaching the fortress by nightfall.

Mahon still away, and my mind too full for sleep, I walked about in a fine drizzle, longing for the days when I felt safe at Kincora, even as I knew it had all been a lie.

A week went by with no news of Mahon. When at last his voice sounded outside his house late one night, I stayed awake, eager to tell him what I had seen at Limerick.

At dawn, pushing his door open a crack, I spied Mahon naked before his hearth, cup in hand. It came to me I was taller than him by half a head—and thinner. Two bundles the size and shape of fat pigs lay on his floor by his feet, wrapped in cowhide and tied with leather straps.

Hearing me, he grabbed up his tunic and covered himself. "You?" he breathed out, not sounding pleased to see me.

"I spied on Limerick, Mahon."

"You did what?"

"I spied on Limerick. On Ivar himself, and two Irish kings."

"They spied you?" He slipped on his tunic.

"No one spied me. I spied them."

Mahon paused. "To what good, Brian?"

"To our good. Ivar schemes with Irish kings, against us."

"Who says? Cúchulainn?" Mahon's lips curled in a sneer.

Mahon mocked me? "Ivar readies for something, Mahon, sure as the sun rises in the sky."

"You woke the sleeping beast?"

I paused. "Pay me no heed and the ghost of our father will strike you dead."

Mahon tilted his head and sneered. "Our father's ghost gifted me the gold pin I gave King Tadg for Úna. An overking's daughter commands a high price."

I sucked in breath, stunned. "You kept a gold pin back from our father's treasure?"

"Had I told you of it," Mahon said, "you would have stolen it from me, like you stole our father's knife."

I commanded myself still, and spoke between my teeth. "I tell you of risking my life to spy on Limerick and of Ivar scheming with Irish kings, and you taunt me for old wounds and grudges? We are men now, Mahon, and you are king of our clan. The Norse will be at our throats in no time."

Mahon flopped down into his chair, pulled on shoes. "I am king and you are my warrior prince, Brian. King Tadg wondered why you stayed back, and I had no answer. Do as you will, but I will rule all of Munster one day, with my chieftains. You will be sorry."

"Your clutch of fawning chieftains cannot win a skirmish, much less all of Munster."

Mahon was set on digging up hurt I had wreaked upon him since childhood. But the threat of Ivar was real and my spying had been daring and brave. Would he not heed me?

He stood and set about unwrapping his bundles. "My chieftains and I will feast this day, without you, Brian. Do not try to join us."

Lifting up a fat bundle, he cut the leather string with his knife and let it fall open to clothing. He picked out a blue-dyed wool brat trimmed with blue satin borders, spotted with many-colored tufts of wool—the finest brat I had ever seen. "You have not asked about my hosting to Connacht, Brian."

"Hosting? Those are your battle spoils?"

Mahon laughed. "No. They are Tadg's gifts to his son-in-law to be."

Mahon unwrapped the other bundle and pulled out a tunic embroidered and stitched with bright colored thread, striped satin breeches, silver-studded leather shoes, and leather gloves.

Piece by piece, he donned his new clothing, changing into an apparition I could only have dreamed in my sleep.

"You are wondering what I promised Tadg in return for his daughter and these clothes?" he asked. As was his wont, he wanted to tell me something, but I would need question him,

"I am not wondering, but you will tell me."

"I promised to bring my fleet against Fergal Ua Ruairc of Uí Briúin Briéfne, Tadg's most fearsome enemy."

"What fleet?"

"The fleet I will build."

"Does Fergal threaten King Tadg?" Mahon hesitated.

"Perhaps."

"How perhaps?"

"They have long been foes, but they have not yet fought each other. Fergal will not like it when he hears Tadg allies with me. What Fergal will do is anybody's guess."

I could scarce believe my ears. "You woke a sleeping beast? Meddling in Connacht feuds?"

"We will see."

"Who will man the fleet you will build?"

"Do not fear, Brian. My fleet will be manned."

"Could you not go for Ivar first? Fergal second?"

"I am king, Brian. I desire a wife, a poet, a manservant, and ties to powerful kings. A battle with Ivar will do me little good. I do not need or want your counsel. Pray do not forget that."

How could I?

☩

Once the feast was over, I followed Mahon and his chieftains into the council house. Their chests were so puffed-up, I was surprised they could all fit.

Mahon skipped the crops and weather and went straight to boasting. His chieftains fought to praise his good looks, his smiles that won the princess and her father to him, his clever strategy, his choice of wife. Mahon—so wise and brave for a king so new.

I waited for a break in their fawning. "The Limerick Norse only feign to sleep." I spoke with no crack in my voice. "They ready for war against us."

Faces turned toward me. "I spied on Ivar's fort," I said. "Our spears and swords would be as sticks against their mail armor." Mahon shot me a warning look. I glanced away.

"The foreigners' arms and necks are giant sized." I stretched my arms out so wide I grazed Mahon's shoulder with my hand. "Their arrowheads are sharp and pronged, their bows so powerful, arrows fly across fields and split trees in two." I sliced the air with my hand.

The chieftains turned their stares to Mahon. "Their warships carry one score men or more in each." I flashed my ten fingers many times to show how great the number.

Conaing's face paled. "Is it so, Mahon?"

Mahon shrugged. "Ivar plots with two Irish kings," I said. "Molloy and Donobhan."

"You know Molloy and Donobhan?" Conaing tilted his head.

"No."

"They could have been somebody else," Eiden said.

"Could have, but most likely they were Molloy and Donobhan." I rubbed my neck, let out breath.

"Ivar may plot with Irish," Conaing said, "but he will think twice before raiding here."

"Twice, but the third time he will come for us."

I paused, slowing my speech. "I have thought of a plan that could stop him." The room went silent, gazes turned to me. I met each one at a time, straight on.

"I will take a band of Dal Cais youth, sturdy and fleet of foot, to the caves above Limerick. We will sling stones at night at the fortress walls and hide from the guards in the day. You are the king, Mahon, and only you can call for sons of farmers to sling stones with me. I trust you will hasten. Meantime, when we are away over Limerick, you will raise an army of warriors to fight Ivar in battle ... if our stones do not drive him away first." Truth, I had only just thought our stones alone might drive Ivar away.

Mahon huffed and frowned. "You command me, Brian?"

"I am asking, Mahon, not commanding."

"You do not know how to sling stones," he said, a frown starting on his face. "The Norse will laugh at you, if they do not kill you first."

"Rónan knows. He will be my general."

"The novice monk? That Rónan?"

"Yes."

"Did I mishear?" Eiden said. "You will sling stones with a monk?"

"A monk and a band of well-chosen Dal Cais youth." My strong voice did not falter. Worried looks passed around the table, but I could see they were not honest. Mahon's chieftains and Mahon himself wanted me gone.

"I say we wish Brian godspeed," Conaing said.

"Slinging stones at Ivar's walls could turn Ivar to a roaring beast," Mahon said, matching his chieftains' false tones. "I am a small king next to him."

"You deem yourself small, Mahon?" My voice lifted in wonder. "I would not have thought it. Indeed, a king who deems himself small will be eaten alive. Big fish, little fish?" Had we been alone, Mahon would have aimed his spit at me, shaken his angry fist. But he could only frown more.

"No harm, Mahon," Eiden said. "A few stones cannot hurt anyone."

Mahon pulled on his beard, looked around the table. "Does anyone think not?" Silence, as the chieftains shot furtive looks one to the other.

"Never say I did not warn you, Brian," Mahon said.

"Praise you, brother."

I stepped over the threshold without tripping, imagining Rónan's thrill when the messenger stepped out on the strand and called his name. Clearly, Mahon had no plan to raise an army against Ivar. He meant to take a fleet against Fergal Ua Ruairc, but he had no fleet and no oarsmen. His promise to Tadg would come to nothing. Meantime, Rónan and I and our band of youth would drive the Norse king from the River Shannon. We would show ourselves brave, skilled, clear-minded, and wise, as worthy as any king, and indeed, far more worthy than my brother and his chieftains.

—Chapter Fifteen—

Rory, the messenger, and his young charge, Félim, came into Kincora thin as sticks and ragged, animal skins tied around their feet for shoes, their hair long and matted. Rory's eyes teared up when Mahon begged him stay at Kincora as his manservant. When Rory asked if Félim could stay, Mahon looked to me for an answer.

"Why not?" I said, seeing hope and fear in the boy's face. "He tends pigs, does he not? Our pigs go every which way when only one swineherd tends them."

"Félim has swineherd blood in him," Rory said. "He is son to Tómas, your father's swineherd, killed in the rout. Félim escaped, but the Norse caught and enslaved him for their own pigs."

"Félim does favor old Tómas," I said. "Do you not think, Mahon?"

Mahon screwed up his face, closed one eye. "Perhaps ... but does he have nothing to say for himself?"

"I can speak Norse like the Norse," Félim said. "Pigs love me. I love them too." I shot a look at Mahon. He could not refuse such a heartfelt plea.

"Stay then," Mahon said. "But swear you will bring more good than trouble, else I will send you away."

"I swear," Félim said, "and again, many times over."

✟

I had hoped Mahon would command Rory to Holy Island first thing, but no, he swore he needed Rory for his journey to Tadg's for his wedding. Would I not come too?

I wanted no part of Mahon's wedding, and I suspected Tadg could well have other plans for Mahon. When I spoke my worries to him, he scoffed. Thus I was both relieved and surprised when, a fortnight later, Mahon and his chieftains rode back in with Úna, a pretty young woman with blackberry-dyed eyebrows and honey brown hair. With them came Mac Liag, a young poet, soft all over with a wart on the end of his nose. Both he and she were fifteen, one year younger than me.

One cold day I went out from my house, forgetting my brat. Turning back, I spied Úna peering into my door, pinching her nose. When I surprised her from behind, she blushed the deep red color of rose and swore she was only doing her wifely duties, keeping Mahon's houses in order. Truth, I felt like a fool, staring at her.

With Úna at the fortress, our cooks readied sweeter cakes and creamier sauces than I had ever tasted, bread so fresh and flavorful I could not stop eating it, vegetables and grains neither rough, tough, sour, foul, or rotten. Our needlewomen worked harder to embroider pillow covers with bright colored thread and sew new tunics for all Kincorans. The sight of Úna brought joy to all of us, a shapely woman with an ivory comb nestled in her thick hair, the only queen I had truly ever known.

By Christmas, word spread Úna was heavy with child. Mahon smiled, but more and more, he spent his time at Bórama. When I questioned him, he swore he watched over shipwrights who built warships for his fleet. Did I not know all kings needed fleets, most of all the king on the River Shannon who had promised to come against the sworn enemy of his powerful father-in-law? I let his words pass without challenge.

✥

On the first of May—Beltane—Mahon sent Rory to Holy Island for Rónan. In a few days' time, they rode out from the river path onto the hill below Kincora. Rónan and I laughed at how much we had grown alike: the same heights and widths, beards starting on both our chins. His hair was dark, mine light, and his freckled spots were still there, but even so, we could have been brothers.

"Rónan, my friend." I reached out to embrace him.

"Brian! I am humbled," he said, his voice as deep as mine.

First thing, we walked to the river to plot, leaning against the chapel wall. "Two score youth should do us," I said. "Fast, strong, hearty, and honest."

Rónan thought, "Fast and strong, we can tell with no trouble ... and hearty. Honest? Not so easy."

I unsheathed my knife. "No man will lie with this pointed at him."

"Point that at him, and he will betray you when you most need him."

"My hound's nose will tell me if he speaks falsehoods." I sheathed my knife.

Rónan hurled a pebble into the river. "We will have three tests of honesty—scent, voice, and gaze. I say we start with gaze. We will send all men away who shift their eyes downward or to the side when we question him." So simple. Rónan's words gave me great comfort.

✥

Mahon put out a call for Dal Cais youth. Meantime Rónan taught me stone slinging on our hurling field. At first, I flung stones every which way save the way I wanted. But by the time youth came in to be tested, I was as skilled as Rónan. He and

I agreed about most of the youth save one named Find—fleet of foot, good with his spear, and crafty with tale telling.

But Rónan shook his head. "Have you not seen Find look to the side when you question him?"

"Yes, but he is son of a poor farmer. His father taught him to look away from a prince."

"He looks away from me too," Rónan said. "Find will do his own bidding over yours."

"A man who thinks for himself," I said. "Is that not more reason to choose him?"

"He may think for himself at all the wrong times. We agreed to the gaze test of honesty, Brian. Find could ruin us."

"Find will stay as true to me as a well-aimed spear in flight. I am the prince, so I have the final say."

"I am the monk you called in to counsel you," Rónan said.

"Ah ... true. Shall we let the smell test decide us?"

"You smell him," Rónan said. "I have not the nose of a hound." Rónan and I bickered, but more like friends, not like Mahon and me.

Find waited for us in the hall. He jumped up when we came in, looking hopeful, but I motioned him down. "I must smell you, Find. Your neck must be as sweet as your words. Pray be still." I put my nose to his neck and sniffed, smelling the scent of a man.

"He is fit," I said, triumphant.

Rónan tilted his head. "Answer this. A Norseman passes close to your cave, his sword at the ready. You could slit his throat or obey your prince to stay back. Which would you do?"

"Obey my prince, of course." Find's gaze shifted.

"Now smell his neck," Rónan said.

Find put his hand out to stop me. "Pray do not shame me with your nose in my neck. Already you chose my brother ... with no smell test."

His brother? I had not known, but I admired Find's courage, denying a prince. "You have passed my tests, Find," I said. "Rónan? What do you say?"

"He is not fit, Brian. But you are the prince."

"He will prove you wrong," I said.

When I looked back at Find, I caught his hate-filled glare at Rónan, and for an instant, I thought we should deny him. But it was too late to say no.

✟

July and most of August, heavy rains kept us back. I cursed the weather, but Mahon's son, Áed, was of no mind to wait. He shot forth from Úna's womb a fine and strong infant. My brother gloated, but still he spent more time at Bórama than Kincora.

The last week in August, my troop gathered on the hillside, ready to leave for Limerick. "You will raise an army against Ivar?" I said, knowing he would shrug and not answer.

"Take care, Brian," he said. "The Norse king will not sit by and do nothing when you fling stones at his walls."

A wave of love swept through me. I knew Mahon's honest voice as well as my own. "We will sling stones until Ivar flees to the Isles," I said, "all the sooner if he hears King Mahon readies an army against him."

"A king calls for warriors when he needs them," Mahon said, "as I have said many times."

"Yes, but when he needs them, it will be too late to call for them."

"That is why it is good I am king, Brian, and you are not."

—Chapter Sixteen—

Leaving Kincora for the hills over Limerick, my spirits were high and my courage strong. But by the time we reached the scrub, both had waned. I had been one man when I spied, now we were two score men and two, grunting, scraping boots through leaves, and breaking branches. Any Norse spy worth the name would know we were coming.

At the stream further on, Rónan and I stood on a high, flat rock, as our men gathered around us awaiting my commands. Lest my voice betray my fear, I whispered my commands to Rónan, who spoke them to the men in his deepest voice. We would divide into three caves of ten men each, and a fourth with twelve men; ten men, including Find, myself, and Rónan. That way, we could keep watch on Find and decide our plans together. From time to time, all of us would move to new caves to trick Ivar's spies. We would snare fish, game, hare, squirrel, and mouse for our meals—but only when no Norse were near.

"Should the men gather outside our cave to be counted every morning?" Rónan whispered to me.

"No," I said, regaining my courage. "Norse will be out looking for us, and we must leave no clues. At dusk every day, I will hoot like an owl. One hoot will mean men in the first cave will sling stones that night, two will mean men in the second cave, and so on. We will take turns night after night, cave by cave."

Rónan nodded and shot me a smile. I loved my friend, who had saved me from shame.

Every night, ten youth flitted down the mountainside, leaping from bush to bog to riverbank, hooting at guards and slinging stones at Limerick's earthen walls. Our goal was to drive Ivar from the River Shannon, not stir him to such rage he would come against Kincora. Norse guards streamed out the gate with torches, straining to see us, but we were away before they could catch us.

A few nights in, one of my stones went astray and hit a guard. He cried out, put his hands to his head, slumped and tumbled down into the river. Certain I had killed him, we moved further away from Limerick.

We had furs and food enough to survive, but we could not light fires for fear smoke would give us away. Always we were cold and hungry. To fool ourselves, we sat shoulder to shoulder in our caves, boasting of our brave deeds, heaping scorn on Ivar and his warriors. Some nights in, story time in our cave became a contest to see whose deeds were the bravest.

One night, Rónan could think of no more brave deeds of his own. He would tell of a warrior more courageous and skilled than any man—the demigod Cúchulainn, who killed horny-skinned Ferdiad, his foster brother, in single combat at a river ford. They had both trained with the warrior woman, Scatach, on the Isle of Skye, and had vowed never to fight each other, even as they found themselves on opposite sides of a feud between Queen Maeve of Connacht and King Connor of Ulster. Queen Maeve, set on besting Cúchulainn, tricked Ferdiad, her best warrior, swearing Cúchulainn spread false rumors about him. Driven to rage, Ferdiad attacked Cúchulainn and the foster brothers fought for three days. On the last day, Cúchulainn rammed his magic barbed sword between Ferdiad's buttocks, the only way into his brother's body. Barbs spread all throughout Ferdiad and killed him.

"Speak Cúchulainn's cry of woe, Brian," Rónan said. "You know it well."

I did indeed, and welcomed my task. "It is to madness I am driven after the thing I have done. You were betrayed to your death, O Ferdiad. Our parting forever is a grief forever.'"

"A brave deed, no?" Rónan said. "The bravest ever."

"Demigods are not real," Find muttered. "Their tales do not count in our contest."

"Cúchulainn is real to me," Rónan said, clearly vexed. "He is real to Brian too. Is that not so, Brian?"

If I nodded yes, I would anger Find. If I shook my head, I would anger Rónan. I chose not to answer, but to end our storytelling.

"Now is the time for sleep," I said. "Story time is over for this night."

Grumbles, grunts, and growls came from men in the circle, but one by one we leaned against each other, slipping down into a heap of bodies. As I drifted off to sleep, I marveled how much Rónan's tale put me in mind of Mahon and me.

☩

At dawn, screams woke us from over the ridge. I strapped on my knife sheath, picked up my sword. The screams were faint, but I could hear they came from youth in our troop.

Rónan took hold of my arm. "Too late. Do not show yourself."

We crouched against the cave's back wall and tried not to breathe. Feet ran up and hands swept aside branches we had piled at the cave opening. Norse voices echoed inside the cave.

A gloved hand reached down and picked up a pouch we had left lying on the floor. Words flew back and forth, but at last they raced away. I bade everyone stay and crept out, almost to the top of the ridge, alone. There I stopped by a tree, imagining Norse laying in wait for fools like me. Leaves rustled behind me.

"Brian?" Rónan's voice.

"Rónan?" He pushed into sight.

"I bade you stay," I whispered.

"Find went out at dawn."

"Out where?"

"I feigned sleep and prayed he was leaving for good. I should have told you."

"I should not have chosen him."

Rónan and I made our way up over the ridge. Through trees, but some distance away, we spied bodies strewn all over the ground, not one moving or moaning. Closer, we stumbled upon heads some arms' lengths from bodies. I knew names, and Rónan knew the Latin words to bless the dead—*Requiescat in pace*. We dragged bodies and heads into the cave, heaped them in a pile, counting nine. The tenth?

We piled branches on top and had started back up the ridge when Rónan stopped me, pointing at two dead bodies wound around each other—Find and his brother, still warm, Find's head axed open, his brother with a spear wound in his back. Rónan kneeled down and crossed himself, his face in deep sorrow.

"It is to madness I am driven after the thing I have done, Find," he said. "You yearned for your brother, not least because of me. May your souls take flight together, on the wings of the holy ghost."

I reached out to help Rónan stand. "From now on, friend, I swear I will heed your counsel."

I called all our men to a clearing, stood before them and spoke truth as best I could. Find had not been careful. He had gone to search for his brother, the Norse had spied him, and followed him. We had a choice: stay and fight or start for home. I was of both minds and would hear every man's thinking.

The first man said he would judge himself a coward if we crept home in fear. The second said Norse had killed eleven of us, and we should do the same. The third said killing Norse would be the surest way to start a bigger battle, but if we did nothing or went home, they would come for us anyway.

So it went, no man sure of his choice, and no man swearing we should abandon our quest. Rónan spoke last. "I say we stay to avenge Find and all our murdered men—no slinking home like whipped dogs."

Those words decided me: no slinking home liked whipped dogs to the sneers of my brother and his fawning chieftains. We moved to new caves further from Limerick and vowed to keep fighting.

—Chapter Seventeen—

I well remember the night I perched in a tree outside my cave, my turn to keep watch. I was cold to the bone and so tired I feared tumbling to the ground asleep. We had been in the hills over Limerick almost a year, and even as the days had grown long once more, we scarce ever saw the sun for the trees. My hair and beard had grown so long, Rónan had taken his knife to them, as I had to his. Even my nose felt bigger to the touch. A scrape on my leg had not healed and pus oozed. I imagined I would die like Lachtna, calling for my mother.

Inside my cave, seven men slept in a pile, half of our men who still lived. The Norse had found another of our caves, killed all ten men, and six more who had stayed back to cover our tracks running back to our caves, escaping guards. We were taking turns risking our lives, and that night, it was Rónan's turn. Even as he was careful and skilled, I worried.

A voice said my name. "Prince Brian!" My heart leapt into my throat. Not Rónan, but who?

"Félim, here." He stepped out from the forest, and I jumped down from my perch.

"How did you find us?"

"I have been spying since you left Kincora."

"You have been watching us die? My brother knows?"

He nodded. "He bids you home for your wedding. A Princess Mór from Connacht waits for you at Kincora."

Anger welled up in me. "One hundred Connacht princesses could not sway me back to Kincora."

My words fell like damp leaves onto the forest floor. Félim stood unmoving and unspeaking, waiting for me to change my answer?

"Pray tell King Mahon I will decide when to come home."

Félim faded back into the trees. I climbed back into my perch to await Rónan's whistle.

☩

He did whistle that night and again at dawn. I made my way to his cave, and he and I sat outside the cave mouth, wrapped in our furs.

"Félim visited me last night," I said. "He says Mahon found me a Connacht princess to wed. She waits at Kincora."

Rónan's frame had thinned, and an open cut festered on his forearm, like the cut on my leg. Yet his shoulders were wide and fire burned hot in his eyes.

"You dreamed Félim," Rónan said.

"No. I smelled him, felt his breath."

"You cannot believe a princess waits for you at Kincora. A princess weds at her father's fort, not her husband's."

I shrugged. "He said her name, Princess Mór."

"Mahon has raised an army against Ivar?"

"I did not ask. We have stayed longer than he imagined. Now he fears we have stirred Ivar to a raging beast."

Rónan lowered his voice to a whisper. "I will tell you something I know is true. Last night, the Norse readied to come upon our last man, but we fell upon them and hacked them to pieces, left them to rot."

"You killed Norse?"

"Seven.

Fear coursed through me. "Ivar will be after us now, with a vengeance."

"But think, Brian. If every night we kill more of his men, he will seek a safer place to thieve and plunder."

"No creeping back to Kincora like whipped dogs in shame?"

"No."

"But are seven dead Norse not enough?"

Rónan shook his head no. "No. But if every night we come upon them and kill more, they will flee."

"You believe that?"

"I know it."

"Then we will try." My doubts were grave, but I had sworn to heed Rónan's counsel.

A light sparked in his weary eyes. "We will take turns," he said. "Tonight I will take your men and show them where and how. On the morrow, you will take mine. They know where and how." He met my gaze straight on.

I unsheathed my father's knife and held it out. "Take this with you, friend. It will serve you well."

He took it and handed his knife to me. "Be proud. There could be no better man than you."

"There is. I look at him now."

✠

I slept hard that night, and at dawn, I whistled, but heard nothing back. The cave where Rónan and my men should have been was empty. Straightaway, his men and I readied for Limerick.

The sun was well up when we came in sight of the Norse fortress, bustling with men dragging broken and burned warships from the water onto shore. Ivar fought, but against who? Our good fortune, if another enemy wrecked his ships.

Rónan's men showed me the place of their ambush two nights before, but the bodies had been taken. Only broken bushes and dried blood marked the spot. We set out for rock outcroppings to wait for dark.

Passing by a thicket, we stumbled upon a corpse—one of our men, his short sword clutched in his hand. Sorrow overcame me as I guessed what we would find next. A trail of blood led to six more of our men, bloodied and dead. Rónan not there to bless them, I recited the Latin words myself. Hope flickered my friend had escaped, but no, a groan sounded from behind a bush. I raced around to see Rónan splayed on his back, eyes closed, my knife gripped tight in one hand, the other pressed up against his skull, blood covering his face. I touched his arm.

"Rónan?" His fingers uncurled and my knife fell loose. I ripped off my tunic and stuffed it into his head wound. In little time, it was blood soaked.

"Leave me," Rónan whispered.

"Never."

We fashioned a bandage around his head and carried Rónan on a pallet of branches and vines, headed toward Kincora. With every sound from his throat, I gave thanks he still lived. At the scrub, we poured water from my pouch into his dry lips, wiped blood from his eyes. At the stream, I felt for his breath, rinsed the cloths, rewrapped his head, and set out once more.

In no time, the rags were blood soaked again. I had walked back to rinse them when Rónan made a noise in his throat. I knew what it meant, even as I had not heard it before. I took hold of his hand, gripped it tight, whispered in his ear. I doubt he heard me as he took his last breath. I laid my head on his warm stomach, my tears blinding me, sure nothing in my life would ever give me such pain.

We had been two score men setting out, but were down to eight and a corpse at the stream. I had paid no heed to the druids' warning, paid no heed to Mahon, wasted the best of our clan's youth, and lost my best and only friend. We had tried to save each other from shame, but the cost had been far too great.

—Chapter Eighteen—

The guard at Kincora shouted into the fortress and Mahon met us in the courtyard, together with Rory, you, poet, and Úna holding young Áed's hand. We lowered the pallet onto the ground.

"The monk?" Mahon glanced at Rónan. "Had you come …"

Lightheaded, my hands cold and my forehead sweating, I spied a young woman floating up to me, her skin smooth as silk, her hair gold as flax, her breasts round as moons.

"Prince Brian!" She flashed a sweet smile, curtsied, and gazed down at Rónan's body. "Your friend?"

I tried to bow, but her cherry lips wobbled and my knees gave way. They say I fell hard, bloodied my head on the courtyard stones.

I woke to the strong smell of perfume—Úna leaning over me, wiping my forehead with a warm wet rag. I tried to sit, but a sharp pain in my head forced me down.

"You fainted and hit your head on the stones," Mahon said from his chair by the hearth.

"Rónan?"

"The priest readies his body."

"My men?"

"Gone home."

"We tried to wake you," Úna said, cradling a bowl of steaming liquid in her hands. "Drink this. Broth."

I lifted my head and sip by sip, strength seeped back into my body. I sat up, swung my legs over the edge of the bed, but once more lay back from pain and dizziness. "We will bury Rónan in the chapel graveyard," I said.

Mahon shook his head. "He is not kin."

"He is my kin." Úna sat by me on the bed and wiped my forehead again, easing my head pain. "Do you not remember your princess, Brian?" she said. "You bowed to her. All is ready for your wedding this day."

"No. Before anything, I will bury Rónan."

"Rónan's brothers will come for him," Mahon said. "He belongs at Tuamgraney. Or with the monks at Holy Island."

I put one foot on the floor and then the other, testing my legs. They held me up, and I started toward the door, my head wound pounding. "Rónan belongs here with me." Mahon blocked the door, glaring at me.

"What harm, Mahon?" Úna said. "Rónan is like kin to Brian. I will fetch the diggers." She draped her wool brat over her shoulders, pulled up her hood, and pushed past Mahon, out the door.

I made a move after her, but Mahon blocked me again. "Not so fast, brother. Shun Princess Mór and she will shun you. Then where will we be?"

Had I been able, I would have challenged Mahon, but I squeezed past him and weaved down the path to the chapel. The priest prayed over Rónan's shrouded body, stretched out on a bier. He looked up. "You did well to carry your friend here, Prince Brian. He would thank you if he could."

My hand on Rónan's cold cheek, I sobbed. "Forgive me, friend." Tears spilled down my cheeks onto his shroud.

"Our Lord God will forgive if you repent," the priest said in a honey-sweet voice.

"Repent?" A woman's voice said from behind me. "Has Prince Brian sinned?" I turned to see Princess Mór standing in the chapel door, a vision of grace and beauty. I bowed my head, more pain shooting through it.

She stepped closer. "A man does not bend to his woman. He kisses her cheeks."

I could smell my foul odor. "Not now, Princess Mór. Before anything, I must bury my friend in the chapel graveyard."

"Ah, no," the priest said. "King Mahon says not. Perhaps the servants' graveyard, behind Kincora? More fitting for a man of low rank."

Mór held up her hand. "Jesus deemed us all brothers and sisters, Father. Is that not so in Munster?" Such wise and wonderful words. The priest blushed, nodded, clutched a silver cross hanging from a cord around his neck.

"I come with a message, Prince Brian," Mór said. "From Queen Úna. King Mahon has given his leave. Rónan's grave is dug in the river chapel graveyard, and the diggers are waiting for the body."

I sighed relief. "Pray help me, Father."

The priest and I grasped the two ends of Rónan's bier and carried it out the church door, through the fortress gate, and down the hill to the river chapel graveyard, Mór following close behind. People stared as we passed, but only Úna and the diggers waited by the open hole. We lifted Rónan's body in, the priest said words and sprayed holy water from his pouch onto the corpse.

"I will love you forever, Rónan," I said, as he disappeared under the mud.

"There could be no better man than you," I remembered him saying. There is, but he is gone forever.

—Chapter Nineteen—

Mór, Úna, the priest and I started back up the hill toward the fortress. Rich smells of roasting beef and baking bread put me in mind it was my wedding day.

"Why such haste to wed me?" I said to the priest, as Mór peeked at me from his other side.

"Do you not welcome your wedding?" he said. "King Mahon swore you would."

"Surely Prince Brian welcomes his new bride," Úna said to Mór. "Mahon promised your father that Brian would wed you the day he came down from the hills."

"Someday," I said, "perhaps. But this day my heart is heavy with grief, as it will be on the morrow." Mór stared straight ahead, no frown, no smile.

"Forgive me, Princess Mór," I said. "My brother made you a false promise. I cannot honor it."

Mór stepped to my side and touched my hand. "You grieve your friend, Prince Brian. I will wait as long as you wish. You need not beg my forgiveness."

"No." Úna said to Mór, "The time is now. Mahon promised your father today would be your wedding day. Is that not so, Princess Mór?"

"It is, Queen Úna," Mór said. "But King Mahon also swore Prince Brian agreed to wed me."

The priest slowed his pace and took hold of my arm. "You must wed today, Brian. Our church laws demand it."

Church laws? I kept walking, paid him no heed.

"Pray, Father," Mór said, staying back with the priest and Úna, "which church laws?"

"No maiden can live unwed at a man's fort with no date set for her wedding. That church law." I turned to stare at him. I knew of no such law.

Mór smothered a smile. "Father, in Connacht, church laws permit a maiden to wait for her man at his fort until he is ready to wed, without fear of punishment. Could it be Connacht's church laws differ from Munster's?"

The priest's face reddened. "Church laws are the same all over our island."

"Priests are not the same all over our island," I said. "A wise priest at Holy Island told me a maiden can wait without sin at her man's fort if he grieves for the death of his best friend in life."

"Take heed, Prince Brian," the priest huffed. "Too many sins and no priest will wed you."

"But is there not a church law that says a king cannot promise his brother to a maiden without his consent?" I asked. "If not, there should be." The priest frowned, shrugged, shook his head.

Úna glanced up at Mahon watching us from the wall. "You will vex Mahon, Brian. He granted you the chapel graveyard for your friend, and now you refuse the princess he won for you?" She hastened up the hill ahead of us.

Mór's gaze found mine, a wry smile on her face. I could not help but smile back. Through the gate into the courtyard, the priest hastened away. I begged a word alone with Mahon, but Mór would not have it. "Prince Brian," she said from next to me. "Should Queen Úna and I not hear your thoughts ... and speak ours?"

I could think of no reason not, nor could Mahon. The four of us strolled to Mahon's house, the men taking chairs and the women, stools.

"You have sinned, Mahon," I started, half in jest. "You promised Princess Mór my hand in marriage, without my consent."

Mahon pulled on his beard, crossed and uncrossed his legs. "Had I not, you would still be in the hills wasting good Dal Cais youth. I found you a princess, but you refuse her, and only to vex me."

"Forgive me, King Mahon," Mór said. "Did you not tell my father Prince Brian agreed to wed me. I heard you speak those words to him." With every word out of Mór's mouth, my heart warmed to her more.

"Brian does agree," Úna said. "He spoke your name in his sleep, as our wedding vows promise a husband and wife will do. Mahon and I both heard him."

"In Connacht," Mór said soft, "we vow to whisper each other's names first thing when we wake, not in our sleep. Are wedding vows not the same in Munster?"

Mór's words made beautiful sense, even to Úna, who smiled in surprise. "No one asked my leave when I was plucked from my father's fort," Mór went on. "I have neither agreed nor disagreed."

Awe swept over me at Mór's bravery, but Úna set her jaw. "Husband—did you not send Félim to ask Brian's leave?"

Mahon cleared his throat, hesitated. "Did Félim not beg your leave, Brian?"

I shook my head. "No, nor did I say I would. Indeed, I said the opposite."

A bell rang out from the church. "Listen," Mahon said. "Your wedding bells." He pushed back his chair. "Look at you, Brian. Can you not smell yourself? No bride will take a stinking groom. Rory will clean you up in my tub."

"I fear not," I said. "Princess Mór does not want a husband who mopes and mourns for his friend."

"But the priest calls, Brian," Mahon said.

"He calls at your bidding, brother."

Mahon blushed. "Princess Mór will not wait forever."

I looked at Mór. "True?"

She tilted her head. "Do you consent to wed me, Prince Brian?"

"I do, Princess Mór. I am no longer in command of my will."

She laughed. "Nor am I."

✛

Rory burned my clothes in the fire pit and took me to Mahon's tub behind his house. He scrubbed me, emptied out foul water and added clean, over and over until the water stayed clear. My matted beard he could cut with scissors, but my hair? Only sheep shears would do for it. My hair cut short, Rory soothed my head wound with poultice. Another dousing in the tub, head to toe, and he spied lice, not fit for a groom.

For endless moments, he scraped my scalp with knife and razor. More doses of bacon grease and at last he declared my head lice free. My head bare, my skin fresh and smooth, Rory stood back and admired his work, even as we both knew the stares my new look would bring.

"Now your leg," he said. "The pus."

I groaned and sat back on the stool as he smeared more poultice—rue, garlic, salt, more bacon grease—into my cut. He bandaged my leg and rubbed me all over with oil and sweet-scented herbs. He turned me around naked, sighing it was the best he could do.

Inside Mahon's empty house, Rory motioned to clothing on a bench—Mahon's gift to me for my wedding. I slipped on tight-fitting breeches, a many-colored striped tunic, and closed a crimson-colored wool brat at my shoulder with a silver pin. Looking about for my ripped shoes, I smiled when Rory handed me fresh, well-fitting sandals—Mahon's doing, so certain I would wed that first day.

Rory held up a shiny metal mirror to my face. I startled at the image, not sure I saw me. But when I touched the top of my head, the hand in the mirror did the same.

"Try this." Rory handed me Mahon's black wool skull cap, more hideous than my bare scalp. I tossed it on the chair. I was ready, but Mór's handmaidens sent word she was not. My mind shifted from Mór swearing she wished to wed me, to Órlaith hiding from her husband-to-be in a slave's hovel. Three times I sent Rory, and three times he came back shaking his head. Once more, and I would go myself.

To my great relief, Mór stepped out from her door, a goddess clothed in green silk, braids of golden hair wound around her head, long strands hanging down in back with tiny gold balls tied to the ends, glinting in the sun. Closer to her, I smelled perfume, and spied her berry reddened cheeks and crimsoned fingernails. From her warm smiles, I imagined she thought me handsome, no matter my new look.

Mór and I followed Rory to the church, where Mahon, Úna, and Áed had gathered to bear witness to our wedding vows. Outside the church door, the priest read our vows from his book, and Mór and I took turns saying them back. We swore to honor each other for life, to always give the first bites of our meat and sips from our cups to each other, and to cry each others' name and smile into into each others' faces the first thing when we woke.

Vows over, Mór, the priest, and I entered the church, where he murmured words in Latin, signed the cross over us, and handed us newly crafted silver rings we slipped on each others' fingers.

Cheers from Kincorans' throats greeted us in the hall for our feast. In my year away, I had forgotten the taste of good food, but memories came rushing back when the cook brought out cheeses, grains, vegetables, meats, puddings, and sweets Úna had no doubt helped him ready. I had heard your bell-like voice, poet, but never such honeyed words. I had not known the blacksmith could somersault, the seamstress dance, the shepherds and cowherds sing, the silversmith joke, or even that I could still laugh. But laugh I did, between mouthfuls of food and swigs of ale, forgetting the fuzz on my head and cheeks. Mór's winsome smile warmed my heart, as did the sight and feel of her soft skin, and the cleft in her chin reminding me of a mountain pass.

Mór and I took leave to my house, newly cleansed, my sleeping nook graced with a new, bigger bed, the mattress stuffed with feathers instead of straw. Fresh pillows and blankets were laid out on the bed, and someone, Rory perhaps, had opened the cowhide curtain, letting in soft light from coals in the hearth.

I prayed my flute would not fail me, but I needed not worry; we were together, in wit and in purpose. Mór's older sisters had tutored her, and she guided me on top. "Try this, Prince Brian," she said, reaching for my flute, and indeed I did, many times, my head pain and dizziness but distant memories.

At dawn, when I stood to dress, I spied a spot of woman blood on the bed. Cúchulainn's tale of Queen Maeve shot to mind, her gush of blood so strong it had turned into raging rivers that swept away all in its path.

"Are you ill?" Mór said from next to me, following my gaze to the spot. "Be proud. You have opened my womb for our children."

I had heard of woman blood and feared it, but had never seen it. "Woman blood cannot harm a man," Mór said. "Touch it. You will live."

I reached out my finger, but she pushed it down. "No. Your flute."

No blackness or sharp pains came over me, only relief and joy that Mór's woman sense had rid me of my fear. Truth, save for nursemaids I scarce remembered, I had spent most of my life in the company of men.

"Mahon brings me the finest jewel in the land," I said. "No better fortune could befall a man."

"Or befall a woman," Mór said, kissing my cheek.

We took our time dressing in clothing laid out for us on chairs. Mór pulled me down next to her on the bed, took my hand in hers. "Promise you will stay?"

"Stay? Why would I not?"

"Úna says you will lead the fight against Fergal, for my father, King Eidne's, sake, and mine." I let go her hand, surprised and fearful of her meaning. "Surely you know the Connacht King Fergal murdered King Tadg, Úna's father?"

"No. When?"

"Only days before Mahon messaged my father. Úna blames Mahon for promising Tadg a fleet he did not have. He made the same promise to my father, for me. Truth, my father doubted Mahon's boastings of a fleet, yet he could think of no better husband for me than a Dal Cais prince with the courage to sling stones at a Norse king's walls."

I sucked in breath. Ivar, downriver, Fergal, upriver, both set against us? My worst fears come true.

Mór touched her finger to my head wound, so gentle I scarce felt it. "When we first met in the courtyard, you were so shy with me, you fell over and hit your head. I could see you were a rare man then, and I loved you for it. But now, I see you are more honest, wise, and courageous than any man. I pray my father lives long enough to know the grandchildren we will give him."

"I pray we live long enough to give him grandchildren. With Mahon king of our clan, deciding our fate, that is by no means certain."

—Chapter Twenty—

Mahon's door opened a crack, I pushed it wide. Úna dropped her knitting into her lap, and Áed startled, knocked his stack of wooden blocks onto the floor, grabbed his mother's leg and yelped like a wounded dog. Mahon, in a chair next to Úna, whipped his head around.

"Caveman? Do you not know to knock? You frighten my child."

I stared down at his face. "You found me a gem of a princess, Mahon, but there is something you forgot to tell me."

"He did not forget," Úna said, picking up her needles and yarn. "He could not tell you for the shame."

Mahon stood, face flushed, and waved his hand at Úna. "Leave us."

She set her knitting down and lifted Áed into her arms, taking her good time to step out the door. Mahon jerked it shut behind them.

"That is how you treat your wife, Mahon?"

"I have suffered enough of her tears for a lifetime. And her blame. I had no warning about Fergal, Brian. Nor would the few boats my shipwrights built for me have done any good. Fergal hosted against Tadg across land, on horse, straight as the arrow flies from his dún to Tadg's."

"So now we have sworn enemies upriver and downriver."

"Fergal will not stray into Munster."

"No? Then why wed me to Mór if not to win the little known king, Eidne, as your ally?"

"Connacht allies can only strengthen me, no matter how small."

"Ivar will not shrink from battle. If his broken and burned warships are any sign, he is in battle now against another enemy."

"Ivar has many enemies. We should not be among them. Nor will we. He has won his little skirmish with you."

"Won?"

"Did he not kill most of your troop?"

"Yes."

"You killed none of his. That means he won."

I paused. Félim had not seen the Norse warriors Ronan and his men had killed. "Call in your chieftains, Mahon."

"Why?"

"I have good reason."

"My chieftains do not journey from their hearths in winter. And winter is upon us."

"You and your chieftains will want to hear what I have to say."

"Tell me now," Mahon said.

"I will tell you when they come. Else you will pay me no heed."

Mahon spat. "You should have stayed in the caves, brother."

☩

That brutal winter, Mór and I sat before our hearth, telling of our lives before we knew each other. We were both the youngest of our fathers' broods, but shared little else. Her mother had died in childbirth, but not from grief. Her father still lived, she had no brothers, only sisters, and none who had lost their heads. Her father's one grandson had been stolen from his cot by a nursemaid, no doubt for the Norse slave markets.

I squeezed her hand. "No such theft will happen to our infants." Mor pressed her face into my shoulder.

☦

One day, the sun shining warm, we walked to the river and watched blue-beaked, orange-breasted birds swooping hapless fish from the rapids. They put me in mind of Ivar, as most everything did. We were sitting on our brats by the river when my fears spilled out.

"Ivar will come for us soon."

Mór glanced at me sideways. "How do you know?"

"He has good reason. Rónan and I killed seven of his men. Perhaps eight."

"Mahon knows?"

"I will tell him when his chieftains come to council in spring."

"Will Ivar wait until spring?"

I gazed at the rapids. "He would be wise to come now, when we least expect him."

A long pause from Mór. "My father once worried every day his enemies would host against him, but now he only worries when his spies say his enemies are near."

"Mahon sets no spies on Ivar. Only on me."

"But can you not set spies on Ivar? Félim speaks Norse like the Norse. He spied on you. Could he not spy on Norse?"

I put my arm around Mór's shoulders and pulled her close, marveling at all she knew. Her wit. A kind of love filled my heart I had never felt before.

✠

Our swineherd hemmed and hawed when I begged him for Félim, but when Félim promised two of his friends would take his place, the swineherd relented. I told Mahon I would be gone one week, setting Félim and his fellow spies over Limerick. His face took on that pensive look, signaling thoughts he did not wish to share.

I had little to teach Félim, and was back three days sooner than I had said. Coming up the hill, I spied Rory on the wall and horses in the pen I did not know.

"Whose horses?" I asked Rory, coming closer.

"The chieftains. Your wife bid me here. She has news."

"What news?"

He shrugged. "Good news, I think. She is all smiles."

Mór heard me coming and met me at the door, bliss in her face. I guessed, but would let her tell me.

"I have missed my bleeding time, husband." She put her arms around my neck and kissed my face.

"So soon?" I said like a fool. "I have been gone only four days."

She laughed. "Enough time for a woman to know, husband. My womb bears our child."

"Our child." The words tasted like honey in my mouth. I kissed Mór's face back.

"You will stay?"

That same question again? Mahon and his chieftains readied for something, in secret from me. Mór suspected. Or perhaps she knew.

"I do not know if I will stay. But I will be here when our child is born."

I made my way to the council house, to eavesdrop on the chieftains' talk before entering. But young Áed spied me and came running, shouting my name. I clapped my hand over his mouth, but too late. All had gone quiet inside.

"What good fortune to find you here," I said, filling the doorway with my presence. "With the air so bitter cold, lesser men would have stayed close to their hearths."

Mahon glowered and bit his lip. No empty chair at the table, I stayed standing. "You speak of the weather and the crops?"

"The animals and the crops," Mahon said.

"And the weather," Conaing said.

"Am I not to know of the weather, the animals, and the crops, Mahon? You called a council in such haste."

"It is best I speak alone with my chieftains."

I kneaded my fingers together, stretched my arms out, unloosed my fingers and let my arms drop by my side. "Now that your chieftains are here, Mahon, I will tell you Rónan and I killed at least seven of Ivar's warriors. If the Norse king ever slept, he does not now."

"You killed Norse?" Mahon's face went white.

I nodded. "Seven. Perhaps eight."

"You told me you had not."

"No, Mahon, you told me I had not. I begged you to call in your chieftains, and lo, here they are, in council without me."

"It is best I talk with my chieftains without your babbling nonsense."

"You woke the sleeping beast, Brian," Conaing said. "Now what?"

"Now I will ride to the father of every youth who died for me in the hills and promise his son's honor-price in milk cows. Then I will speak of our next battle to come against the

Limerick Norse and the booty we will share with our warriors. The farmer's face will tell me if he is of a mind to give other sons."

Mahon banged the table with his fist. "Our brithem will judge you a lawbreaker."

"Our brithem will judge you a coward and a fool."

Our laws did not allow public slander, and Mahon did not dare call me a caveman. He pursed his lips. The chieftains shifted their gazes between Mahon and me.

"Mahon," Conaing said, "We do owe honor price for our farmers' slain sons. Why not agree to Brian's plan?".

"No law says Brian cannot speak for us," Eiden said. "He could suffer our farmers' grief. Instead of us."

Mahon pulled on his beard, swiped sweat from his face. "Brian could save us much time," Conaing said, "when the time comes."

"Time?" I said. "What time?"

"Any time, Brian," Mahon answered. "You may go, but be sure to tell our farmers you speak for their chieftains. And their king. Remember, you are my warrior prince."

I turned to leave, grateful for their leave, even as I knew they plotted. "Do not come begging for my help," Mahon said to my back.

I turned. "I would never, Mahon."

—Chapter Twenty-One—

I set out in summer to Dal Cais farms with two bodyguards, a carpenter and a butcher. Neither knew fighting, yet both looked fierce in their leather helmets, vests, and weapons hitched to their horses' rumps and manes. Mór cried more tears at my leaving than water in the lake, but I promised I would visit every fortnight, without fail.

My bodyguards and I headed west over forested mountains, passing through clearing after clearing, meeting turtles, hares, and badgers sunning themselves. Begging their pardon, we kept on.

Down into farmland and pasture, I hoped to meet youth who had come back alive from the caves. But more often we met fathers and mothers whose sons had not come back. Supping and drinking at their ringforts, I told tales of their sons' bravery and promised fair honor-prices—a one-year-old heifer for every farmer who owned two milk cows, or one milk cow for those who owned no cows.

Morning come, I turned my talk to King Ivar and the booty Mahon and I would take in our battle against him. I took my time leaving, for fathers and mothers to wonder if others of their sons might yearn to join our army. I made a notch in my mind if they nodded maybe, and a deeper notch if they pledged a son.

Some months on, my bodyguards and I came to a river. Downstream, the river widened into a lake-like body of water, where it met the River Shannon. Across the lake, we saw an island with a ringfort, but with no boats, we could not reach it.

We rode back to a narrow place in the river, crossed, and rode back down. A wary farmer appeared on his ringfort wall and I called my name, holding out my open hands to signal I meant no harm. We boarded his currachs and let our horses go free.

The farmer had no sons, dead or alive, but for many days I stayed, listening to him tell of land west of him, pocked with rocks. If a man kept going, the farmer said, he would come to stone tombs where ancient men buried their dead, and then to cliffs where men could see the vast sea meet the sky. A careless man could be swept away by waves crashing against those cliffs, but still, I wished to see it all, smell and feel it all. I thought to go, but Mór's time was coming, and she would be wanting me home.

My bodyguards and I were back to the river crossing when Rory appeared on his horse. Our horses splashed through water to meet him.

"Your child, Prince Brian," Rory breathed out. "A boy. He is born."

My hand flew to my chest. "When? It is too soon."

"Three days ago. But for your horses' piles, I would never have found you. Your son is well—scrawny, but full-throated."

A flood of fear filled my chest. "Mór?"

"She bleeds, but the midwife swears she will heal."

"Swears? The woman is not certain?"

Rory hesitated. "Perhaps certain."

"How scrawny?"

Rory drew his finger from wrist to elbow. "But his lungs are strong." I turned my horse's head toward Kincora, leaving my bodyguards and Rory behind.

A full moon lit my way through plains, bogs, forest, and clearings. The sky was graying dawn when I rode up the hill to the gate, jumped off my tired steed, and made haste to our house. The midwife stood outside, cradling my cloth-wrapped son in her arms.

She called back to Mór. "He is here."

I took my son into my arms, stared into a face ruddy and splotched, his head misshapen, his deep blue eyes open. Gazing at me? I touched his feather-soft cheek with my dirt-smeared finger, but snatched it back before he could take it into his mouth. I handed him back to the midwife and stepped in to Mór.

She smiled at me from her bed, pale, but I saw only roses in her cheeks. I kneeled and kissed her forehead.

"Our child," I said. "Shriveled, but well. And you?"

"I will strengthen, now that you are here."

"Forgive me. I promised to be here." I willed my tears away too late.

She lifted her finger to my face. "Only a rare man weeps." I put my head on her chest. What more could a man want?

The priest blessed our child, and we named him Murrough, after Mór's grandfather—a good, strong name. The midwife warned we should take time between births, but our yearnings were stronger than our vows.

☩

I was still at Kincora when Félim brought news of Ivar. He had seen what I had seen. Norse warships left Limerick, headed downriver, but when they came back, they were battered and burned, fire-breathing serpents missing from prows, oarsmen struggling to row half-sunk warships up the strong river current.

A blessing for us. But who? Time and again I asked Félim, but he did not know. One day, I shouted at him and called him useless. His face drained of color and he swore he would do better next time.

Mór's womb did swell again, but our twins were born far too soon, the size of my hand, and died within a day. We named them Connor and Flann and buried them in the river chapel graveyard. Murrough, up on his feet, stuck his blond curly head out from behind a stone—once, twice, three times—bringing a smile onto Mór's sad face.

I crawled into bed with my sweet wife and swore she would bear us more children, sons and daughters, so many we would lose count. She loved me for that and before long, was up chasing Murrough in and out of our house and all around the fortress.

One night in bed, Mór whispered to me about Úna, who had become like a sister to her with me away. "Úna envies me. She pouts and says I give you hope for more children. Mahon has lost hope."

"Mahon could use more children to strengthen his kingly ties," I said. "But truth, it has been long since Áed."

"She is scarce to blame. Mahon saves his seed for bondswomen at Bórama."

"Ah." I had suspected as much. So much time spent at Bórama watching over shipwrights.

Mór hid her shy face in the blanket. "Úna says how handsome and kind you are, next to Mahon."

"What do you say to comfort her?"

"I say you are taken; you are mine."

"No pity for a wretched woman?" I touched Mór's chin and smiled.

"Not one who eyes my husband. At least she has a friend in the poet. They visit together in his island house ... did you know?"

"No, but I do now."

"They are not lovers, only friends. Swear you will tell no one?

"Your secrets are safe with me." I kissed her forehead.

—Chapter Twenty-Two—

Mór heavy with child for the third time, I stayed back at Kincora and called in pledged warriors for training. Mahon stood at the gate, holding a wax tablet, counting and putting faces to names and places. I needed no list.

I had killed a Norseman by mistake at Limerick, and I had seen beheaded corpses, but never had I twisted my knife's blade in a man's gut or hacked a head loose from a body. My tutors had taught me the tactics of Julius Caesar and Alexander the Great—useless against Norse. So I invented my own.

"Norse wear metal helmets and mail shirts to their thighs. They carry wooden shields with metal braces, wield axes, bows and arrows, spears, swords, and knives. Yet there is always a way in. When he raises his arm, go for his bare skin—his armpit, groin, legs, feet. That first move will decide the winner. When he falls, go for the kill."

Those words flowed more easily from my mouth each time I spoke them. "Never turn your back," I went on, "and do not let his friends surprise you from behind. Never meet his gaze, never gloat. Move on to the next foe, until all have fallen. When the battle is won, take no trophy heads. You will need space in your sacks for spoils—silver, gold, silks, fineries such as you have never seen before."

Murrough and Áed watched from the side of the field, copying our warriors' moves with wooden swords and spears crafted by our woodworker. Thrusting, chopping, charging, slashing, grunting, Murrough held his own with his much bigger cousin, twice his age. Not once did I see them try to truly harm each other. At battle's end, they laughed and chased each other around the field. I slapped both boys on their backs and told them, "Well done."

Those days, after training, I lay in bed next to Mór and rested my hand on her swollen belly, fingered the mountain pass in her chin.

⊕

True to his word, Félim hastened into Kincora with more useful news. He had crossed the river above Limerick and mixed in with Norse talking around night fires. His head covered, no one suspected him from the few words of perfect Norse he spoke. He heard little of interest until one Norseman said the name, "Haroldssons," fierce Norse enemies of Ivar's from the Isles. Félim listened close as the Norseman swore he yearned for battle against easier prey upriver—Mahon, Irish king of Dal Cais, at Kincora.

"Good," Mahon said when we told him. "The Haroldssons keep Ivar busy."

"That Norseman yearns to fight you, Mahon. He deems you easy prey. Does that not give you pause?"

"One Norseman's yearning is of no concern to me." Mahon waved me away.

⊕

Mór and I counted three fortnights before our infant was due, ample time for one more outing. The farmer on the river island had told of giant men sheltering in cliff crags at sea edge, feasting on fish and creatures washed up on rocks and sand. He had never seen them, but had heard rumors they wrapped themselves in seal skins and grazed skinny cows on tiny patches of grass.

"Those giants would not be Dal Cais," I had said. "Why would they fight for Mahon?"

"They will fight for any king, for a bull." The farmer was a known tale teller, and I doubted such giants existed. Yet truth, I welcomed new warriors, whatever size, and the chance to see cliffs and the line where sky meets sea.

My horse picked his way over rocks to the edge of our island. I gawked at the endless sky, watched clouds chase each other from one side of the earth to the other. Scores of birds circled, others clung to cliffs, all different sizes, short and squat, long and thin, orange beaks and feet, black and white with pointy beaks. I had seen gulls, but not such birds as those. No giant men showed themselves—indeed, no men at all.

Turning back, cold rain and hail came out of nowhere and pelted us. My horse would go no further, no matter my prodding. The only shelter was an ancient tomb covered by a rock slab, open at one end, closed at the other. I had crawled in to wait out the weather, when I heard Rory's voice.

"Prince Brian!"

My heart sank. Only bad news could bring him looking for me so far from Kincora.

"By God's hands, you are here," he said, sliding down from his horse. Shoulder to shoulder under the slab, he shouted into my ear. "King Mahon has taken his fleet ..." A blast of cold wind covered his words, and we squeezed further back.

"King Mahon has taken his fleet against King Fergal. He said to tell you he could not wait."

"Oarsmen?"

"The tablet," he shouted.

I howled. Of course. Mahon and his chieftains had plotted all along to take warriors I trained to fight Ivar into battle against Fergal. When the time came.

"King Mahon is safe at Holy Island," Rory shouted.

"But his fleet is wasted, and his oarsmen." Had Mahon been anywhere near, I would have taken my knife to him.

"The midwife bids you home," Rory shouted, fear in his face.

Fear surged through me. "You wait to tell me this?" I threw myself out the tomb and climbed onto Rory's horse, leaving my stubborn steed behind.

—Chapter Twenty-Three—

I sprinted through the sick-house door to nursemaids gathered around Mór's body, her shroud in their hands. Pushing them aside, I put my face close to her still warm lips, whispered her name, once, twice, many times. But in vain—her lips cooled.

My head on her chest, I cursed myself. Could you not have held back? Stayed? A vile odor seeped into my nose from blood-soaked rags in the corner. I leaned over, wanting to retch. The priest took my elbow. "Stand outside," he commanded.

In the sunlit courtyard, I fell onto my knees. A new infant cried, and a nursemaid thrust a cloth-wrapped bundle into my arms. I clutched it to my chest.

Murrough, age four, rounded the corner of a house at a run. I leaned back on my heels, the bundle in the crook of one arm, the other stretched out to stop my son from leaping on it. The infant whimpered, and Murrough's face changed to shock. I pulled him close.

"Look." I lifted the cloth to a head not quite round, a tuft of wet hair matted flat on top. At the sight of Mór's mountain pass chin, I pushed back a sob.

"See, Murrough? Perfect."

Piece by piece I unwrapped the bundle. A small crowd had gathered in the courtyard, watching in a silence so deep the world seemed as if it had stopped.

A nursemaid spoke. "A girl. Your daughter, sire."

"A girl." I muttered.

Yes," the nursemaid said. "And so sweet."

I inhaled a deep breath. "Your sister, Murrough. What name will we give her?"

"Sweet?" he said.

"Yes, Sadb, sweet like her mother."

Sadb turned a deep pink, knotted up her face and wailed. Murrough backed away as I wound the cloth tight around her body, looked up at the staring faces.

"I will need a wet nurse ... and an honest farmer for a foster father."

I had not noticed Úna standing close. "The daughter of a prince belongs with a noble family, Brian," she said. "A chieftain. A lord. Not a farmer. Wait for Mahon—he will choose for you." From her swollen eyes I could see she had been weeping.

"Mahon will not choose for me, nor will Sadb be raised by any of his chieftains. His sheep."

"Sheep? I do not think so," Úna said. "Mahon's chieftains are brave, loyal men. Mór would not have wanted a farmer for her daughter."

"Mór wanted what I want."

Úna held out her hands. "Give her to me. Your mind will clear when you are fed and rested."

Murrough put out his arm. "You cannot have her. She is my sister."

My knees aching from hard stones, I struggled to stand. "Here, Murrough," I said. "Sit."

He plopped down cross-legged and I placed Sadb in his lap. He gripped the bundle tight, set his face in firm purpose.

"Let no one touch her," I said. "Not anyone. Yell to me if anyone tries."

I stepped back into the house, to Mór. The priest stood to the side as I leaned close to her ear and whispered. "You have done well to bear a healthy girl. We have named her Sadb—sweet, like you."

Did I see a smile on Mór's lips? I took her cold hand. "If only you could speak, Mór. I would heed your counsel."

The priest put his hand on my shoulder. "Leave her soul in peace. She cannot counsel you now. But her last words were for you. 'Pray tell Brian to keep our daughter safe.'"

I leaned close to Mór's ear, whispered. "She will be safe with a foster family, an honest farmer family."

Shocked breath shot out from the priest's throat. I leaned even closer, spoke so soft I could scarce hear my own words. "Mahon will never touch her." I kissed Mór's head.

Outside, Murrough and Sadb were circled round by Úna and the crowd of onlookers. I pushed through and reached down for Sadb, but Murrough would not let go.

"Can we not share?" I said. Murrough held tighter, pursed his lips. "No?" I said. He shook his head. I gently lifted Murrough to his feet and led him clutching Sadb to our house. There would be time on the morrow for Murrough to see his mother's shrouded body.

⊕

I slept little that night, listening to my daughter suckling at her wet-nurse's breast. At first light, the door opened and someone stepped into my hearth room.

"Brian? May I come in?" Úna's voice.

I pulled on clothes and stepped into the hearth room to see Úna bending over Sadb's cot. "I will have good news for

Mahon when he comes back in," she said, sitting herself down in a chair.

"My heart yearns for good news." I bade the wet nurse leave us and sat down in a chair next to Úna.

"Mahon and I will foster Sadb," Úna said, her voice lifting high. "I can think of nothing he would like better than to foster your child, Brian. We will give her the royal family she deserves."

There were so many flaws in Úna's plan, I could not begin to challenge them. "Will? Have I agreed?"

"No, but surely you will." Her sweet tone turned fretful. "You know I loved Mór like a sister, and I will care for Sadb like she was my own daughter."

Úna bent close to Sadb's face and raised back up with a look of wonder, as if she had uncovered a rare secret. "Her chin is so like her mother's. No farmer woman would see that likeness or love Sadb as much as me."

I swallowed hard to keep from howling. "My brother will never touch Sadb, much less foster her. He is a traitor to you and to me."

Úna stayed silent, pondering. I braced myself for angry words or heartfelt pleas, but no, she spoke in a somber voice. "May I speak truth to you, Brian?"

"Pray do."

"Sadb could save me. Mahon wants many wives and many children to tie him to powerful kings all over the island, but if he takes another wife or tries to divorce me, I will set my brothers on him, Cathal and Connor. I will not be parted from Áed. If I could give Sadb to Mahon, he would beg me to stay. He could gloat he is a better father than you, and that Sadb loves him more than you. That is all he wants anyway, to be better than you."

If Úna imagined those words would sway me, she was mistaken. Mahon would never touch my daughter, nor would I give her to Úna as a weapon in her wars against her Mahon.

"I understand," I said, "but I promised Mór I would keep both our children safe."

Úna rose from her chair. "You are my best and only hope, Brian. Mahon listens to you more than anyone. No wonder Mór loved you so." She gave a long look at Sadb, her tiny fist in her mouth, and stepped away, out the door.

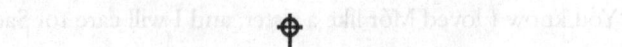

☥

Murrough came from behind his curtain, wide awake. I dreaded telling him of Mór. "Your mother will not be with us anymore."

He furrowed his brow. "I know."

"She left us sweet Sadb in her stead." Murrough stared hard at his sister.

"We will bury your mother's body in the graveyard. But I have a secret to share—she will not be in her body."

"No? Where?"

"Up here." I pointed to his head. "You can bring her back anytime you want. Close your eyes and think of her."

Murrough squeezed his eyes shut, opened them straightaway. "She spoke to me."

"Oh?"

"She said beware of Uncle Mahon. He will not keep Sadb safe. Or me."

I could not help but smile. "One day you will make a good spy, Murrough—like Félim." Murrough pressed his arm close to mine.

I did believe Mór's spirit would live in my head and my heart, not in the stiff corpse the diggers dumped into the hole at the river chapel graveyard. I held tight to Murrough's hand as the priest said words: Our Lord God, eternal life, Patrick, Mary and Jesus, Heaven. But my throat did not tighten nor my eyes fill until my gaze wandered to Rónan's gravestone. Sadb's foster-father would indeed be a farmer—a brother of Rónan's at Tuamgraney. There could be no better choice for my daughter.

Burial over, I closed myself inside my house with Murrough, Sadb, and the wet nurse, chiding myself an unworthy friend, husband, and father.

—Chapter Twenty-Four—

That afternoon, the swineherd and the cook's son dragged Félim up our hill. I heard their voices and ran out to help. Together we carried Félim to the sickhouse, laid him on a bed, and raised his swollen foot onto a pillow. He tried to sit but fell back clutching his side.

The physician turned Félim's foot this way and that, called for wet rags to cleanse his side wound, poked around on his belly.

"How bad?" I said.

"A scratch and a strain. He will heal." Alone with Félim, I asked what happened.

"Three armies are coming," he breathed. ... "to squeeze you."

"Three armies?"

"Ivar, Molloy, and Donobhan."

"Where? When?"

"Here. Under the full moon."

"Tonight?" Panic swept over me picturing Ivar's longboats.

"The next full moon."

I let out breath, started out the door. "Félim," I said, turning back, "you have proved yourself worthy ten times over. No king or prince could ask for a better spy."

Straightaway, I sent Rory to Holy Island with a message. "Tell King Mahon that Ivar and his Irish allies are coming for us," I said. "No matter his wounds, I will expect him at Kincora on the morrow."

✠

Indeed, the next evening, Mahon, Marc, and Rory rode up the hill below Kincora. In the dying light, I could see Mahon's bandaged thigh, his bruised face, his half-closed eye. He glanced up at me with such a piteous look, I vowed to leave him in peace.

In the courtyard, Mahon slid off his horse, stood an arm's length from me. I had dreaded the moment, but when it came, neither of us had the strength to fight.

"I am sorry for you, brother," he said. "For Mór."

"I am sorry for you too. We will talk in the morning?" He said nothing and started off. I called after him. "First light, Mahon." He limped off, not speaking.

Left alone with Marc, I guided him to the hall for soup, ale, and talk. Since I had seen him last, his mousy brown hair had streaked with gray. But the brother I knew was still in him, quick to know what was best for me and everyone else. What I had to say to Marc was urgent.

"You remember Rónan," I said, "the novice monk?"

"The harp player? Yes."

"The Norse killed him. He was the best man who ever lived."

"I warned the abbot not to send him, but he would do what you asked."

"As I pray you will now. Ivar and his Irish allies will be at our gates by the next full moon."

Marc put his cup down. "So Rory said, but Mahon is of no mind to heed that news. He suffers mightily from Fergal."

"I pray you will carry Sadb to Tuamgraney, to Rónan's brothers. I mean to foster her to a good farmer family, and

I trust you will choose the best of them ... one with a good wife."

Marc frowned. "Mahon will not agree."

"Mahon need not agree."

Marc gave me a fierce look. "Take my word, Brian. Brother fighting brother will come to no good."

"The time for fighting Mahon is past. But meantime, will you help me?"

Marc sighed. "As always, you pay me little heed, brother. But I will do your bidding."

At first light, Marc and Sadb's wet nurse rode out of Kincora's gate with Sadb strapped to Marc's chest in a pouch. My heart defied my vow not to weep. I took time before walking to Mahon's house—empty save for Úna's handmaiden, sweeping, and Áed at a table with his chessboard and pieces. They glanced at me.

"King Mahon is away," the handmaiden said.

"Away where?"

"To his boats," she said.

"What boats?" I asked. "They are sunk."

"They are not sunk," Áed said. "It is a lie."

He put me in mind of myself at his age, wanting to believe my father truthful. I chose not to challenge him.

⊕

Our cook readied a hearty midday meal for Mahon, his first day back—broth, hazelnuts, barley cakes, carrots, and parsnips—but neither he nor Úna appeared. I ate Mahon's portion and went in search of him again. Úna sat sewing in a chair by her hearth.

"Mahon?" I said.

"At Bórama." The look on her face warned me not to ask more.

At sunset, Mahon rode up the hill on his horse. I climbed down from my perch on the wall and met him in the courtyard.

"Such haste to visit your boats?" I asked.

He slid off his steed, readied to move around me. I blocked him. "Much damage?"

"Some."

Such a lie I could not let pass. I grabbed hold of his arm. "We know what happened, Mahon. Speak truth."

He jerked his arm free, tried to move past me. "Leave me, Brian. I am not to blame."

"No?"

Mahon sneered. "Those men did not know a prow from a stern." He spat and kept going.

"Ivar and his allies are coming for us, Mahon. By the next full moon."

—Chapter Twenty-Five—

I was still awake when Mahon appeared at my door, a jug in one hand, a calfskin in the other. I grabbed up my brat and followed him to the council house. We lit kindling, set logs, and pulled up chairs to the hearth.

"Mac Liag composed a poem for me," Mahon said, ale strong on his breath. "It speaks of what should have happened in my battle with Fergal."

I pushed down the urge to rip the calfskin from his hands, as he lifted it to his eyes:

O Mahon! That is well!
O son of Cennétig
Thou has put your enemies to rout
Thou has brought slaughter upon them
In this great battle, O Mahon.
Not false the tale! Tis a tale of truth.
Hundreds, there they fell.

"This verse will do for many a battle to come," Mahon said. "The numbers may change—thousands instead of hundreds—but the sense will stay the same."

"Yes," I said. "But perhaps scores, not hundreds or thousands?"

"Scores, hundreds, thousands." Mahon shrugged. "No matter. Whatever men believe centuries from now will be the truth."

Mahon placed the calfskin on the table and picked up his jug. "We were too late," he said, swigging down ale. "By the time my fleet left Bórama, Fergal had already plundered Eidne's dún and killed him."

Eidne dead? I gave silent thanks Mór had not known. Or had she? "You had little warning," I said.

"No, I had good warning from Úna's brothers. But with you still at Kincora, I had to wait to call for oarsmen. You would have tried to stop me, blathering on about Ivar."

Every word from Mahon's mouth stirred more anger in me. But I would stay calm. "My men were trained to fight Norse on land, not Irish on water. I would have tried to stop you."

"Those men did not know a warship from a currach," Mahon said. "A shame." Flames licked the logs in the hearth. I fixed my gaze on them.

"I was too late for Eidne," Mahon went on, "but I promised Tadg's sons Connor and Cathal I would avenge their father against Fergal. I failed, but I tried, and they will come for Úna when I renounce her. She is barren."

"She bore you a son."

"In ten years? Your wife bore you four infants in three years."

"Too many." We stared together into the hot coals.

"Ivar, Donobhan, and Molloy are coming for us in less than one month," I said, "under the next full moon. We must be strong together."

Mahon huffed. "I told you not to stir Ivar's nest."

"You did. But now time is short."

Mahon rocked forward, set the jug down, then rocked back in his chair. "The Norse have been on this river for two hundred years and will be two hundred years from now. I set my sights on Irish in Connacht, not on Norse who will be on this river forever."

"That may be, but do we want to gift our territory to the Norse?"

"I wanted to win against Fergal, Brian. A victory for the annals."

"Indeed." Our talk was going nowhere, save in circles.

Mahon shot me a wary but pleading look. "You chided me for Úna and Mór. What do you say now?"

"I say you chose well for me."

His voice lowered to a whisper. "Not so well for myself."

"Perhaps you should put your seed in Úna's womb instead of your bondswomen's."

Mahon cleared his throat. "I will do what I want with my seed. They are mine." Mahon tilted the empty jug upside down over his gaping mouth, trying to coax phantom drops into his throat.

"I will not speak of your seed again," I whispered.

"Pray do not." He stared back into the fire.

"We have both wasted men," I said. "Can we agree to that?"

Mahon shrugged. "You wasted more than me."

False, but I would not challenge him. "Ivar and his allies together could be one thousand strong—in truth."

Mahon knotted up his forehead. "One thousand strong and we are lost."

"Not if we fight Ivar before he can join with his Irish allies."

Mahon sat up straighter. "A king calls for warriors when he needs them, and we need them now. How many in Ivar's army alone?"

"A few hundred."

"By when did you say?"

"We should fight Ivar under the next new moon. Ten days from now."

Mahon leaned back, let the jug drop to the floor. "I will put out a call for warriors. Many Dal Cais still live, despite the men we both have wasted."

"Hundreds still live?"

"Scores. But I have friends in other places, and I can call our mercenaries home to fight for their king."

"What other places?"

"The Muscraige Tire, King Eiden's clan, and the Delbna ... the Delbna ..." Mahon's voice was rising high at the mention of the Delbna.

My head was spinning. "Who are the Delbna?"

"Distant kin of Dal Cais at Lake Owel in Meath Kingdom. Surely you know of Lake Owel? No people hate Norse more than the Delbna at Lake Owel."

I did know the tale of Turgésius, the most hated Norseman ever to trample Irish ground, drowned by a king of Meath in Lake Owel a century before. Mahon spoke rare sense.

"I forget the Delbna king's name," Mahon said, "but he will remember me from childhood. If we lose this one, Brian, there will be no more Kincora."

I kept my face straight, even as a surge of good feeling washed over me. I had soothed Mahon's pride and stirred his desire to fight Ivar.

"Work your magic, brother," I said. "This fight we must win, the two of us together. We have not done so well apart." Mahon's eyelids drooped. I shook his shoulder, helped him stand. "I will not blame you, brother," I said, "whatever happens."

"Nor I you."

"On the morrow, we will make a plan together?"

"I will make a plan," Mahon said.

I held Mahon's forearm, steadying him. "You will make a plan, and I will agree." We made our way out the door, into the light of a waning moon.

—Chapter Twenty-Six—

Mahon woke me at dawn, the faint smell of ale on his breath. He and Félim had sketched out a battle plan in the hurley field dirt. Murrough and I pulled on our tunics and set out to see it, shivering in the morning cold.

"We will fight Ivar at Sulchóit," Mahon said as we stood over the patch of soft dirt. "It is an inland hill, far from the river."

Félim drew a curvy line—the River Shannon. "Kincora is here, Limerick, here." He jabbed two holes along the wavy line. "Sulchóit is here, east of the river." A third jab. "A triangle, if you connect these three holes."

Mahon took the stick. "Sulchóit hill slopes into a bog that runs into a flowery plain. If we can ambush Ivar on the hill, slow them down in the bog, we can finish them off on the flowery plain."

"You have seen this place?" I asked.

"Félim has," Mahon said, "tending Norse pigs."

"Ivar is at Limerick," I said. "How will we fight him at Sulchóit?"

"We will set fire to Norse farmers' barns and kilns," Mahon said, "Ivar will come out after us and chase us to Sulchóit hill."

"A few fire setters will not stir Ivar out of his fortress," I said, "unless, of course, he hears that King Mahon himself sets the fires. Then he might come out in force."

"Yes," Mahon said. "Once Ivar's men are chasing me, I will cross over the bottom of Sulchóit hill and turn up through the trees to where you will be waiting for me. When they lose my tracks, they will camp on the hard flat ground at hill bottom."

"Hard flat ground?" I said. "Did you not say bog?"

Félim drew a picture in the air with his finger. "Hill, hard flat ground, bog, flowery plain."

"When they put out their fires for the night," Mahon said, "we will attack from above."

Mahon, so proud. A plan better than any I had crafted.

"We have ten days to raise an army, Mahon."

✛

Mahon did raise an army, four hundred in all from Dal Cais, Muscraige Tire, and mercenaries. Not a peep had come from the Delbna by the time he and a handful of men rode out to set fire to barns and kilns. Félim and I and the bulk of our army headed toward Sulchóit on foot, in small groups, taking different paths.

From my first sighting of Sulchóit hill, I knew our plan would fail. A strip of hard ground divided hill from bog, but it was scarce wide enough for three men to stand shoulder to shoulder. The Norse, if they camped, would spread out all over the hill, so close to us in the trees they would smell us.

"I remembered the hill bigger," Félim said, coming up next to me.

"So now?"

"Now I will put myself down the path, that way, the way we just came, and yell in Norse. They will think I am one of them and come looking. When Ivar hears sounds of skirmishing, he will send more men, or all of them, and himself. When I hoot four times, you will start after them, from behind."

"What if Ivar does not do what we think?"

"We will think more."

"Ah. Four long hoots from you and four short hoots from me to signal we are coming." Félim was not Rónan, but his wit was sharp, his courage boundless. Without doubt, he was not useless.

☦

The day was fading when Mahon and his small troop found me at hill top. By his count, Ivar's army was twice the size of ours. Surprise would be our best weapon.

"You saw Ivar?" I said.

"No, but I will know him when I see him."

"I have seen him," I said. "Short, squat, with a square-looking head. I should be the one to take him."

"No," Mahon said. "It will be written in the annals that Mahon, king of clan Dal Cais, killed Norse King Ivar of Limerick, at Sulchóit hill. His three sons will be mine as well."

"Three sons watching their father's back," I said.

"As you will be watching mine."

"And you mine."

We clasped hands. For that brief instant, it seemed we had always been brothers together and always would. At dusk, Ivar and his warriors streamed onto the hill from Limerick way, pointing at marks Mahon had made in the dirt. Commands rang out and tents and fires sprang up. Norse warriors gathered around them, their armor and weapons put to the side.

Mahon and I crouched at the tree line, the bulk of our warriors huddled some distance behind us in the trees. From a tent on the hill, a man started up toward us, alone. Closer, I saw the man was Ivar. I moved my hand to my knife hilt, but

Mahon grasped my arm. A few paces from us, Ivar pissed like a dog on a tree trunk, and turned back down.

"Our best chance to kill the Norse king and you stop me?"

"Kill Ivar in sight of his army?" Mahon said. "What do you think would happen next?" True. Perhaps Mahon was not such a fool. He had saved my life, and his.

Fires had dimmed when Félim's Norse shouts rang out across the hill. Ivar's warriors sat up, tent flaps flew open, and generals stepped out, Ivar among them. More shouts from Félim, and Norse at hill bottom streamed onto the path, headed toward Félim. All was happening as planned.

I had faded back into the trees to warn our warriors, when I heard more shouts from Félim—but in Irish—followed by screams from men and horses. I scrambled back to Mahon. Norse on the hill strapped on weapons and marched off toward the screams.

"Your horses?" I said to Mahon.

"No."

I started back to our men when Félim came crashing through scrub, his face and hands scratched, his eyes wild.

"Did you not hear me?"

"Yes ... no ....whose horses?"

"The Delbna."

"What?"

"The Delbna, with Eiden and Conaing. But they are outnumbered. You must go now."

"Are you mad? The Norse on the hill are far too many. They will slaughter us."

"Then all is lost." Félim's face dropped.

"No." Men listening behind me sparked an idea. "Take some of our men and ambush the Norse midway down the path, before they reach the Delbna. Ivar will send more warriors when he hears that fighting. Then we will come from behind. Go now."

Félim hastened off with ten of our warriors, and I dove through the trees, back to Mahon.

"Did I not tell you the Delbna would come?" he said, preening himself.

—Chapter Twenty-Seven—

The Norse poured onto the path, and Mahon and I and our men started after them. The few Norse left on the hill ran at the sight of us. Some fled down the path toward Limerick, others tried to escape through the bog onto the flowery plain. I swept up a Norse axe from a corpse, and fought like a madman, slashing at groins and armpits, cracking helmets, leaping away from shadows coming at me from the sides.

Mahon had sworn we would watch each others' backs, but I saw no sign of him, Ivar, or Ivar's sons.

The fighting went on all night. Had it not been for the cloudless sky and the dim light from stars, we would not have known Norse from Irish, save for their shouts. Screams and grunts rang out around me all night, but other than bodies crashing into me, boots knocking me down again as I tried to stand, I escaped injury.

In the dawn fog, I scoured the field for Mahon. I was standing amidst a heap of bodies when Félim appeared and spoke my name. My relief was so great, I hugged him and wept. He and I and others lifted our wounded onto Delbna horses, and dragged our dead into ditches. The slain Norse we left on the plain to rot. In my strongest voice, I commanded Félim back to Kincora in charge of the wounded. I could not suffer losing him, my best spy and battle strategist.

Daylight dimming again, I and my able-bodied men began a long march to Limerick.

✠

Smells of charred grain and animals tortured us as we marched toward the island fortress. At Norse ringforts, we slaughtered pigs and roasted them on makeshift spits. At a stream, we splashed and gulped down water. Hours later we spied a glow from Limerick. I commanded a halt on a ridge, where we took turns sleeping.

At dawn, we marched to Limerick and crossed to the fortress in two longships, the only boats in the harbor. Muffled sounds came from behind the shut-tight gate. I sent men up and over the wall, and the gate opened to the sight of a handful of wounded Norse warriors escaped from Solchóit, young women, children, and old people, amidst cows, horses, sheep, goats, chickens, dogs, cats.

"Take all able-bodied Norsemen downriver to Saingel Hill," I commanded my men, "and slay them. Bind the young women and children and ready them for Kincora. Ferry the old people to shore and leave them. Search every house and building for silver, gold, jewelry, saddles, cloth, fineries, pots, cups, jugs. Bring it all here." I motioned to the ground by my feet.

All the while, I solaced myself with Rónan's words. *There is no better man than you, Brian.*

If Ivar lived, I would burn his fortress to the ground. If he was killed or was captured, I would leave the fortress whole and take it for Dal Cais.

I walked about, marveling at the straight-sided houses, the cobbled pathways, gardens, and paths leading off wider paths like spokes. I saw no people in the houses, only coals burning in hearths. In a stone-paved square, I pictured Norse readying

Irish women and children for the slave markets. Pushing down rage, I kept going.

Down one path, I came to a house larger than any I had yet seen. A child's shoe lay on the ground near the door. I pushed on the door, but it was blocked from inside. My ear to it, I heard nothing inside. But walking away, a man's voice sounded from inside, as clear as day. I turned back, pulled out my axe and swung at the door, splintered a plank. Through the hole, I spied an old man circled round by women and children, all with square heads like Ivar's. I widened the hole with my axe, stuck my leg in, and pushed away a chest.

The old man glared at me. Not Ivar, but his father? Uncle? My mind slipped into a rage I could not keep down. "Murderer," I shouted.

No answer.

"I will burn your filthy town to the ground."

The old man spat at my feet, let out a stream of angry sounding Norse words.

No fear? I shoved him backward with my boot, knocked his head against the floor. With a swing of my Norse axe, I hacked off his head. He was not Ivar, but great pleasure washed over me. Revenge for my father, brothers, Rónan.

The women and children whined and pled, whined and pled. Enough, Brian. You do not want the blood of women and children on your hands. I hitched my axe to my belt and turned to leave. A woman hissed at me in perfect Irish. "Cur."

I turned on my heel, scanned the faces. Who? They are innocents, Brian. Leave them.

Cúchulainn's battle cries flowed through my mouth like water. "Red is this house with slaughter, when Brian mac

Cennétig comes into it. Like the sands on the strand." I swiped at a woman's head, left it hanging from her neck.

"Like the stars in the sky." I sliced the head off. Blood splattered.

"Like the dew in May." I split a skull.

With each hack and swipe, I felt more joy, more vigor. I narrowed my eyelids to blot out faces.

"Like snowflakes and hailstones." (swipe)

"Like leaves of the trees." (hack)

"Like buttercups in a meadow." (swipe)

"Like grass under a cow's foot." (hack)

Silence fell in the room, the only sound, my panting. I had turned to leave, one blood-covered boot out the door, when I spied an infant's head on the threshold, her face beautiful, sweet, putting me in mind of Sadb.

I clutched at my throat and stumbled out the door, heaving. Kneeling in the dirt, I retched and sobbed.

A young Norse boy knocked into me, running in fear. I struggled to stand, breathing in dust. Forcing myself away from the old man's house, I knew my battle rage, my wasp spasm kicks, Cúchulainn's battle cries, and the infant's sweet face would stay with me forever.

Around the next corner, a house with a high thatched roof loomed large, pustule-like bumps swelling out from both sides. Ivar's house, no doubt. An unmistakable form leaned against a door post.

"Mahon!"

He straightened up, startled at the sight of me. "There was nothing I could do, Brian," he said. "Ivar escaped."

"His sons too," Eiden said, coming out from Ivar's house, Conaing behind him, their fiery red heads covered in dirt and ash.

"How?"

"We were fighting Norse, like you," Mahon said. "They escaped."

"They jumped on horses and rode off," Conaing said. "They were long gone by the time we found horses for ourselves."

I howled, long and loud. "We chased them to the river," Mahon said. "But they got away in boats. We saw the cut ropes."

"All this, for nothing?" My voice rose in pain.

"Not for nothing," Mahon said. "We have taken Limerick. Forget Ivar."

"No!" I stepped into Ivar's house, kicked a half-burned stick from a hearth and set fire to every silk tassel I could find on every pillow in every room. I dashed back outside as the house burst into a ball of flames.

"Norse warriors wait for you downriver at Saingel Hill, Mahon," I growled. "Go there and kill them. Earn your victory. Then kneel and pray for Cennétig's forgiveness, that the corpses in front of you are not Ivar or his sons."

Did he go? I did not wait to see. I headed to the gate, gave orders to our men to burn the fort. All of it.

—Chapter Twenty-Eight—

I passed a sleepless night on the hillside across from the fortress. Each time my mind drifted asleep, the infant's perfect face woke me with a start. Ivar laughed and jeered in my mind, calling me a fool as he skimmed out the River Shannon mouth in his currach with his sons, to safety in the Isles.

At first light, we filled the two Norse longships with booty and sent them upriver. The rest of us set out on foot toward Kincora. At the top of the hill, I took a last look at Limerick. The stench of death drifted into my nose.

"The greatest victory in Dal Cais history and you pout?" Mahon said.

"Ten years fighting Ivar and you let him flee?" I could scarce force the words from my mouth.

"I saved your life at Solchóit, Brian. Do not forget."

"But for what?"

"For what? We burned Ivar's town, slaughtered his people, took more booty than ever in history." He pointed to the line of bountiful young Norse women, soon to be bondswomen at Bórama. "Our men will love us for them," he grinned. "Smile, Brian. It is time to reap your reward."

"I will leave the reaping to you, Mahon".

※

We kept on to the stream where Rónan had taken his last breath. "Trout swim in this stream," I said to Mahon. "Tasty fish eggs under these rocks will make a good meal."

Mahon called a halt, and I stepped through the water to the spot where Rónan died, by a holly bush. Stretched out on the ground, I put my arms behind my head, closed my eyes.

"I swiped off heads in an old man's house, Rónan—Ivar's kin. An old man, women, children, and an infant girl. Cúchulainn did it to me. It was not me."

Not your hand on your sword?

"Cúchulainn seized me. His wasp spasm battle rage. My grief will never leave me."

Cúchulainn fought waves to cure his grief. Can you not do the same?

"One hundred days I could fight waves, and my grief would stay. I am no demigod, Rónan. No Cúchulainn. He is only a tale. Find spoke truth. He is not real."

No? Then who are you, friend? "A man. A flawed man."

Mahon called my name from across the stream. I wiped my eyes as if I had been sleeping and sat up.

☥

At Kincora, Murrough rushed out from the gate and jumped on me. "You won," he shouted. I pried him loose and kept walking. Rich smells of food tempted me, of beef, bacon, bread, barley, sweets, all mixed together—a feast awaiting the victors. We had won against Ivar, and perhaps he was dead or dying from festering wounds. I had started toward the hall when I heard an infant cry, either in my head or the crowd, I was not certain. I shouted at it to quiet. People in the courtyard went silent and stared.

Murrough pulled on my arm, nudging me toward the feast. "Not now." I growled. I guided him fighting me all the way to our house.

He looked down at me on my bed. "Why?"

"Only fools feast when a battle is not won."

"But the battle is won."

"King Ivar escaped Mahon's clutches. He will be back tenfold."

Murrough paused. "Áed feasts."

"You must learn to wait."

I rolled over, turned my back, and feigned sleep. Perhaps he would leave me be. The door to our house opened and closed—a blessed relief.

My eyes closed for sleep and I was back in the old man's house at Limerick, crawling through heads, matching them to bodies. I spied the infant's head. Ah, good ... I can fix her.

Searching for her tiny body, I stumbled upon Mahon's head. No, not you, I whispered.

His lips moved. "Why, Brian?"

A mistake. I will fix you too.

"Liar," Mahon's head whispered. "You want me dead."

No! I lifted Mahon's head and crawled across the blood-splattered floor to his body, crumpled in a corner. With all my strength, I pushed his head to his body. Mahon sat up and turned his dead face toward me.

I screamed, woke up shaking. "Why do you yell?" Murrough stood next to my bed.

I breathed in deep. "A dream."

"You missed the feast."

I pulled Murrough down next to me and bade him stay. His breath rose and fell and lulled me back to sleep.

Rory called into my doorway. "Visitors. Many." I stumbled into the courtyard, Murrough behind me. Dal Cais mothers and fathers streamed through the gate, searching for their wounded sons.

"Fergus?" a man shouted at me. "Is he here?"

I shook my head. I did not know Fergus. A chorus of other names rose up.

"Search for yourselves." I waved my arm into the fortress.

Murrough and I made our way to the hall, old food on tables from the feast. I was scraping bits of bacon and bread into my mouth when Mahon appeared in the doorway, his bloodshot eyes the same rust color as his knotted hair.

"Here you are," he said. "A strange woman came into my house. You gave her leave?"

I closed my eyes, thankful Mahon's head had not come loose from his neck. "The woman seeks her son. I did not think to warn her away from the king's house."

Mahon stepped closer, screwed up his nose. "You eat old food?"

I held out a piece of cold soggy bread. "For you."

"Vile." He swatted it onto the floor.

The hall door flew open, and a man and woman burst in. "Our son?" the woman cried. "We cannot find him. Pray do not say you buried him at Sulchóit?"

I had seen that woman at her ringfort—skinny, black hair to her waist, puffy skin under her eyes. She and her husband had lost a son in the hills with me and Rónan, and I knew another had died fighting Fergal. A third? Ah, I remembered him too, his body trampled on the field at Sulchóit.

Seeing my face, they guessed their son's fate. The woman sobbed harder. Her husband, white haired and weathered, pulled her to him.

"Three sons we have lost to your wars," the man said. "We have one more, and you will not have him."

Mahon straightened up. "Our wars are your wars, old man. Are you not proud of our victory?"

The man stared at the floor. The woman whimpered.

"Your chieftain will pay honor price for your sons," Mahon said. "How many did you say died?"

The woman wailed. Her husband pulled her close. "Three," he muttered.

"They died for good cause." Mahon's voice rose higher.

The woman buried her face in her husband's neck, sobbing. "I knew all three of them," I said, keeping my voice low. "They fought hard and well—like Cúchulainn."

The woman stopped her sobs and new looks came over their faces. "Cúchulainn?" the man whispered. "He slew whole armies by himself, in single combat. Our sons did that?"

"No, but they were strong and brave like Cúchulainn," I said. "Fearless."

"Cúchulainn!" the woman said.

The man's face softened. "Cúchulainn used magic. His sword was barbed."

"You know his tales," I said.

The man nodded and blushed, wondrous, as if he had seen Cúchulainn himself. "He is my hero."

Murrough tugged on my arm. "They fought like Cúchulainn?" I covered his mouth, but he pried my fingers away. "Then why did they die?"

"For their king," Mahon said, scornful.

The man smiled at Murrough. "Bad things happen in war, son. Men die—the fate of brave warriors. You will learn that some day." He aimed his gaze at me. "We will tell our kin what you said, Prince Brian. Our sons fought like Cúchulainn."

Arm in arm, the man and his wife walked away, out the hall.

Mahon kicked a bench out of his path, stepped over rubbish, and spat into the black embers of the hearth.

"My cause was just," he growled. "Ivar threatened me. I burned his fortress and slaughtered his warriors. I took more booty and slaves than our father, or any king."

"Yes, and now our men are wasted," I said. "Ivar is alive and free to fight us again."

Mahon spat again. "He may be alive, or he may be dead, but in either case he will not be back anytime soon."

"His Irish allies are fresh," I said. "If you put out a call for warriors, no one will come. You heard that man—no more sons for our battles."

"A mere farmer. What does he know?"

"That he will give no more sons."

"If he holds back his sons, I will take his land and he will starve. Dal Cais men will be glad to fight.for me."

"Why is that, Mahon? Why will they be glad to fight?"

"For their king."

I whispered. "We will see."

Mahon kicked a wooden tray across the floor, cracked it into pieces. "You will see. Irish all over this island will hear of my victory and beg me to be their ally."

Murrough looked from one of us to the other, moving ever closer to my side. Mahon frightened him with his loud shouting and kicking. But Mahon was right and I was wrong. Dal Cais men would be glad to fight. I had seen the pleasure on warriors' faces and felt it myself—my battle rage. The pride of victory rang loud in Eiden's and Conaing's voices. Blades slashing flesh and axes hacking skulls would always thrill a man, and battles would always follow battles. It would take every bit of wit I possessed to craft a plan for peace in Munster, but at that moment, the idea alone gave me reason to smile.

"Can we not have peace, Mahon," I said, "for once in our lives?"

Mahon sneered. "For this one day, brother. But I need a warrior prince to fight for me. I do not see such a man in this hall."

PART FOUR

—Chapter Twenty-Nine—

For weeks, well into summer, wounded men healed and hobbled away on the arms of their kin. For others, wounds festered, fevers came, and screams started up for their mothers, a sign they would die. We had not enough nursemaids to tend to them all, not enough hands to mix poultice or fashion bandages. Marc loaned monks and the Holy Island physician, but Úna swore even they were not enough. Why not call in bondswomen from Bórama? We had many more since Limerick, and surely they would better serve wounded men than cows or shipwrights.

Úna did not falter speaking those words to Mahon, nor did he falter doing her bidding.

Little cheered me amidst the stench and the screams, save Marc's news he had chosen the most worthy of Rónan's Tuamgraney brothers for Sadb's foster father—a farmer who had sworn to care well for her, protect her from thieves, and forego knowing her blood father's name for the thirteen years our laws allowed for fosterage.

"And the wife?" I asked.

"She is good, too," Marc said with a smile.

Marc, Mahon, and I counted our booty from Limerick. From written tables, we figured numbers of milk cows, dry cows, calves, and bulls owed to warriors who had survived, and to families of those who had not. But no table told us how many and what kind of cows equaled one piece of bright-colored cloth, one jeweled saddle, or a bondsman with a limp. I had not known until we studied the tables that one bondswoman could be traded for five bondsmen.

In the end, Mahon kept a good share of everything, and all of the gold. I kept a silver pin, a brooch for a future wife, and a fine-sewn pouch. The rest we divided amongst the Delbna, the Muscraige, and our chieftains, who kept the greater portion for themselves and gave what was left to their warriors.

Félim deserved more than anyone, but he refused it all. He had no wish for booty, only a yearning to spy. But with Limerick burned, I could see no use for a spy.

⊕

The last of the wounded gone home on the arm of his father, Murrough and I dropped our clothes near the river chapel, and slipped into calm water, readying to swim the rapids further out. For the first time in weeks, I felt free of the stench of blood and death. For that rare moment with my son, I was content.

"Lie flat on your back," I said, "feet first, brace for rocks, but do not fight the rapids. Let the current take you to calm water and then make haste to shore before you freeze to death. Watch me first, and then we will go together."

I bumped along in the rapids, swam to shore, and pulled myself out. I had headed back to our starting place when I spied Murrough's head bobbing in white foam. A mere seven, and he defied me? My heart in my throat, I watched him pop up in calm water some thirty paces downriver.

I was in the water again, ready to follow, when a ship's prow peeked around a bend in the river—a warship followed by another, square white sails billowing.

Murrough had taken hold of a tree root and was pulling himself out when he saw the ships, sank back down, clinging to the root. I motioned him to me, but he shook his head, terror on his face. The oarsmen lowered sails and aimed their ships' prows toward our shore. I raced down the path to Murrough, grabbed his arm, and yanked him out. Naked, we ran back to our clothes, swept them from the ground, dove through the river chapel door, and slammed it shut.

We pulled on clothes, listening to boats scraping up on shore and oarsmen shouting commands in Irish. I peered out a small window and saw Irish oarsmen standing in shallow water, tying their ships to posts. Men trekked up the hill toward the fortress, no weapons drawn, one with golden hair, boots made of fine, carved leather, and a tunic stitched with gold and silver thread. No doubt a king. But who?

I pushed open the church door and stepped out. "Hello?"

Heads whipped around. "King Mahon?" the king said.

One quick glimpse told me he was young, scarce any beard on his chin.

"No, I am Prince Brian. The king's brother. And you?"

"King Donal mac Diarmait, Corcu Bascind. A friend. I bring news for the king." "

"For King Mahon's ears only?" I said.

"His ears first. Perhaps he will share it."

A horn blasted from the fortress wall. I looked up to see Mahon, Áed, Úna, and Marc standing on top.

"This is Murrough, my son," I said, my hand on his shoulder, "and up there," I motioned with my head, "King

Mahon, his wife and son, and Brother Marc, our monk brother."

The horn blew again. "My brothers call," I said. "We should not keep them waiting."

Striding up the hill, I chided myself. Had I heeded Mór's counsel and set Félim to spy, he could have told us warships were coming.

✠

Greetings flew all around in the courtyard. Marc remembered Donal's father, a friend to Cennétig from the days before Norse at Limerick blocked passage between their territories.

"What good fortune," Marc said to Donal, "that my brothers have rid the river of Ivar. Our clans can visit again, without fear of attack."

"That would be good fortune indeed, Brother Marc, if it were so," Donal said. "Where shall we talk, King Mahon?"

"If it were so?" Marc said, looking to Mahon.

"It is so," Mahon said in haste. "King Donal and I will talk in the council house." He nodded his head toward the place.

"If it suits your pleasure, King Donal," I said, "Marc and I will come too. Your news will reach all our ears, but it will be better heard from you."

Mahon shot me a sharp look, clearly wanting Donal for himself. But was I not his warrior prince, and Marc, the tender of his soul?

"It suits me," Donal said. "if it suits you, King Mahon." Mahon had the wit not to speak against Marc and me in Donal's presence. He shrugged, and we three—Donal, Marc, and I—followed him into the council house.

Rory had known to bring cups and a jug of water to the council house, and to offer Donal's oarsmen food and drink in the hall.

All settled in our chairs, Donal grasped his empty cup, stood, and held it out. "King Mahon, you have won a great victory for Munster. I raise my cup to you."

He sat back down. "The Bascind people are grateful for Sulchóit and Limerick, King Mahon, but I am here to tell you Ivar and his sons shelter on Scattery Island, at Saint Sénan's monastery, in plain sight of my territory at the river mouth. Ivar and his sons are not alone."

No! I had wanted Ivar gone forever from our island.

"Ivar still lives?" Marc demanded of Mahon, shocked. Mahon reddened and looked to me.

"Ivar escaped," I said.

"Escaped how?" Marc asked.

"Like a coward." I would not shame Mahon in the presence of a king wanting to be his ally.

Mahon flattened his hand and drew it across his throat. "If Ivar is at Scattery, he is as good as dead."

Marc signed the cross over his forehead and chest. "Not by your hand, I pray. At a saint's monastery."

A pause, as Donal readied his words. "The Munster overking's fort at Cashel stands empty, as it has been since Callaghan died from lightning strike. Your fame has spread across this kingdom, King Mahon. The Bascind people would welcome a friendly king at Cashel. We are fishermen and traders, not warriors, but we will help where we can."

I squeezed my fingers into fists. Did Mahon fathom the import of Donal's words? His cheeks bulged and shifted, his thoughts banging into each other. Once again he looked to me, but I would not answer for him.

"I am honored, King Donal," Mahon said at last. "Yet Dal Cais are weary of battle. Our farmers will give no more sons."

Confusion spread on Donal's face, and he ran his fingers through his golden hair. "You know the Greek tale of the Hydra, King Mahon?"

"Cut off one head, and more will grow," Mahon said. "But perhaps it is your turn to fight our enemies now."

I narrowed my eyes at Mahon. Donal's offer made good sense for us, a path to survival and peace through strength one day.

Donal shook his head. "Scattery's harbor seethes with warships, far too many for Bascind fishermen and traders."

"Whose warships?" Mahon said.

"Ivar and his Irish allies, Donobhan and Molloy. You, King Mahon, are our best hope. Pray do not say you mean to do nothing."

Mahon pulled on his beard. His face took on that faraway look I knew too well. "'Nothing', King Donal," Mahon said, "is exactly what I want. My wife is barren and I need time to seek a young princess who will bear me children. And time to waste King Fergal of Connacht. He wasted my fleet and I mean to waste his. My brother Brian here did not teach my warriors how to fight on water."

"King Fergal of Uí Briúin Bréifne?" Donal said.

"Yes." Mahon said. "That King Fergal."

"You need not worry about him. King Fergal is dead."

"Dead?"Mahon said, truly shocked. "By whose hand?"

"By our Lord God's hand. Fergal died in bed, only last month."

Mahon leaned back in his creaky chair, triumph covering his face. "Our Lord God's hand moves for me. I say it is time to feast."

"Does that mean you will take Cashel for Dal Cais, King Mahon?" Donal asked.

Mahon fixed his gaze on me. "You and Marc begged to join us here, Brian, yet you have nothing to say?"

"We have lost many good men in battle," I said, "but Eóganachta cannot agree on a king to take Callaghan's place, and Cashel is empty. Eóganachta may pout, but once you are at Cashel, Mahon, all of Munster might well accept you as overking—the first Dal Cais overking of Munster Kingdom in all of history."

I did not know what would happen if Mahon occupied Cashel, but to stay at Kincora, anger Donal, and tempt the Norse and their Irish allies, would surely end in slaughter. Donal had brought us a gift and we should take it.

"Marc?" Mahon said.

"If you take Cashel from the Eóganachta, they will come together as one, in no time."

"So," Mahon said, "have you a better idea?"

"Wait for Eóganacht clans to waste each other," Marc said, "and then decide."

"It is too late, Brother Marc," Donal said. "Molloy, Donobhan, and Ivar are more together than ever before."

Marc sighed. "I am but a lowly monk, but I can think of another reason you should not take Cashel in haste, Mahon, or indeed, at all."

"Which is?"

I could hear the vexation in Mahon' voice. My words had decided him, and no naysaying from Marc would change his mind.

"The overking at Cashel protects Emly," Marc said, "the most powerful monastery in Munster. The abbot there is Eóganacht himself. He and Molloy are like vines twisted around each other, and neither will suffer usurping Dal Cais at Cashel."

"Usurping Dal Cais?" Mahon said, sitting up straighter. "Cashel is our birthright, Marc. Eóganachta usurp, not Dal Cais."

"Indeed, King Mahon," Donal said, hopeful, "you could be the vine that strangles Emly and Molloy."

Marc signed the cross over himself again, shaking his head.

"I will take Cashel, King Donal." Mahon thumped his chest with his fist. "And now, we feast."

I gave thanks for small favors. We stood and touched our cups to each other.

✠

Let me tell you, Mac Liag, my recollection of the feast. The cook carried broth, fresh roasted lamb, garden vegetables, breads, and sweets to the king's table in the hall. Úna on one side of me and Donal on the other, we looked across the table at you, poet, and Marc and Mahon. Áed and Murrough sat far down at table's end.

Donal praised our risky battle against Ivar, hoping for the day Mahon's strong hand would free us of the Norse. Mahon listened and nodded, washing his food down with ale.

I spoke under my breath to Úna. "Donal showers praise upon your husband."

She kept silent. I whispered louder. "Donal deems Mahon worthy of the Munster overkingship. He begs him to take Cashel. For Dal Cais."

"Mahon brings me grief and shame, Prince Brian," Úna said softly. "Need we speak of him?"

My gaze met Úna's—the first I had looked deep into a woman's eyes since Mór—bottomless, shimmering, like a freshwater pond.

"No, we need not." I paused, searching for different words. "You keep busy with your sewing?"

Úna licked her finger. "I keep busy visiting Mac Liag, a friend and a learned man. I share my secrets with him."

You flushed, poet, hearing Úna speak your name from across the table. I whispered. "May I ask what secrets, Queen Úna?"

"You may ask, but secrets are secrets, are they not? Perhaps you have forgotten the secrets I already shared with you?"

I shook my head, feeling foolish.

"What of your secrets?" Úna said.

"I would trust no one with my secrets, save Mór and Rónan, both gone. Úna gave me a look of such pity, I pitied myself. My gaze fell upon her hand, resting close to mine. Perhaps I might touch it by mistake, reaching for the ale jug.

Donal kept on. When he stopped to chew and swallow, Marc broke in with talk of Holy Island, Mahon spoke of the mail-clad warriors we had beaten back at Sulchóit, and Murrough fought to keep his eyes from closing. The day had been long since our swim in the rapids. I swigged back ale and crooked my finger at Murrough, a signal we would leave. You rose to your feet, poet, to praise Mahon, but Murrough and I were out the door before you began.

—Chapter Thirty—

Donal and his oarsmen boarded ships for Corcu Bascind, their sails billowing in a brisk summer breeze. I watched him go, daring to imagine my life if and when Mahon was chosen overking at Cashel. I could be clan king at Kincora, marry again, and breed many children, all who would live to ripe old ages without constant fear of battle. The thought cheered me, even as I knew Mahon and I would face many dangers. Eóganachta would not welcome us and we would starve unless the Eóganacht Caisel agreed to share cows and fields all around Cashel.

Musing, my mind had drifted elsewhere when Murrough came up next to me. He carried a message from Mahon, but I did not want to hear it. My brother would be full of smug pride and wanting to know my thoughts so he could speak them as if they were his own—unless, of course, they proved wrong or ended badly. Then I would be to blame.

"Let us walk in the hills," I said to Murrough, remembering my father. "I have places to show you and tales to tell."

"But what of Mahon's message?"

"You can tell me later."

Murrough smiled, and I took his hand. It was time he knew of my father's lies and Mahon's tricks when I was his age. I would even tell him of the toy spear Mahon had given me to hunt deer. Perhaps he would laugh, or show me pity.

✛

We stayed the night in the woods, sleeping on beds of leaves, wetting our mouths with water pooled on top of a rock from the last rain. We had started back to Kincora the next morning when I thought to ask about Mahon's message. Did Murrough remember it?

No, only that I should hasten to Mahon's house. When I came up to Mahon's door, I spied him and Úna before a table heaped with tunics. They were pointing at one, lifting another, squinting at others. I stayed still, not wanting to ruin my brother's time with his woman.

"Brian," Úna said straightaway. "Come in." I stepped through the door.

Mahon stared at my tunic and breeches, dirty and damp, but with no rips. "You will need better than those clothes if you wish to stand behind me under our sacred tree. At my óenach."

Mahon held up Úna's basket, filled with bright colored balls of thread. "Choose your colors."

"An óenach, Mahon? Do we want all of Munster to know our plan for Cashel?"

"Why not? We have won a great battle and we will march in triumph, as we should. I know your mind, and I heed it. Now, what colors?"

⚜

At Magh Adhair, Mahon stood in front of our sacred oak tree, his back straight as an arrow, his fine linen tunic sparkling with gold and silver, his king's silver circlet firm on his head. I stood two steps to the side and behind him, my tunic stitched with red and blue threads. Before us swelled a sea of eager faces, stretching into sheep fields well beyond the raised ridges saved for men of highest ranks.

"Welcome Dal Cais," Mahon shouted.

"Welcome," they roared back.

"I am here to claim my birthright," Mahon shouted louder.

A stillness came over the crowd. "Everyone here knows of Ailill Ólum?"

Heads nodded. No one dared admit he did not know of our famed ancestor from the mystical past, said to rule the southern half of Ireland.

"Everyone knows Ailill had two great-great grandsons, Eóghan and Cas?"

Nods turned to rumbles, grunts, and growls. "Have Dal Cais ever ruled from Cashel?"

"Nay!"

"Will Dal Cais always give way to usurping Eóganachta?" A louder nay swept like a wave through the crowd.

"Raise your hand if you mean to forsake your birthright." No man raised his hand. "I, Mahon, son of Cennétig, worthy fruit of Cas's seed, am here to claim Cashel. It is my right."

Cheers sounded so loud they dulled my hearing. Men leapt to their feet and roared. I imagined the assembly over, but Mahon was not finished. He kept speaking. "All men who will ride with me to Cashel, raise your arms."

A few arms went up, then many. "Raise arms if you will farm land around Cashel?" Many arms raised. "And pay rent to the king of Eóganacht Caisel?"

Fewer arms raised, puzzled looks and scowls came over faces. He had tried to slip in rent without notice. "All who will raid cows for me at Cashel, raise your hands," Mahon shouted.

Scowls turned to smiles and hands flew up for cow raiding. "Brave men of Dal Cais," Mahon shouted. "Ready yourselves for my call."

Mahon strode away to his horse, and Dal Cais clansmen burst into loud, excited talk, clapping each other on the shoulders, celebrating.

☩

That evening, the sun sinking below trees in the west, Mahon and I sat by the river on a log lying amidst scattered piles of water-soaked twigs.

"You are wise to leave our cattle behind," I said. "Prodding horses, donkeys, and oxen to Cashel will be hard enough without cattle."

Mahon slid down and leaned his back against the log, his gaze fixed on the river rapids. "King Eóghan might lend us land to farm," I said, "if we pay rent—no matter our clansmen's scowls. Eóghan is no friend of Molloy or Emly."

Mahon shrugged. Perhaps he agreed. "But he will not welcome us if we raid his cows." My voice flat, I tried not to sound chiding.

Mahon looked back at me. "Are you finished counseling me?"

"For now."

Mahon lifted himself back up on the log and gave me a triumphant look. "I have news, brother, from Félim. The Haroldssons raided Scattery Island and captured Ivar. Félim thinks he has been taken prisoner in the Isles."

"You set Félim out to spy on Scattery Island?"

"I could not keep him back. He is gone again, with Eiden and Conaing to King Eóghan's dún, with my pact."

I scooped up twigs and flung them into the river. Mahon loved to surprise and shame with news he had gotten and deeds he had done without my knowing. His message was clear; I was not needed—indeed I was useless. But I would not give him the pleasure of my surprise.

"Our good fortune," I said. "We will be safer with Ivar gone."

"I would have sent you to Eoghan," Mahon said, "but Eiden and Conaing honor my wishes. They will not invent a pact of their own." I bit my tongue to keep from speaking. A sad tone came into Mahon's voice. "I wish it were not so, Brian, but you do not heed my desires, unless they match yours." He gazed out at the river.

I snapped a twig in two. "The pact?"

"I will not raid Eóghan's cows, in return for leave to farm his land ... for no rent."

"No cow raiding? What of those who raised their hands for cow raiding?"

"They will be content with free farmland. Perhaps Eóghan will share his cattle as well, when he comes to trust us." Mahon turned his gaze back to the river. "No swords drawn, Brian. Is that not your way?"

Heat had long reddened my neck, but I would not let my voice betray me. "If Eoghan agrees to your pact, we will not starve."

Mahon stood and stepped backwards over the log, as if ready for escape. I clutched my fingers, fearing what he had to say next. "Eiden and Conaing will keep watch over Kincora and Bórama when I am at Cashel."

"Truly?" I could no longer hide my surprise. "Our nephews will never leave Kincora."

"They are no traitors, Brian. I am king at Kincora and will be until I die."

"At Kincora and Cashel?"

Mahon rolled his eyes. "I will need many forts to house and feed me on my circuits."

"Kincora is no mere stopping place for your circuits, Mahon," I said loud. "It is the fortress of our ancestors. The resting place of our kin. The resting place of my wife and best friend."

"Calm yourself, Brian. Our nephews will tend Kincora well. I mean to start for Cashel soon, before leaves fall from these ash trees. You may join me, if you wish." He turned on his heel and started walking away, up the hill.

"Take Conaing and Eiden with you to Cashel," I said to his back. "I will keep Kincora safe."

Mahon stopped and looked back at me with narrowed eyes. "Only a fool would take that risk."

"Risk? What risk, Mahon? Leaving me here? Or taking me with you?" Mahon spat and kept going.

—Chapter Thirty-One—

Eiden and Conaing rode back in with news King Eóghan was wary but willing to try Mahon's pact. He would lend his land, milk cows, and houses for Dal Cais farmers and warriors, in return for protection from Emly and Molloy. But ash leaves had already fallen from their limbs, and we would wait for spring to make our move.

Beltane, next, three score Dal Cais men and women, together with as many animals, started for Cashel. At our farewell feast, you read a new verse, poet, praising Mahon:

For Munster, hast thou well contended, O Mahon! Thou great chieftain!
Thou hast given, O king, a stern defeat
To banish the foreigners from Erin.
King of Munster, methinks thou art.
High King of Cashel, renowned. Bestow gold upon those who merit.
There are many, O Mahon?

Mahon stood and thanked you, warning he was not yet king of Munster or high king of anything, even as he meant to be.

"Gold I do have," he said, "and you will see me use it well with the abbot at Emly monastery—no swords drawn."

✠

Leaving Kincora, we loaded our heavy loads onto flat metal slipes, fixed with ropes to horses, donkeys, and oxen. The slipes bumped and scraped over hard rocky ground to the shallows next to Bórama, where we moved the loads to the backs of animals our herdsmen nudged across the rocks. Ourselves, our women, children, and you, poet, rowed across in currachs, through calm lake water above the shallows. Your many bulging sacks weighed our oxen down, but since you said they were filled with precious vellum for Mahon's praise poems, we did not deny you.

On the far shore, we reloaded the slipes and set off through the forest toward Cashel. Birds, squirrels, and badgers noticed us, as did deer and boar, but no people, or at least none we saw.

At a narrow path leading off to King Eóghan's ringfort, we met Ailill, the king's son, who together with a pack of his friends, carried a message from his father. He would tend to our entourage while Mahon, Úna, Áed, Murrugh and myself, went on alone to Cashel fort.

The forest thinned and opened into a long, empty field. Nothing could have readied me for the sight of Cashel at the field's far end. The limestone rock rose up like a small mountain out of flat land, a stone and mud wall circling around the top, and a round tower pointing to the sky. Chills ran through me imagining our long-ago ancestors coming upon that sight for the first time, without warning. Only one steep, narrow path led up, and straightaway I understood the good of it. No enemy could hope to attack Cashel with the threat of rocks and spears hurled down upon their heads long before they reached the fortress entrance.

We had started across the field when a bell sounded three loud bongs. A lone monk appeared atop the wall, followed by a host of more monks.

"Emly's monks." Mahon said.

"No doubt harmless," I said.

"We cannot look like cowards," Mahon said. "I will go in first."

"I will come behind you," I said.

"I too," Áed said.

"So will I," Murrough said.

"Well, then," Úna said, "we will all go."

Mahon fixed his king's circlet on his head and we rode on, step by slow step up the steep path, ending in flat ground outside the wall. A thinner path led around to an arched opening, out of sight from below. I had reached the flat ground when a monk rushed out from the opening, waving his hands. My horse reared up and scrambled to keep from falling backwards, down the side of Cashel rock.

"Stop!" I shouted. "Are you mad?"

The monk bowed many times, begging forgiveness. He had only come to tell us the abbot waited to bless us. We entered into a sea of brown-robed monks massed in a stone-paved courtyard. The abbot in his black-dyed robe, a heavy wooden cross hanging around his neck, came up close. We slid down to our feet and handed our horses' reins to monks.

"Kneel," I whispered.

"Welcome, King Mahon," he said. "I am Fáelán mac Cáellaide, abbot of Emly. We have cleansed the fort for you." I stared at his pointy shoes and many-colored stockings, as he laid hands on our heads and muttered Latin words.

I gave Mahon such a look, he took my meaning and begged the abbot's pardon. We climbed a ladder leaning against the wall and gazed west, the way we had come, and south to forested mountains. This was a Munster we had not known and it was truly vast. The sky was clear and the setting sun warmed our face.

"That monk tried to kill me," I whispered to Mahon. "Agree to nothing the abbot says."

He may have nodded, but I could not be certain. We climbed back down to the abbot, who led Mahon away with Úna and Áed.

"Come," I said to Murrough, nudging him toward the back of the fortress. "We can choose our own house. It will be better that way."

Strolling about, we passed by the round tower, a hall, a church with a graveyard attached, a council house, empty smithies and houses, a cesspit, and a rubbish heap. Already I yearned for the vegetable gardens at Kincora, the heather and gorse on the hill, the river.

In the far back, we came to a house much like ours at Kincora: round, with a hearth room and sleeping nooks and beds at both ends. Murrough jumped on a flea-infested straw mattress and a mouse ran out from under, did circles in the dirt floor, and raced out the open wicker-wood door. We laughed and threw the mattress out after it.

We lit turf in the hearth and ate dried pork from our pouches. A foot scraped outside our door, and a man's cough sounded so close it seemed as if he was in the room with us.

I waited for a knock, but when none came, I shoved the door open wide. It met a monk who fell whimpering onto his back side, scrambled up and started running. I lunged and grabbed a piece of his robe. He freed himself from the robe and raced down the path in his under-breeches, leaving the robe behind in my hands—proof we should not trust the abbot of Emly or his monks. I held the robe up to Murrough, who had curled up in a ball, trembling behind his bed.

Dawn the next day, the abbot and his monks filed out of the fortress. I hastened to Mahon's house, cleansed, as the abbot had said, of spiders and animal droppings, but leaning to one side, like his wooden-box chairs. Mahon was sitting on one, pulling on boots, while Úna moved about in their sleeping nook behind him.

"Walk with me, Mahon," I nodded toward the door.

"Why? I keep no secrets from Úna."

A lie I chose not to heed. I waved the monk's robe in his face, tossed it at his feet.

"That monk had his ear to my door."

My brother shrugged. "I sent him with a message for you to join us here, but you ripped the man's robe from his body. Truth, I was shamed."

"He skulked at my door and fled when I opened it. No messenger does that." Mahon kicked the robe out of his way and pulled on his other boot.

"You were not surprised to see Emly here?" I was stunned.

"I am pleased monks cleansed the fort, and pleased Emly welcomed us here."

"We did not invite him."

"Invite him? Emly needs no inviting. He and I agreed a pact, not so easy after what you did to his monk." My small glimmer of hope turned to fear. "I promised the abbot gold and protection."

"Molloy protects Emly," I said.

"I am closer than Molloy."

"What does the abbot promise?"

"A feast, for Munster flaith who will choose me overking. Your way, Brian, without a weapon drawn."

"Molloy and Donobhan?"

"If they wish. But no matter. Munster kings, chieftains, scholars, brithems, brehons, poets, all with high ranks, will come to my feast."

"When?"

"When we fix this fortress. You can see this house leans, as do many others."

"Emly will drain you of every ounce of gold and then deny your feast."

"You mistake him, Brian. He is my friend. You may know how to pen sheep, but you are not twice as smart."

I closed my eyes, struggling to remember where and when I had heard those words ... our father's words, the night of the sheep. I had been six. and Mahon, twelve.

"You speak truth, Mahon. I am not twice as smart, nor was I ever. I want you to be chosen overking, and I want to be chosen clan king at Kincora. With you here and me there, we could live in peace. But believe me, Emly schemes against you, no matter your pact."

Mahon sneered. "He and I agreed to our pact your way, Brian, with words, not swords. I heed you, even as you do not heed me."

"I do heed you, Mahon, and I pray I am wrong."

"No need to pray, Brian. You are wrong."

—Chapter Thirty-Two—

No date set for the feast, Áed, fourteen, carried messages on horse between Cashel and Emly. Mahon asked when the feast would happen, and the abbot sent one of two replies: either Munster flaith were stubborn and swaying them would take more time than he thought, or Munster flaith could only be swayed with more gold. Mahon frowned at both, but without fail, he sent more gold. Still no date was set.

Meantime, when King Eóghan saw the yield from his fields double in size with our farmer's help, he opened his arms to us like long lost friends. It was not long before Dal Cais and Eóganacht Caisel farmers worked side by side, tilling land and milking cows.

Murrough found his way to Ailill, and roamed the king's territory with Ailill's pack of friends. Had it not been for my son's eavesdropping, I might not have known Eóghan dressed and lived like a poor farmer to trick Molloy, who collected church taxes far beyond what Eóghan owed and stole women and children for the slave markets. Félim became Eóghan's spy, and Molloy's raids slowed to a trickle. But Eóghan would not enter Cashel until he was certain the raids had stopped.

✠

One late spring day, Mahon and Áed burst into my house. I was sitting by my hearth polishing my knife hilt with cloth and ash.

"Norse thieves raided Emly," Áed spat out. "Limerick Norse."

"True?" I said. "When?"

"Two days ago," Mahon said, breathless.

"Any thieves will be long gone after two days," I said. "They burned the monastery?"

"They stole gold," Mahon said. "My gold."

I scratched my head. "Ivar escaped the Haroldssons?"

"His sons raided Emly," Mahon hissed. "We promised to protect the monastery."

"We?"

"Are you not my warrior prince?"

Best not to answer. I went back to polishing.

"I will chase the raiders," Áed said, "but I need help."

"It is a trap, Áed," I said. "Emly means to ambush your father."

Mahon spat. "Take Félim, Áed. He cannot refuse you. Say his king commands him."

Áed stole a look at me, nodded to his father, and left.

"You send your son and Félim into danger meant for you?" My knife hilt sparkling, I stood and sheathed it. "Shame on you, brother."

"Shame on you, Brian. You are no use to me." Mahon hastened out after Áed.

☦

Mahon scoffed at me as we watched Áed, Félim, and their small troop gallop across the field into the copse. But three days later, with no word from Áed, my brother knew better than to ask me to help him search. Rory would come with him.

Within hours, they were back, Áed bent over with his face in Rory's steed's mane, and Mahon with a wounded man on his horse's rump. Five more of their troop walked alongside Mahon's horse. I searched in vain for Félim.

"Not one of them is whole." Mahon cursed as he came into the courtyard with Áed's gashed and scraped arm around his shoulder.

"Félim?" I stepped close.

Mahon snorted. "You should have gone, Brian. Do not put your ugly face in mine."

"They were Irish, not Norse," Áed muttered. "Félim held them off, else we would all be dead."

"Félim?"

"They killed him."

"You saw him?"

"We heard him go silent."

I stepped out the arched opening, howled and wept.

☦

Evening come, Murrough and I visited Mahon in his house. He sat slumped in his chair, Úna behind him on a wall bench.

"Now what do you think of Emly?" I said.

Mahon stayed glum and silent. "That ambush was meant for you," I said. "Not Félim or your son."

"The ambushers were Norse," Úna said. "Why blame Emly?"

"Áed said they were Irish," I answered.

"They were Norse, not Irish," Mahon muttered.

"They were Irish," Murrough said softly. "Áed was there and he said so."

Mahon's anger filled the room like a cloud so thick we could scarce breathe.

The next day, his wounds bandaged, Áed rode with me to the ambush spot. I hoped to find Félim alive, or at least his corpse, but all we found was a trail of smashed, bloodstained undergrowth, leading into the forest.

Riding back to Cashel, I questioned Áed. Could the ambushers have been Norse pretending to be Irish? Could the abbot have spoken truth when he swore Norse raided Emly?

Áed shook his head. The ambushers spoke Irish like the Irish, not Irish like the Norse. Had they been thieves, they would not have searched for him and his troop in the forest all night. No thieves would have bothered to tie horses belonging to their victims to the monastery gate. Áed had seen the ambushers come out of that gate, mount their own horses, and ride away. They were Irish, not Norse.

"The feast will be more of the same," I said. "You will warn your father?"

A long pause. "No, he is set on his feast, and the overkingship."

"Emly set ambushers to kill your father."

Another long pause. "I suppose they could have been Norse thieves. Would an abbot lie?" I stayed silent. Why speak useless words?

—Chapter Thirty-Three—

I warned Murrough. "If it drops, the dogs will get it."

"So?" He wiggled his sandal closer to the end of his toe.

"Our leather worker has better things to do than make new sandals for the king's nephew."

"I shall bid him to."

"He will laugh at you and do nothing."

We leaned against slotted timber ramparts atop Cashel's earthen wall, our knees to our chests, save the one leg Murrough held out straight over the sheer drop of two hundred lengths to the ground. Two long hours we had waited for Emly and his guests. The sun sinking below the trees in the west, we had little time before dark.

One week after the ambush, the abbot had set a date for the feast, swearing he had swayed Munster flaith to Mahon without the promise of more gold. My eyebrows shot up high, but my brother rejoiced. At last the feast would happen. Munster flaith would pledge themselves to him, and the abbot would bless him overking. It was our good fortune Emly stayed his friend, after all we had failed to do for him.

Murrough lifted the sandal from his toe, shifted it to his other foot and stretched that leg over the abyss. He did not have my leave to fetch it if it fell, not with strangers coming in.

Murrough's dog barked from the courtyard—Flann, my dead son's namesake.

"Pray may I go?" Murrough said.

"If you bring me food from the kitchen. And ale."

Murrough edged along the wall and climbed down the ladder. He was growing faster than weeds, three fists wider in the shoulders than when I last looked, and much ruder to his father. With Murrough gone to the kitchen, I pondered King Edgar's court in Wessex, my chosen place of escape. Mahon would do better without always needing to show himself wiser than me. You had mentioned Edgar's court, poet, a haven of peace and safety on an island swarming with Danes. I would start for Wessex as soon as the feast was underway, when I was satisfied Mahon could survive the night without me.

Turning sideways, I stretched out my legs and wrapped my arm around a post. Úna dashed about in the courtyard below, joy on her face, readying for the feast to begin. The sun stirred a glow on her cheeks, a sight I would truly miss.

✠

Emly and his entourage rode out below Cashel just as light left the sky. Up through the arched opening, he and his monks made haste to the church. Munster flaith began to arrive, their manservants commanded to stay below with their masters' weapons. In the distance, Eóghan's warriors lined up behind stands of trees—close enough to hasten to Cashel if trouble broke out, far enough not to be seen by anyone. Cheer filled me. I had been my brother's keeper far too long.

Blessings begun, Murrough and I took to our house, cleansed and tidied ourselves. and recited the pledge: Worthy King Mahon, overking of Munster, we swear to honor, obey, and sacrifice ourselves to you, for as long as we shall live.

I had not yet told Murrough of my plan for Wessex, for fear he would let it slip. But surely he would welcome it.

At the church, a monk led us to the front of the long line. We knelt before my brother and the abbot, but a croak came out when I opened my mouth to speak the pledge.

I clutched my throat and nudged Murrough. "You say it."

Murrough squeaked. "I swear to honor, obey, and sacrifice you for as long as we shall live."

Mahon waved us away. Did he hear?

I hurried Murrough back to our house and sat him down in a chair. "Tonight we leave for Wexford, a Norse trading town on the sea. From there, we will seek passage to Wessex, in Britain."

Murrough tilted his head, not understanding.

"We are going to Wessex, to King Edgar's court."

"Why?"

"Uncle Mahon is overking and we are free to travel the world." I smiled, opened my eyes wide, expecting excitement back.

"Leave here forever? What of Flann? And Ailill?"

"Rory will be Flann's new friend. Ailill will visit."

Murrough frowned, not liking what I said.

"We will need peasant clothing, tunics and breeches. The cook and his family are busy in the kitchen. You will make the better thief." I spoke in my most secretive voice.

At last a spark shone in Murrough's eye. In little time, he was back with peasant tunics and breeches for both of us.

"Now, scissors for our hair," I said. "The seamstress." But one foot out the door, I stopped. "No. She keeps dogs."

"Your knife?"

My heart full with love for my son, I lopped off clumps of hair, leaving his head like a vegetable garden in spring. I covered it with a hat.

"Now, your turn." I knelt down, praying Murrough's hand would not slip. Time come for my beard, I scraped it off myself.

"How do I look?"

"Ugly."

"Good." I covered my head with a hat. "We are ready—save for the dirt."

I stepped outside, smeared both of us with mud. "We are travelers and have not bathed for days."

"You stink," he said.

"So do you."

✢

The guard away from his post, we strolled down the steep path and headed east, away from the manservants feasting in the field. A bright moon lit our way, and Murrough skipped ahead.

"Not so fast," I said. "We are out for a stroll."

He slowed, his spirits lifting mine. Well into the forest, we stopped at a stream, laid our sacks out for pillows, and wrapped ourselves in brats. "If anyone comes," I said, "do not speak. I can sound like a peasant, but you sound like a prince."

At dawn, we ate from our pouches, drank from the stream, and kept going. At a crossing, I stopped to think, north or east to Wexford, when boots pounded toward us from the south.

"Do not speak," I warned Murrough again.

A woodsman appeared, an empty sack and axe in one hand, a spear in the other, a mangy short-haired dog the size of a goat by his side. The animal lowered his head, bared his teeth, and growled. The woodsman commanded him quiet.

"Who are you?" he asked.

"Two tired travelers."

He eyed our pouches. "Where might you be going with that young lad?"

"To Wexford and Wessex."

He frowned, pondering. "A long journey. You come from which way?"

"That way." I pointed west.

"Cashel way?"

"River Shannon way."

"The woodsman furrowed his forehead. "Where on the River Shannon?"

I cursed I had not crafted my false tale. "Tuamgraney. Lough Derg."

"Ah, we get travelers from Lough Derg all the time. Come sleep the night with us. Wife makes a hearty hare stew."

"God bless you, man."

"I will be back," he said, striding north with his dog.

Murrough let out a breath. "Run?"

"No, we could use good food and a hearth. And there is much he can tell us. Remember, say nothing."

✠

Murrough and I kept dry from drizzle under a tree. Fighting sleep, I wondered what would I say to King Edgar in Wessex? How I would say it? I doubted he spoke Irish, and my Latin and French were not good enough for much talk, nor my Greek. I had some Norse, but not much, and any I had would be different from Edgar's Norse. We would learn fast, but what use would I be to Edgar? Peace reigned in his land, but perhaps not for strangers. If we stayed away forever, Sadb would never know her father or brother. If we tried to come back, Mahon would shun us as traitors. And Úna? I took joy from her, even as she was Mahon's woman.

Enough doubts, Brian, my braver self said. You have made your choice. The woodsman skipped back with a squirming hare in his sack. His dog nuzzled his nose up to Murrough.

"He smells a friend in you," the woodsman said.

Murrough stayed silent, his thin frame shivering from damp. The woodsman tilted his head. "Your mouth is stuck shut?"

I pointed to my throat, grimaced. "His throat pains him."

"Ah," he said. "At least one of you talks."

I fumbled to pick up our pouches, fighting for time. "A new king rules from Cashel," I said. "King Mahon, Dal Cais. You know of him?"

"Do I know the sun rises in the morning? Be glad you did not stop at Cashel. I would wager my dog the king does not last the night. But then again, he has his brother to protect him."

Murrough brushed against my arm and whined. "You put the fear into my son." I pulled Murrough close, stepped back under trees.

"Come warm yourselves at my hearth." The woodsman turned south, the way he had come.

Murrough followed, but I held him back. "Our thanks, but no," I said. "We have far to go." I tugged on Murrough's arm.

"Wait." The woodsman reached into his pouch and pulled out a whittled wood dog on a looped leather string. "Take this, son. Púca will bring good luck if you treat him well, if he likes you." He lifted the string over Murrough's head.

"Púca?" Murrough said, loud and clear.

"Ah, so you do talk."

"No," I said. "The day grows old."

✛

I nudged Murrough a short way north and stopped in a copse. The woodsman gone, I pointed us back toward Cashel.

"Why?" He planted his feet.

"There is trouble at Cashel."

Murrough stood still. "You said we were going to King Edgar's court."

"Another time."

"Pùca and I will go without you."

Murrough turned on his heels and kept going north. By the time he came back, his head lowered and his eyes swollen, the sun was midway across the sky. I handed him my last piece of bread. If we ran, we could be back at Cashel by dark.

—Chapter Thirty-Four—

It was dark when we spied torches from Cashel. The manservants gone from the field, we stopped to listen, but heard only rustling leaves and animal cries. We had started up the steep path, our hats pulled down as far as they would go, when three drunken men weaved into sight, coming out from Cashel toward us. One slipped onto his buttocks, bringing howls of laughter from the other two. They edged around us, stinking of ale. I watched them mount horses and ride away south, in the direction of Molloy's territory.

The guard at the gate blocked us, an empty jug at his feet.

"We come to pay our respects to the new king," I said.

"He is feasting." The guard slurred and wobbled. "Why the hat?"

"I broke my head in a fight."

"Him too?"

"Uh huh." I pushed Murrough through the arched opening. "Run."

Inside our house, we threw on our princely tunics, and I bade Murrough still as I ripped holes in the cloth of my knife.

"Do not ask," I said. "Just do what I say." We set out for the hall.

✠

The second night of the feast, the hall thick with smoke from the hearth, I could see only Mahon sitting with you at a table, poet, and Úna with Marc. I had not seen Marc come into Cashel, but was not surprised he would strive to be at his brother's feast. Further back, voices sounded, but I could not see faces.

We crept in and stood behind Mahon. I called his name. His head jerked around, and I ripped my hat off, then Murrough's.

"Brian! Where have you been? What happened? A demon?"

"No demon. We pulled out our hair and planted these weeds. And these holes? Rent with my own hands. Penance for my croak at your blessing."

I kneeled and Mahon put his arm around my shoulder. "You are maaad, brother," he slurred.

"A tiny frog jumped down my throat," I said. "Even now my gullet pains me." I put my hand to my throat and swallowed hard.

Murrough knelt down beside me, and we spoke in one voice; "King Mahon, we shall honor, obey, and sacrifice ourselves for you for the rest of our lives."

Mahon stood and raised his cup. "A drink to Brian and Murrough, my long lost brothers." He took a swig from his cup, sat down hard in his chair, and winked at me. "No bad feelings, Brian. Tiny frogs will have their way."

✠

You went out from the hall, poet, and Murrough and I stayed on with Mahon. "I was wrong," I said. "The feast was honest. But tell me. Who came?"

"Many ... Munster flaith."

"Molloy? Donobhan?"

Mahon shook his head. "Not those cowards ... but their emissaries." He burped a foul odor.

My eyes made out two men through the haze, strangers to me, but others were further back—far too few to rout Cashel.

The light outside graying, Úna steadied Mahon and they walked out together.

Murrough, his head on the table, woke at the sound of Flann whining at the door. I nodded my leave and he raced out to his dog with a bone from the table.

Alone with Marc, I asked about Sadb. The monks who brought gifts to her foster parents spoke of her uncommon feistiness and wit for a young girl, putting me in mind of her mother. Marc's words tore at my heart, and I vowed I would take her back not more one day after she turned thirteen.

Daylight shining in, Marc shuffled off to his mat in Áed's house. I followed him out and climbed to wall top. The sun lit the tops of trees in the west, and little by little, crept across the field toward me, heralding morning. The feast had ended in triumph, without rout, murder, or theft, Emly had blessed Mahon overking, and soon my brother would put me forward as clan king at Kincora.

☦

Inside my house, I peered behind Murrough's cowhide curtain at his empty bed. Guessing he slept with Flann. I pulled off my clothes, wrapped myself in a blanket, and lay down for sleep. Yet Murrough worried me and I forced myself up, pulled on my breeches, and set out to search for him. Flann slept nights in an empty house, so I headed there. But no Flann and no Murrough.

Another path, and then another, past the church, behind the hall, to the cook's house, but still no Murrough. I picked up my pace and was almost to the courtyard when boots hurried across the stones, then a cry—Rory's voice. I broke into a run, spied him bent over a still form on the far side.

"Flann," Rory called out. "His skull is smashed." A sharp-edged stone in his hand, Rory looked up at me in shock as blood pooled around the dog's head.

"Murrough?" I breathed out. "Have you seen him?"

He stared, shook his head. Such fear came up in me, I could scarce think. I made haste to the arched opening and shook the slumped guard. He opened his eyes and blinked. "What? You?"

"My son," I said. "Did he go out?"

He glanced behind me at Rory.

"He does not know you. Your hair."

"Prince Brian's son, Murrough. Did he go out?"

I wanted to squeeze words from the guard's throat. He stumbled to his feet. "That was Murrough? I thought it was a dog or a goat. In a sack."

"What sack?"

"Two men from the feast. I did not know them." The guard opened his hands, shook his head, backed away from me.

Murrough stolen? "Which way?" Rory said.

"It was dark. I heard them ride off on horses."

⊕

I pushed through Mahon's door and swept open his curtain. He and Úna bolted up in bed. "What is wrong?" Mahon said.

"Who were those men behind us in the hall?" I demanded.

"Which men?"

"You tell me. They took Murrough."

Úna clapped her hand over her mouth.

"Two men carried Murrough out in a sack," Rory said from behind me.

"By Christ's blood," Mahon said, standing naked. "I do not know who they were."

205

"Molloy's men," Úna said.

Mahon slipped on his tunic and breeches. "Why are you not out chasing them?"

"What is all the noise?" Marc stood in the doorway, Áed behind him.

"Murrough," Úna said. "Molloy's men took him."

"True?" Marc looked to me, his hand on the door jamb, steadying himself.

"I heard scuffling outside my house," Áed said. "I thought they were drunkards."

"When did Emly leave?" I said.

"Dusk. Some time before you came in," Rory said. "With his monks."

"Áed?" I said. "Go after them. If they have Murrough, take him. If they do not, take the abbot. However you can. I will ride south."

On my way out with weapons, I met Mahon in the courtyard with his helmet dangling from his arm.

"I will ride with you," he said.

"Pray no." I could not bear the sight of him.

"I am sorry, brother," he said.

"Sorry is not enough, Mahon. If Murrough is harmed, I will slit your throat."

—Chapter Thirty-Five—

I galloped south toward Molloy's territory. Acorn mast covered the ground, and if horses had ridden through, they would have left tracks. I found none, save from deer. I wound back and forth, using the sun to guide my way. If the thieves had headed south to Molloy's dún, they had taken a route I could not find.

I slid off my horse and leaned against an oak tree trunk. I had let Murrough out of my sight with strangers inside Cashel fort. They had needed no weapons. Keeping on to Rath Rathlainn tempted me, but Molloy would be expecting searchers. Two of Mahon's kin—myself and Murrough—would be far better for Molloy than one.

Cold drizzle started up, and strong wind. I galloped and trotted my horse through the mountain foothills down into the field. By the time I reached the steep path, blasts of hard driven freezing rain and hail pelted me. I covered my head with my brat, hastened to my house, and slipped on dry clothes. My hearth cold, I ran to the church—a warm place to sit, think, and wait for Áed.

From a bench in the nave, I fixed my gaze on candlelight bouncing off copper holy water basins, conjuring all the horrors happening to Murrough. The priest rushed in and busied himself pouring water into the basins, blessing and dusting the crucifix. All black in my brat, I prayed he would not see me. But no, he begged my pardon and hastened away.

Thinking myself alone again, I startled when a throat cleared behind me—you, poet, on a bench by the hearth, quill in hand.

"You surprised me," I said, walking over to you. I had given up being alone.

"Forgive me," you said. "I come here to think."

"So did I." I sat down on the bench. "What do you write?"

"King Mahon's praise poem, with a new verse for you. I read it at the abbot's feast, but you were not there to hear it."

"The feast was a lie, Mac Liag. Do you not know? Murrough is gone, stolen by men from the feast."

The quill dropped from your hand and you leaned down to pick it up. "Emly schemes with Molloy," I said. "They want us gone from Cashel."

"Emly?"

"Molloy does his dirty work for him."

You fumbled with your calfskin. "If you like, I could read the verse I wrote for you."

"I am of no mind to beg crumbs of praise from you, Mac Liag. Tell me your honest thoughts—not your poet's thoughts."

"They are the same. It pains me you think not."

"Yet Queen Úna is privy to your secret thoughts, is she not?" You picked up your quill and twirled it many times.

I leaned closer. "If you are speaking, I cannot hear you."

"King Mahon could see us here. He will deem it unseemly that we speak alone."

"Mahon does not decide who speaks to whom."

"It is best I go." You clutched your writing things to your chest and took a step away.

I reached up to stop you. "Pray stay."

You sank down onto the bench, cast your gaze to the side.

"I will slit my brother's throat if Murrough is not found." I prayed you would comfort me, but you shot me a fierce look.

"You may go," I said. "I cannot keep you here."

You squeezed your brows.

"I cannot read brows," I said. "If there is something you wish to say, pray say it."

"Is there no one Emly fears," you asked?"

"No," I said, resigned, "Our Lord God is on Emly's side."

You tilted your head. "Our Lord God does not take sides, Prince Brian. Is there not a cleric who can sway Emly? A more wealthy, more powerful cleric?"

"Not in Munster."

You stood. "Forgive me, Prince Brian. I need to piss."

For an instant, I forgot my woes and smiled. "To the cesspit then. The priest will not be pleased if you piss in his fire."

You hastened away, quill, ink, calfskin, clutched in your hands. I stared into the fire, an idea forming. A cleric more powerful than Emly? The Great Abbot at the See of Saint Patrick in Armagh?

☦

My idea was still a green shoot when shrieks and cries came from the courtyard. I raced through puddles to see Mahon, Úna, and Rory on the wall, their gazes fixed on the field below. The rain and hail had stopped.

"Áed is coming," Mahon shouted down at me. I kept going down the steep path and met Áed as he slid from his horse.

"No Murrough, no abbot," he huffed, "but I found this."

He lifted a pendant from his neck. "It hit me in the face, from a tree branch. Is it Murrough's?"

I took the pendant, my heart beating so hard I could scarce breathe.

"Púca. Where?"

"Emly's cow pasture."

"You searched for Murrough?"

"Of course."

He turned to walk up the path, but I put my hand out. "You will show me where."

☦

Mud and roots slowed our pace to Emly's cow pasture, where I hooted and called my son's name, but heard nothing back. Strains of chanting from the monastery told us monks were at prayers, all save three cowherds we spied in the field—one a monk from his brown robe, and the other two with short fair hair and gray tunics. Norse slaves?

I slipped down from my horse, plotting how to steal past the cowherds unseen, so as to search the monastery for Murrough. But seeing no way around, I made up my mind to go, and pray.

"If those cowherds see you," Aed said, "the whole monastery will come out after you."

"They will think I am a farmer or a pilgrim."

"No farmer or pilgrim wears fine boots and clothes. The monks will set dogs on you."

"I am a tired messenger, come a long way. The abbot cannot refuse me hospitality."

"The abbot knows you."

Your words came to me, poet. I secreted my swords, knife, and fine leather boots in the scrub and handed my horse's reins to Áed. "I am a messenger from the Great Abbot of Armagh." I started out into the field, barefooted.

"Our Lord God help you," I heard Áed say.

"Stay," I said over my shoulder. "Hide."

✠

I stepped barefooted through thorn-pocked grass to the cowherds. The two fair-haired boys moved closer together.

"I have a message for the abbot," I said. "Is this Emly?"

The boys looked one to the other, but did not answer. The young monk came up beside them.

"I have come from Armagh," I said. "Have you food?"

"Armagh? Armagh is that way." He pointed north. "You came from that way." He pointed east.

I shrugged. "I lost my way. My message is for the abbot of Emly, from the Great Abbot of Armagh."

"He is at prayers."

"May I wait? I am hungry." I pointed to my stomach.

"I cannot go asking for food now," the young monk said.

I tilted my head. "Emly does not obey laws of hospitality?"

A frightened look spread over the young monk's face.

"What will the Great Abbot think," I said, "when I tell him a monk at Emly denied me food?"

An intake of breath. "Wait here," the young monk said. "I will find bread."

"Tell the abbot I bring a message from the Great Abbot of Armagh," I called after him.

✠

I was truly hungry, but not for food—for my son.

"Do you speak Irish?" I said to the two fair-haired boys standing shoulder to shoulder. Neither answered. "No Irish?"

One shook his head, the other shrugged. Clear signs they understood what I had said, in Irish.

I took steps away, pretending to head for the monastery gate. "We speak Irish." A boy's voice from behind me.

I turned. "Ah, good. When that monk comes back, pray tell him I have gone in search of the abbot. My message is urgent."

"The abbot will be wanting his midday meal after prayers," one boy said.

"Then I will wait by the refectory," I said.

"After his meal, he will be wanting his walk," the other boy said.

"Walk where?"

"Wherever," the first boy said, "but no one speaks to him during his walk. After his walk, he will be busy with afternoon prayers."

"And after that?"

The boy smiled. "I will take your message to the abbot … if you mind my cows."

"Will you now?" I studied him closer. "Strange. You look Norse, but you speak Irish like a prince."

Whispering started up between the two boys. "We are three-part Norse and one-part Irish in blood, but all Irish in our hearts," the older-looking boy said. "Our Irish grandfather is Donobhan, Uí Fidgiente. He sold us here, out of spite."

Donobhan's grandsons? Slaves? "Your names?"

"Eric."

"Stefan."

"And yours?" Eric asked.

"Pádraig. I am a messenger, from Armagh."

"Ah, Pádraig," Eric said. "We would have guessed your name was Brian."

I flushed. "How?"

"Your hair," Stefan said. "Like Murrough's, exactly."

My heart skipped beats. "He is here?"

"In a chicken coop," Eric said. "We can free him ... but look there."

Over my shoulder, I spied the young monk running toward us with a long loaf of bread in his hand.

"Have you a message for Murrough?" Eric asked me.

"This." I pulled the pendant from my neck, pressed it into Eric's hand. He slipped it into his pouch.

The young monk stopped in front of me and handed me the bread. Eric spouted a stream of Norse words to Stefan and took off running toward the rear of the monastery.

"They do what they will," the young monk said. "I cannot stop them, what with them having no Irish and me having no Norse."

I sat on the grass next to the monk, my heart pounding so hard I could scarce breathe. I tore pieces of bread for both of us. "You are a novice?"

He nodded, his mouth full. "My first month. You know the Great Abbot?"

"Yes."

"Truly?"

"A most holy man."

The chanting stopped, the young monk stood. "My abbot will be going to the refectory now. I will tell him you are here." Off he went running again.

Stefan looked over his shoulder. "They are coming."

I turned my head to Eric and Murrough walking up behind us. I locked gazes with my son, started toward him, but Stefan motioned me still. "No. The monks will see you."

"Which way, messenger?" Eric said. I nodded east, toward the path from Cashel.

"Stoop down behind these cows," Eric said.

Murrough and I crouched, and little by little, edged toward Áed and our horses. Murrough looked wiser and braver than the night before. I would praise him, after I begged his forgiveness for leaving him prey to thieves.

☩

Out of sight of the monastery, I pulled Murrough to me, squeezed his shoulder, ruffled his hair shoots. "You were frightened?"

Murrough's chin wobbled. "No."

"Not afraid?"

"I knew you would come."

"Thank Áed. He found your pendant."

Murrough glanced at Áed, gave him a big smile.

"Púca hit me in the face," Áed said. "I banged right into him."

"It was the last branch before the monastery." Murrough said. "My last chance."

"Good thing," I said, "else you would still be in your coop."

"The chickens are running everywhere," Murrough said. "The monks know by now."

Indeed, hastening toward us on foot were the young monk and two others. I hefted Murrough behind Áed on his horse, and bade Eric and Stefan take mine.

"Go. I will meet you at Cashel."

The four boys galloped off. I swept up my boots and swords, dove into the trees, hid behind a massive tree trunk, and prayed. All quiet, I crept out and started toward Cashel on foot, through trees.

✠

I was glad for the time to think. We had rescued Murrough and freed Donobhan's grandsons from slavery. It would take the two kings and the abbot some time to craft a new strategy to rid Cashel of us, but in the meantime, Mahon and I would craft one of our own. Surely Mahon could no longer pretend he had swayed the abbot to his side. He would be angry and shamed, ripe for revenge. But to what end?

As I pushed my way through undergrowth, my green shoot of an idea opened into a beautiful flower. The Great Abbot was indeed our best hope. The seanchaie and my tutors had spoken of a long-ago ancestor who pledged church primacy in Munster to Armagh. Mahon was not yet overking, but he was at Cashel, looking strong.

I hastened up the steep path to Mahon's house and met Marc stepping out the door. Mahon was in a rage, planning to send mercenaries against Uí Énde, a weak king and neighbor of Emly. Marc shook his head.

I burst into Mahon's house, not bothering to knock. He sat stiff in his chair, in a rage. Úna and Áed behind on a wall bench.

I tried to stay calm. "Uí Énde, Mahon? Why?" My voice rose in wonder.

Mahon leaned back in his chair. "Emly shamed me. I will shame him back."

"The Uí Énde king has done you no harm. He is not Emly."

Mahon spat onto his floor. "Shame one Eöganacht, shame them all." He stroked his beard.

"We have shamed Emly enough. Now we need to sway him to our side."

Mahon's frown deepened. "You did not ask my leave."

"For what?"

"Donobhan's grandsons. He and I will be close kin ... or might have been had you not stolen his grandsons."

One glance at Úna's stricken face told me he plotted marriage ties with Donobhan's kin.

"Where are Donobhan's grandsons?" Mahon said, demanding.

"Ask Áed."

"At King Eóghan's," Áed said softly.

"Fetch them," Mahon growled. "I will send them back to Donobhan."

"Donobhan sold them to Emly," I said. "His grandsons are not his, and he does not want them back."

Mahon glared at me. "What is your better idea, Brian?"

I would speak my idea as best I could. "Pledge church primacy in Munster to the See of Saint Patrick in Armagh. To the Great Abbot there. He of all clerics can sway Emly to you and away from Molloy."

Mahon shook his head. "I am not fit to pledge anything to anyone. The feast was a lie."

"We know that, Mahon, but many in Munster and across our island do not." Mahon stayed quiet.

"Pledge to Armagh and you will have Emly, Molloy, and Donobhan begging for your mercy. The Great Abbot will ask your advice when he metes out Munster's share of taxes to our clerics."

A tiny light flickered in Mahon's eyes, but sputtered out. "The Great Abbot has wealth enough. He will shun me."

"You can promise him laws banning Norse. Armagh has been sorely plundered by Norse."

Mahon shook his head again. "Half the kings in Munster have Norse blood. We cannot ban half the kings in Munster."

"What harm trying, Mahon?" Úna's voice, innocent, soft and sweet. "Why not pledge to Armagh?"

Mahon shifted in his chair. "Who would carry my pledge to Armagh?"

"Marc," I said.

"He agrees?"

"He will."

"What of my mercenaries?" Mahon said. "No battles, no booty."

"Perhaps you will not call for them."

Mahon hesitated, sighed. "I will think on it."

For Mahon, those words meant yes. I took my cue and left, my hopes raised high as the sky.

—Chapter Thirty-Six—

Mahon stood before the cook and smiths in the hall. "On this calfskin is a pledge from me to the Great Abbot of Armagh, granting church primacy in Munster to the See of Saint Patrick. My brother will read it."

I pushed my hat firm over my hair shoots and stood. "Emly schemed with King Molloy to steal Murrough."

Knives were set down and silence fell. "We cannot trust Emly to watch over our souls." The silence deepened. "Brother Marc will carry this calfskin to Armagh. If the Great Abbot agrees to King Mahon's pledge, our souls will be well tended."

I held the calfskin to my eyes, the better to read your fine hand, poet. I, Mahon mac Cennétig, king of my clan, Dal Cais, and overking of Munster at Cashel, do pledge myself and my kingdom to the See of Saint Patrick at Armagh, together with all the tributes, taxes, and duties our church laws require.

Murmurs of pleasure and praise filled the hall. "Will Munster pay double church tax?" Marc? Would he naysay Mahon's pledge?

"One tax," I said, "to Armagh. The Great Abbot will share his taxes with all Munster clerics, even clerics at Holy Island."

I caught your eye, poet. You had put me in mind of the Great Abbot of Armagh, and I was deeply grateful.

☩

Marc left at dawn with Mahon's pledge in his pouch. I rode to King Eóghan's ringfort, to share the news and fetch my son. Back at Cashel that night, Murrough and I ate scraps meant for dogs and cats from the kitchen and fell sated into our warm beds.

Morning come, my nose felt prickly cold to the touch. I readied for a dash to the woodpile, but the door was blocked by wet snow—an ill omen. Early snow meant a late spring, poor harvests, hunger and pestilence, a poor planting season, one after the other.

I scooped up a handful of snow and tossed it onto Murrough's foot. He jerked it under his blanket, but to no use; I pulled him out of bed. We squeezed through the door and slogged down the snow-covered path to the hall. We pushed through to find Rory and the cook staring at us with sour faces.

"So glad to see us?" I said.

"You," Rory said, "but not this snow."

The cook nodded. "Our grain stores run low."

One by one, Mahon, Úna, Áed, you, poet, and every man, woman, and child at Kincora sought warmth at the hall hearth. We had wood enough to keep it going for some weeks. But after that?

Snow fell and melted to slush that froze to ice, soon covered by more snow. In April, rains started, turning the ground to mud. Our only visitors were monks from Holy Island, who brought news from Marc. He had made it to Armagh and back before the worst of the weather.

The Great Abbot had welcomed Mahon's pledge, the monks said, but only if Mahon could prove he commanded respect. Mahon's face reddened." Respect? Why?"

"Brother Marc did not say why."

Mahon stepped away to the cesspit, and I pressed the monks. "Brother Marc did not travel all the way to Armagh for so few words?"

I had expected more, but not such an earful. The Great Abbot knew of Sulchóit and Limerick and praised Mahon for those victories. But he also knew of Ivar's escape, the Fergal rout, Emly's ambush and his theft of Murrough. Could such a man as Mahon rule a kingdom? The Great Abbot would wait for proof.

☩

The rains washed seeds from the fields and rotted seedlings. In summer, rain kept on heavier than ever, flooding stream banks, pooling water in fields, ruining pasturage. By Lughnasa, the first of August, we knew there would be no harvest. By Samhain, streams found their banks and fish were plentiful, but not enough to feed us all.

No one at Cashel died until the pestilence started up in early winter—a fever and racking cough our physician called scamach. He bade everyone stay inside their houses, but visiting the sick, he himself fell ill and died within days.

Mid-winter, Úna's face turned white and her forehead burned with fever. Mahon bedded in Áed's house, fearing to fall ill himself. Áed, mad with worry for his mother, rode through frosty mud to Emly and stole sacks of grain from the monastery kiln. Rich, sweet smells of baking bread wafted from our kitchen, and word came Úna's color was back.

In March, more than one year after Marc's journey to Armagh, the ground began to dry and open its arms to our seed. It was our good fortune farmers lived to plant it. Sprinklings of newborn lambs and calves appeared in the fields, and for the first time in months, we had fresh meat. We raised glasses of honeyed mead to spring and our health.

—Chapter Thirty-Seven—

The last week of April in the year of our Lord, 975, I was scraping stirabout from my bowl in the hall when Murrough ran in.

"Warriors from the east," he huffed out. "On horses."

"How many?"

"Six. Irish."

Mahon and Áed already up the ladder, Murrough and I followed. Six leather-armored warriors pulled to a stop at path bottom. They dropped weapons and opened hands. Mahon beckoned them in, and we slid down the ladder to greet them.

"We are from Osraighe," the lead warrior said, coming in. "We carry a message from our king, Donnchad the Fat. Invaders threaten and our king begs help from Munster's overlord."

Mahon beamed with pride. We both knew of Osraighe—a strip of hotly contested land between Munster and Leinster kingdoms.

"I am Munster's new overking," Mahon said, "Mahon mac Cennétig, Dal Cais. Invaders from where?"

"Dublin and Leinster. The invaders will be upon us by Beltane, one week from now."

"You have come far," I said, picturing the route in my mind.

"Two days journey," the warrior said.

"Dublin?" Mahon said. "Old Norse Olaf of the Sandals?"

"Forty years a king, in Dublin and Northumbria," the warrior said, "but now he bends to the will of his new wife, young Gormlaith, the princess daughter of the Leinster king, Murchad. Truth, Gormlaith puts Queen Maeve to shame."

I dreaded Mahon would speak of his young princess, but no, he looked to me. "The Great Abbot wants proof? This is proof."

I said nothing, certain this was not the time to speak of the Great Abbot's doubts of Mahon.

"Proof? The Great Abbot?" the Osraighe warrior squeezed his brow, tilted his head.

"Proof Munster is Osraighe's best ally," I said before Mahon could say more.

"I will be taking a young princess," Mahon said, smiling. "But not a Queen Maeve. You may promise your king I will bring an army to Osraighe, by Beltane."

"He will be grateful," the warrior said, "as I am also. I am his son, Gilla Pádraig."

I had suspected the warrior was of high rank. Surely no farmer's son. We could not have imagined better fortune.

"You are named for our patron saint?" Mahon asked.

"Yes, Saint Patrick," Gilla Pádraig said.

"Then you and I share a tie to the saint. I have pledged Munster to the See of Saint Patrick at Armagh, to the Great Abbot there."

"Truly?" Gilla Padraig said, his voice raised in wonder. "Emly has pledged to Armagh?"

"The pledge is so new," I said, "Emly does not yet know of it."

"But thanks to Osraighe," Mahon said, "Emly will soon know if it, and he will pay taxes to Armagh."

Gilla Padraig blushed, once more not grasping Mahon's meaning.

"You are hungry?" I said, eager to end our talk.

"Yes," Gilla Pádraig said. "A bite to eat, and we will be on our way."

Mahon crooked his finger at Rory. "Meat and ale for Gilla Pádraig and his men. Pray tell the cook."

☩

True to their word, the Osraighe warriors downed meat and ale, and straightaway mounted their horses for home. Mahon and I stood side by side on the wall, watching them ride away. I did not believe in fate, but how else to explain this best of all possible gifts dropped in Mahon's lap? It would behoove Mahon to act with haste and cunning—both more likely if I rode with him.

"I will ride with you to Osraighe," I said. "Murrough too. He is past fighting age and well trained by me."

Mahon thought a moment. "No, Brian, I would rather you stay back to guard the fortress—and content Úna."

I had a soft place in my heart for Úna, but Mahon hinted at something more than kindness and care. I stayed silent.

"I have offered Úna divorce, on my terms, of course, but she will not leave Áed, nor will I grant her our son. I can take a second wife, but Úna has threatened me with her brother, King Connor, overking of Connacht. So you see? I can scarce leave Cashel with Úna free to plot against me. Her mind is always scheming. You have a way about you, Brian, that will soothe her ... if you would, while I am away." He cast his gaze out over the fields and the mountains.

"Does your new young princess have a name?"

"Not yet. She is but a gleam in my eye."

"Donobhan's kin?"

"As I said, a gleam in my eye."

"When do you mean to wed this gleam in your eye?"

"When the Great Abbot comes and goes from my council."

"Oh?"

"It is best I not vex him. The church frowns on more than one wife at once. When he is come and gone, I will act with speed."

"When will your council be?"

Mahon set his face in thought. "I will need time to chase away invaders, time for the Great Abbot to learn of my deeds, to agree to the pledge, to sway Emly, and time for Emly to sway Munster flaith. Five months? October? What do you think?"

"October it is." I was greatly cheered. Mahon himself had listed the steps we would need take for my plan to happen.

"Meantime, Brian," Mahon said, "When I am overking, Áed will be my warrior prince. You have served me well, but my son is of age and well tested."

"True, and I will be your best ally as king of Dal Cais at Kincora, the loudest of the many voices who seek to flatter you."

Mahon scratched his cheek. "Did I not say I would stay as Dal Cais king?"

"You did, but you will need my help when King Connor hosts down the River Shannon against Kincora. Eiden and Conaing are loyal chieftains, but you and I are brothers. No stronger bond exists."

"Ah ... then you will content Úna?"

"Whatever you want, Mahon."

Mahon let out breath. "So humble, Brian? It is true we are brothers together. I may not always do things to your liking, but I try to heed your counsel, and I always have."

I nodded. A good way to end our talk.

—Chapter Thirty-Eight—

The last horse in Mahon's troop out of sight, the day fading, I hastened to your house, poet, and knocked at your door. My purpose was to ask help wording laws for our council. I had thought of three: one banning Norse mercenaries from Munster, one banning Norse from Limerick, and one giving Irish leave to burn Limerick when the Norse paid our ban no heed.

"Brian?" You cracked your door open and put out your head.

I started forward, but no, you closed the door and bade me wait. I drew back to sounds of creaking and scraping. A few moments passed, and you bade me enter.

I walked into a room dimly lit by wall candles, and one sweet smelling beeswax candle. I could scarce make my way between upside-down wooden crates piled high with calfskins, covering most of the floor. Your hearth in the middle of the room was stuffed with bulging leather pouches, and your writing table, chair, bed, and a bench took up the rest of the space. Air came in through a wicker window and a hole in the ceiling.

Your skin sallow and pasty from months, perhaps years, of little sun, I noticed gray hairs peppering your head and beard, too soon for a man my same age.

I sat on the bench, you in your chair, your table between us. "I am here for help wording and writing laws banning Norse, for our council in October."

You paused, shifted in your chair. "The king gave me no such leave."

Heat crept into my face, remembering your words in the church. I reached for your ink pot, meaning to pen the laws myself.

You put out your hand to stop me. "Pray no, my only ink."

I pushed your hand aside, tried again to take hold of the pot. "Pray stop." You grasped my wrist. "I will help you, if you tell King Mahon you threatened me."

"Threatened you? I only ask for your ink."

It came to me to wonder about the piles of calfskins. I had heard two verses of praise you had written for Mahon, and I imagined the calfskins held false starts.

I stood and edged through spaces between boxes, seeking skins I could read. You leapt to your feet, faster than I had ever seen you move. But I had seen blank calfskins atop piles, and scrapes in the dirt floor where boxes had been pushed here and there.

I lifted one blank calfskin from a pile and spied fine writing on the skin beneath it. I could not read your scratchy hand.

"Pray read this to me." I held the calfskin out.

You stared at it. "I cannot."

"You cannot read your own writing?"

"I can read it. But I cannot speak it."

"Why?"

"It tells of King Mahon."

"A praise poem?"

You shrugged, clearly hiding something. I lifted a blank calfskin from another pile, spied my name written in giant letters on the one beneath.

"What is this?"

"Pray forgive me." Your voice lowered to a whisper.

"These skins speak of me?" I pointed to the bottom calfskin. "Pray read that one to me."

You pulled out a skin yellowed with age, and we sat back down.

"This one tells of when I first saw you at Kincora. Forgive me. Had you been king, I would have written it in verse. Still, there is praise at the end."

"Pray read it."

"Prince Brian came through the gate after months of fighting Norse King Ivar from the hills over Limerick. Five young warriors trailed in behind him, stinking like rotting fish. Ninety-five had died from hunger and cold. A fair young woman waited in the courtyard—Mór, a princess from Connacht kingdom. She lifted up her dainty hand and squeezed her nose shut with her fingers."

"Stop."

You glanced up at me. "I am almost to the praise part, where you bowed to the princess in your filthy tunic, your hair knotted up …"

"Enough. I will hear no more falsehoods."

You held the calfskin close to your chest. "I write only truth."

"Seven warriors, not five. Thirty dead, not ninety-five. The smell was of rotting flesh, not fish. Mór did not squeeze her nose shut. She was so taken with me she did not notice my smell. The whole kingdom will believe your lies. These calfskins will last for centuries."

You stood, clutching the skin. "These calfskins hold my musings, Prince Brian. Queen Úna counseled me to write them."

"Truly? Since when?"

"Since the first day she and I came in from Connacht."

"All these years you have written falsehoods about me?"

"I only write what I see and hear. King Mahon will not be pleased if he finds out."

A truth had dribbled out your mouth. I had been slow to fathom you wrote about Mahon too, without him knowing, as I had not known.

"The more so if he discovers his wife counseled you to write about him."

Such a downcast look, I took pity. "Take my counsel, Mac Liag. Bury these skins in the copse before Mahon comes back in a fortnight from now. Leave them to rot in their graves."

You shook your head. "King Mahon will see my house is empty."

I had never seen Mahon visit your house and I doubted your words. I gestured to the pile with my name on top. "Those calfskins tell falsehoods about me. If you do not bury them, I cannot promise not to tell Mahon." I meant those words as a threat.

"Queen Úna will see my floor is bare. She visits me often. Did I say?"

"No, but she told me herself, as did Mór."

An idea came to me in our silence. "I will help you bury these damning skins, Mac Liag, if you will write my honest and true tale, words that I say, on new calfskins. We can put the new in place of the old." The thought brought me joy.

"Queen Úna will see the skins are fresh."

"The light in here is dim. Everything seems yellow, no matter how old."

Your face fell. "King Mahon will take my head."

"We will hide my tale in the round tower before he comes back, in a fortnight."

You stayed mute. I had answered all of your worries.

"We must hasten," I said. "Fourteen days, fourteen piles of calfskins."

I made my way to your door and looked back. "You may craft a note of your own, to place on top of mine in the round tower. That way, the tale will belong to both of us."

You nodded, grim-faced.

"On the morrow then?" I stepped out your door.

—Chapter Thirty-Nine—

The second day of May, in the year of our Lord, 975, I began my tale to you, poet. You kept your face straight and scribbled fast, wiggling the wart on the end of your nose only when I told of sadnesses and tragedies—Órlaith's head, my mother, my father, Rónan, my sweet wife, Mór, the infant I beheaded at Limerick.

One late afternoon that first week, while burying calfskins in the copse, my gaze fell upon words I could read. A thorn in my flesh. I handed you the skin.

"What thorn? Whose flesh?"

You studied the calfskin. "A thorn in my flesh," you said. "Thorns pricked my fingers." You paused. "Blood can ruin a precious calfskin."

"You waste your precious ink and calfskin telling of a thorn prick?"

"All scribes should know the dangers of thorns."

Your words were false, poet. Mahon had said I was a thorn in his flesh. Or perhaps Úna told you. But I would not challenge the man who wrote my tale—most of all, not when I was so full of cheer. Mahon would soon return, victorious, ready for the next step in our plan.

✛

The fortnight came and went, and it was not until mid-June, three fortnights later, that riders come into the field from Osraighe—Áed and four warriors. They tied reins to posts and walked up the steep path. I worried for Mahon.

"My mother?" Áed said first thing.

"Your mother? Well, I think." Truth, I had scarce seen Úna since Mahon's leaving.

"Your father?"

"In Osraighe." Áed marched off toward the king's house.

I sat with Áed's warriors as they downed their barley bread and cheese in the hall. The invaders had turned away at news of Mahon's coming. King Donnchad had feted Mahon and his troop, and promised one score Osraighe warriors to swell Mahon's army for his circuit.

"Circuit? What circuit?"

My gut knew before my mind: Mahon betrayed me. "His circuit around Munster," the warrior said.

I closed my eyes. A circuit around Munster would take much longer than October.

Áed came in scowling, collapsed into a chair. "My mother raves and weeps. She wants me here with her."

"Why not stay? Your father will be back soon enough."

Áed sneered. "He has all of Munster to conquer by next spring. Not soon enough for my mother."

"The Great Abbot of Armagh will be here in October."

"My father has sent new messages to the abbots and kings. The council will be next spring."

My mind caught up with my gut. Mahon never meant to follow my plan. We would never be brothers together.

"Tell your father I dislike traitors."

Áed sneered, beckoned to his men, and started for the door. "If my mother falls ill, send for me. I mean to bury her at Kincora."

"You are not king at Kincora," I said in a flat, steady voice.

"But I will be."

Áed gone, I knocked at Úna's door. Had her son told her a different story?

"Is that you, Brian? Or a ghost?" She sat in a chair by her hearth, no sewing in her hands, no raving, no weeping.

"Only me." I sat down on the hearth stones, close to her knees.

"I hoped you would visit," she said, "what with Mahon and Áed away. I thought you might be ill."

"Your son said you were ill."

"From heartbreak."

"He plans your burial at Kincora."

Úna searched my face. "You do not know what Mahon means to do?"

"Mahon agreed to a council with the Great Abbot of Armagh in October. Áed says next spring. Is it so?"

Úna smiled. "Mahon will do what he will, no matter what anyone prays. I see in your honest face you do not know what he means to do."

"Tell me."

"He will subdue Munster kings and chieftains with his sword, and seek a young princess on the way." Her smile turned to tears. The coward would send his son to tell Úna of his young princess?

"More of Mahon's idle talk, I would think."

Úna dabbed at her eyes with a cloth. "No idle talk. I will be gone when he comes back in spring. I could not bear the shame of another woman in my husband's bed."

Spring! Then it was so.

"I will go to my brother in Connacht. Will you carry my message to him? I have no one else." She reached out and took my hand. "I have always trusted your good heart, Brian." She hesitated. "Even loved you—truly." She stroked my face.

A desire so strong came over me, I fought to keep myself from carrying Úna to her bed. But I would not turn her into an adulteress, a weapon for Mahon to use against both of us. No doubt his plan all along.

I held her hand to my lips and kissed it. "If you mean to divorce Mahon on your terms," I said, "adultery will not help you."

She ran her fingers down my face again. "Mahon swears I am barren. I wish to prove him wrong."

Every word from Úna's mouth brought me closer to her bed. "Yes," I said. "We should prove Mahon wrong."

I lifted Úna from her chair, and lay her down on Mahon's bed. She put her arms around my neck and kissed me all over my face, smiled as I pulled off our clothes and pressed my body on top of hers, guiding my flute in. Nothing mattered then—not Mahon, not the Great Abbot, not Munster, not Ireland.

I do not know how long we stayed together, skin to skin, not speaking, only touching each other, as I had yearned to do so many times before.

✠

Murrough called my name from the courtyard. It was midmorning, and I had promised to meet him and his friends in the field for training. Only a cowhide curtain blocked his sight of Úna and me. He knocked and called my name, and I prayed he would leave. But no, he opened the door, stepped in, and sat down no more than two paces from me in Queen Úna's bed.

"Someone there?" Úna said, as if he had awakened her.

"Murrough. Have you seen my father?"

"No, but pray go. I am not dressed."

I slipped out the bed and pulled on my breeches and tunic. Úna opened the cowhide curtain a crack, enough for me to see Murrough standing by the hearth fire. I was shrouded in shadow.

"Try the poet's house," Úna said. "Your father spends every moment of every day with Mac Liag."

"Ah, yes." Murrough left without another word.

✟

"What did Áed tell you about Mahon's plans?" I asked Úna as I readied to leave.

"Mahon means to host through the lands of Déisi near Waterford, into Molloy's territory, through the lands of the Ciarraige, through King Donobhan's territory, into the lands of Uí Énde, and then to Emly. In the spring he will ride into Cashel for a council, no doubt with a young princess who will bear him many children."

"He will not win friends that way," I said, pinning my brat at the shoulder. "The Great Abbot will refuse his pledge, as he should."

Úna settled into her chair. "Will you carry my message to Connacht?"

"Mahon's young princess is but a gleam in his eye. If he finds one in truth, you could stay at Cashel as first wife." I did not want Úna gone.

"Mahon's princess is more than a gleam, Brian. She is granddaughter to King Donobhan, daughter to King Ivarr of Waterford, and great-granddaughter to King Ivar of Limerick. A prize for Mahon, no? I will not be stuck atop this rock while Mahon beds another woman. I may be old, but there is much life left in me—as you can see."

Donobhan? Ivarr of Norse Waterford? Ivar of Norse Limerick? A true gem of a wife. But with that lineage, she would be sister to Eric and Stefan. They had not mentioned a sister. I doubted she existed.

I stood for a moment by the door. "Will Áed join you in Connacht?"

"Áed means to be king at Kincora. So, no, he will not. But when my brother avenges me against Mahon, Áed will take Mahon's place as Munster overking. Perhaps then I will stay at Cashel. We will see."

Úna's mind was as muddled as mine. I did not answer.

—Chapter Forty—

I went in search of you, poet, my heart raw as uncooked meat. You were downing broth when I knocked on your door, earlier than usual.

"What? So eager?" you said.

"Pray read what I told you yesterday."

You picked the top calfskin from the pile behind your chair and sat down. "Yesterday you told of Mór whispering something Queen Úna confided in her. It pleased you to remember it."

You held the calfskin up to your eyes. "These are Mór's words. 'Úna envies me, husband. I tell her I have given you but one healthy infant, yet still she pouts. I give you hope for more children, but Mahon swears Úna is barren.'"

I narrowed my eyes. "It does not please me to remember Mór birthing children. She died birthing Sadb. Did I say I was pleased?"

You shook your head. "No, but I supposed it."

"Did you write it?" I could see color rising in your face.

"Not yet."

"You dare write what does not please me?"

You lowered your gaze. "Shall I read what you said back to Mór?"

"Yes."

"'It would be a miracle if Úna bore Mahon another child.'"

"No! I would never speak of miracles in Úna's womb. How do I know you have not changed all my words?"

A wounded look came over your face. "I write only what you tell me to write."

"Prove it."

You shuffled behind your chair, pulled another calfskin from the middle of my pile, held it up under the light of the beeswax candle.

"This one tells about the night of the sheep."

"Read it."

You squinted. "I found Mahon herding sheep, but one at a time without a sheep dog. I could scarce believe he did not know sheep move only in a clump."

"Did I not say Mahon was a fool?"

You held out the calfskin for me to read. "You may read it yourself. I write all and only your words."

I batted the calfskin away. "If I did not say it, I should have. I thought it then, and I think it now."

Perhaps I had said fool, perhaps not, I could not remember. Truth, my heart had been cheered when I told of the sheep, but it was no longer. It would never be.

"Fool, fool, fool, Mac Liag. Write that now." I squeezed my arms tight around my middle, pushing back pain.

Pity came into your eyes. "You are troubled, Brian. We should stop for today. New words here and there will ruin these calfskins."

We sat in strained silence. "My tale is a lie, Mac Liag. Every word of it. Mahon was a fool the night of the sheep and every night since, whether I said it or not. Anything good I have said about him is a lie."

Your brow furrowed. "We could start again, with fresh calfskins."

"Only a madman changes his mind every day. You speak facts, and I speak lies? Words that change every day?"

"I did not say that."

"Is it a fact you pricked your finger with a thorn?"

You lowered your eyelids, blushed.

"I will tell you some facts, Mac Liag. About now. Pray write them."

You reached for a fresh calfskin, grabbed up your quill, readied your ink.

"Mahon betrays me. He does not mean to honor our pact with the Great Abbot—never did."

Your hand stayed still.

"He is a fool and a traitor. And he has been, forever. Those are facts, no matter what day I say them or do not say them, no matter if you write them or not."

You rested your quill on your table. "Irishmen centuries from now will yearn for your truth, Brian, not dull facts."

"You do not have my leave to counsel me."

I had broken my own rule, telling of Mahon's betrayal out of order in my tale. Perhaps by the time I came to laying with Úna in my tale, I would have forgotten all about it.

I stepped out the door, slamming it against its frame.

✥

The next many weeks I took refuge at King Eóghan's, helping with his harvest. Murrough, Eric, Stefan, Ailill, Eóghan, and I worked together tending crops, milk cows, chickens, hogs, and ploughs and kilns. Eóghan offered me space to sleep in his ringfort, but I chose an empty hut nearby.

Our only visitors those weeks were monks from Holy Island with grim news. The Great Abbot would not honor

Mahon's pledge, as I thought. There would be no tie between Armagh and Munster. Not in October. Not in the spring. Not ever. Brother Marc, a monk said, could not make sense of what had happened. Could I help?

No, I could not. My voice sounded hard, and the frightened monk scurried away.

—Chapter Forty-One—

Samhain, the harvest in, I came back into Cashel. I had not seen Queen Úna since the day I lay with her. She seemed quite well that evening in the hall, her cheeks pink like dog-rose flowers in summer. I sat across from her and asked about her health.

"Save for a sick stomach, I have been quite well. It is a wonder you ask."

My mind flew back to Mór: well when I rode out that last time, but a corpse when I came back in. Had Mahon followed my plan for the Great Abbot, I would have been on my way to Kincora, clan king, Murrough with me and Sadb in my sights. Indeed, my dreams of Sadb were coming almost every week, with her looking and acting so much like my sweet wife, I struggled not to wake. But of course, I always did.

Úna swallowed her barley bread and rested her hand on the table, well within my reach.

"So?" I said.

"No need to fear, Prince Brian. We both know what can happen when a man lays with a woman."

The cobbler one table over glanced our way. I put my finger to my lips.

Úna lowered her voice. "I said what can happen, not what did happen. We do not know what did happen, only what might have happened."

"If this child lives," she said, "I will stay at Cashel. Mahon is well pleased. He will be a father again."

"Mahon messages you?"

"We message each other. A husband to wife, and she to him."

"Ah, then the child is his?"

"Of course. Did I not say it would be? It could be."

I warmed my hands at the hearth fire. Úna had chosen Mahon to be the father of her new infant—no adultery, no cuckolding. Yet Úna was scarce a woman who would bear him many children, while his new young princess could bear him many and tie him to three of the most powerful kings in Munster—Ivar, Ivarr, and Donobhan—if his young princess existed. Truth, I felt helpless in the face of Mahon's and Úna's scheming. They both had plans for themselves, and perhaps for me, that I could not fathom.

When next I looked back at Úna, the cook's wife was sitting with her, both smiling as Úna rubbed her slight swelling.

☩

That night, I drifted in and out of a torturous dream: Úna, in a doorway with an infant in her arms, holding it high as its head wobbled and fell off. I woke myself, shaking and sweating. Like Mahon had said of himself, I was not fit for anything. I started up my tale with you again, poet, but found myself shouting at you for no reason. Murrough stayed away from me, and I could scarce shout at the cook. Often when I was angry, your writing would slow and you would say you were tired, put your pen and ink away. I knew what you were doing, trying to save me from myself. Had I not felt that kindness from you, I might well have quit my tale. Still, I could not tell you I had laid with Úna. It brought me great shame and I kept hoping something would happen to stop me from ever telling it.

✠

Late March, I was in your house, poet, when Rory pounded on your door. It was no secret where I spent my days.

"Queen Úna's pains have started. She calls for you, Prince Brian."

I cursed, but made my way to the sick house. I poked my head in and spied Úna's face glistening with sweat. She looked over at me. "Brian, pray come in."

I bade my feet forward, but they stuck in place. "Go in," her handmaiden said. "She wants you."

But my feet would move only backwards. The midwife squinted and spoke in harsh tones. "You block our light. Come in or out."

I backed away, and escaped down the steep path. Rory followed close behind. "Leave me," I said, walking faster. "It is not safe."

"Safe?"

I stopped to face him. "You sit for the infant."

He shrugged and started back up. I kept going to path bottom. But when I thought of telling you of my cowardice, poet, I turned back up the path to Úna.

✠

"Is it born?" I said to people gathered at the sick house door. They smiled and nodded. "Alive?"

"They were a bit ago," a woman said.

Úna sat up in bed cradling an infant. No stench of blood came into my nose.

"Now you come," she said, spying me.

I walked boldly to her bedside. "Forgive me. I am a coward." I stared down at the infant.

"A girl," Úna said, smiling at her daughter's smashed face, the wisp of light brown hair sticking up, the tiny brown mark on her left cheek.

"Here," Úna said, holding her out to me. "Her name will be Brigit. It means noble, like yours. Mahon will agree." I hesitated. "Take her," Úna said. "Your chance."

I took Brigit into my arms, light as my feather pillow. A smile flitted across her lips, gone in an instant. Was she trying to tell me I was her father? I handed her back, certain I would hold her again.

Úna touched the birthmark on Brigit's cheek. "A mark of high birth."

"You will stay at Cashel?" I asked.

"Of course. All is changed." I walked toward the door.

"Where will you will go?" Úna said to my back.

"Go?" I stopped.

"Áed says you will seek your own dún, no? He will be Mahon's warrior prince."

"I will go one day. But not this day."

☦

In April, eleven months after Mahon rode out to Osraighe, he sent a messenger with a plea. Pray, would I ready the fortress for his council meeting one month from then, with clerics and kings?

The man and I were sipping ale together in my house. With studied calm, I nodded yes. Any such council without the Great Abbot would be useless, but nevertheless, I would agree.

The messenger went on telling me of Mahon's circuit, a stream of words making little sense. Mahon had chased King Molloy hiding at Emly, and taken Molloy's youngest son, a youth named Cian, hostage. A willing warrior? I wondered. Or tied and bound?

Murrough showed his face at the door, wanting to hear the news. I warned him with my eyes. Anything we said would make its way back to Mahon.

"King Mahon means to hold two councils," the man said. "One at Emly, one at Cashel. King Molloy and King Fáelán of the Déisi will host both of them."

"Hosts? At the point of Mahon's sword." I could not help but say it. Neither king on their own would choose to host Mahon's council, or anything Mahon put forward—Molloy, our sworn enemy, Fáelán, a victim of Mahon's circuit.

"Someone has worked magic," Murrough said, downing his own cup of ale.

"Perhaps the Great Abbot of Armagh?" the messenger said. "He will be at both councils." My calm frayed. Had Mahon spoken those words? Or did the messenger make up lies to trick me?

"No," I said at last. "I think not. The Great Abbot denied King Mahon's pledge."

"I only say what King Mahon bade me speak, Prince Brian." He licked his lips.

I could play his game. "Pray tell King Mahon I am pleased to ready Cashel for his council. When did you say?"

"One month from now."

"Both councils one month from now?"

"Yes, both. I will tell King Mahon. And I thank you for your sweet tasting ale."

Certain the messenger was out of earshot, I bade Murrough bring me one score of Ailill's most skilled warrior friends, Eric and Stefan among them.

245

"For training?"

"For scouting. We will see for ourselves what Mahon is doing, and with whom."

PART FIVE

—Chapter Forty-Two—

Cashel. Two years later, in the year of Our Lord, 978

You remember my last visit to you two years ago, poet? It was early morning, the day Mahon came back from his circuit around Munster. Only hours before, in the dead of night, we had carried my tale's calfskins to the round tower and placed them on the rungs of metal steps leading up to the top. I was certain Mahon would never think to look inside the round tower, and even less, to look for my tale.

Much has happened in the two years since then, and I see you have readied fresh calfskins. I thank you for that.

✢

That morning, I had finished telling of our visit to the round tower when my scouts ran in with news Mahon was moments away from Cashel. I left you in haste and found a place on the wall where I could see my brother's entourage, but no one would see me. I could not bear to look upon Mahon's treacherous face.

Helmet back, burnt red hair flowing to his shoulders, Mahon led his troop into the field, looking like a victorious warrior. Áed came next, looking older and much like his father. Four clerics followed: Marc, Emly, an abbot I had been told was Colum from Cork, and a man dressed like a shepherd, with a large, shaggy, black and white dog loping beside him. The Great Abbot.

Three kings followed on horse: my friend, Donal of Corcu Bascind, and two kings I guessed were Molloy and Fáelán. A long line of monks and warriors came after on foot.

I bided my time, waiting for quiet in the courtyard. I could not hide forever, but I would choose when and how I would be seen. I ventured forth, only to be spied by Marc and King Donal, waiting for me. I cursed, and not under my breath.

"You were not at Emly," Marc said. "Why not?"

"I was not summoned."

"Strange," Donal said. "Much was decided there. Mahon spoke his pledge to the Great Abbot and he accepted it without conditions, save for the laws."

"He does not fathom the laws," Marc said.

"Nor do I," Donal said. "Only a spear through Ivar's gut will keep him from the Shannon." Donal paused, studied my face. "You knew Ivar escaped the Haroldssons? He is back at Scattery Island."

Running footsteps sounded behind me. I turned to see Rory, bearing calfskins. "Mac Liag says to give you these, Prince Brian. The laws for the council."

"Aye, I thank you."

I was grateful, Mac Liag, but I did not need the calfskins. The laws were etched in my head.

✠

The kings, clerics, Áed, and Úna settled themselves in the council house, all save the Great Abbot, who asked for food and water for his dog. I slid behind chairs to an empty seat at the far end of the council house table, keeping my gaze away from Mahon. But the room was small, and I could not help glance his way. Smug pride covered his face, sickening me.

We sat in awkward silence, my mind drifting to news of Ivar back at Scattery, and to Mór, who would not have left our infant alone, as Úna had, with the wet nurse. The Great Abbot stepped in and sat in his chair by the door, his dog at his feet. I looked to Mahon to begin, and found him looking to me, nodding to my calfskins.

I stood, ready to speak the laws. The Great Abbot raised his hand. "Your brother speaks for you, King Mahon?"

"The new laws, holy father."

The Great Abbot gave me a stare. "No need for your calfskins, Prince Brian. Say what you have to say, and I will say what I have to say. Then we will feast."

I put the calfskins down. "Norse in Munster are like midges in a summer twilight. They swarm everywhere, seeking blood. These new laws will ban them from Limerick, give leave to Irish to burn the fortress at Limerick if need be, and ban Norse mercenaries from Munster. Irish who break the new laws will be fined."

The Great Abbot gazed around the table as I spoke. He seemed not to be listening.

"I did not agree to ban Norse," Abbot Colum said, fingering his wooden cross. "Nor did I agree to fines."

"A law is scarce a law if no man can be fined," the Great Abbot said. Abbot Colum fumbled with the hood bunched around his neck, silenced.

"King Fáelán," the Great Abbot said. "Are you not wed to a Norse woman?"

Fáelán flushed. "Not all Norse are evil, holy father. Only trouble-making Norse."

"Ah, trouble-making Norse. Do Norse make trouble in your territory, King Molloy?"

"If King Mahon and Prince Brian say so." Molloy looked at me, and for the first time, I spied his different colored eyes—one brown, one green. A monster.

The Great Abbot paused. "Even a dog has thoughts of his own." He reached down to scratch his dog's back. "King Mahon, pray tell us. Who are troublemaking Norse? Where are they?"

Mahon leaned back in his chair and smiled. "Norse King Ivar escaped us at Sulchóit, and now he has escaped his enemies, the Haroldssons, in the Isles, and is back at Saint Sénan's monastery on Scattery Island. But he will not escape me again. I mean to wed his great-granddaughter, who also happens to be granddaughter to King Donobhan, Uí Fidgiente, and daughter to King Ivarr of Waterford—three of the most powerful kings in Munster."

"Forgive me, King Mahon," the Great Abbot said, "but your thoughts are at odds with one another. You would ban troublemaking Norse, but at the same time take a woman more Norse than Irish into your bed? Your own children will have much Norse blood."

My fingers laced so tight, they turned white. I stole a look at Úna's face, expecting a frown—but no, a proud sneer.

"My Irish blood will tame my bride's Norse blood." Mahon paused, as if waiting for high praise.

The Great Abbot nodded to Úna. "This woman is your wife, is she not?"

Úna nodded, her smug satisfaction matching Mahon's.

"Yes," Mahon answered, "but Úna is barren."

"Barren?"the Great Abbot said. "Did I not see a wee one in her arms? And this young man?" He glanced at Áed, then back at Úna. "He seems to favor her. Pray speak words I can fathom, King Mahon."

Úna shot me a sly look, sat up straighter in her chair. "King Mahon and I have agreed a pact, holy father. As you say, I have given my husband two healthy children ..."

My mind shot back to Mahon saying he was pleased Úna bore him a child, yet still he claimed she was barren?

"My husband slanders me," I heard Úna say. "He swears I stole my infant daughter from a serving woman. At this very table is a witness to Brigit's birth, who could swear she came from my womb ... if he would."

I stayed silent, thinking it best not to speak of Úna's womb or her infant.

"By law," Úna said, shifting her gaze back to the Great Abbot, "a woman who does her wifely chores and bears her husband's children cannot be put aside. I have more of a right to divorce King Mahon than he has to divorce me."

The Great Abbot nodded, clearly struck by Úna's wit. Úna's lips spread in a wide smile. "If King Mahon tries to divorce me now, he will forfeit much wealth, not to mention the battle he will need fight against my brother, King Connor, from Connacht. So, as you see, holy father, our marriage laws favor me."

"You know our marriage laws well, Queen Úna," the Great Abbot said, soft.

Úna shot me another furtive look. She feared I would speak of her adultery, the ruination of her scheme.

"So, to the pact," Mahon said. "Perhaps I should speak it, Queen Úna?"

"Pray do, husband," she said. Úna glanced at me again. I was part of her plot.

"Úna has agreed not to divorce me," Mahon said. "She will stay at Cashel, with all the rights of first wife ... save my bed. That will go to my new young princess."

The Great Abbot rubbed one side of his nose, then the other. "Our Brehon laws do permit two wives, King Mahon, yet our church laws say a man can wed but one woman at a time. Most likely you misspeak? Or speak too soon?"

Could even Mór have outwitted this man? "My counsel, King Mahon?" the Great Abbot went on. "Keep Queen Úna as your only wife. If you must take another, do not boast of her to the church."

Mahon scowled.

"Another bit of counsel," the Great Abbot said. "Beware of Norse women in your bed. One day you will wake up and find Munster more Norse than Irish, troublemaking or not."

Ah, he and I were of the same mind. "We are finished here?" he asked.

Mahon cleared his throat. "Pray no, holy father. Emly here deserves to be punished. He ambushed my son and stole my nephew. I outwitted him, but I will punish him for trying."

Had that matter not been decided? At Emly?

"I understand, King Mahon," the Great Abbot said. "But I will judge Emly. He is my friend now, and yours—unless, of course, you fail to protect him, or fail at your duties as Munster overking. Then I will have to rethink my pledge to Munster. Pray spare me that trouble."

"Of course." Mahon's ruddy face flushed more than I imagined possible.

The Great Abbot rose to his feet. "A feast awaits us. If any man or woman wishes to speak to me alone, I will be in the church after I eat. But only until dusk. It is a long way back to Armagh." The Great Abbot did not say my name, but I was certain he meant me.

—Chapter Forty-Three—

I caught up to Úna at the doorway to her house. "May I come in?" She held the door open and I stepped in. Úna waved the wet nurse away, and I sat in a chair by Brigit's cot, lightly touching her cheek. Úna leaned over and tucked her daughter's blanket close around her body.

"So many knowing looks at the council," I said.

She straightened up and stared at me. "Surely you took my meaning?"

"That you have agreed to stay as Mahon's first wife? With all rights save his bed?"

Úna frowned and pulled her cowhide curtain back, motioning me to follow her into her sleeping nook. I sat on a wall bench across from her bed.

"For our sake, Brian. I pray you understand, else I shall weep."

"For our sake? I would hear it from your lips."

Her frown deepened. "Perhaps I misjudge you?" She studied my face. "Perhaps you misjudge me as well."

Little fussing noises came from Brigit in the hearth room. "Plain words, please," I said. "We have little time."

Úna fetched Brigit's cot, set it down by my knees, and put herself next to me on the bench.

"Look," she whispered. "Our daughter. We need not be husband and wife to share love of our child."

I shook my head. "Of course, but as you have said, Mahon is her father." I paused. "It is likely, no?"

"Who can say?" Úna put her hand on my knee. Brigit sucked harder on her fist, and a yearning came over me to whisper I would care for her, no matter whose child she was.

"She chides you for your doubts, Prince Brian. She is strong and healthy, thanks to the good seed I coaxed from you."

Seed coaxed from me?

She kept on, her hand rubbing my thigh. "You have helped me show I am not barren, but Mahon thinks I am too old for all the children he wants."

My flute wanted to grant the temptress more seed, but my mind told me not.

"Do you not praise my clever wit?" she was saying. "My pact with Mahon? It is perfect for you and me."

"How is that?"

"I will stay at Cashel as the old queen who can do as she wants. You and I will be free to be together, in plain view under Mahon's nose. He can have his princess, and I can have you." She shot me a triumphant look.

I looked away. I had misjudged Úna—sweet and long-suffering on the outside, a seed-coaxing schemer on the inside.

"My brother deems it unseemly for me to speak alone with his poet," I said, "much less lay with his first wife in plain view under his nose."

"But surely you know he slanders you? He deems himself a great warrior and king, and you, nothing. But we know better, do we not?"

I stayed quiet. Úna's sweet touch, her weeping, Brigit, her mocking of Mahon—all weapons to use against my brother. I was a mere pawn in that battle, as Mór had guessed from the start.

Brigit fussed more. Úna jiggled her cot. "I will divorce Mahon if you would rather, and take what I am due. Then you and I can wed. Any brithem will judge me a wife of equal lordship and grant me Brigit. Mahon will rue that day, not to mention the enemy he will make of my brother in Connacht."

My gaze fixed on Úna's cunning look, her gleaming teeth. She placed her fingers on my arm, kneaded it. "You know the tale of Queen Maeve and King Ailill? I would counsel you and Mahon to heed it."

My skin felt as if fleas crawled on it under Úna's hand. I lifted it off and slid further down on the bench, away from her. "What would you have us heed?"

"Strong women will raise armies to right the wrongs men wreak against them. You take my meaning, no?"

"I have done you no wrong," I said. "Indeed, I may have gifted you a child."

"Ah, yes," Úna said. "Briget will tie me to you forever." Úna reached for my hand, but I kept it away, swiping my arm to wipe away the very memory of her touch.

"You know Queen Maeve's tales well," I said, my neck on fire.

A smile crept onto her lips. "Mac Liag and I speak of many things." She tried again for my hand.

I stood away from her. "Surely he told you a seed-coaxing queen cedes all divorce rights to her cuckolded husband?" A blow soundly struck. Strength seeped back into me.

"I will decide what to tell Mahon," Úna hissed, her sweetness turning sour. "You will never speak of laying with me to anyone, else damage your own good name."

I sensed victory. "I do not worry about my good name. A man can lay with many women and keep his good name. A woman risks her head when she cuckolds her husband. Has Mahon not told you of Órlaith?"

All pretense of sweetness fled from her face. "Perhaps you do not know Queen Maeve's tale? A spurned woman has many ways to fight back, Brian. Not only armies. Remember that when you plot against me."

Maeve had taken her husband's head when he lay with another woman. But I did not fear Úna—I would pay no heed to her threat. I had not truly known her until then.

Brigit squealed, Úna picked her up, and I turned away in fast retreat.

—Chapter Forty-Four—

Walking toward the hall, to the feast, an urge came over me to retch. I had not known Úna was a fork-tongued adder, like those snakes my tutors taught me lived in Britain. I had never seen a snake, but I knew they slithered in silence, waiting for the right moment to strike their heedless prey.

I poked my head through the hall door to see Mahon, Molloy, Fáelán, and Áed at one table, and the four clerics, including Marc, at another. Further back, Donal and Murrough sat alone together—friendly faces for me to join. They greeted me, and went back to eating, swigging cupfuls of ale, enjoying each other's company.

I leaned back in my chair, keeping the Great Abbot in my sights. I was plotting a way to pry him away from the feast when Queen Úna appeared in the doorway, her braided hair propped on top of her head, held up with golden twine and shiny combs. Her berry-dyed black eyebrows and rose-colored cheeks put me in mind of that first time I saw her at Kincora, when she came in like a breath of fresh air, bringing cheer to all the fortress.

Úna kissed cheeks with Mahon, just as Molloy and Fáelán rose and bade the king and queen goodbye. A scraping of chairs at my table startled me. Next I looked, I was alone.

You waved your calfskin in the air, poet, and called for quiet. I would have stayed and listened had the Great Abbot not chosen that moment to move toward the door, his dog close behind him. I followed after them, begging forgiveness under my breath that I would miss your praise of my brother.

I cleared my throat at the church door. "Ah, Brian," the Great Abbot said from his bench facing the hearth. "Come in." His dog raised up from the floor, lowered his head and growled. "No," the Great Abbot said, "a friend." The dog settled at his master's feet.

I sat two arms' lengths away on the same bench. "I feared you would not come," he said. "Had you not, my journey would have been for nought." I waited, uncertain of his meaning. "You are puzzled?"

"Truth, yes."

"Are you not the man who crafted the pledge your brother Marc carried to me at Armagh?"

"If Marc named me, he misspoke. Mahon's name is written on the calfskin. In his hand."

The Great Abbot smiled. "His name in his hand, but your words. Mahon tests me sorely, and now you as well? I am not a witless man, Prince Brian. We have little time here. It is best you speak truth."

An honest face, an honest voice. Clearly the Great Abbot had come for a reason I still could not guess. "I did craft the pledge," I said, "and I believed Mahon understood the good of it. Yet he betrayed me once again and chose his own way. I was not surprised you denied his pledge, but I was surprised you came. You are aware that Molloy and Fáelán are not honest?"

"Ah, again you question my wit? I am no stranger to brothers feuding or to kings swearing one thing and meaning another." He paused, studied me with his sharp, blue-eyed gaze. "Shall we get to the point?"

The Great Abbot was steps ahead of me. I would take care.

A knock came at the church door. I whipped my head around to see Abbot Colum peering around the door frame.

"A few moments, Colum," the Great Abbot said. "Your turn is next." Colum pulled back his head and shut the door.

The Great Abbot lowered his voice. "Your pledge holds promise, Prince Brian, not only for Munster, but the whole island. Tie the churches together and the kings will follow—if the Munster overking who pledges to Armagh is clear-eyed about that vision. That is not what we have here at Cashel. Which is why I came."

I took moments to ponder the Great Abbot's words. I had not thought of tying clerics and kings together across our island. Munster, yes, but our island was far out of Mahon's reach, and mine. "Mahon may be clear-eyed about a vision, but not one that ties kings and clerics together in peace. Indeed, the opposite. His vision is to fight and win as many battles as there are kings to fight."

"I am aware, Prince Brian."

"But there is more. Mahon opposes my vision for lasting peace, not only because he wants to be seen as a great warrior flush with battle spoils, but because he wants to believe himself wiser, braver, and more worthy in every way than me. It has taken me all this time as his warrior prince to understand that simple fact. He is skilled at pretending to heed and agree to my way, while secretly plotting to do the opposite."

"Again, I am aware."

"This time, there can be no doubt he set out from the beginning to ruin my plan. No matter that the Great Abbot of Armagh agreed to help. Mahon will be better off without me. Munster too. Murrough and I will go somewhere else other than Munster, as we should have long ago."

"Oh? Where?"

"Edgar's court in Wessex. We started on a journey there once before, but turned back. Next time, we will not turn back."

Colum knocked again. "Another moment, please, Colum." The Great Abbot waited for the door to close. "King Edgar of Wessex died last winter. News does not come to Cashel?"

I flushed. "News comes to the king, not to me. Died how?"

"Poisoned, perhaps, like his brother, Eadwig. Many suspected Edgar of Eadwig's murder, and now many suspect Eadwig's young sons' councilors of Edgar's murder. In any case, you will not be welcomed at that court."

I narrowed my eyes. "Mahon and I are not set on murder. We have our own special ways of wounding each other—many ways, save murder."

"Tell me."

"Mahon pretends he thinks well of me, but then he acts as if I mean nothing to him."

"And you?"

"I stand by him. But I will no more. I will leave him to his ways. If not in Wessex, then somewhere else far away."

The Great Abbot shifted on the bench, gazed into the hearth fire. "My brother shows me pity, Brian. Even as he deems himself wiser and braver, as you say. Can you not show Mahon pity?"

"Pity? Mahon?" The last thing I wanted.

"Saint Patrick preached brotherly love, Brian, no matter a brother's sins."

I flushed, my neck growing hot at this turn in our talk. Was the Great Abbot testing me? I reached down to scratch the dog's head, but drew my hand back when he jerked his head up and growled.

"I do owe Mahon my life," I said. "And long ago, before he became king, I believed he cared for me."

"Perhaps he still cares for you, and you for him. As you say, neither of you has poisoned the other."

"Betrayal is a strange way to show he cares for me," I said. "Or for Úna, the wife he has threatened with divorce since the day after Áed's birth."

The Great Abbot cast a glance at the church door, and lowered his voice. "Your quest belongs to all of us on this island, Prince Brian—not only to you or to Mahon or to Munster. Take yourself far away, and you will have me and all the gods, old and new, to answer to. I will leave you to imagine that fate."

"All the gods?"

"I have my ways of knowing things. But do not worry. I take heed of the old gods' tales as much as any man."

I felt small next to the Great Abbot, a man who had spoken more truth to me than anyone in my life. But he had more to say. "Not all Norse are troublemaking, Brian. Someday, you will seek them as friends. For now, we can pretend to ban them in Munster."

I let out breath, spent. "Remember," he said, "blame will get you nowhere. I trust you will find a way to do what you must."

I wanted to ask what I must do. But the Great Abbot's dog lifted his head, barked and snarled, as Abbot Colum moved slowly toward us, no longer waiting for leave. The Great Abbot beckoned to him, and our talk was over.

—Chapter Forty-Five—

I left the Great Abbot and walked about. Dusk was falling when he, Emly, and Marc mounted horses and rode off together, the abbot's dog loping along side his master's horse. Emly had agreed to spend time at Holy Island, a safe enough place, Marc said, for Emly and Armagh to bond. Abbot Colum of Cork stayed behind, keeping watch on his gospel book and Saint Finnian's ashes.

I walked to my house, yearning to be alone, but Murrough and Donal sat before my hearth, telling stories and laughing. They nodded to me, the old man of thirty-five, and went on with their talk. I pulled the cowhide curtain closed and lay down on my bed, smiling when Murrough told Donal how his warships had sent us fleeing naked into Kincora's river chapel.

I was half asleep when I heard the scream. Not sure if it came from my head or outside, I opened my eyes and listened. Another scream—Úna. I would not hasten to her side. A third scream, and the cowhide curtain flew open, swept back by Murrough. "Úna," he said.

"We will hear soon enough what vexes her."

"You are not coming?"

"You go. Come tell me."

Murrough and Donal hurried out the house. I put my hands behind my head, prayed the screaming would stop, but it kept on, battering my ears. Other voices mixed in, shouts, men and women. Footsteps pounded up and the door to my house burst open.

Mahon!

I sat up, swung my legs to the floor, and stood.

"Are they here?" He stepped behind Murrough's curtain, then back to my nook, his face red and twisted.

"Who?" I asked.

"Brigit. And the nurse. They are gone. Stolen. Are you so careless? Again?" Mahon was shouting at me.

I stepped forward and swung my fist at his head, knocked him against the wall. He tried to steady himself but fell onto one knee. I had lifted my foot to kick him down when Donal and Murrough pushed between us. Not until they blocked me did I know they were there.

Mahon raised himself up, drew his knife, waved it at Murrough. I pulled my short sword from its sheath on a wall hook. "Touch him, and I will take your head."

I moved around Murrough and Donal, meaning to threaten Mahon, he with his puny knife and I with my sword, when Áed appeared in the doorway.

"What?" he said, staring.

"We do not know what, do we Mahon?" I said, lowering my sword. I kept my gaze on his hand still gripping his knife.

"I know," he breathed out. "So do you. So does everyone."

"Know what?" Áed said. "Why the weapons?"

"Know what, Mahon?" I said. "Why the weapons?" Would Mahon dare tell his son I had cuckolded him? That his son's mother was an adulteress? That his own seed was weak?

His face smoldered hot and he did not answer. "We must go now," Áed said, taking hold of Mahon's arm. "They have a long lead."

Mahon put his knife away, looked at me. "I trusted you, Brian. I will not anymore."

"Take him away," I said to Áed. "Or I will myself." I lifted my short sword higher.

Mahon backed away and Áed guided him to the door. They vanished into the night.

☩

"It is too late," I said to Murrough and Donal. "They will not see tracks in the dark."

"What does everyone know, Brian?" Donal said.

"Nothing. You misheard."

Donal shook his head, kept his gaze fixed on me. "I did not mishear. Mahon near killed you for it. Is it Brigit? There are rumors she is yours. You cuckolded your brother?"

"I need not confess my sins to you."

Murrough cast questioning looks at me.

"Any fool could see those kings were not honest," Donal said. "And Mahon's young princess? What nonsense is that? Donobhan is not to be trusted. If Mahon truly believes such a thing, you should warn him. Will you?"

"If he seeks my counsel."

"What does that mean?"

"It means I will do what I must." Donal swept his golden hair back behind his ear, rubbed the back of his neck.

"Meantime," I said, "dawn on the morrow would be a good time for you to start for home."

I could not share my honest thoughts with Donal, nor did I want or need more counsel. He gave me a long look, starting for the door. "I pray Brigit is found alive. For your sake, friend." We kissed cheeks, and he left.

"Is Brigit my sister?" Murrough said.

I squeezed my eyes shut. I had not meant to have that talk with my son. Not yet. Not then. "She could be," I said. "I did lay with Úna. Once. I wish I had not, but it happened. One day you will know how that is."

"One day?" Murrough smiled.

His face went somber. "Had Donal and I not come in, Mahon could have killed you."

"Perhaps."

"If he tries again," Murrough said, "he will have me to fight as well."

My rest ruined, I peered into Úna's open door. From her chair next to Brigit's empty cot, she looked at me with reddened eyes, wiped tears from her rose-colored powder smeared with wet.

Her voice quivered. "Why are you not out looking for her?"

"I will be, at a better time."

She turned her head away from me. "Go. You are no use to me now."

I shifted my feet, searched for words that might solace us both. Yet no amount of spring rain could bring dead seeds back alive. Out the door, I heard Úna sob loud and pitiful. I paused, but kept going.

—Chapter Forty-Six—

Mahon and Áed were back the next morning, empty handed. A late May rain had started up in the night, and any tracks the kidnappers might have left had been washed away. Mahon said we would wait for news. Indeed, news soon came that both Fáelán and Molloy had hosted out against rivals, taking hostages and breaking pledges they had made to Mahon and the Great Abbot of Armagh.

Mahon shouted all was my fault. He had done everything my way, but Molloy and Fáelán had betrayed and shamed him. The rain still falling, he and Áed rode off with a clutch of warriors to punish Fáelán. Molloy, they said, would be next.

The rain stopped, and spots of dry ground peeked up through the wet. Mahon and Áed rode back in with the head of King Fáelán's grown son, Cormac, in a sack. He had been out fishing with his dog, with no weapons or warriors to protect him.

Mahon planted the putrid head on a pole at the bottom of the steep path, where everyone would see it, coming and going. Surely Fáelán would seek revenge, but I would counsel Mahon no more. He would do what he would, no matter what. With the blessing of the Great Abbot of Armagh, I would do what I must.

☩

July that year, the sun bright and warming, a messenger rode into the field from the west. Mahon mounted a horse from the pen and met him in the field, where they sat on their horses and talked for some time. The messenger wheeled his horse around and rode away.

Mahon hastened up the steep path, smiling to himself. Seeing me on the wall, he called out the man's purpose, a message from Donobhan, of no matter to me. Mahon shut himself up in his house with Úna and Áed.

At evening meal, Mahon and Áed smiled at me with uncommon calm, as if dark clouds had parted in their minds. Chills ran down my back when Mahon asked if I would join him for a talk in the council house. Murrough could come too, if he wanted. Mahon's words boded ill, but at least I would know his mind.

Murrough and I sat across from Mahon and Áed in the council house, the dying sun streaming through the window. Even so, Mahon lit the beeswax candle for a matter of great importance.

"Kincora has long been empty," he said. "Eiden and Conaing keep squatters away, but now it is time for a new clan king at Kincora."

Hope leapt up in me, but turned fast to fear, then gloom. Mahon cleared his throat. "I have messaged Eiden and Conaing to gather the names of all Dal Cais with rights to the clan kingship."

All Dal Cais?

"We have many nephews and cousins," Mahon said, "but I have been thinking. You and I are the only two of our father's sons to outlive him, Brian, save Marc and poor Lachtna, who died. Only I have been chosen king. Surely our next clan king at Kincora should be from my line, do you not think?"

Needless words. I did not answer.

He breathed deep. "I will put Áed's name forward to the chieftains. He has proved himself quick-witted and courageous."

I warned Murrough still with my look, but to no good. He jumped up and shouted, the hurt thick in his voice. "The Dal Cais kingship is my father's right. You would not dare."

Áed smirked. "It is decided, Murrough. You need not worry—I will keep the River Shannon clear of Norse."

"I would put you forward, Brian," Mahon said as if noting a passing cloud in the sky, "but we both know I cannot trust you, with my wife or anything else. I once believed you knew better than me, but all your great ideas come to nothing."

"No matter, Mahon." I said, matching his calm. "Murrough and I will soon be away. I will no longer trouble you with my counsel." Murrough rose to his feet, kicked the door open, stepped through, and banged it and shut. Mahon waved Áed away and motioned me to stay. I stayed seated.

"King Donobhan invites you to my wedding," Mahon said.

"Wedding?" Of course I knew what wedding. I would hear him say it.

"To Donobhan's granddaughter. His manservant brought your invitation long ago. I forgot to tell you. Will you come?"

A lie. Donobhan's man had come that day, and I still doubted his princess existed. "When is this wedding?" I asked.

"I leave on the morrow," Mahon said, "with Áed, Abbot Colum, and six bodyguards. We will all dress as Colum's bodyguards. No Christian will dare harm us in the presence of his gospel book and Saint Finnian's ashes. If I could bring an army, I would not need you. But to show I trust Donobhan and Molloy, I will bring no warriors. I would feel better if you came with us, my warrior prince."

Mahon spouted words he could not possibly believe. "Molloy will be at your wedding?"

"He regrets the trouble he has caused me, and promises a gift. I have reason to think the gift is Brigit. You will want to be there when that happens."

I could not help myself. "Need I remind you of all the reasons you should not trust Molloy or Donobhan?"

"Old deeds, Brian, forgiven and forgotten."

The slightest promise of Brigit tempted me, but I suspected Mahon plotted my murder. Again, I kept my face straight, my voice calm. "Úna agrees Brigit is your daughter," I said. "Brigit proves your seed is good, your wife is faithful, your brother loyal, and yourself not cuckolded—all things you want, no?"

"Yes, and that is why Una and I have agreed to divorce on equal terms. Something for her, something for me."

"Did she not agree to stay at Cashel as first wife?"

"Ah, no longer. We will divorce. Úna will swear Brigit is my child and take her to Connacht as part of what she is due from our marriage—no small sacrifice on my part. In return, she will admit her sewing and housekeeping skills and her pouty face are unsuited for any queen, much less wife to an overking. I will be free of Úna at last. So I ask you again, Brian. Do you not wish to be at Donobhan's when Molloy gifts Brigit back?"

So honest sounding. Had I not known better, I might have thought he believed his words. "Does your new young princess have a name?"

"Of course. Brunhilde."

"Brunhilde?" I said, truly surprised. "The same name as Donobhan's daughter, her mother?"

He nodded, pursed his lips. "Mothers and daughters often share the same name."

"Why does she not wed at her Norse father's palace on the sea? In Waterford town?"

"Ivarr of Waterford has children enough to spare."

"Eric and Stefan would be her brothers, Mahon. They know nothing of her."

Mahon shrugged. "A mystery, I agree. But despite your naysaying, Brunhilde does exist, and I will wed her, whether you come or not. Will you?"

"Donobhan invites Murrough too?"

He shook his head and shrugged. "No, not Murrough. He will stay to protect Úna, with the rest of us away. But Donobhan does invite his grandsons. Their names again?"

"Eric and Stefan?"

"The same."

"The grandsons he sold into slavery?"

Mahon scowled. "So suspicious, Brian. Donobhan hopes to make amends with his grandsons. I will honor his wish. Do not make a liar of me."

A clear falsehood. My plan was simple. I would only need quiet my son. "In the morning, Mahon," I said. "I will give you my answer."

I left Mahon and hastened to my house. Opening the door, I spied a chair splintered into pieces on the hearth stones, Murrough pacing the floor.

What was wrong with me? he shouted. Had I not sworn I would fight Áed for Kincora? I let him rage. He was right to be angry. But I could not share my plan with him. I prayed he would never know it. "Trust me, Murrough. I will do what I must."

—Chapter Forty-Seven—

In the wee hours, I chased my thoughts like bees back into their hive. But they swarmed and stung me. You need not raise a hand against Mahon, Brian—without your counsel, he will end his own life. Even Jesus does not condemn a man to a lifetime of brother-keeping. You need no barbed sword, like Cúchulainn against Ferdiad. No sword at all. Mahon's foes will do him in.

You startled when I came early to your house for help, poet. Still in your bed, you opened one eye. I took my usual seat, and you took yours. You grabbed up your ink and quill.

"Mahon swears he wants me with him at his wedding. Either he is tricked or he plots to murder me."

You went white, poet. My first mention of murder in my talk about Mahon.

"Eric and Stefan know of no such sister," I said.

You were not scribbling, only listening. Truth, I was speaking nonsense. A man cannot line up reasons to let a brother go to his death or not. I would not go with Mahon to Donobhan's, nor would I counsel him one way or the other. His choice would tell me all.

I went from your house to the hall, where Mahon waited for my answer. I could see his eager face from the doorway. "You have decided?" he asked.

"I will not come with you, Mahon. Murrough and I will stay until you return, to keep Úna and this fortress safe. Your wish."

"I want you with me."

"You will have Áed with you."

"And Abbot Colum," he said.

"Ah, wise."

"Do you think?"

"I do. No Christian thieves will harm you in the presence of such a holy man and his gospel book and saint's ashes."

"Yet not all men are Christians, are they? Perhaps you will come after all?"

"I think not."

Mahon sighed. "Úna believes you are the better warrior, Brian. With the promise of Brigit, she will be doubly vexed if you stay back."

I shook my head. "It is not my duty to please Úna. You should have the honor of bringing Brigit home."

Mahon sighed again. "Úna and I would both rest easier if you would come."

"You will do better without me. I am careless, remember?"

Mahon paused. "I am sorry for that, Brian. But Brigit will be safer on our journey back to Cashel if you are by my side."

I scratched my cheek.

"Do you think I should not go to my wedding feast?" Mahon said.

"You seek my counsel?"

"Úna is so certain I should go, I wonder if I should not stay back."

"Úna swears you will do what you will, no matter what anyone else thinks."

Mahon smiled. "You counsel me to go?"

"I counsel you to do what you will."

Mahon pulled on his beard. "Well then, I will go."

The abbot, his six bodyguards, Mahon, Áed, Murrough, and I gathered in the courtyard. My brother and his son were dressed like the bodyguards in full garb, their long hair stuffed up under helmets.

"Remember when you and Murrough cut your hair short and pretended to be peasants?" Mahon said. "I cannot wear my hair short for my wedding, but still, no one will know us."

I let out a long stream of air.

"Rory fetches Donobhan's grandsons now," he said. "Two grandsons for one granddaughter? A fair exchange."

"Eric and Stefan."

"Yes. They will meet us in the field."

Rory would not find them. They knew to hide.

"It is not too late to change your mind, Brian," Mahon said. "And Murrough can come after all, if he wants."

I shook my head. "It is best this way, Mahon."

He put his hands on my shoulders. "When I come back, we will feast, eh?"

My face burned. "We will."

Mahon and his troop strode down the steep path, past Cormac's stinking head to horses waiting down below. Murrough and I watched from the wall as Rory galloped back in from Eóghan's ringfort. We could not hear words, but we both knew he was saying Eric and Stefan were nowhere to be found. Mahon looked up at me, and I hunched my shoulders. I thought to wave him back in, but the moment flew by.

—Chapter Forty-Eight—

Five days into Mahon's journey to his wedding feast, I began a vigil on the wall. I came down only to piss, eat food, drink ale, and sleep in my bed at night. Úna darted about the fort, a spurned woman plotting revenge, raising armies. I imagined myself leaping out from behind a door and scaring her. But of course, I did not.

I was asleep in my house at dawn on the fourth day of my vigil when Rory rushed in through the door and called to me. "Prince Brian?"

"What?" He pushed aside the cowhide curtain, his face drained of all color. He nodded toward the door.

"Mahon?" I stood, pulling on my breeches and tunic. He shook his head, held the curtain back, waiting for me to pass. "Murrough?" Still no answer. I stepped around Rory, looked behind Murrough's curtain, and spied him in his bed. He opened his eyes, sat up.

"What?"

"I do not know. Rory cannot find words to tell me."

Murrough threw on his tunic and brat and we followed Rory to the top of the steep path, scanned the field. The day, mid-June, was dawning cloudless. I saw nothing strange.

Rory unpinned his brat and handed it to me. "Take this. You will see it. Down there." He pointed to the path bottom and stepped back into the courtyard.

I started down the steep path with Murrough, toward Cormac's head on its pole. Closer, the head turned to two. Mahon?

Another few steps forward and I saw the head was beardless and bald—not Mahon. An infant ... Brigit. I stopped my feet and thumped my chest, bidding my heart to beat.

"Brigit." The name caught in my throat.

"Pray no," Murrough said from behind me.

We made our way down, forced ourselves to look. Her eyes were open, her lips parted, her face gray. Brigit, but not Brigit.

I spied the brown mark on her cheek, choked and heaved.

"Molloy?" Murrough said.

I could not speak.

"Look." Murrough stepped behind the heads, picked up a long sword from the ground. He lifted it to his eyes. "Norse letters."

I took the sword from Murrough, squinting at runes carved into the blade, an animal head for a hilt. "Whoever did this wants us to believe he is a wealthy Norseman."

"Who?"

"I cannot say, but Ivar is back. You have readied Eric and Stefan?"

"Yes."

"Warn them again, and sixteen more men—the best. Bring them here. By noon."

A nod of his head and Murrough broke into a run across the field. I set down the sword and lifted Brigit's head—cold and hard—into Rory's brat. I wrapped it around her face, praying she had not suffered. Bundle in one arm, Viking sword in the other, I started back up the path. Úna came out the arched opening and stood staring, arms crossed.

"Brigit," I said, coming up close. "Norse, I fear." I lifted the sword to show her the runes, and held out the bundle. She kept her arms folded.

"Could you not have gone?" Her voice rang clear like a bell.

"No."

"You murdered her." She spat at my face, fled back into the courtyard.

Úna's spittle missed its mark and fell harmless at my feet. I clutched the bundle to my chest, pushing back the urge to shout she was to blame, leaving Brigit alone with the wet nurse. When at last I stepped into the courtyard, Rory stood waiting to help me, color back in his cheeks.

"Pray fetch the three-legged baking pot from the cook," I said, "and bring it to the church."

I woke the priest and set the bundle down on the altar. "Queen Úna's daughter, Father—Brigit. This Norse sword took her head." He went pale and crossed himself.

"Rory comes with a burial pot. I trust you will pray over Brigit and bury her in this graveyard. When I am able, I will carry the pot to Kincora, to our river chapel graveyard."

"The queen?" he said.

"She grieves."

"And you?"

"I will grieve alone." He nodded, crossed himself.

One last look at the bundle and I strode to my house. The Viking sword in my hand, I sat in my chair, my head in my hands, my heart heavy in my chest. Whoever took Brigit's head, and I believed he was Ivar, had challenged me with that sword. I would avenge Brigit against him, and then go for Molloy and Donobhan.

I bounced the sword in my hands, rubbed my finger over the dried blood, the sharp tip, grasped the handle with both hands, stood and swung the sword in a wide arc—scarce missing Murrough who came in without warning. His face was whiter than snow, his eyes wild, his breath short.

He stepped back out of the sword's reach. "What are you doing?" I readied to speak, but he paid me no heed. "Come. It is Áed. I found him half dead in the field." I dropped the Viking sword on the table and hastened after him.

Women in the sick house pulled off Áed's mud-caked clothes and gathered rags, bowls of water, poultice, bandages. Úna sat in a chair by her son's head, speaking softly. His gaze fixed on her face, he grimaced with every breath.

I kneeled across from Úna, catching her gaze, Murrough kneeling next to me. "Dead," Áed whispered. I looked up into Úna's stoic face.

"Brigit?" I said. Áed whispered something soft. I put my ear to his lips. "Again?"

"My father."

"Mahon?"

A nod. Murrough gasped. Úna shot me a look of pure hatred. I rose to my feet, spoke to a nursemaid. "Pray send for me when Prince Áed is able."

People had crowded into the courtyard on news of Áed. I climbed the ladder to the wall top. "The king is dead," I shouted. "Murdered." I waited for faces to settle, murmurs to quiet. I put my fist to my chest, raised my voice louder. "The murderers will forfeit life for their deed, else I will forfeit mine."

The sight of Murrough and you in the crowd, poet, gave me courage. "King Mahon gave his life for Munster. He will not have died in vain." Truth, poet, I did not know what my own words meant. For what did Mahon give his life? You fathomed my muddle, poet. Your smile was my reward.

Úna stepped out the sick house door with her handmaidens and mouthed "murderer" at me. I shrugged. Who would believe her?

—Chapter Forty-Nine—

Did Mahon know he was walking into a death trap? Did he think of me when they came for him? Had he truly plotted to kill me?

I prayed to wake from those thoughts, only to find I was awake. Nor could I escape Murrough's questions. Why had I not stopped Mahon from going? He would have. Was I not pained and wretched at Brigit's beheading? Mahon's murder?

I nodded and said I was pained and wretched at both. In our house, Murrough lifted the Viking sword and was bouncing it, feeling its sharp edges, fingering the dried blood and the sword tip, as I had done.

"This will do for me," he said. He stepped into his sleeping nook, came out with his old metal sword made for him as a youth.

"No murderer will run from this toy. But he will run from this." He picked up the Norse sword again, swung it around.

"They will, but it will be in my hands." I took it from him, carried it into my sleeping nook, put it next to my armor and other weapons. Bringing out my old sword, I held it out to Murrough. "This has served me well. It is yours, for now."

Murrough's face showed a kind of doubt I had not seen before, darker, more than a child's sulk. I prayed it was fleeting.

☩

I kept awake for fear of visions, but flashes of heads—Brigit's, Mahon's, the infant's at Limerick's, Órlaith's—tormented my mind.

In the morning, Murrough pushed back my cowhide curtain. "Úna says Áed can talk now."

"I am coming. No matter Úna."

We walked to the sick house, stepped through the door. Women bathed him, lifting his bandaged head, spooning broth into his mouth. His eyes were brighter than the day before, but his breaths still pained him. The women had wiped his body clean of blood, wrapped bandages around his girth, and rubbed poultice on his welts and in his cuts. I knelt close to Áed's head, Murrough across from me.

"It was an ambush." Áed grimaced. "We had no chance." He looked down at his ankles. "Shackles."

He squeezed his eyes and lips tight, forced out words. "They had Brigit at Donobhan's." Tears welled up and spilled out onto his cheeks. Soon sobs wracked his body. Úna reached over and wiped his face. "She knew us. Started screaming." Áed eyes went wild, his voice pleading for solace. Úna coverd her mouth with her hand.

"Who had Brigit?" I asked..

"A woman ... who looked like Ivar."

Beads of sweat dripped down Áed's cheek, mixing with tears. A nursemaid handed me a rag to wipe his face.

"Ivar took Brigit. He held her up to my father. 'This is for you, King Mahon. An eye for an eye.'"

A long pause, and then a bleating cry: "What did he mean?" Tears spilled out, and Áed panted for air.

"Ivar dropped Bridget on the ground and axed her head off. It happened so fast ..." Áed fell silent, his fist opening and closing, over and over.

Úna moaned and yielded to the nudging of a handmaiden. I leaned back, gripping my gut. Spent, Áed closed his eyes, a signal he could say no more.

Murrough and I stepped outside, climbed the wall again, a place to talk. "Whose eye for whose eye?" Murrough said.

"Ivar will tell us more when he is begging for mercy."

I climbed down the ladder, took myself to my house, and sat on my bed. A pillow by my hand, I pushed it into my face and wept.

A short time later, Murrough came to fetch me again. I pulled on a clean tunic, strapped my knife around my waist, and walked with my son back to the sick house. Neither of us mentioned my swollen eyes, my blotched face.

He and I knelt in our places around Áed's bed, but this time, Úna stayed away. "Donobhan's men unshackled us and marched us out the gate," Áed said, his voice steady. "They tied us to a long rope—all save Abbot Colum, who walked free behind us."

"With his gospel book and saint's ashes?" I whispered.

"No ... my father carried the abbot's pouch. I was behind him, but when I tried to talk, they beat me." He nodded to his cuts and bruises on his ankles and feet.

"They marched us until sundown, into a mountain gap—somewhere. Colum went off into the woods, and Molloy and his warriors came up on top of the ridge. My father tossed me the pouch and I fell down on top of it—just as something hard hit me in the back of my head and everything went black."

Pain came into my head hearing those words.

"When I woke, my ears were ringing and everything was spinning around. I could not see with the blood in my eyes.

When I dared wipe them, my father's body was an arm's length from me—headless." Áed let out a long, whining cry.

I pressed his hand. "Saint Finnian saved you. Your father's gift to you." Áed clutched my hand. We stayed like that for some moments.

"When next I woke, I was face down on a farmer's ox, tied on with a rope. He dropped me where you found me in the field." I had many questions I would save for later. Once again you have proved yourself brave, Áed," I said. I nodded to Murrough, no words needed.

⊕

Passing by Úna's open door, I slowed and looked in. She sat in a chair with her sewing.

"Have you words for Ivar or Donobhan?" I said through the open door. "Murrough and I will go for them first. Molloy can wait and stew."

She nodded. "You can thank them for Áed's life."

I took a moment. "Should I thank them for Brigit? Mahon?"

She shrugged. "You might have saved them both, had you gone."

I could not force my feet away. "If I had gone, I would not be here to avenge your husband and your daughter and your son. Mahon left me that gift." Úna picked up her sewing, lowered her gaze.

I had done what I must, and I would do what I must. Surely that thought had solaced Mahon, knowing the battles I would need fight. He would have his way, even in death.

PART SIX

—Chapter Fifty—

Eric and Stefan knew the way to Scattery Island. We were twenty men on horses, riding due southwest from Cashel over forested hills and mountains, down into valleys, around lakes and across streams and rivers into the rough territory of the Ciarraige.

The third day, we came to the Shannon River mouth, Scattery Island in sight. Wide stretches of mud and sand sloped down into the river, but we could find no fishermen's currachs to take us across to the island. We were setting up camp for the night when Murrough, Eric, and Stefan, my "scouts," raced in with news of driftwood in a nearby inlet. Dusk falling, we strapped logs together with vines and horses' bridles—five rafts for four men apiece.

Under a darkening sky, we pushed off into water churning from tide meeting river current. Close to the treeless, windswept island, we guided the rafts with our makeshift paddles into a rock-rimmed harbor. Two Norse warships floated amongst monks' currachs, ten rowing benches in each warship, five to a side.

Moving through tall grass, we set off roosting starlings into a waving, rushing cloud of twittering birds. I bade us still. But the birds settled and no bells rang out. Did Ivar not expect me?

My men stayed put while my scouts and I crept around the back of the low stone monastery wall. A guard dozed against it, sitting, his sword on the ground, his head drooped down. Eric and Stefan slipped out from bushes and slit his throat. His hand raised and fell, his legs jerked, but no sound came forth.

I hooted, my signal to attack. My orders were to kill only Norse, no monks, no abbot. Screams rang out from monks as my men shoved them out of their way. I took hold of a monk and put my knife to his throat.

"King Ivar? Where is he?"

No answer? I twisted the monk's arm behind his back and pushed his forehead against the church wall.

"The oratory," he gasped.

"Show me."

He pointed across a sheep field to a small, bug-like stone building, a round body with a smaller round head stuck on.

"Saint Sénan's bed," the monk said, crossing himself.

Murrough and I heard Ivar howling before we spied him kneeling on a flat stone slab inside the oratroy, his long gray hair wild in the dim light, his two hands pressed down on his head. Eric and Stefan were standing over him, swords raised.

Skum! Morder! Eric was shouting.

Coming in through the door, I yelled at Eric to stop. Ivar spewed out Norse gibberish—*Nei! Hvorfor er du her?*

Eric shouted back. "Why are we here? We come for your head." *Du betaler med hodet.*

"Show me your face, King Ivar." I opened a long, thin wound across the back of Ivar's hand pressed over his square-looking head. He gripped his bloody hand with his other and turned a desperate face to me.

285

"You escaped us once, Ivar," I muttered. "You will not again." My sword tip at his neck, I picked at the skin.

More Norse words. I understood only two—Mahon and Limerick.

"Speak Irish, Ivar."

"He waited nine years," Eric said. "Mahon's infant at Donobhan's for his infant at Limerick. An eye for an eye."

My steady hand shook. Ivar murdered Brigit in revenge for the infant I beheaded, but he had given the infant and my deed to Mahon. I dragged my sword tip from his neck to his chin, along his jaw line to his ear, drawing more blood.

"Look at me, King Ivar. I am Brian, King Mahon's brother. You murdered my infant. I murdered yours."

Ivar pressed his bleeding hand to his jaw. "You?"

I twisted my sword tip into flesh behind his ear. Blood dripped down the side of his neck.

"Me. Brian mac Cennétig."

His lips parted. "The runt."

I glanced at Murrough. "This pitiful king calls me a runt?"

Murrough lifted his sword, but I pushed his arm down. "He belongs to Eric and Stefan." I kicked Ivar backwards, his head finding the flat stone of Saint Sénan's grave.

Nei! he whimpered, clutching his head with both arms. Eric's spear found Ivar's heart, silencing his howling and mumbling. He body went limp.

I motioned to Murrough. "Help your friends carry this corpse to the abbot." I took one long last look at the man I had stalked one score years. The end of Ivar, but not the end of those pictures that tortured my sleep; not the end of avenging Mahon and Brigit; not the end of countless more battles I would need fight for a moment of peace on my island.

One foot out the door, I heard a scuffle behind me: Eric blocking Murrough. His sword aimed at Ivar's neck, I snatched it from his hand. "Behead a corpse? Shame. Your turn will come."

Gold rings, silver chalices, cups, jewels, all manner of booty piled up at my feet in the courtyard. I stood across from the pale, silent abbot, two of Ivar's sons' heads and Ivar's corpse at his feet. He crossed himself many times.

"You shelter Norse?" I said to him.

"Norse Christians."

"Indeed," I said. "Ivar did the Lord God's work—an eye for an eye, one infant for another. As do we—Ivar, for countless of our kin."

"Who are you?"

I paused, breathed deep. "You do not know me?"

"Your name?"

"Brian, son of Cennétig, brother to King Mahon. Remember me the next time you think of sheltering murderers."

The abbot slinked back two steps, clearly shocked. I ordered my men to set fire to all thatch in the monastery and the fields. We raced to the harbor as flames plumed to the sky.

"Saint Sénan, forgive me," I muttered.

We loaded sacks of booty into currachs, tied the small boats to the sterns of Ivar's warships and rowed hard away from the island, headed toward Corcu Bascind and Donal's dún on the far bank.

—Chapter Fifty-One—

Up the west side of the river, we rowed under low hanging trees into a harbor the size of a small lake. Donal and torch-bearing warriors lined the far shore. Hungry for food, praise, even awe from my friend, I pointed my oarsmen to a landing spot near him and jumped onto hard ground. He would be amazed when I told him Ivar and the abbot said they did not know me, and that Ivar called me a runt.

We kissed cheeks. "That was you at Scattery?" Donal said, no praise or awe in his voice.

"You have heard about Mahon?" I said. "And Brigit?"

"Yes."

"Then why the surprise? What did you expect from me?"

"I prayed the Haroldssons set those fires, not you. You killed Ivar?"

I hesitated. "He was hiding in the oratory. We killed him, two of his sons, and Norse guards, but no monks."

"You murdered Ivar in Saint Sénan's bed?" His voice rose in disbelief. "Every Christian in this kingdom will fault you for that."

I knotted up my face. "This is scarce the welcome I hoped from you."

Walking away, Donal nodded over his shoulder. "Come. My house is over there, behind the rise."

Murrough started after us, but I motioned him back. This talk would be between Donal and me.

Donal's servant, a young man named Henri, led us down a long winding path to the king's house and left us at the door. In no time he was back with a jug of red wine and two painted earthen-baked cups.

We sat in chairs at Donal's table, sipping in silence, waiting for Henri to light wood logs in the hearth. Many times he tried with flint and steel, but each time the spark sputtered out. His hair seemed long for a king's man, and the thought came to help him. But I copied Donal and waited.

I glanced around the room at clay pots on shelves, warrior figures clinging to their sides. Glass bowls the colors of the rainbow sat on other shelves and cups. Many tries later, Henri won his battle with flint and steel. He coaxed the flame to life with dry twigs, then bigger sticks and branches. Warmth flowed into the cold room. *Merci*, Donal said to Henri, who went out.

"My French is better than his Irish," Donal said. "We teach him boatbuilding, and his vintner father in Poitou sends us wine." Donal poured himself another cup of red wine.

"The bowls and the cups? From Poitou?"

"Rome. You know of Bobbio?"

"The famed library."

"My scholar brother at Inisfallen visits Bobbio often, but he is more tempted by painted glass from Rome than manuscripts from a library. I keep the cups and bowls safe from Norse thieves. As you see, I need more shelves."

I walked over to a bowl and lifted it to my eyes. "Ah, pray no, Prince Brian. My brother will blame me if you break that."

I set it down, sat back down in my chair. "Would Inisfallen deep in the mountains not be safer from Norse thieves than here? On the river?"

289

"Norse raiders could ruin my brother's precious annals at Inisfallen."

"Norse raiders could ruin you." Donal's words were making little sense to me.

"If I die before him," Donal said, "he will write my name and my deeds into the annals. I tend to my name now, while I am alive. Truth, Brian, for all the black deeds scribes could write by your name, be thankful you are not a king."

"Black deeds? I came for praise and warships, not to hear you recite my black deeds."

Donal poured himself a cup. "I have only begun. The whole kingdom suspects you for Mahon's murder. If not the deed, the plot. You said you would do what you must, and the next thing I hear is that Mahon marched into an ambush. What am I to think?"

"Think what you want." Truly, I was vexed. "When I am chosen king of Dal Cais, I will live out my life in peace, with Murrough and Sadb. No need for you to visit."

"No man who sullies a saint's bed will be chosen king of anything," Donal said. "Not in Munster. Not anywhere on this island."

The wine was loosening my tongue. "The Great Abbot is a seer and a sorcerer. He deems me the savior of our kingdom and our island."

Donal let out breath, shook his head. "Do not speak of the Great Abbot as a sorcerer, Brian. Úna and Áed have enough reasons to blacken your name."

Henri came in with a second full jug. I drained my cup and filled it with more. "I have no fear of Úna, a seed-coaxing schemer. What brains Áed ever had were axed by Molloy."

Donal shifted in his chair. "I will forget you ever spoke those words."

"Mahon deserved to die, and so did Ivar."

Donal sighed. "We kings cast long shadows, Brian. Your words will stay here with me, but others might not be so tight-lipped. My counsel? Keep your thoughts to yourself, and trust no one."

Donal reached for the jug, but my hand grabbed it first. "You are no druid, King Donal."

"True, I am a king."

"You are a king who guards cups and bowls and tends to his name. Meantime, I do what I must ... until I must no longer. That is the day I will feast."

My eyes closed, and my head wobbled. Donal stood and shook me. "Sleep there." He pointed to a cowhide curtain. "We will talk on the morrow." He guided me up with his hand.

✢

A storm raged in the night and made its way into my head. I had stolen Sadb from her cot at Tuamgraney, but a storm came and swept her away. She called for me, but I could not find her.

I woke blurry eyed to sun shining through my open window, a cool breeze blowing on my face. No matter my black deeds, I would step forth like a sleek buck and seek good air outside, savor the smells of salt from the sea, animal dung in the fields, and the fragrance of the summer flowers all mixed together in the sweet sunshine. And then, with the help of Donal's warships and warriors, I would go for Donobhan, but a short way upriver.

—Chapter Fifty-Two—

Five warships carried my one score men and thirty of Donal's to Donobhan's territory. The sun was down to the treetops by the time we pulled up on shore and dragged our warships into the trees. With my leave, my scouts went looking, but it was dark when they rushed back, breathless with news.

"The fortress is empty," Murrough said.

"You went in?"

"The gate is open," Eric said.

"The hall door is open," Stefan said. "We smelled roasting pork."

"We have a plan," Murrough said.

"Oh?" Since when did Murrough make my battle plans?

"It is a trick," Murrough said. "Donobhan no doubt hides outside, waiting to attack us on the bridge. We will go in first with half of our men and slam the gate shut. You and the rest will come behind Donobhan when he chases after us on the bridge. He will try to escape through the ditch, but it is pure muck.."

"Ah."

"We will cut them down like saplings." Eric's eyes glowed with excitement.

Murrough—tall, long haired, sharp-edged face, wide neck, arms and legs bulging with strength—looked and spoke like a seasoned general, certain of his words. Too certain.

"Donobhan will keep men back," I said. "And come after us on the bridge."

"You will keep men back, and come after them."

Murrough's idea was brazen, and his tongue quick. I could think of no better plan. But the next time Murrough tried to take command of my army, I would stand my ground.

All went as Murrough imagined. Donobhan and his men, half in Norse mail armor, rushed the bridge, too late to catch Murrough before he slammed the gate shut. I kept Donobhan himself in my sight and fought my way to him, his back to the shut gate. One thrust and I would have had him, had the gate not opened behind him. I glanced for an instant at Murrough's face at the gate, and the king escaped onto a narrow strip of ground between the fortress and ditch, sliding into the ditch's tall grass. I leapt after him, but met a large, sharp-edged rock hidden in the grass. A searing pain shot up my leg and I screamed and cursed, trying to drag my leg after a vanishing Donobhan.

⊕

I remember only brief moments awake in the boat bottom, hearing my own voice yelling in pain, other voices urging me to drink, hands holding my head still. Blessed ale touched my lips, and I swallowed it, slipped back into blackness.

I opened my eyes to see Murrough and Marc looking down at me, swimming in and out of sight.

"Ah, there you are. Thank the good Lord. We feared you had gone mad, raving on about Sadb."

I tried to shift my body, but could not. "Where am I?"

"The abbot's house," Marc said. "Holy Island."

"He is here?"

"The abbot? We buried him some months ago. Did you not know?"

"No.". I moaned with pain.

"You have a broken leg and a head wound," Marc said. "Nettles and water scorpions did the rest. In the ditch."

A fiery mountain rose up from my skull, but my shoulder pain would not let me touch it. Marc stepped out of sight.

"I had Donobhan in my sights," Murrough said, "when someone screamed you were wounded. By the time I got to you, they had dragged you into the trees."

My sight of Murrough steadied. "You rowed me here?"

"No, two of our men. You raved the whole way."

"Water scorpions?"

"Under your vest and down your pants."

I grimaced.

"Poultice will ease those stings, but your head wound and leg will take time." Marc, Eric, and Stefan appeared in my sight. Marc put ale to my lips, and I gave myself over to blackness once again.

I slept, woke, sipped broth, drank ale, pissed, and slept more, dreaming of the abbot naked in his house. When next I woke, Murrough and Marc hastened to my bed, eager to fill my ears with rumors of my black deeds. Murder, sacrilege, and one more Marc had heard from Eiden and Conaing at Kincora. They were loathe to tell me.

"What?" A lie, whatever it was.

"A rumor. That you will set Dàl Cais against Dal Cais. Your loyal clansmen against Áed's."

My wounds pained me so, I could not speak Úna's name, so clearly the source of that rumor. A spurned woman had more ways than armies to best their enemies: her words. But perhaps she did not thnk her plan through. Áed and I could both die in such a fight, Dal Cais against Dal Cais—a gift for Molloy.

I fell back asleep and dreamed of Sadb, full of wit, beauty, and love like her mother. The words were on my lips when I woke. "Pray, Marc, your monks can do double duty. Carry a message from me to Bórama, to my men who guard Donobhan's warships, now my fleet. On their way back, they can fetch Sadb. It is time."

"Sadb?" Marc said. "Must you burden yourself with a young girl? Now? With all your woes?"

No matter his naysaying, I would say those words again and again until he did my bidding.

—Chapter Fifty-Three—

When next I woke, feeling more myself, Marc stood over me with his arms crossed, a stick in his hand, and a twinkle in his eye.

"A stick for you, Brian. Try standing. My monks have come and gone. And our visitor."

"Sadb?"

"Pádraig, her foster father, Rónan's brother. He came to see for himself, and was well satisfied with what he saw, save for that gash in your head. I promised you would be up on your feet in no time."

"When?"

"In no time. Now. Sadb is here."

I lifted my head and glanced about, "On the strand, with your scouts. Shall I call her here? Or will you join them there?"

"She will stay the day?"

"The day? Did you not call for her?"

"To meet her. Scarce to keep her."

"She means to keep you, brother. My counsel? Take this stick and go, else you will lose her to your scouts. When I left them, they had only begun to boast about their victory at Donobhan's, how they beat back the king and his mail-clad warriors on their own, with you in a ditch. You would do well to thank your son for your life, now that you are able."

I would praise Murrough and thank him, but first, I had a daughter to meet. I sat up, felt myself able, and with Marc's help, raised to standing. The stick in my hand, I took one step and then another, imagining Sadb on the strand. My broken leg still bound to wood, I could not bend it, but with Marc by my side, I hobbled out the door and down the path, to a place where I could see the strand and my daughter. She and my scouts were sitting in a tight circle, and I paused to stare. All three scouts were talking and gesturing at the same time, and Sadb, a copy of her mother, smiled, laughed, squinted, frowned, seeming fixed on their every word.

I stepped out into the open, Marc behind to catch me if I fell. All four gazes turned toward me, startled. Sadb, full-bosomed and ruddy-cheeked, her golden hair wild in the wind, leapt up, shoes in hand, and skipped over to me.

"Shall I call you Prince Brian? Or Father?"

It had happened so fast, I could not decide.

"I will call you Father. The man who made me, not the man who raised me."

Ah, a challenge. "Shall I beg forgiveness now or later?"

Her smile lit up my heart. "Forgiveness? Why?" I did not know why. I took her hand and kissed it.

"Come," I said, forgetting I could scarce walk. "I will show you where Rónan and I pulled cows' teats together."

"If you wish, but can we sit and talk first, then look about."

"I know a place down there."

One slow step at a time, Sadb at my arm, we made our way around a bend to a weedy patch of ground between trees and water. A struggle to sit, I planted my stick, and lowered my bottom down, feigning no pain. We sat on the ends of my brat, some two arms' lengths apart.

"Women are not welcome at Holy Island," Sadb said. "Only pilgrim women. Brother Blat told me. Do you know him?"

"Yes—the monk who whipped me."

"He brought me gifts and news about you and my mother who died birthing me, and Murrough and Mahon and Úna and Áed. I could scarce wait for the day you would send for me. I cannot wait for what we will do next."

"Next?"

"Tonight. We will not stay here, will we?" We? I had not thought what I would do with Sadb, that day or any day.

She leaned back on her elbows and a plotting look on her face. "I am not a cow. You cannot trade me for anything you want more." She grinned, as if she had discovered my secret plan.

"No, but neither are you a warrior who can fight King Molloy."

Sadb's face crumpled in grief, and tears started in her eyes. "Pray do not say I cannot come with you."

"The dangers are too great."

She wiped her cheek and looked away, silent.

"What is that around your neck?"

Sadb turned back and lifted a pouch from the front of her tunic, the size of my thumb. "It is a gift for you. From Rónan. But you can only have it if you take me with you." She clutched the pouch as if I would snatch it from her.

"A bribe?"

"I did not mean it to be, but it is now." She moved off my brat onto the weeds, out of my reach.

"You tease me?"

"When you know what is in here, you will want me with you, no matter what." My heart's armor had sprung leaks.

"Turn around," she commanded. "Face the water."

I did her bidding. She leaned her back against mine. "Close your eyes." She paused. "When I rub Rónan's magic stone inside this pouch, a vision will come. You must not speak, or you will frighten Buí away."

"Buí?"

"Druid wife to Lugh." She sighed. "Need I teach you about Lugh? Or Buí?"

"No, you need not."

"I will rub the stone, and if Buí comes, I will whisper what she says. Do not speak." I stayed silent. "Shhh. She comes." My heart beat faster. "She speaks ... 'You will rule, Prince Brian, and Queen Gormlaith will rule. Over all the island.'"

"Queen Gormlaith?"

"Shhh ... You frightened Buí. She is gone."

Sadb put the pouch back under the front of her tunic and moved away again.

"You conjure prophesies?"

"The stone speaks, if you rub it the right way. Pádraig saved it for you."

"May I try?"

She held tight to the pouch. "If you promise to take me with you."

"How do you know of Queen Gormlaith?"

"From Buí."

I closed one eye, tilted my head. "Only Buí?"

She blushed. "Everyone knows of Queen Gormlaith. She is just right for you."

"Last I heard she was wed to the Norse King Olaf of Dublin and Northumbria."

Sadb frowned. "Buí will tell you more, if you take me with you. But she will tell you nothing if you try to take the stone without my leave. You cannot fool her. Or me."

No. I guessed I could not. "Well, then," I said, "You may come with me. But only if I can rub the stone."

A radiant smile shone forth from Sadb's face. "When the time is right."

—Chapter Fifty-Four—

Two fortnights later, my head and leg better, my four young counselors and I rowed in curraghs to Bórama, to my warriors guarding my fleet. They had awed Eiden and Conaing, rowing upriver through the rapids, and I bade them bring my fleet to Kincora's shore. I would awe my nephews again, at the very moment my counselors and I arrived to meet them and nine young chieftains, sons and nephews of those I had known at Mahon's councils.

Splendid in their bright-threaded tunics, carved leather headbands, and silver pins, the chieftains parted their lips in surprise when I presented my four counselors—Murrough, Eric, Stefan, and Sadb.

Conaing spoke their names: Conor, Eoin, Turlough, Darragh, Donncha, Callum, Oisín, Ceallaigh, and Fionn—all younger than me.

I was kissing their cheeks when my fleet pulled up on the river bank. Fearsome in their leather armor, my men started up the hill. "Those are my warships and warriors," I said, "and my men are hungry."

Eiden shook his head. "We have food, but not for so many. Scraps, perhaps?"

Sadb looked to me, wide eyed. "Scraps? Scraps are for pigs and chickens. Our men want more than scraps."

Eiden feigned not to hear. "I will bid the cook to bring the scraps here, to the hill."

"The hill? No man eats scraps on a hill," Sadb said, her voice raised higher. "No man I know. Cows, maybe. Sheep. But not men."

"Prince Brian?" Conaing said, vexed.

I pushed back my smile and looked to Sadb for an answer.

"We could take turns," she said. "A few at a time in the hall."

"Yes," I agreed, "we will take turns, a few at a time in the hall. And pray, nephews, no scraps."

The next morning, my men, well fed, rowed my fleet back to Bórama, and started their treks on horseback to Eóghan's farms, their homes. My counselors and I gathered in the council house with the chieftains.

"We do not believe the rumors, Prince Brian," Conaing said, "but Áed's loyal chieftains do. With Dal Cais divided, King Molloy will outnumber us ten to one."

Frowns, cheek scratching, and beard pulling started up all around the table. "It is so," I said. "Molloy will be the better for it if Áed and I fight each other. We will lose any battle we fight against Molloy, unless all Dal Cais come together against him."

More cheek scratching and throat clearing as the truth of my words settled in. "Is murder not a crime in Munster?" Sadb said. "My foster father says it is." Was that not Mór speaking? Through Sadb?

"To kill a man in battle is not murder," Murrough said.

"Did King Molloy kill King Mahon in battle?" Sadb said. Murrough flushed. "No."

"Then King Molloy is a lawbreaker." Sadb said.

"Yes," I said, "but Molloy bends only to his own laws."

"But do law-breaking murderers not pay heavy fines?" Sadb said, firm in her purpose.

"Fines so heavy they would beggar Molloy," I said. "He will not pay. But bickering back and forth could buy me precious time to bring all Dal Cais together. What does everyone say?"

My words rang so true, no one could say anything.

I chose Corccarán, younger brother to a chieftain, to carry my message to Molloy at Rath Rathlainn, It was simple; I would hold back from battle if Molloy would pay a fine—five herds of bulls, milk cows, and calves, ten ounces of gold, and twenty crates of red wine from a vintner in Poitou, France. An answer of no would mean war.

A fortnight in, the guard announced Corccarán. From the wall, I studied his face—a trick I learned from you, poet. Good or bad, news sits better in a man's gut if it is tasted before it is chewed.

To my surprise, my messenger was not alone. Beside him rode a long-haired chieftain with bright blues and reds in his tunic and breeches, fine leather boots laced up to his calves, spiral and circle carvings on his sword sheath. Not Molloy, but who?

"King Molloy will pay no fine," Corccarán said. "He scoffed when I told him your message. Prince Cian here will tell you more." Cian—Molloy's son.

"My father begs for more time." Cian said, staring at my counselors next to me. "Can we speak alone, Prince Brian?"

"Yes, but know that I will tell my counselors every word you and I speak alone."

"As you wish."

"Queen Úna promised my father your head on a stake," Cian said, the moment we sat down.

Such nonsense, I smiled. "Queen Úna will take my head?"

"From your corpse. When you die in battle against your own clansmen, Prince Áed's Dal Cais."

I took a moment. "Your father is a fool to think I would fight my own clansmen."

Cian blushed. "He no longer thinks that. Your message swayed him. Indeed, he welcomes pitched battle to end all battles against Dal Cais. Skirmishes and raids could go on forever."

"He will lose pitched battle against me," I said, hoping to put fear in Molloy's son.

Cian shook his head. "One thousand or more Eóganachta could take the field. Have you that many? My father doubts it."

I cursed under my breath, knowing we did not. "Pray tell your father I do not trust him. He killed my best spy, stole my son, ambushed and killed my brother, and schemed with Donobhan and Ivar to behead an infant. Would you trust such a man?"

"I cannot speak those words to him. He will take my head."

"A pity for such a fair head." I paused. "I will agree to more time, if he will agree to one year and six months."

Save for the lift to his lip when he spoke, Cian looked nothing like Molloy. He frowned. "I cannot ask for so much time. I am but one year out of fosterage."

"He will suspect you of treachery?"

Cian wrinkled his nose. "No. How could that be?"

"I do not know, but perhaps you will find a way to please us both."

The next morning, Cian stepped into the horse pen, readying to mount his horse for home. Sadb hastened in after him, a halter and yew rod behind her back. With her free hand, she held out hay to a horse, and murmured soft words as he swept the straw into his mouth with his giant top lip. In one swift move, she slipped the halter's two bands across the horse's face, his forehead and nose, fixed the bit between his teeth, and tossed the single rein between his ears. Her left foot up on the horse's front knee, she took hold of the mane and was pulling herself up when Cian reached out and gave her a push on her bottom, stirring a loud shriek. Up on the horse's back, with the rod against his face, she wheeled the horse around and out the pen gate.

"Race me if you dare, Prince Cian," she called behind her.

Cian stared, seeming struck by lightning.

"Coward," Sadb shouted back.

"Coward?" he muttered.

He leapt onto his horse and galloped after Sadb. Hooves pounded down the hill, mixed with shouts and laughter. I hastened to wall top and stood behind a post. At the river, Sadb was far ahead of Cian. The two passed each other, he going down, she going back up. Through the gate into the courtyard, she pulled her horse to a stop, swept her honey gold flecked hair back and tied it in a knot on top of her head. A smile covered Cian's face when he rode back in.

"Again?" he said.

"Next time," she answered. "When you come back?"

"Ah," he said. "Yes. When I come back."

—Chapter Fifty-Five—

Winter come, Cian came back in with Molloy's answer. He would agree to one year and six months if I would agree to pitched battle at Belach Lechta, a field in the mountains near his dún, where slabs of granite marked old graves of his ancestors fallen in battle.

My reply? "We will scout Belach Lechta. Then I will give my answer."

Cian was slow in leaving, swearing his horse did not do well in cold and wet. But the weather was not so harsh as to stop him racing Sadb, over and over again, each time losing.

"Try a different horse," I said, taking pity on the prince.

He had tried different horses, but still Sadb came out ahead.

"Just one more race," he begged her.

"One more," Sadb said with her plotting face.

My brat wrapped tight against the wind, I watched their horses stay even with each other to the river. Their race would be close, coming back up through the fortress gate. Yet they did not turn back up, but started off down the river path and vanished from sight.

Ah ... so.

That same visit, I heard Cian speaking with Murrough outside my house. I stepped out to join them, taking but a few moments to pin my brat and pull on boots, but they were gone halfway down the hill by the time I stepped out. Their heads bent together, that was the first of many walks Cian and

Murrough took together at Kincora. I imagined Murrough envied Sadb's time with Cian, and wanted some for himself.

✠

Eiden and Conaing, at my bidding, visited Eóghan, and came back with news his men were eager to fight for me again. But Dal Cais chieftains loyal to Áed still came and went from Cashel. Their leader, a chieftain named Tadgh, had cobbled together an army to fight me, of how many warriors, no one knew.

Eric, Stefan, and Murrough scouted Belach Lechta, as good a place as any for a pitched battle, they said. A nearby lake would be well suited for my army's gathering spot. But I saw no reason to hasten, what with Dal Cais still divided. The year and six months passed by, and Cian warned his father was losing patience. He visited often, and each time vanished with Sadb, no longer bothering to race her to the river, or she to tease him. I was growing fond of Molloy's son, whose spirit and love for my golden-haired daughter put me in mind of myself and Mór. And on those visits, Murrough and Cian kept up their walks, but what they said to each other, I did not know or ask.

✠

Summer in the year of our Lord, 976, Cian and I decided a day for the battle to begin in one week. Without glancing Sadb's way, he mounted his steed and galloped away. I had hoped he would pledge himself to me, but when the moment came, he chose his father. I was no stranger to betrayal, and I could see it in the set of my daughter's jaw, and the flick of her wrist. She hurled the silver pin Cian had give her to the ground.

I messaged Donal and all Dal Cais chieftains, loyal to me or not, to meet at the lake one day before our battle time. Their choice to join my army or not, the message said, would decide their fates and their sons' fates for years to come.

Murrough and I set out for the lake alone, one day early. When the path widened and we could ride side by side, Murrough swore the battle would begin with single combat. Molloy would choose his best warrior, and he, Murrough, would be ours. He was not asking; he was telling me. Our victory against Donobhan, had gone to his head.

Pitched battles often did begin with single combat, I agreed, but this battle would not. He was the best of my warriors, but the battle itself would be danger enough.

We reached the lake at sunset, its wide flat shore edged all around by mountain forest, a sight of beauty. We tied our horses to trees, and walked to a dry spot to fill our stomachs with food and drink from our pouches.

We were there but little time when a voice called my name from the lake's far side. Two men, strangers to me, stepped out from the trees, not more than ten paces from our horses. We had been careless wandering far away from our weapons. Molloy's men?

But no. As they came closer, the two men dropped their weapons and stopped a safe distance from us.

"I am Tadgh," one said, "and this is Aengus, my manservant. Forgive my dull mind, Prince Brian—I did believe Queen Úna's lies, and when your message came I feared you meant to ambush us here at this lake. But my scouts have rid me of that worry. King Molloy does indeed ready for a pitched battle at Belach Lechta. The chieftains and warriors I command will be here on the morrow, ready to fight with their fellow Dal Cais, as one."

Such relief swept through me, I could scarce speak. "How many?"

"Hundreds."

"And you, Tadgh, will be their general."

Tadgh's his face lit up in a smile. "I feared your wrath, Prince Brian, but instead, you reward me. I will show myself worthy. I swear."

Midafternoon the next day, Eiden, Conaing, Donal, Eric, and Stefan, rode in with warriors. To each one, and to Murrough once more, I gave the same command; the battle would begin at dawn the next day, not with single combat, but in the manner we would agree together at dusk, in a clearing I had found in the trees. Murrough knew the place and would lead them there.

At dusk, I took myself to the clearing and waited. But by nightfall, I was still alone. I made my way to fires lit on the shore, and to my shock, spied my generals sitting with their heads together, Murrough talking. I crept up behind in silence. Moments went by before Eric noticed me.

"Prince Brian!" Heads shot up.

"We searched for you," Murrough said.

I doubted that. "You are talking without me?" Not one spoke. "Well?" I said, staring at Murrough.

"Well, now that you are here, I will tell you. The battle will open at dawn with single combat, between Cian and me."

My son, betraying me? "Need I say it again? No single combat. The Cian I know would not agree to his death, fighting you."

"It will be a draw," Murrough said.

"You cannot know that."

"If Cian does not keep his word," Murrough said, "he will pay for it with his life."

"A draw? Then what?"

"Warriors in Molloy's army will do Cian's bidding, when he bids them."

I shifted my gaze from one general to the other. One by one they looked away. Clearly, Murrough's plot with Cian had gone far beyond single combat.

"Molloy will smell traitors in his army."

No use speaking. Their minds were decided. Men nearby on the strand turned their heads and strained to listen.

"We pray you will stay back from battle, Prince Brian," Eric said. "We can fight, but only you can rule our kingdom."

Stay back? Wind picked up over the lake water. I rubbed my eyes, seeing seven treacherous Mahon's before me, not one challenging Murrough.

"It is not what you think," Murrough said. "But the plan is made and we cannot change it now. If you show yourself on the battlefield, all will be lost."

"Pitched battle is not like a cow raid," I said. "There are rules to follow."

"Cian and I have agreed rules, and I will trust him until I do not."

"I will stay back with you, Brian," Conaing said.

"Staying back will take more courage than fighting," Eric said. I sighed in defeat. They were all agreed, and I could scarce fight a battle without generals.

"Whatever the plan, Murrough, it had better be good."

☩

I stayed awake all night, my mind going in circles. My son, a traitor? Eric and Stefan? Donal? Cian? All traitors?

At dawn I stood amongst our men on the shore and bade them follow Murrough. He would command them. Quizzical looks broke out on faces, but I showed no doubt or fear.

Murrough shouted words, and he and my men marched off toward Belach Lechta. Conaing and I followed to a path leading to Cashel. We would spend the day moving horses from the lake to a spot down that path, to carry ourselves and our wounded at battle's end. A good plan, but one I could not follow. My first glimpse of the battlefield struck such fear in me, I bade Conaing go on without me.

I perched in a tree at the edge of the field. If Murrough and Cian fought in single combat, their fight was over, and the front lines of the two armies were clashing, men behind them moving forward to fill in for their dead and wounded. Murrough nowhere in sight, I imagined him wounded and calling for me. Nor did I see Cian or Molloy. Conaing passed by many times on his circuit, but I stayed hidden in my perch.

The fighting went on all day, but it was not until dusk that I came to my senses. A huge rear flank of Molloy's army waited to move forward, but we had no rear flank, all our men either dead, wounded, or fighting—a slaughter in the making. I slid down from my perch, and hastened to a hillock at the entrance to the field. My hands cupped around my mouth, ready to shout retreat, when the rear flank of Molloy's army turned and ran from the field.

I hid in scrub, nursing shame and fear. I had not trusted my son. No doubt he was dead. Conaing's voice sounded on the path, and I hastened to meet him.

"Eiden is killed," he said, his voice breaking. "And Tadgh."

"Murrough?"

"I said Eiden and Tadgh."

I looked over Conaing's shoulder to Eric and Stefan coming up to us, their pale yellow heads looking like moons, Stefan's hand was thrust up under his jaw, blood oozing between his fingers.

"It is over," Eric said. "They have fled."

"Murrough?"

"I do not know. We lost Eiden and Tadgh."

"Donal?"

"Alive." I pushed past Conaing, Eric, and Stefan, and started toward the field.

"Take care," Eric shouted. "Those bodies can rise up and kill you."

My head down, I butted my way to the field, through moaning and limping warriors all struggling toward the horse gathering place.

Pale moonlight shone on bodies, enough for me to see faces. I picked my way through, calling Murrough's name, but no. More than once, a voice called my name, and I hastened toward it, but still no Murrough or Cian.

A flat empty stone caught my eye. I sat on it, pulling my brat over my head, hiding from the sights and stench. Those same visions of Murrough came back to mind—wounded, beheaded, alive, calling for me. His voice spoke my name as if he was standing next to me, bidding me to look. He touched my shoulder.

"I am here," his voice said into my ear.

A hand ripped my brat off my head. I opened my eyes to Molloy hanging from Murrough's hand, his two different-colored eyes bulging wide open. I looked up into my son's face, and tears overflowed onto my cheeks. I stood and hugged Murrough. He was no vision, and neither was Molloy.

We sat side by side on the stone, Molloy's head hanging between us. I forced myself to look at the gray face pointing up at me, hair and beard matted with blood.

"I was looking for you," I said.

"I saw you picking around out there. Did you see Cian?"

"No."

"Then perhaps he lives. He saved us, you know."

"Yes."

The moon cast an eerie glow on Molloy's head. Murrough's lips curled up in a smile. "Cian told me where to look for Molloy. Once he came, the rest was easy."

"Easy how?"

"He was leaning against a tree. You should have seen his face when I came upon him."

"I see it well enough now."

I stood and lay my brat flat on the ground. Murrough dropped the head into the middle and tied up the ends into a sack. We sat back down, set the head between us again.

"Promise you will not scheme behind my back again?" I said.

"Your heart was not in the fight ... not in any fight, as you have sworn many times." Murrough glanced at me. "I thought you would praise Cian and me for our cunning."

"You showed much cunning. But all the kingdom will know I stayed back— another reason I will be deemed unfit for the overkingship, We won this time, but from now on, I will command my armies."

Murrough gazed across the field. "We feared you would call a retreat at the worse time. Would you have?"

I hesitated. "Indeed, I was one moment away from doing just that." I stood and reached for the sack. Murrough put out his arm out to stop me.

"I must look for Cian."

Murrough walked out amidst the dead and dying men, calling Cian's name, but for nought. He came back frowning.

I handed him the sack. "You take it, but I will carry it into Cashel."

"Yes, of course." Murrough hefted the sack over his shoulder and followed me from the field, stepping around bodies and heads, my eyes blurred with wet.

PART SEVEN

—Chapter Fifty-Six—

At the horse gathering place, we tended to our wounded, wiped blood and grime from our bodies in a cold mountain stream, and started back to Cashel—a long, slow, trek. Murrough took the lead, the dripping sack tied to his horse's mane. Mountain people stared from the woods and raced off to tell their neighbors. Word of our victory would reach Cashel long before we straggled in, and surely all the fortress, save Úna and Áed, would greet me as Munster's future overking.

The day was old when we rode into the field below the fortress. A horn blew, and a lone man appeared on the wall, rust-colored hair hanging to his shoulders, dark against his bright red brat.

Mahon? A shock ran through me at my mistake: not Mahon, but Áed, with Úna close behind, a peahen next to a peacock. I had not known Cashel without my brother. Life without Mahon.

"Why do we wait?" Murrough said.

"For a friendly face." It was my turn to take charge, and I needed time to ready myself for my new role.

More people appeared on the wall, among them six old men—bent, with long gray hair blowing in the breeze, their many-colored brats speaking of high rank. I could not think who they were or why they were at Cashel.

Rory loped down the steep path, stopped in front of us. We slid off our horses, and Murrough untied the stinking sack from his horse's mane, lowered it to the ground. Rory pinched his nose shut from the stench.

"King Molloy," I said, nodding at the sack.

"He will do you well with the elders," Rory panted, out of breath.

"Elders from where? Why?"

"I do not know from where, but they are here to choose our next overking."

"Who sent them?"

"Emly came in with them, at the behest of the Great Abbot." Rory said.

"The choice is made," Murrough said. "There is no choice."

I spat. "Áed is a choice, and he has no black deeds tied to his name."

Rory's cheeks flushed red. "Pray, Prince Brian. I did not mean to anger you. Only to warn the elders will be wanting words with you."

"Emly is here?" I asked.

"No," Rory answered. "He came with the elders and left."

"The Great Abbot?"

"No."

"Brother Marc and Sadb?"

"No."

"Any word?"

"Not that I have heard."

"King Donal?"

Rory's face brightened. "Word came only this morning that he nurses wounds, but he will come if you need him, when he is healed."

"If I need him?" Did Donal not know I needed a friend?

I picked up the sack and held it out to Murrough. "You carry it in. You took it."

He glanced up at many more people standing on the fortress wall, and thrust the sack back at me. "No, you. People are watching."

I let it fall to the ground. "My heart tells me not."

"Let me," Rory said, lifting the sack from the ground. "It is good air you are both needing." I shrugged. Better air would never heal my heart or cure my gloom.

Up the steep path, we came through the arched opening to silence. Áed stood straight and tall, with Mahon's kingly red brat thrown over his shoulders. I did not see Úna. Others from the fortress stood around, watching.

"Dump it," I commanded Rory. "There." I pointed at the ground in front of Áed's feet.

"I dare not." He set the sack down.

"I will do it," Murrough said.

"No, I will." I picked up the sack and stepped close to Áed. "King Molloy is in here, Áed, would you like to see him?"

I half opened the sack to dump the head, but instead I set it down by his feet and nodded Murrough toward our house.

I had gone but a few steps when gasps sounded all around me. I turned to see the misshapen, oozing head poured out on the ground, Áed swiping his hands on his tunic. Maggots crawled from the eye socket.

Áed kicked the head across the courtyard dirt. "Bury it," he commanded Rory. "In the rubbish heap."

Murrough and I kept going, but the elders blocked our way.
"Emly called you here?" I asked. "The Great Abbot?"

"Yes," a big-chested elder said, "and from what we have just seen, we are needed."

"May we pass?"

"You may, but we mean to hear your case, Prince Brian. You, and all who claim rights to the overkingship, Dal Cais and Eóganachta."

I tried once more, but once more they blocked me. "We have come a long way, Prince Brian," Big-Chested said. "Surely you will not deny us?"

"Need I unsheathe my sword?" I said.

"Not if you hope to sway us."

"My hope is to pass by you."

Big-Chested shrugged. "Tonight, we will meet with Prince Áed. On the morrow, with you, and your son, Murrough, and the next day with your nephews and cousins. The day after that, with Eóganachta—kin to Callaghan, kin to Molloy ..."

I closed my ears to his words, spied an opening between the elders and took it. Murrough loped along behind me as we hastened to our house, praying it still stood after two years away.

Weary to the bone, I spread my brat before the cold hearth and lay down, my arms behind my head. Murrough pulled up a stool.

"Áed called us liars and cowards."

"Yes."

"I could have struck him down."

"Just what he wants," I said. "More cause to blacken my name."

"No matter ... those old men will choose you over him."

"I will not put myself forward for the overkingship."

A long pause. "What did you say?"

"Nothing I do is enough, or will ever be. Áed is Mahon's son and he will rule Munster like an Irish king, with the sword, the kind Munster wants."

"Munster does not want another Mahon. Munster wants you. Emly and the Great Abbot at Armagh want you."

"Oh? I have done what I must and now I must make my case to elders? Emly and the Great Abbot betrayed me, like everyone else in my life."

"Then I will put myself forward. They want to hear my case." Hurt and anger rang out in Murrough's voice.

"They will not choose the son of a prince over the son of a martyred overking. Cian might have spoken well of you, but he is likely dead."

Murrough spat onto the mud floor. "Naysayer." I breathed relief at the sound of his footsteps fading away.

I was still lying on my brat when you came in, poet.

"Forgive me," you said. "I have brought you food and drink. Rory comes behind me with fresh turf and new bedding."

You set down a cup of ale, bread, and a bowl of beef. I had not eaten since before Belach Lechta. The mere smell of food turned me to a ravenous animal.

When I had downed it all, you said, "I have readied fresh calfskins and a pot of ink for your tale."

"I will bury my tale. It shames me."

"Not my calfskins."

"My words."

"On my calfskins."

I was of no mind to play games with you, poet. "Those old men ... Emly called them here? At the Great Abbot's urging?"

"Yes."

"When my turn comes," I said, "I will counsel them to choose Áed."

A sigh? What use were you, poet? I wanted to hear shock in your voice.

"But no, a sigh. Did the Great Abbot not counsel you to do what you must? I wrote those words on calfskin."

"I have done what I must, and he betrays me, calling in elders. Áed is fit. Úna and all of Munster believe so."

I could hear the hesitation in your voice when you next spoke. "Beware the hawk, Brian."

"What hawk?"

"The hawk that ate the wren who flew high on the eagle's back, the king of the birds. Need I say more?"

"If you want me to fathom you."

"An old tale, Brian. You would do well to heed it."

An urge came up to swipe the wart from your nose, poet. I knew the tale, and I knew what you meant. But I was of no mind to hear you.

"No worries, Mac Liag," I whispered. "I will be wary of hawks."

We sat in bleak silence. A long time went by, with you deciding to speak or not. You could not help yourself. "One last lesson, Brian. Had the wren not insulted the owl, the wise old bird might have judged the wren the winner, king of the birds. But as it was, the wren hopped off in fury onto the forest floor, easy prey for the hawk."

I yawned, and you had the good sense to leave. All night, I drifted in and out of sleep, and when morning came, I thought to seek a better place to think alone. Not the wall, the church, the round tower, the hall. Then where?

—Chapter Fifty-Seven—

The graveyard. A grassy space with flat stone slabs and stone Celtic crosses remembering Eóganacht Munster overkings from centuries past. A path led from the church back door to a rusted metal gate in the graveyard's low stone wall. No one would stumble upon me there by chance. A long bench stretched along the back wall of the church and I headed toward it, the quiet broken only by a bird singing from the branch of a white-barked tree in the graveyard center.

Laying down on the bench, I caught sight of a dirt mound topped with hairy-leaved purple flowers, wilting with age. I guessed Brigit's head was buried there, still in its three-legged bread-baking kettle. I would carry the kettle to Kincora, to the river chapel graveyard there, but then what? Bobbio near Rome? I could not picture Murrough there. A farm? My time at Eóghan's had solaced me, but a lifetime of farming? Murrough and I were both too old to become novice monks. And what of Sadb? She yearned to live the life of a princess, as she was meant to be. I had no plan that would please me or either of my two children, no glimmer of a plan.

Footsteps? I cursed under my breath. The graveyard gate creaked open and shut. I stayed flat on my bench, praying not to be seen. From the corner of my eye, I spied a woman glide up to Brigit's grave, a hood pulled over her graying hair: Úna, with fresh purple flowers in her hand.

She kneeled and put the new flowers in place of the old, then crossed herself. I closed my eyes, scarce breathing, hearing only muffled whispers. A long silence told me I had been seen.

"You? Sleeping?"

I sat up. "I prayed not to be seen."

"Why are you here?" She stood as if guarding Brigit's mound, her feet apart.

"I swore I would carry Brigit's kettle to Kincora. I will keep my vow."

Úna stared at me. "When?"

I expected snarling, not a simple question. "So innocent, Queen Úna? I know the hateful rumors you have spewed about me."

Úna fiddled with the limp flowers in her fingers, then lifted her head, a tiny smile on her lips. "What mother would not scheme for her son? But I will no more."

She stepped closer, leaning up against the white bark tree trunk. "Áed is healed from his wounds. You saw him. He tells me he does not need me anymore. Indeed, the elders must not see him weak and guided by his mother."

"You have poisoned the elders against me."

Úna's face softened into wistfulness. "I did try, and the list is long of your grievous deeds. Sacrilege, cuckolding, plotting your brother's downfall. But even so, it seems the elders wish to hear from you."

A pitiful sight, Úna leaning against a tree, gripping limp flowers, confessing failed schemes to undo me. "I will share a confidence with you, Prince Brian." A lift started in her voice. "I am glad, indeed relieved, the elders have come to decide the overkinngship. Had they not, the new path I have chosen would not have opened up to me. It brings me much cheer."

"Oh?"

"I will take myself to Clonmacnoise, to a house for hermit women who choose to live alone, down the lane from the monastery and blessedly out of sight of the monks. My brother, Connor, protects that monastery, and the abbot has agreed to let me stay. I am widowed, of an age not to marry again, and sister to the most powerful king in Connacht. It is my right to live at Clonmacnoise, and I shall." Her face lit up in a smile.

"You will become a nun?"

Úna snorted. "No. I could, but I choose not. I will do as I please. For the first time in my life, I will heed no man's bidding."

She sat down on the far end of the bench from me, set the purple flowers between us. I cursed the envy rising in me. I too wished for a house down a lane from a monastery where I could do as I pleased.

"You know Clonmacnoise?" she asked.

"I know of it—from Mahon."

"The River Shannon at Clonmacnoise spreads out into shallow grassy marshes with water so clear the fish and the pebbles are in plain view. The birds' songs and nuns' voices mix together in in a chorus of angels. I will sing with the birds and the nuns when I am not drawing or firing my pots."

"Will you be singing when Áed hosts against Clonmacnoise?"

She smiled. "Áed can take his silver chalices and jewelry. I will have no use for them, nor will he worry me."

I studied Úna's face as she spoke. "No more husbands, Queen Úna?"

"I have said. I will not wed again. I only pray you will take Brigit to Kincora. She did not deserve her fate, nor should she spend eternity in the company of old Eóganacht kings. When will you?"

I hesitated. "After I tell those old men I will not contest the overkingship. Indeed, you may tell Áed he can ready for his enkinging feast. All that is left for me is to imagine a good life for myself, as you have done for yourself."

Úna narrowed her eyes at me. "Now who plots and schemes?"

"Áed will make the better overking, following in Mahon's footsteps."

"Áed will seek revenge against you, first thing, if he is chosen overking. He blames you for Mahon's death."

"Revenge is the way of all Irish kings. But he will not find me. I will hide myself, on the far side of revenge."

Úna sighed. "My brothers' warriors will be here on the morrow to escort me to Clonmacnoise. You will not see me again."

"Truly? I envy you."

Úna picked up the wilted flowers from the bench and held them out to me. "These will keep you in mind of Brigit … and me."

I took the flowers, watched Úna slip out the graveyard gate. A sadness came I did not expect or welcome. I stuck a wilted flower behind my ear and lay back on the bench.

Not a moment more went by before I heard the sound of many footsteps. I made haste over the low stone wall, knelt down behind it.

"Brian?" Marc's voice?

"Father?" Sadb's voice.

"He was here moments ago." Úna's voice.

I stayed down. More footsteps strode into the graveyard.

"Marc. Sadb. You are here." Murrough's voice, excited.

"Have you seen your father?" Úna said.

"No."

The footsteps and voices faded. I stood and brushed leaves from my tunic. Dread came over me, knowing I would need tell Sadb she would never be a princess daughter to a king, and that surely Prince Cian was dead.

"I knew you were hiding!" Sadb's voice.

All the blood in my body rushed into my face, as Sadb stepped out from behind a monument, grinning.

"It seems I am found," I said.

We looked at each other and laughed. We sat on the bench together, I, with the flower behind my ear, and she with the pouch holding Rónan's flat stone around her neck.

"I came here to craft words to the elders," I said.

"They will choose you over anyone."

"But I have something to tell you," we both said at the same time. We laughed again.

One after the other, Murrough, Marc, and Úna came out from the church, stepping through the graveyard gate.

"You would make a liar of me, Brian," Úna said. "Here, and then not?"

"He was hiding," Sadb said. "I have forgiven him already."

"Hiding from what?" Marc said.

"In a graveyard?" Murrough said.

I meant to answer, but my gaze fell on Sadb rubbing her hand across letters carved into a monument base.

"Callaghan," she said. "Did he not die from lightning strike? My grandfather's murderer?"

"Yes." I said. I had told Sadb many things, but not that I may have spawned an infant with Úna. She was one grave away from Brigit's mound, and I struggled to think what I would say, with Úna standing silent right there.

325

"Where is King Molloy's grave?" Sadb asked. "Is he not buried here?"

"King Molloy's head is in the rubbish heap," I said, "where he belongs. Come ... we will find him."

Sadb pried my hand off her arm. "The stones in this graveyard cover Prince Cian's ancestors. I would see them all."

Sadb moved to the next cross, muttered the name, then almost tripped over Brigit's mound with the fresh purple flowers on top.

"And this?" Sadb said. "Why the tiny mound? For a Munster overking? I see no name." I shot a quick glance at Úna, her gaze fixed on Sadb looking at the purple flowers.

"That flower behind your ear," Sadb said to me, "is the same as these."

"It is indeed," Úna said, stepping over to Sadb. "My infant daughter Brigit is buried under this mound—your father's namesake." She tugged on Sadb's elbow. "Come, I will tell you all about Brigit, and your mother too. I knew her well. Shall we leave these men to themselves?"

Sadb's gaze found me, questioning. "I made a promise to Queen Úna," I said. "These flowers keep me in mind of it." I took the flower from behind my ear. "In return, she has sworn to speak no more of my grievous deeds. Is that not so, Queen Úna?"

"I believe it is," Úna said.

"Well then, Sadb," I said, "surely you will want to hear Queen Úna's memories of your mother. You and I will talk later."

"Yes, I do ... and we will."

Sadb followed Úna out the gate. Murrough started after them, but I shook my head at him. "Leave them be."

"Why?"

"Woman to woman. Better that way."

In the distance, I could hear Úna's voice. "Your mother was a Connacht princess. I knew her even before your father came down from those hills ..."

Murrough frowned hard at me. "One of us must save Sadb from Úna. And one of us must keep watch on Áed. He meets with the elders again, this day." He turned on his heel and slammed through the rusty gate.

Left alone with Marc, I told him of Úna's plan. "I envy her," I said.

"You have chosen a different path, brother. You will have little peace as Munster overking."

"I will not seek the overkingship."

"Not seek it? Why?"

"I will not follow our ten brothers to the grave, in needless battles. Perhaps you have forgotten your counsel to me at Holy Island? I should have followed it."

Marc frowned. "Did you not pledge Munster to the Great Abbot? I carried that pledge to him myself, in the cold and wet."

"Mahon's pledge. It does not bind me. No brithem would say it does."

"The Great Abbot deemed you honest, Brian. You would prove him wrong?"

"The Great Abbot betrays me."

"Did Murrough and Prince Cian not risk their lives for you at Belach Lechta?"

"They did, and it pains me Cian died doing it."

Marc tilted his head. "Died? He is very much alive. Sadb and I have been with him these last days at Emly."

I stared at Marc. "If you lie, brother, I will take your head."

"I do not lie. Have I ever?"

Truth, I could not think when he had. "Cian is well?"

"Yes."

Our gazes shifted to the gate—Murrough coming back through it. "Áed is out from the elders. Your turn is next."

"I have good news for you, Murrough," I said. "Cian lives and is well at Emly. Marc and Sadb have been with him there."

A huge smile broke out on Murrough's face. "True?" Marc nodded. "Why is he not here?"

"He sends word he will come when your father is chosen overking and Áed is well away."

Murrough looked from Marc to me and back. "Did my father not tell you? He will not seek the overkingship."

"He did tell me, but I pray he will change his mind."

Murrough sat on the bench with us. "The elders want to hear from me. My case for the overkingship."

I shook my head. "I have been thinking, Murrough. We will journey to a place where we can wed beautiful women who will bear us many children, who will all live long lives in peace."

Murrough shot me a look of pity, spoke in scorn. "There is no such place."

"Why not try?"

"Seek it by yourself," Murrough said, standing. "I will meet with the elders."

I sighed. What else could I do?

—Chapter Fifty-Eight—

The knock came on my door, a light hand I knew to be Sadb's. I had scarce opened my mouth when she burst in, holding a cloth-wrapped package tied with a string. I pushed open a window and set turf to burning. The fire brought warmth and a sweet smell into the room.

"I have something to tell you, if you swear not to tell anyone," she said, sitting on a stool before the hearth. "Until the time is right."

"Perhaps you will tell me now," I said, finding a seat on a hearth stone.

"The time is right to tell you, but not for you to tell anyone else. Do you swear?"

"I swear."

"You go first," she said. "You have something to tell me."

"I have forgotten what."

Sadb reached up and felt for the pouch around her neck. "Buí could help you remember. I pray you have not forgotten her prophesy."

"I have not. I will be ruler of all the island, with Queen Gormlaith, wife to Olaf of the Sandals, king of Norse Dublin and Northumbria." I smiled wide at the thought.

Sadb's face darkened. "You laugh at Buí's prophesy?"

"No, her words please me. But Queen Gormlaith is content with Olaf and their young son, Sitric."

"How do you know?"

"I am guessing. Olaf has been king many years. I am but a prince."

"You will be king of Munster when you sway the elders."

I shrugged, shook my head. "What? You will not try?"

"Perhaps yes, perhaps no." I spoke truth.

Sadb handed me the small package. "This will help you decide. Unwrap it, gently."

I squeezed the soft and squishy package, sniffed it, but found no scent.

"Open it," Sadb said.

I untied the string, peeled back the cloth, and spied two strands of braided hair, one the honey-golden color of Sadb's hair, the other a dark brown like Cian's, the ends tied tight with string.

"You and Cian?"

"We wish to be wed." Her voice sang in happiness. "We will be wed." I held the braids out to Sadb.

"Keep them," Sadb said, pushing my hand away. "Cian says they will help you with the elders."

"Cian says? How will they help me?"

"They will show you have turned him to friend—son of your brother's murderer … but …"

"But what?"

"Queen Úna says the elders might choose Áed."

I put the braids on a shelf and sat back down. "Did Queen Úna tell you not all husbands do well by their wives?"

"She did, and if you swear to keep her secret, I will tell you what else she said."

"I swear."

"I will be welcomed as a hermit at Clonmacnoise, if one day I see the good of a place like that."

"And you said?"

"I said the men I know have been good to me."

"Ah."

"You have been good to me, and Pádraig, and Prince Cian loves me, no matter that I am better with horses. And Buí prophesied you will love Queen Gormlaith."

As crafty as her mother, knowing how to sway me. Sadb lifted the pouch with Rónan's flat stone from her neck. "Here. Take this too. For courage."

I took it and put it with the braids on the shelf. "I will meet with the old men on the morrow," I said.

Sadb stood to leave, the top of her head reaching to my chin. Fifteen, full-bosomed, and tall—a woman.

"If you see Queen Úna sneaking away from Cashel," I said, "pray come for me. I wish to bid her goodbye."

Sadb laughed. "No one could sneak away with all those bulging sacks and bags. But if I see her trying, I will come for you. I promise."

✞

The next day, my turn come for the elders, I put the braids in the pouch with Rónan's stone, hooked it to my belt and set out to meet them. I was down the path when a horn blew, heralding Úna's escorts arriving. No doubt the elders had heard the horn as well. I changed course to the courtyard to bid Úna goodbye, glad for a chance to show myself in a manner befitting an overking—better than the picture of me threatening to drop Molloy's stinking head at Áed's feet.

The Connacht warriors stepped through the arched opening, four men in leather armor with helmets and weapons. Áed greeted them as Úna's handmaidens swept out from the king's house, bearing her bulging sacks and bags, Úna herself close behind. The elders, as I had suspected, could not stay away, and watched with the rest of the fortress.

I had imagined Úna eager to escape Cashel, scarce heeding those left behind. But no, she had words for every one of us. At Sadb, she paused, whispered in her ear, then moved on to Murrough. She might have passed him by, angry he had ruined her scheme with Molloy, taking his head, but no—she took Murrough's hand between both of hers and kissed it.

Then she came to you, poet. I could not see her face, but I could see your lips pressed together, your chest rising and falling, your eyelids squeezed tight. I had long known you and Úna were confidants, and I felt your sadness.

At Marc, Úna crossed herself and bowed her head. At the cook and his family, she gave each person squeezes of the hand, from the youngest to the eldest. She greeted the first elder by name, the furthest from me in their line, and thanked him for coming so far a distance. She swore her brother Connor would be friends with Munster no matter their choice of overking. I snuck a look at the old man's face, saw him smile, like the other five old men when Úna spoke their Irish names in turn and remembered some small detail about each of their tiny territories.

My turn come, I stepped out in view of everyone, so they could see and hear me. "Prince Brian." Úna said, struggling to steady her wobbly voice.

"Queen Úna." I kissed her cheeks, noting her stretched thin lips, her eyes cloaked in sadness. I had meant to speak with passion of the excellent ties Munster would make with Connacht, and to praise her choice of Clonmacnoise, a famed, holy place that Irish kings everywhere should respect and keep safe.

Instead, I took Úna's hand and kissed it. "Godspeed, Queen Úna." I stepped back into my place.

"Godspeed to you, Prince Brian," Úna said.

Then she was gone through the arched opening, the warriors carrying her sacks and bags, Áed guiding his mother down the steep path to her horse.

—Chapter Fifty-Nine—

The elders, garbed in their well-sewn, many-colored robes, led the way to the council house. The table taken out, the elders sat in six chairs at the far end of the room. A seventh chair was placed for me some two lengths away, facing the elders. Light drifted in from a high window, but most came from the giant beeswax candle perched on its brass base in the corner. The room was otherwise empty, save for spiders weaving webs in the corners. My stomach told me noon had been a poor choice for our meeting time. I would try to be brief.

The long-bearded elder began. "Brian mac Cennétig, Prince Murrough took the head of Molloy, your brother's murderer, at Belach Lechta—a deed that will be written into history. If you are chosen overking, will you name Murrough overking-in-waiting?"

I hesitated.

"No words?" Long Beard asked.

"A wise man chooses his words with care," I said, "else he risks others mistaking his meaning."

The old men shifted in their chairs, pulled on their beards. I had tried their patience. "To name a son king-in-waiting," I said, "is to invite him to seek the kingship before his time." I would not mention Murrough usurping my army command before his time.

Quizzical looks covered the elders' faces.

"I will give way to a son when I have won peace among Munster's warring clans, when all Irish and Norse kings on this island pay me tributes."

Had they heard me say, on this island?

"There are many kings beyond Munster's borders," Big-Chested said in a deep voice. "Irish kings and Norse kings, small kings and big kings, low kings and high kings. They will not submit and pay you tributes without a fight—many battles."

"How will you heal the wounds of war?" a wrinkle-faced elder asked. "You have ravaged and killed Ivar, Donobhan, and Molloy. Their kin will seek revenge."

"I will reach for the far side of revenge. I will seek true loyalty from my people, the kind that lasts beyond fear of vengeance, the kind that means stars are lined up together, that one wants for the other what the other wants for itself."

Wrinkle-Face paused. "We do not speak of stars, Prince Brian, we speak of Irish kings and chieftains. What or who can line them up?"

My hand at my pouch, I felt for Rónan's stone, rubbed it. "Our Lord God, nature, a miracle, or a wise king who uses war and proffered peace together. Proffered peace is to war as the left hand is to the right, and war is to proffered peace as the right hand is to the left. A king cannot win with one hand or the other. The two must work together, hand in hand."

The elders leaned forward, cupped their ears, strained to hear. "Proffered peace? How shall you proffer peace?" the elder with a right-cheek hair-mole asked.

"I will turn my enemies to friends, not to corpses."

"But how?" Hair-Mole asked, just as a furtive-eyed elder, last in line, opened his mouth to speak.

"You wish to ask a question?" I said to Furtive-Eye, taking my cue from Úna to heed every man the same.

"Yes," he smiled. "How will you turn enemies to friends?"

"A wise king does not scold, but praises. He does not hoard, but shares. In this pouch, I have proof of a third, most excellent way of turning enemies to friends."

I unloosed the pouch from my waist, withdrew the braids. The elders squinting in the dim light, I stood and carried them closer. Big-Chested opened his hand and I placed the braids in them.

"These braids speak of a love union between a prince and a princess," I said. "Their kin have been enemies since time began. If they wed—or I should say, when they wed—battles between Eóganachta and Dal Cais shall be things of the past and Munster will be much the stronger for it."

Big-Chested passed the braids to Furtive-Eye, who held them close to his eyes and studied them. "Murrough?" he asked.

"No, I speak of my daughter Sadb and Prince Cian, son of my brother's murderer, King Molloy—a bond so rare between Dal Cais and Eóganachta, it has not existed until now."

Such pleasant thoughts filled my head, I scarce noticed the elders' faces turn grim. Not until I heard chairs scrape did I see the tight circle they had made, their heads together, whispers too soft for me to hear. My heart sped up and fear took the place of courage.

I reached down and rubbed the stone in its pouch again—a small rub, so as not to be seen. My eyes half-closed, I conjured myself ruler of the island, Queen Gormlaith by my side, the two of us at the king's table at Kincora, Sadb and Cian there with us, Murrough, Eric and Stefan too.

"Prince Brian?" Big-Chested speaking to me. I opened my eyes. They had stretched their chairs back into a line.

"You have been tricked," Big-Chested said.

"The oldest trick in the world," Furtive-Eye said. "I should know. I am among the oldest men in the world."

"It suits Prince Cian," Big-Chested said, "to feign love for your daughter."

"To steal your power," Long-Beard said.

"There is poison in Prince Cian's tongue," Wrinkle-Face said. "You had best warn your daughter."

"The braids tell the tale," Missing-Tooth hissed. "Prince Cian means to bind Sadb to him, like a slave, so tight she cannot escape. Surely you suspect Prince Cian of ill-doing, a man who betrayed his father in battle?"

"No young girl fostered by a farmer could resist the love call of a prince," Hair-Mole said. "It is an old story, no?"

All six were agreed. Had I been tricked? Sadb tricked? Murrough? Marc? "May I have a moment to think?" I said.

Long-Beard looked to his fellow elders, who shrugged. "One moment," he said, "but not more."

I closed my eyes, calling up Cian in my mind. Murrough, Sadb, and I had deemed him honest, and he had showed himself trustworthy at Belach Lechta. Did he mean to steal my power? Were the elders right to suspect him?

"My son Murrough says you wish to meet with Prince Cian."

"It is so," Big-Chested boomed.

"You have messaged him? He knows of your wish?"

"The priest goes now to Emly," Big-Chested said, "with our message."

"You suspect Cian of treachery, yet you deem him worthy of the overkingship?" The elders looked from one to another. I had caught them in a trap.

Long-Beard smirked. "What seeker of power is not guilty of some treachery?"

The other five elders smiled and nodded. What? Outwitted by six old men?

"Prince Brian." Big-Chested's voice. "Friendship between Dal Cais and Eóganachta would serve Munster well, but braids are scarce proof."

I let out a breath, thankful for the plan in my mind. "Prince Cian will deny your bidding. Proof he does not seek to be overking." Missing-Tooth frowned, as did Hair-Mole and Wrinkle Face. "If I am wrong and he comes," I said, "you will have reason to deem me unworthy."

Once again, the elders made a tight circle with their chairs and whispered. I was so sure of my test of Cian, I felt no need to rub the stone. At last, they broke apart again, stretched back into their line. "Some of us suspect Prince Cian of stealth," Big-Chested said.

"Stealth?"

"No matter if he defies our bidding," Missing-Tooth hissed, "he could wend his way into your overking's nest as your daughter's husband, and strike at you when you least expect it."

A weariness came over me. "Prince Cian does not wish to strike at me. He and I share a vision for our kingdom, peace among all the clans, for the first time in history." I hoped that was true.

The elders pondered, each man to himself. Clearly, they were not all of the same mind. I stepped over and picked the fallen braids from the floor.

"My daughter deems these proof of Prince Cian's love. The same as a marriage proposal. If Sadb believes Prince Cian loves her, then he loves her. They will wed no matter if I am overking or not."

"Time will tell," Long-Beard said. "Meantime, we will meet with Murrough. Your son has shown himself a great warrior and a leader of men. His youth could bring Munster many years of strong rule."

"My son Murrough will not put himself forward, now that he knows my will."

"Prince Murrough doubted your will?" Hair-Mole asked.

"I doubted it myself and told Murrough so. But my mind is changed, as must happen for a wise king when something new casts shadows upon his doubts."

A pause, each elder pondering to himself. "We will wait and see," Long-Beard said, his voice signaling our meeting was over. I stood to leave, stuffing the braids back into my pouch.

"Your nephew, Áed, makes a good case for himself," Big-Chested said. "Is there more you wish to say for yourself, Prince Brian? Perhaps something more about Murrough?"

Ah, something more about Murrough? A hint? "When I am chosen overking, Murrough will be my best general and closest counselor, my warrior prince. Choose me ..." I started to say two are better than one, but it came to me to say, "and you will have chosen Murrough and Prince Cian—three better than one." The elders nodded, smiled, frowned, grunted. I took my leave.

✥

I stepped out the council house into the bright midday sun and made my way to the corner of the smithy, from whence I could see Rory carrying bedding from Áed's house to the king's house, then empty. My first thought was to take a different route to my house, sight unseen by Áed. But on second thought it came to me to try to make peace with my nephew. We had once fathomed each other. Perhaps we could again.

"The king's house is my right," Áed sneered as I walked up, "if you are here to stop me."

"I am here to propose a truce, before the elders divide us more."

Anger came across his brow. "Divide us? Did you not tell my mother I could ready my enkinging feast?"

I picked the braids from my pouch, held them up. "I did, but these have changed my mind." I nodded to the king's house. "Shall we talk alone, in there?"

We stepped in and shut the door behind us. Brigit's cot and Úna's hand-carved wooden chest caught my eye, her most precious things left behind for her son.

I held out the braids. "These speak of a love bond between Sadb and Prince Cian. The elders have sent for Cian at Emly, but I suspect he will not want to make an enemy of either of us. He wants Sadb and his clan's kingship at Rath Rathlainn, not the overkingship of Munster. I am praying for both our sakes he will deny the elders."

"If he does not come, it will be because he fears me," Áed snorted. "If he does come, I will kill the traitor on sight."

"Traitor to your father's murderer, his own father, but friend to us. Kill Cian, and you will have ruined Munster's best chance to come together as one, no matter if the elders choose you or me."

"A traitor to anyone is not to be trusted. Nor are you to be trusted, for so many reasons I cannot name them all."

Did Áed not have ears? Did he not hear me say Cian would be ally to either of us? Áed spat, waved me away.

I put the braids back in my pouch. "I will think on your counsel."

Next time, I would take more care before I proffered peace with a hornet.

—Chapter Sixty—

Scarce any time passed before Cian came into the field on his horse, with two monks from Emly. Sadb ran down the steep path to greet him, and Áed and I climbed the ladder. We watched as the lovers fell into each other's arms.

"Cian will make a strong case for himself with the elders," I said to Áed. "Eóganachta have always ruled from Cashel. Perhaps they always will again if your sword does not get Cian first."

Áed spat. "I will kill him, but not in plain sight."

"Ah. Should I warn him?"

"If you like."

"I do like, if he has reason to fear you." An eerie silence from Áed. Truth, I had reason to fear him.

"What will you do when the elders do not choose you?" Áed asked, his voice in a studied calm.

The question surprised me. "I will wait to know our new overking's mind, and then decide. And you, if they do not choose you?"

"I will do what my father would have done."

"Seek my counsel and do the opposite?" I could not help but say it.

Áed stiffened, glowered. "Had he only done the opposite when you counseled him to his wedding feast."

His voice dripped with blame. But I so wanted to know Mahon's thoughts, I would keep on.

"Did your father say I counseled him to go?"

"You deny it?"

"I counseled him to choose his own path, as I knew he would no matter what I counseled him. Did he ask your counsel?"

"My father did not listen to me. He would do what you counseled him. He lived and died for you. His warrior prince. You could have stopped him. You should have stopped him. Why did you not?" Áed had lost his studied calm and was talking in a loud, excited voice. "I might have tried harder, had I known what would happen. But truth, it is a mystery to me, why he went. Did he truly believe a young princess waited to wed him at Donobhan's dún? That Molloy would give him the gift of Brigit? Molloy, our fiercest, most cunning enemy? Or that Donobhan, Ivar's close ally, had turned from enemy to friend? Pray tell me, Áed. You knew your father's thoughts better than anyone."

A hubbub had risen, Cian greeting Murrough in the courtyard. Áed stayed silent, staring at me. Had I pushed him too far?

Turning toward the ladder, I heard him speak in a low growl. "He went because you did not try to stop him."

"What?" I turned to face him.

"You asked what he thought and I am telling you."

"His words? Or your imaginings?"

"His words. I told him I feared a trick. Grave danger. But he did not listen. He said, 'Brian knows. He would stop me if he believed the dangers were too great. We are brothers together and always have been.'"

Stunned, I could scarce breathe.

"So you see?" Áed said with smug satisfaction. "You are to blame."

Murrough and Sadb calling to me from the courtyard, I closed my eyes and whispered a silent prayer of thanks to Áed. I could choose to believe my brother thought I wished him to live, but did not fathom the dangers he faced. Mahon would never know I had chosen to let him die for the good of Munster, our island, and my quest. I had done what I thought I must with the leave of the most holy abbot on the island, the Great Abbot of Armagh.

✠

I hastened down the ladder to the courtyard, skipping rungs, but only Murrough was there, with monks standing near.

"Sadb is in the church," Murrough said, "confessing her sins."

A lie so plain, I could not help but smile. "And Cian?"

"With the elders."

"I will seek them out."

Murrough took my arm. "No," he said, blocking me. "We must show these monks hospitality."

"You tend to them. You and Áed."

A plot was afoot. Murrough's gaze turned away, I set out to the church. But the closer I came, the more I pictured scowls from Sadb if I did find her there. It was best she came to me.

I was in my house, pondering my talk with Áed, when Cian's voice called my name. I opened my door wide to him; his face much older and more weathered than I remembered from Kincora.

"You made your case to the elders?" I asked as he passed by me into my hearth room.

He stood by a chair, unpinning his brat. "Yes, but not the case they imagined."

"Oh?" We sat facing each other.

"I bade the priest speak his message three times."

I folded my arms, leaned back. Clever of Cian to feign surprise. He studied my face. "You doubt me?"

"You came in great haste."

"For Sadb."

"And the overkingship."

"No."

"Then why meet with the elders?"

"I thought it best I tell them myself. You are my choice."

He flattered me. All the more reason to doubt him.

"Áed is Mahon's son," I said, "and he has shown himself clever, brave, and battlewise—a worthy choice."

"Yet not such a good ally for me when I am clan king at Rath Rathlainn. I told those old men they should choose you if they hope to see the day when Dal Cais and my people come together as friends."

I smiled at those words. "Did they mention your theft of my power?"

"No. Why would they?"

"I swore you would wed Sadb no matter who they choose as overking."

"I will, this evening, in the church."

"And then?"

"Then Sadb will be queen at Rath Rathlainn."

"The elders suspect you of trickery, Prince Cian. Is it so?"

"No. Is that what you think of me?"

"You would not be the first man in Munster to seek power through his woman."

Cian stared at me. "No, I would not be ... nor would you. My marriage to Sadb will be good for both of us."

Bold words, to an overking-to-be, who would be his father-in-law. Cian's gaze shifted to the door, to Sadb, standing quiet inside it.

"What is this?" She stepped behind Cian, put her hand on his shoulder. "You were talking about me? Our marriage?"

Cian covered her hand with his. "It is nothing."

"You mean to marry me for power?"

Cian shook his head, but too late. Tears had begun in Sadb's eyes. "Do not lie. I heard you."

She came around to face him. "You swore you loved me." A quick turn of her heel, and Cian was up on his feet, blocking her from the door.

"Pray stay. I am here to wed you."

I edged around them, out the door, into the air. It was true I had used Sadb's braids for my own good, to sway the elders. I had gained courage from her prophesy. But I had not chosen Cian for Sadb. She had chosen him herself. I had treated her well, much better than my father treated Órlaith.

Sadb's and Cian's voices rose and fell. His stayed steady, hers changed from sobs, to anger, to sadness, to pleading, to questioning, to whispering. I moved closer to the door, the better to hear.

"I would wed you even if you were daughter to a cow." Cian's voice.

"You would not," Sadb giggled.

"We could wed now," Cian said. "Why not?"

My heart sped up. Not without my leave.

"The priest?" Sadb said after a long while. "We agreed sundown."

"The priest will do our bidding."

"But the elders," Sadb said. "You invited them."

"I will say you denied me."

"No wedding? Then what?"

"We can be wed in secret and be gone. Or we could be gone and then be wed."

A weight lifted from my heart. Cian had met the test. I might well be chosen, but I might not. Cian could scarce steal my power if I had none.

A long silence from Sadb. "If we wed in secret, the elders will not know my father turned you to friend. They will think he lied to them, and choose Áed."

"Hmm," Cian said. "And if they do?"

"If they choose Áed, I will be but a cousin to an overking. I wish to be daughter to an overking, and wife to his son-in-law."

"You seek power from our marriage?"

A pause and a laugh. "Yes. Shhh. Listen."

I backed away, around the side of the house. Whisperings, footsteps, and I pressed my body flat against the outside wall, trying to become part of the wattle and daub.

But no, hurried footsteps. First Sadb, then Cian, she coming from one way, he from the other. No escape.

"What have we here?" Sadb said, smothering a smile.

"Prince Brian?" Cian said. My face went red. I tried to move around them.

"Wait," Sadb said, blocking me. "Cian has something to ask you."

"I beg your leave to wed your daughter at sundown, here, in Cashel's church," Cian said, over Sadb's shoulder. "Will you give it?"

Such power he granted me. I would feign surprise, uncertainty and doubt. "Wed? Then what?"

"Then we will be husband and wife, on our way to Rath Rathlainn—with your blessing." Cian raised an eyebrow at Sadb, who crossed her arms, planted her feet firm in the dirt.

"Your leave is yours to give," she said to me, "but ours to take, if you choose not to give it."

"I do give it." I stepped over and kissed her cheeks, then his, each one twice to be sure they fathomed my meaning.

—Chapter Sixty-One—

Sundown, time for the wedding, came with a heavy rain. Sadb rode on Cian's back to the church to save her feet from the muddy path. In his wisdom, the priest bade Sadb and Cian speak their vows inside the dry church, at the altar, not outside the church door as was our custom. The elders not yet arrived, I suggested we wait, but Sadb and Cian would not have it. They spoke their vows, exchanged rings, kissed cheeks, all with only Marc, Murrough, and I there to bear witness.

Within moments, the elders filed in, the six of them, their tunics new and clean since that afternoon. I was nodding my greetings when I caught sight of Áed striding in through the door in his father's red brat, the king's circlet upon his head. He sat himself down on the front bench, blocking my view. I poked him on the shoulder, whispered for him to move over.

The priest's blessings began, and my mind drifted first to Mór and me, and then to Órlaith, no doubt speaking the same vows. I had not known my sister, but from tales Mahon had told me of her protests, hiding in a slave's hovel, I imagined her strong-willed like Sadb. But clearly not as crafty, for Sadb would have escaped me had I tried to wed her against her will to a brute.

You came in late, poet, paler and pastier than ever. I would have nodded to you, had I not needed to keep my gaze fixed on Áed until Cian and Sadb were safe away from the church.

No time to ready musicians, dancers, acrobats, or magicians, Cian promised Sadb a proper feast when they became king and queen at Rath Rathlainn. But that night, what they wanted most was a bed. In his most kingly voice, in earshot of the elders, Áed offered the couple his old house, then empty after his move to the king's house. Sadb's and Cian's gazes met across the table, and off they went.

The six old men licked their lips, drained their cups, and bade us all good night. Marc caught himself nodding off and left the table, taking the priest with him.

Murrough swore the night was too young for sleep. He would go in search of his friends at King Eóghan's. I begged him wait and drink a horn of ale or two with me first. And we did, more than one, although I did not keep count. Alone at last, I made my way to my house, visions of Gormlaith playing in my head. At last at my bed, I sighed relief. The day had been long and full.

✟

I was deep asleep when a hand touched my shoulder, poked me twice. I swiped at it and cursed, deeming it Murrough's. I was not ready to wake.

A man's voice spoke to me. "Prince Brian, pray wake."

I reached out into the dark, touched an arm. I sat up, slipping my hand over my knife I kept in ready reach. "Who?"

"Félim mac Ruadh. We wait for you in the council house." Long-Beard? My eyes found him in the dark.

"Now?" I said.

"Now." He backed away. A swish of my cowhide curtain, a creak of the door, and he was gone.

Real? Or a dream? Either I was drunk or mad. I lay back down, clutching my knife, hearing Murrough's snores. No sound of birds outside, I guessed the time about halfway between midnight and dawn. Truly, I had no choice but to make the trek to the council house, at least to see. I groped about for my boots, tunic, breeches, and brat. Reaching for my brat pin on my shelf, my hand brushed the pouch holding Rónan's stone. I hooked it to my belt and crept out the door.

The rain had stopped, but clouds covered the stars and the moon. I stepped through puddles to the empty courtyard, to spy a dim glow coming from behind a smithy, the place of the council house. All was quiet—no wind, no wolves, voices, no sounds of a snoring guard. But still I crept. Was I walking into a trap, an ambush—a fool, like Mahon? Had I dreamed Long-Beard? No matter—no one was about and no one would know.

I peered around the corner of the smithy to the council house, some five lengths away. The door wide open, there sat Áed in a chair in the middle of the room, an empty chair next to his. His tangled hair on the back of his head told me he too had been awakened from sleep. Two elders, Long-Beard and Hair-Mole, faced him and the empty chair that I guessed was for me. Small animal fat candles burned in cups on the floor, flickering light onto the elders' faces. The beeswax candle in the corner stayed cold.

At the door, I cleared my throat, made myself known. Long Beard nodded me to my chair. I sat in the silence that followed, my thoughts flying. If the elders had decided, why not wait for daylight to tell us. Why not all of us together in the hall? The name of Munster's new overking could not be kept secret. If they had not chosen, why wake us? Whatever their purpose, I would wait for their signal to speak. I had learned that lesson long ago at Holy Island.

I glanced to my side, spied Áed staring at me. Both of us looked fast away. The first to speak was Long-Beard.

"Patience," he said, "is much needed in an overking—patience and tolerance for the unknown. Both of you fidgeted in our silence, but neither of you spoke. Had you, we could have chosen the other and gone back to bed. As it is, we will try our second test."

I glanced again at Áed, spied him staring at his fingers. "One of you will be chosen overking," Hair-Mole said, "the other, not." He lapsed back into silence.

A trick? I let my eyelids droop. "Prince Brian." Long-Beard—his voice so strong it startled me. I sat up straight, my eyes wide open. "If we choose Prince Áed, will you swear fealty to him as overking, for life?"

The thought stirred pain in my gut. I crossed my arms and squeezed them into my middle. Think before you speak, Brian. He is testing you.

"Your words have fled?" Hair-Mole asked, his voice sounding like a man who favored Áed.

"My words did flee," I said, "but now they are back. If you choose Prince Áed overking, I will pledge myself to him, no matter if he and I agree about nothing."

I turned my face to Áed and held out my hand in a gesture of peace. No movement, no sound.

"Prince Áed?" Long Beard said. Áed frowned, stayed silent. Did he not know it was a test?

"If you asked my counsel, Áed," I said, "I would urge you to accept my pledge."

"Ask your counsel?" Áed said. "I would rather die." His eyes—droopy, red, sad—put me in mind of a sick hound.

Long-Beard and Hair-Mole pulled their chairs all the way to the far wall of the room, faced it, their backs to us. They whispered and gestured to each other.

From the corner of my eye, I spied Áed move his hand to his knife hilt. Mine strapped at my waist, I thought to do the same, but instead, I rubbed my pouch, felt the stone inside. New courage flowed in, coming from Rónan, Sadb, Buí, Lugh, all together in one stone.

The elders' silences grew longer, flurries of words shorter. They pulled their chairs back, turned to face us, but both men started to speak at the same time. Hair-Mole paused. "I will take my turn, and then Félim here will take his turn—a lesson to be learned."

Hope flickered inside me—my way, a difference mended with words.

"Some of us favored you, Prince Brian," Hair-Mole said, "and some of us favored you, Prince Áed. We argued and came close to blows."

My stomach churned. Could they not speak their choice? My name? Brian mac Cinnétig, overking of Munster kingdom?

"Prince Brian," Long-Beard said, "Some of us think Prince Cian tricked you with the braids—a simpleness on your part unworthy of an overking. Now we are swayed to believe he is honest. He makes no case for the overkingship, and we have not stated our choice, yet still, he has wed Princess Sadb."

Were they so old they had forgotten their purpose? Their choice?

"Prince Cian divided us," Hair-Mole said. "And so did the fact and the manner of King Mahon's murder. Some of us suspect he might be alive today were it not for you, Prince Brian. Others of us suspect the same about you, Prince Áed. We have looked at that thorny problem from every side, and still cannot agree."

"Me?" Áed said. "I am suspected?"

"Some of us believe you might have known better than to march with your father into an enemy ambush."

Ah. They had not chosen, and never would.

"So," Long-Beard said, "we crafted these tests. You both passed the test of silence. But only you, Prince Brian, passed the second test, pledging loyalty to your foe for the sake of your clan, kingdom, and island."

Worthy. Yet still they did not say it?

"Prince Áed," Hair-Mole said, "I deem you a worthy choice for overking—son of Mahon, an excellent king and overking himself."

Hair-Mole—an elder not suited to his weighty task.

"I, too, deem you worthy, Prince Áed," Long-Beard sighed. "But more of us than not are swayed by Prince Brian's promise of peace in our kingdom. Too many of our sons, nephews, grandsons, and cousins have died in needless battles, and more will die in times to come, if a new way is not found to rule on this island."

"You have three choices, Prince Áed," Hair-Mole said. "You can raise armies to fight Prince Brian and his many allies—not wise, in my mind, given your lack of warriors and skill in battle, but still a choice. Another is to pledge yourself to Prince Brian, our new overking."

Had he said it? Yes! I let out breath.

"Or," Hair-Mole went on, "you can steal away from Cashel this night. That was my idea, Prince Áed. With everyone sleeping, no one will see you and shame you. Of course, it is your choice."

No overking worth the name would stay silent after Hair-Mole's words. I would be bold.

"Worthy elders," I said. "I have held my tongue, not wanting to speak too soon or put words into your mouths. But only an instant ago, I heard my name and the word overking mentioned together in the same breath. You have chosen me overking of Munster kingdom."

I had stated it. Both Long Beard and Hair-Mole nodded.

"King Brian," Long-Beard said. "I feared this, our final test, might fly by you unnoticed. But it has not. You have listened and spoken our choice out loud, without fear."

"Shall we tell him together?" Hair-Mole asked Long-Beard, who nodded with a smile. Áed, meantime, looked nothing like a man who would thank Hair-Mole for his thoughtfulness, giving him leave to sneak away. He looked more like a man who would leap upon the elders and flatten them on the council house floor with his boot.

"Brian mac Cennétig," Hair-Mole and Long Beard said together, "in our great wisdom, we choose you to rule our kingdom as overking. Do you accept?"

"I do, and I will strive to prove your choice well-taken. My first deed will be to spread your good names throughout our kingdom, together with all the virtues you have shown here at Cashel—patience, tolerance, wisdom, fairness, and every other good quality known to men and the gods."

I knew my words to be true. The elders bent their heads in thanks. "My second deed will be to write your names into history. Penned by my poet on calfskin."

I was thinking, poet, of a calfskin placed atop my tale in the round tower, with the elders' names and worthy qualities penned on it, in your best hand. On top—not mixed in with my skins, or your note beginning my tale, our tale, where it would ruin the flow.

Long-Beard and Hair-Mole nodded and smiled, stood and bowed to me a little. They had taken steps to leave when Áed sprang back to life. He stepped over in front of them.

"Your words mean nothing to me, old men. Who are you, anyway? You have no right to decide Munster's fate."

I readied to come between him and the elders, but they moved around Áed and kept going, not slowing their already slow pace toward the door.

Áed raised his fist at me. "If you are hoping to befriend my Connacht kin in your all-island quest, Brian, nothing untoward will happen to me on my journey there. I will leave Cashel this night, before sunrise."

Ah, a promise to be gone. "You may call me King Brian now, Áed. Overking of Munster. As for your journey, I promise it will be as safe as any man can promise another. I will not watch you leave, this night, in stealth before dawn."

"We will state our choice to all who are at morning meal," Long-Beard said to me at the door. "We will feast at midday meal, and by evening, we six old men will be headed home."

Such rare contentment I had not heard in their voices until then.

"Your enkinging will happen in good time, King Brian, with all the musicians, dancers, acrobats, and magicians in Munster," Hair-Mole said. "If you invite me, I will come, if I am still alive."

"I shall," I said, pressing both elders' hands in mine.

I waited for Áed to leave the council house, doused the candles, and stepped out into a night that was dark, but brighter in my mind and heart than noon on a cloudless day.

—Chapter Sixty-Two—

I made my way slowly to my house, pushed hard on the door, hoping the sound would rouse Murrough. But no, his snoring told me not. I felt my way behind his curtain, to his bed.

"Murrough!"

No change in his snoring, I sat down on his bed's edge. I could see he lay on his stomach, his face turned to the wall. I put my hand on his shoulder and shook him.

"Wake up. I have good news."

The snoring stopped. I waited for him to turn over and open his eyes, but it started up again. I shook him again and he rolled over onto his back, swung his right arm out to the side, found my shoulder. I stood and looked down at him.

"It is only me."

"What?"

"The elders have chosen me overking. King Brian mac Cennétig, overking of Munster kingdom." Silence. "Did you hear me? I am chosen overking. It is over. We will celebrate."

A long, low groan came from his throat. "Pray no more ale. Enough."

Ah. He deemed me drunk, wanting more ale. I leaned over close to his face. "No ale. Smell me."

Murrough turned back onto his stomach, his face to the wall. "You imagine it," he said. "No one chooses overkings in the middle of the night." He pulled his pillow over his head.

I sighed. I might have done the same had I been he.

I stepped into the hearth room, thinking to light a fire. The tinder was in its bucket by the hearth, but the flint and stone were not on the shelf. I sat, pulled my brat tighter against the cold, waiting for dawn.

I thought to wake you, poet, to see your face when I told you the elders had looked at the thorny issue of Mahon's death from every side, and still could not agree. Surely you would fathom the cheer that brought me. I did not tell them what I said to Mahon when he asked my counsel. Why court blame when the elders' blindness suited me better? Had they not chosen me, I would have stopped telling my tale. No one years from now would care about the musings of a prince who abandoned his quest. But I have not, and for that I am grateful, even as I suspect my journey thus far has been easy, next to what is coming.

No fire in the hearth, I pulled my brat tight and pondered the dangers I would face turning enemies to friends across the island. Cian and I had sworn friendship and loyalty, but those were mere words. Actions would be something else.

Surely dawn was not long away. I stole out the door, walked down the path to the courtyard and climbed the ladder. I sat on the wall and hooked my arm around a post, as I had done many times before.

"Mahon? Are you listening? I want to thank you. Had you not saved me from the rout, lifted me high on your kingly shoulders, I would never have risen to the place I am now. The overkingship of Munster." I waited. A gentle breeze touched my face.

"Something else, Mahon. I will fly high on my own wings to the kingship of all of Ireland. Every king, lord, and chieftain on this island will pay me tributes. I will use my sword to help me when nothing else can do, but more, I will turn enemies to friends with wit. Remember, Mahon? My way? Forgive me. I had to let you die."

A howl sounded in the west. A wolf. "I know you blame me. We tried to outdo each other all our lives. Everything was a contest between us, no? I confess to it, and so did you, if I remember. Wiser men than I may deem you the winner after all. We will not know until it is written. We have no old owl to tell us."

Wet starting in my eyes, I rubbed my pouch, still at my waist, praying for a voice to guide me.

Why look west, sweet prince? I am east, where the sun rises.
Gormlaith? Her voice in my head.

Always I had looked west from the wall, toward the River Shannon, or south, toward Molloy's Rath Rathlainn, or north toward Armagh, but scarce ever east. I rose to my feet and made my way along the wall to the east side of Cashel fortress. I passed by the round tower, the church, the graveyard, the rubbish heap, your house, poet, the cook's house, the hall, spied the council house, and found a new place on the wall to sit, looking east.

The sky above the trees had streaked pink. *You will always find me here, sweet prince. I will wait for you.*

I am overking now, Queen Gormlaith. You will not need wait long.

I pray not, but your journey will be hard. Many men will seek me. But if you look close, you will see my hand moving always for you.

I took in a deep breath, fearful I might frighten Gormlaith away, my heart so full. I am alone now, Queen Gormlaith, save for my son, who oft times wishes to be away from me, and the poet who hears my tale. I will feel much pain telling of the slaughter I wreaked to avenge Mahon and Brigit.

I will be here for you, sweet prince. But now I must go. Until later.

No. Gormlaith?

Enough now, Brian. What if someone hears you? Overking of Munster, speaking out loud to no one?

Ah, true. The sun is up. I will wake the poet.

Author's Note

Brian Bóraime, known in English as Brian Boru, is the only Irishman in history to have held power over all of Ireland, if only for a short time. He is best known for a battle against Norse and rival Irish at Clontarf in 1014, at which his army, led by elder son, Murrough, defeated their opponents, but at which Brian himself, Murrough, Murrough's son, and all others who could have carried on after the great king were killed. The island returned to its former state of division, rendering it vulnerable to the predations of foreigners, most notably, the Norman English.

Brian was a skilled warrior and battle strategist, but a close reading of the annalists' descriptions of his activities after his brother's murder leads to the inference that Brian tried all his life to avoid fighting in favor of diplomacy. He yearned for lasting peace in his kingdom and on his island, having suffered the loss of many close kin and experienced the horrors of battle. He understood that lasting peace requires both a show of power and ways of turning enemies to friends.

Far Side of Revenge is a plausible account of Brian's journey to this epiphany, in the company of older brother, Mahon, with whom he had both a dependent and rivalrous relationship. In the novel, Brian's journey begins with his childhood dealings with his father and Mahon, and continues through his eventual attainment of the overlordship of his kingdom of Munster. Although he may or may not have realized the connection, Brian's early conflicted relationships with his father and brother

Mahon prepared his mind for later conflicts and solutions on the political stage.

A fictional account of the second half of his life and career, featuring a wiser Brian, his third wife, Gormlaith, queen thrice over, and their respective sons, Murrough and Sitric Silkenbeard, king of Viking Dublin, is a work currently in progress.

All major characters in Brian's story are historical figures. I have invented his friend, Rónan, the infant, Brigit, Mahon's manservant, Rory, and Rory's charge, Félim, as well as the name of Mahon's wife, Úna.

My primary sources include the *Annals of Inisfallen, Annals of Clonmacnoise; Annals of Ulster*, the *Cogadh Gaedhel re Gallaibh (The War of the Irish with the Foreigners)*; Sean Duffy's *Brian Boru and the Battle of Clontarf*; Darren McGettigan's *The Battle of Clontarf, Good Friday 1014*; Maire Ni Mhaonaigh's *Brian Boru, Ireland's Greatest King*; Roger Chatterton Newman's *Brian Boru: King of Ireland*; Benjamin Hudson's *Viking Pirates and Christian Princes;* P.W. Joyce's *The Social History of Ancient Ireland*; the Penguin Classic, *Early Irish Myths and Sagas*; Lady Augusta Gregory's *Cuchulain of Muirthemne*; Daibhi Ó'Cróinin's *Early Medieval Ireland*; and Michael Richter's *Medieval Ireland*.

Acknowledgments

I would like to acknowledge the rotating members of the Barnes and Nobles writing group in Eugene, Oregon, the first to take me seriously as a fellow writer. I would not have persevered without the introduction to this group by Susan Swanson, and without the input of Anna Willman, Daryl Lynne Evans, Valerie Ihsan, Rex Moody, Patricia Graap, Shiela Pardee, Joan Fulton, and especially those who still continue on with me—Sondra Kelly-Green, Ross West, and Randy Luce. Certain of these individuals read entire earlier drafts, some more than once.

The novel benefitted greatly from the input of Tex Thompson, my writing coach, who faithfully read pages every week for several years, making cogent suggestions while at the same time navigating rush hour traffic in Dallas, cooking dinner, and learning the trade of expert locksmith.

Molly Malone, Jessica Morrell, and Sarina Dorie also contributed their professional opinions, as did workshop leaders at Aspen Summer Words—Tony Marra, Laura Fraser, and Luis Alberto Urrea.

I am fortunate to have long-time friends from childhood, some of whom spent their careers teaching English and writing, who read and commented upon my earlier drafts during COVID and beyond. Specifically, I wish to thank my first reader, Susan Wall, and subsequent readers, Lalise Melillo, Joan Starr, Karen Perschall, Donna Apgar, Jack and Mary Sue Roniger, and Joey McCloskey, who I hope will be pleased with the changes I have made as a result of their insightful suggestions.

I want to thank my children for refraining from commenting about their mother's bizarre behavior researching and writing a novel about a tenth century Irish king, an enterprise I am certain they believed would never end. My daughter, Sophie Therrell, and my niece, Sarah Evans, came to my rescue when it seemed I would founder on the rock of the impossible synopsis and query letter. I will be forever grateful to Ross West for introducing me to GladEye Press (Jeff Bolkan and Sharleen Nelson), who freed me from those onerous tasks by agreeing to publish this novel.

In Ireland, author Darren McGettigan and Irish language experts, Rónán O Dochartaigh and Andrew MacGiolla Easbuig, were of great help in setting me straight about pronunciations and obscure pieces of information about tenth century Ireland.

My husband, Mark, accompanied me on my many journeys to Ireland, where we examined numerous mounds of dirt with historical significance. He continues to exhibit understanding and patience as I move on to the next writing project, isolating myself from the world in my backyard writing studio.

About the Author

Anne Labouisse Dean grew up in New Orleans, the city she still calls home. After ten years away in the east, earning her BA in political science at Wellesley College, and PhD in psychology from Catholic U. in Washington, DC, she returned to New Orleans to raise a family and teach developmental psychology at the University of New Orleans. In the meantime, she trained to become a clinical psychoanalyst at the New Orleans Psychoanalytic Institute, and practiced both in New Orleans and Eugene, Oregon, where she and her husband now live with no pets.

In the late nineties, as a visiting scholar at Queen's University, Belfast, Anne and her husband conducted an ethnographic study of the Northern Ireland Troubles. Irish history, Brian Boru, and the continuing but failed efforts of subsequent Irish heroes over the last millennium to unite the whole island under Irish governance, has intrigued her ever since.

MORE BOOKS FROM GLADEYE PRESS

The Time Tourists Trilogy
Sharleen Nelson

Follow the adventures and missteps of time-traveling PI Imogen Oliver as she recovers lost items and unearths long-buried stories and secrets from the past in this exciting series! (*The Time Tourists is available on Kindle Unlimited.)

*The Fragile Blue Dot
Ross West
Veteran science-writer and journalist Ross West's collection of award-winning short fiction touches on the human aspect of living in a world on the brink of ecological disaster.

*Quilts of a Feather
Arlene Sachitano
An innocent birdwatching festival hosted by the parks and recreation goes terribly sideways when one of the event volunteers is found dead from a fentanyl overdose on the hiking trail. It's up to amateur sleuth Harriet Truman and her quilt group, the Loose Threads, to solve the mystery?

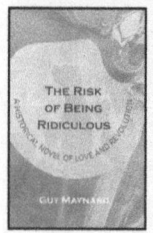

Join 19-year-old Ben Tucker for a passionate and revolutionary tale of protests, parties, trials, and a band of idealists who set out to build a countercultural utopia in the southern mountains of Oregon.

The Risk of Being Ridiculous Trilogy
Guy Maynard

*Available as an ebook on Kindle Unlimited.

All GladEye titles are available for purchase at www.gladeyepress.com and your local bookstore.

*Federation of the Dragon
*Footman of the Ether
Jason A. Kilgore
Enter the ancient world of Irikara for high-stakes epic fantasy adventure in a mythical land filled with dragons and demons, dwarves and elves, magic and mages and gods.

*Dye. Run. Don't Die
K.J. Kolsen
Chased by shadowy figures, Winnie and Jimmy re-unite somewhere between Oklahoma and Colorado and embark on a wild ride filled with disguises, stolen vehicles, murders, truck-stop perverts, a sex-cult, deadly shootouts, and rediscovered love.

Coastal Coffee Club Mysteries
Patricia Brown
Five cozy mysteries follow retired poet Eleanor Penrose and her band of quirky friends as they solve mysteries along the Oregon coast.

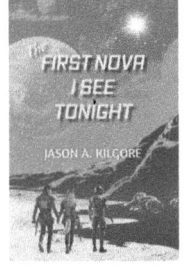

*The First Nova I see Tonight
Jason A. Kilgore
Firefly meets Indiana Jones in this spicy space opera when rogue space jockey Dirken Nova and his cyborg sidekick Yiorgos accept a risky gig to transport a mysterious item in a locked safe box to another planet in a far corner of the galaxy.

COMING later in 2025 *from*
GladEye Press

Dying for Romance
Patricia Brown
In this sixth book in the Coastal Coffee Club Mysteries series, Eleanor, Angus, and the gang take to the woods to solve a knotty crime.

Black and Tan Fantasy
Randall Luce
In the turbulent and often violent nascent civil rights movement of the Mississippi delta, racial identities, culture, and attitudes collide and shift in this taut drama.

The Extraordinary Voyage of a Tall Ship in a Tiny Pool Far from the Sea
Donovan M. Reves
With gentle absurdity and copious humor, Donovan Reves weaves an exciting adventure yarn with a tender love story all set in a ridiculous landlocked tallship built in a tiny pond. As hard to describe as it is to put down, this tender fable evokes the magic of *The Princess Bride*.

RERELEASES FROM JASON A. KILGORE

Around the Corner from Sanity: Tales of the Paranormal
Fourteen short stories of spine-tingling horror will scare you AND tickle your funny bone!

Guide Me, O River and other poems

www.ingramcontent.com/pod-product-compliance
Lightning Source LLC
LaVergne TN
LVHW031114070525
810573LV00003B/13